"Annie, I don't want to talk about this anymore," Kevin said, putting his arms across his chest.

"Neither do I. Should we talk about the weather? No. Let's talk about football." Annie was not calming down. The more she thought about it the angrier she became.

"Calm down." Kevin raised his voice. "I've had enough of this. Don't blame my mother. I admit she was out of line about the abortion thing, but I made it clear we were not considering it. Shut your mouth and listen for a minute. I have to ask you a question." Kevin paused for a breath. He had been pointing his finger in Annie's face.

"Well," Annie said, taking a deep breath, "as much as I would love to hear what you want to ask me, Kevin, I'm afraid I have to leave. Go talk to your mother like that." Annie pulled open the door and started to get out. She felt her head jerked back into the car and slammed against the headrest.

THE
BREAKABLE
VOW

KATHRYN ANN CLARKE

⬧ AVON BOOKS
AN IMPRINT OF HARPERCOLLINS*PUBLISHERS*

The Breakable Vow
Copyright © 2004 by Kathryn Clarke

For information address HarperCollins Children's Books,
a division of HarperCollins Publishers, 1350 Avenue of
the Americas, New York, NY 10019.

Library of Congress Cataloging-in-Publication Data
Clarke, Kathryn.
    The breakable vow / by Kathryn Clarke.—1st Avon ed.
      p.   cm.
    Summary: After eighteen-year-old Annie becomes
unexpectedly pregnant, she marries her boyfriend, but
slowly realizes that he is abusive and that she must decide
what she can and will do about the relationship to keep her
daughter and herself safe. Includes information on the
characteristics of abusive relationships and how to end
them.
    ISBN 0-06-051821-9 (pbk.)
    ISBN 0-06-051822-7 (lib. bdg.)
    [1. Wife abuse—Fiction. 2. Emotional problems—Fiction.
3. Jealousy—Fiction. 4. Pregnancy—Fiction.] I. Title.
PZ7.C55368 Br 2004   2003007533
[Fic]—dc21   CIP
                                                       AC

First Avon edition, 2004

*This book is humbly dedicated to
the united hearts of our Savior, Jesus Christ,
and His Blessed Mother Mary.*

Prologue

Perched on the front porch, Annie McGowan nestled a bowl of candy in her lap and distributed treats to the relentless stream of trick-or-treaters. Inside was a blitz of slamming doors and yelling voices as four other McGowan children prepared for the evening's activities. Their father, a widower, supervised the pandemonium.

As usual, the weather was hostile. A light but determined drizzle conspired with a brisk breeze to sabotage the evening for the ballerinas and princesses. Forced to don outerwear, they wore deflated looks and marched from house to house with glazed eyes. Streetlights did little to illuminate the evening. Except for a small glow at the top of each pole, the darkness remained intact. Annie glanced at the sky. A light mist was acceptable. Downpours could spoil the night.

After an eternity, Marla and Rene, her closest friends, arrived. The girls melted into the river of children heading toward the park. Their extended group of friends, boys and girls, fought a valiant war that evening. A new boy in particular interested Annie. Kevin Griffin. His dark curly hair and soft brown eyes were hard not to notice. Dark olive skin belied his Irish name. Approaching six feet, his frame was evenly distributed, and he moved smoothly. Observing him, Annie noticed he was watching her.

After exchanging a smile, she approached him.

"You're pretty small," he observed with a grin.

At just over five feet, Annie was indeed on the short side. It was not until this split second in time, however, that she noticed her size.

"Compared to some." This she delivered with a smile. He grinned down at her and was about to say more when Annie was pulled back into the fray. Throughout the night, Annie glanced at him often. He seemed always to be looking back at her, and they smiled when their eyes met. Annie felt a happy drop in her stomach each time.

She was rummaging through her pillowcase for her last can of shaving cream when Rene approached. Damp hair straggled around Rene's tense features, and Annie laughed out loud at the sight of her best friend. The girls conferred in whispers until a shout forced them to look up. One of the other girls was crying. Hastening to her side, they asked in alarm, "What happened?"

"That jerk kicked me," said their schoolmate through sobs.

"What jerk?" Annie asked.

Indicating Kevin, their friend continued to cry while Annie took control. "Don't give him the satisfaction. We'll get Julie to walk you home."

In minutes the injured reveler was dispatched. Annie looked at Rene grimly, and Rene nodded.

It was time to go home.

The girls began their trek across the park. Riddled with sodden toilet paper, the dreary landscape matched their mood. Halfway home, they heard their names called and turned to see Marla approaching with their friend Terry. Kevin Griffin ambled slowly behind them.

"Thanks for leaving without me," Marla greeted them. "Did you hear what Sue did to Kevin?"

Annie and Rene exchanged a glance. "No," Annie replied. "But we heard a nasty story about what Kevin did to Sue."

"Well, you heard it wrong," Terry Joyce said with feeling. A core member of the St. Malachy's group of eighth grade boys, his opinion carried weight. "She came up behind him and smashed an egg right into the back of his head."

Kevin kept his head down.

"You didn't have to kick her," Annie said to Kevin.

Kevin appealed to Rene. "You saw what she was doing to me. I asked her to leave me alone about a hundred times."

"That's true, Annie," Rene swayed. "She was driving him nuts."

The group merged and walked home, discussing the event. By the end of the journey, Annie was persuaded that Kevin had been sorely victimized. When they arrived at Annie's home, the others casually withdrew, leaving Kevin with Annie.

"I'm glad I met you, Annie," Kevin offered shyly.

"I'm glad I met you," she returned playfully. "I'm sorry Sue was such a nightmare."

Kevin held up his hand. "It was my fault. I should have left. I feel terrible about the whole thing."

"Don't be ridiculous," said Annie. "It wasn't your fault, Kevin." She looked up into his dark eyes.

Smiling down at her, Kevin spoke gently. "I think you are the nicest girl I've ever met, Annie."

Something tightened in Annie's throat. Since the death of her mother, she carried a dull but constant ache of loneliness. It shifted just the slightest bit. As Kevin bent down to kiss her gently on the forehead, it shifted again.

Chapter One

For the next three years, Annie and Kevin dated. Like most couples, they occasionally disagreed. Annie sometimes worried that their relationship was unlike that of other high school couples. Kevin could be jealous. He once pushed a boy for talking to Annie. While he said he trusted her, he was often suspicious. The fact that Rene was dating a delightful senior did not help matters. Annie felt that Rene's romance had shined a bright light on her own. She did not like what she saw.

In mid-July, Rene called Annie with a proposition. Rene's older sister, Patty, was attending a camping weekend sponsored by her college. It was being held at a campground two hours from Chicago, and Rene thought it would be a great chance for them to get away together. They would not have to socialize with her sister's friends but could put their tent close enough for safety. The girls could swim, read, talk, and eat. It sounded great to Annie. The McGowan family had never taken expensive vacations, but they had gone camping every summer, often at this very campground.

Briefly thinking of Kevin, Annie sighed. A year ago he would have been furious at the very idea. Thankfully, when she called to relay her plans, he said he would miss her but it was only for three days and the change would do her good. He made her promise she would not let any college boys flirt with her.

Annie laughed. "Kevin, I hate to break it to you, but I'm not half as appealing as you like to think."

"Give me a break, Annie. Those guys are vultures, and you are the most attractive girl I've ever seen."

"Thanks for the vote of confidence," she said lightly. "I'll be the most conceited one there anyway."

On the day of their departure, Rene picked up Annie in high spirits. Patty was driving with her friends, leaving the car to Rene. Their parents assumed the two sisters were driving together, and the girls had not enlightened them. It was a great adventure. Rene had been driving for a year but was currently allowed to use the car only for trips to the grocery store.

The girls loaded their gear quickly into the car. Rene surveyed the McGowans' large tent with misgivings.

Annie noted her friend's apprehension and said confidently, "I've watched my Dad put it up a thousand times. It's easy. It looks ghastly, but it will keep us dry, and if we want to invite the whole campground over for a party, we'll have enough room."

Annie ran in and said good-bye to her father. Mr. McGowan assumed Patty was the driver. When they were pulling away, Annie noticed him looking out the window.

"Annie," Rene said tersely, "does he know it's me driving?"

Annie thought quickly. "Smile, Rene. Smile and wave. Pretend we think he is waving."

The two girls waved and smiled. As they pulled out of sight, Annie noticed her father was no longer waving but shaking his fist. She gave him a huge smile and continued waving. "C'mon, Rene, move. Bye-bye, Dad." When they were out of sight, the girls burst out laughing. "Rene, I swear I'm going straight to hell," Annie said, wiping her eyes. "I'll call him tonight and let him know we got there okay. He might call your parents."

"Don't worry, Annie. We're already gone. This is something they haven't covered. Patty and I will act innocent and basically say, 'Oh, now we get it. This is, like, a new rule, right?'"

"Well, Rene, I will say this. It's nice to know you guys are as evil as we are!"

"Annie, all kids are like that with their parents. It's just your family that feels so guilty about it."

"I know, but my dad has enough to worry about. We really don't like to add to his problems. That sounds funny, doesn't it?"

"Not at all. When my dad was gone for a month, it was that way with my mom. We felt like we had to take care of her or something. And he was only on a business trip. I can't imagine how it would be if he was dead like your mom." Rene always understood.

This was going to be a great weekend. The girls headed for the expressway and merged into traffic.

"Let's open the windows and smoke in the car," Rene said recklessly.

"Rene, you're dangerous today," Annie said laughing.

"I'm not that crazy, Annie." Reaching under her seat, she pulled out a can of air freshener. "I have a true criminal mind and have planned everything down to the last detail."

The girls settled in to enjoy the ride. Rene was not confident on the highway and alternated between speeding in the right lane and creeping along in the left. They ignored the honking horns and discussed everything from funerals to boyfriends. After what seemed like a short time, they spied their exit. At the campground, they cheerfully greeted Patty and agreed to set up their tent just up the hill from the crowd. After two hours their temporary home was "viable," as Annie put it.

"It looks like a circus abandoned it," Rene said with a chuckle.

"A very sad and depressed circus," Annie agreed. "Let's get our stuff inside, make the beds, and go swimming. We should also stop at the campground store and buy some wood. We want to have our own fire tonight, don't we?"

"Definitely," Rene answered with a shudder. "Can you imagine sitting with that group all night?"

Annie glanced down the hill and concurred. Patty's friends had set up volleyball nets and a huge scoreboard. "Too collegiate for me."

After donning swimsuits, they bought their wood and spent the rest of the day at the beach. Later they crashed the college wiener roast and thoroughly enjoyed the free meal. After dinner they enjoyed the free campfire. A young man named Harold approached them and struck up a conversation. Surprisingly, he was quite pleasant. They talked about college and camping. He was interested in their college plans, and Annie noticed she had not said a word about Kevin. For some reason she did not want to. This thought made her feel guilty.

"Rene, it's getting late," she said abruptly. "We should go and start our own campfire."

Startled, Rene jumped up. "Yes, we should, I suppose." She gave Annie a quizzical look but said nothing more.

Harold protested that the night was young, but the girls were adamant. Annie could not shake the mental picture of Kevin. Harold was certainly smooth. He was so smooth that Annie would have liked to sit by the fire with him all night. She could absolutely envision herself going out with him. How did Kevin know these things? This was exactly what he had said would happen. Annie thought about Harold and realized she would love to get to know him better. She felt twinges of disappointment as she and Rene built their fire.

"Annie, do you ever get the urge to go out with someone other than Kevin?" Rene asked casually.

"I'm just curious. Do you think you can marry him without dating anyone else?"

"I don't know, Rene," Annie answered thoughtfully. "My dad is getting a bit frantic about it. He keeps insisting I date other guys. He even said there was 'no way in hell' I could go to the same college as Kevin." Annie paused. "I could still see Kevin, just date a few other people. Kevin would never agree, though."

"No. He sure wouldn't," Rene agreed. "Harold really seemed to like you. It seems like a shame, doesn't it?"

"Yes. It does," Annie said quietly. "But, Rene, I would hate to think of Kevin dating other girls."

"I wouldn't worry about that somehow," Rene said with a smile. "More likely he'd follow you on your dates. I could not help thinking, if Kevin pulled up and saw us sitting there he would automatically assume you were about to start making out with Harold. Did you think of that?"

Annie looked startled. "Yes, I did. That's why I came back up. That's an ugly thought, isn't it, Rene? What would Tom think if he pulled up?"

Rene rolled her eyes. "You know Tom. He would grab a hot dog and introduce himself to Harold. Tom is not the jealous type. It makes me wonder sometimes." Rene looked pensive.

"Surely you don't think he has to be jealous to like you a lot? Don't compare him with Kevin. Kevin has a lot on his mind from home. It makes him more possessive. I think Tom is more normal. Don't you?" Annie spoke with feeling. She had often wondered why Tom was not jealous. On the other hand, he and Rene did not have huge fights like Annie and Kevin. Their relationship was more peaceful.

"I know what you mean, Annie, and I agree," Rene said slowly. "It's just that you and Kevin seem so romantic. We're not like that. Sometimes I would like Tom to be passionate about me. You know?"

"Yes," Annie sympathized. "When it's good with us, it's good. But when it's bad, it's bad. Kevin has gotten over a lot of that stuff, thank God. You know, Rene, there is nothing stopping you from dating other people." Annie was about to continue when they heard someone shouting her name.

"Who is that? Did you hear someone call your name?" Rene asked.

"Yes," Annie said, smiling. "It must be Harold. We're over here, Harold," she shouted into the darkness.

Two figures approached from down the hill. One of the figures was quite tall. "I hope that's Harold, Annie," Rene said nervously.

"Of course it is. Who else could it be?" Annie said confidently. "Harold, is that you?" she called out.

As the figures got closer, Annie gasped. "Rene, tell me that's not Kevin. How did he find us?"

Rene was aghast. "At least we're sitting up here by our own little fire. Did he say he was coming, Annie?"

"Of course not. I would have told you, Rene. Do you think he heard me calling out to Harold?"

"Don't say anything, and we'll act like he's mistaken," Rene advised.

"I don't believe my eyes," Annie called when they were close. "Kevin, what are you doing here? Hi, Terry," Annie said on recognizing Terry Joyce. "How did you find us?"

Greetings were exchanged all around.

"I hope you don't mind us crashing your campout," Kevin began. The girls assured them they were most welcome. "We decided we needed some country air."

"But how did you get away?"

The boys began to laugh. "Kevin is staying at my house, and I'm staying at his," Terry answered. "We did not know where you were so we parked down the hill," Terry continued. "We have to go pull the car up and unload the cooler."

Just then a voice rang out of the darkness. "Annie?" Harold called. Kevin shot Annie a level look. She felt a chill as Harold entered their circle of light.

"Hi," he said pleasantly, looking at the two unexpected visitors. "My name is Harold." With this he extended his hand to Kevin.

Ignoring him, Kevin looked at Annie. "Who's the loser?"

Harold looked stunned. Rene gasped. Terry shifted his feet around, and Annie said angrily, "Kevin. How rude. This is Harold. Harold, this is my boyfriend, Kevin, and his friend Terry. They surprised us." Looking at Kevin, Annie explained,

"Harold is a friend of Rene's sister Patty. We met him at dinner." Turning to Harold, she said pleasantly, "What can we do for you, Harold?" Immediately assessing the situation, Harold said quickly, "I just wanted to see if you needed anything. It's kind of lonely up here, and I wanted to make sure you were okay."

"Well, you can see that everything is hunky-dory, Harold," Kevin said briskly. "No need to worry yourself. See you later."

Harold began to stammer, and Rene jumped in. "Thank *you*, Harold. Terry, why don't you and I go get the car? We can walk down with Harold. We'll be right back." Rene spoke cheerfully, and everyone hastened to follow her plan. Harold could not leave quickly enough, and Terry looked like he did not relish the thought of pulling Kevin off Harold. Annie gave Rene a grateful wave as they started down the hill. Turning slowly, she faced Kevin in a rage.

"Kevin, how could you? I don't know what to say. I'm glad to see you?" Her voice dripped sarcasm.

"Are you, Annie? I guess I'm wondering if Harold was glad to see me."

"Don't start this, Kevin. I am not going to defend myself for something I haven't done. Please, for both of our sakes, don't start accusing me of anything." They gazed at each other with intensity. "I'm getting my sweater." Annie turned sharply and entered the tent. Inside, she sat down and put her head in her hands.

"Can I come in?" Kevin asked sweetly from the door.

"It depends," Annie answered grimly. "Are you rational?"

"Of course. Why do you always assume I'm going to overreact?"

"Experience, I guess."

"Well, I'm not. I'm glad to see you. I'm glad to be in a tent in the middle of Wisconsin with you. By ourselves. Alone." Kevin assumed a lecherous tone, and Annie laughed. "I'm sorry I was rude to Harvey, Annie. He seemed like a nice guy, but I do not miss him at the moment." Sitting beside Annie, Kevin pulled her into his arms. "Are you mad?"

"His name is Harold. Yes, I'm mad." Kevin kissed her. "I'm not too mad, Kevin, as long as you're not going to be suspicious. Actually, I am happy to see you. If you get caught, you'll have to face the firing squad, you know."

"It would be worth it. How long do you think Rene and Terry will be gone?" he asked, becoming more passionate.

"At least thirty minutes. Actually, Rene will stay away longer. I'm sure she thinks you're having a fit about Harvey. Er . . . Harold. Kevin, maybe we should go back to the fire," Annie suggested. Kevin was a little too pleased to be alone with her.

She and Kevin had discussed the subject of sex and agreed to abstain until after they were in college. Kevin did not feel it was a sin as long as two people loved each other. Annie remarked that most eighteen-year-old men would agree. Kevin laughed but contended it was only wrong if someone was using someone else. Annie pointed out the church's clear mandate on premarital sex. Kevin thought that many things they did could be considered sins. Annie understood his logic but felt there was sin and there was SIN. Just because a person stole a candy bar didn't mean he might as well rob a bank.

"Let's stay in here for a little while," he said, kissing her again. "You never let me near you. I know what you're worried about, Annie, but I won't let anything happen. I promise."

Knowing Kevin's feelings mirrored her own, Annie relented. Almost immediately the situation went too far. She could have stopped it. Kevin always scrupulously respected her wishes in that regard. For some reason, she let it continue. Later she wondered what was different about that night. She and Kevin were no strangers to passion, but they had always restrained themselves.

Afterward they dressed and sat silently by the fire.

"You're beautiful, Annie," Kevin said lovingly.

"I don't feel beautiful," she whispered.

"Are you sorry?" he asked.

"I don't know. I can't think straight. Kevin, we shouldn't have. I mean . . ." Annie struggled for words, but her voice cracked. Kevin pulled her into his arms and held her. "Annie, it will never happen again. I promise you. It was my fault. Do you hear me?" He pulled back so he could look into her eyes. "Do you hear me, Annie? I won't let it happen again. Okay?"

"Kevin, it was not your fault. There were two of us in there. Whatever else we do, we're not going to blame you. It's just that we decided not to do this. We shouldn't have stayed in the tent."

"I love you, Annie. Do you believe that?"

"Yes," she answered truthfully.

"Then believe me when I tell you it won't happen again. I would never hurt you. You know that. It's all right now. Maybe we got it out of our system."

"You're right, Kevin. We'll be more careful from now on. No more campouts for us."

"Annie, I think we can make a case for blaming Rene," Kevin joked. "She ought to be horse-whipped for leaving us alone. I hate Rene. Don't you?" Annie burst out laughing in spite of herself. "That's better," Kevin said kindly. "Now, let's have a beer while I plan my next seduction."

"That's not funny, Kevin," Annie said with a hurt look.

"Oh, God. Sorry. It was supposed to be." Kevin had a wild look on his face. "Help me out here, Annie. I'm not sure what to say."

"I'm sorry, Kevin. I'm just feeling a little sensitive. I guess I'm waiting for someone to call me a harlot."

"Let's see if we can make Harvey say it," Kevin

suggested brightly. "That will give me an excuse to kill him."

"You're outrageous." Annie chuckled. "His name is Harold, and I'm sure he'll run the next time he sees me coming. Honestly, Kevin. Calling him a loser like that . . . what were you thinking?"

Kevin smiled. "He was after you, Annie. Couldn't you tell? Let's not talk about Henry, though. Let's get a beer and walk down to meet Terry. Are you okay now, Annie?"

Annie was able to look at him and answer honestly, "I think so. Let's go anyway." Taking her hand, Kevin led the way, and they went off to meet their friends.

The boys stayed for the weekend. Much to everyone's relief, Harold stayed discreetly away. Kevin and Terry were at their funniest, and it turned out to be the best weekend of the summer. Tender and sweet, Kevin made a constant effort to amuse Annie. Rene voiced her surprise at the turn of events. She candidly admitted that she had been prepared for a midnight flight if Kevin got too aggressive with Harold. "He's certainly acting like a gentleman, Annie," she observed grudgingly. Annie nodded in agreement. He certainly was.

Summer wore on, and Kevin and Annie prepared for their senior year. College scouts monitored Kevin's progress. He frequently asked Annie about her college plans. Annie was not concerned about making a decision yet. She still had time and figured she would attend school downstate with

17

Nellie. Mr. McGowan was watching Kevin's choice carefully. If Kevin chose the downstate school, Annie could count on a battle.

One evening Annie made Kevin drop her off early. They had gone to a party at Rene's boyfriend's house. Annie had begun to feel sick. Certain she was coming down with something, she asked Kevin to bring her home. Kevin complied and promised to call her later.

On the way up the stairs to her bedroom, Annie doubled over. She felt a sharp pain in her head. Waiting a few moments, she continued up the stairs to her room. Pausing at the doorway, she noticed Maureen reading on her bed.

"Hi," she said weakly. "What are you reading?"

"Nothing good," Maureen answered shortly. "What are you doing home so early?"

"I'm not feeling well," Annie said. She leaned against the doorway and tried to focus on Maureen's face. Strangely enough, it was gone. Annie could see only the bed. "I'm sick," she muttered as she doubled over again.

Annie was vaguely aware that Maureen was screaming for their sister Nellie. It seemed like hours before she felt strong arms pulling her up from the floor. "Annie, Annie, wake up!" Annie tried to focus on Maureen's face but gave up. Everything was swimming. She heard Nellie's voice from a thousand miles away. Nellie and Maureen were trying to lift her onto the bed. Annie thought idly that she could not help them. She was concentrating on a more pressing sensation.

"I'm going to be sick," she heard herself say.

Disembodied hands brought her into the bathroom. Someone held her hair, and someone else stroked her arm. Annie felt extremely loved, in a detached sort of way. The nausea passed, and Annie's head cleared.

"Can you put me in front of the fan?" she asked weakly.

"Sure. Grab her under the arm, Maureen," Nellie instructed. "Get that washcloth wet, and we'll put it on her head." Nellie was all business, and Annie could only surmise that Maureen was in a panic. Maureen was great in a crisis unless blood or pain was involved. Annie was grateful that Nellie had been close by. Moments later they propped her up on Nellie's bed with every pillow in the house under her head. The sisters kept vigil, waiting for Annie to respond.

"Sorry," she accommodated them.

"No need to apologize," Nellie said gently. "What happened?"

"I'll tell you what happened," Maureen volunteered. "She came to the bedroom door and her face was the most ugly gray I've ever seen. Then she doubled up and fell down. I couldn't get to her in time, and she hit her head on the floor. Does your head hurt, Annie?" Maureen shouted.

"Why are you screaming at me?" Annie moaned,

putting her hands up to her head.

"She is not deaf, Maureen. She's sick," Nellie snapped. "Annie, did you hit your head?"

"I'm not sure. I felt sick at the party and came home," she answered. "I had sharp pains in my head when I was coming up the stairs. Then I don't remember anything. I'm feeling better now."

"Annie, Dad is riding his bike," Nellie said reassuringly. "He should be back in a few minutes, and he can take you to the hospital. Maureen, hop in the car and find Dad." Nellie spoke calmly, but the suggestion put Maureen into a panic.

"Oh, my God. Do you think it's a brain tumor? Should we call an ambulance?" Maureen was poised for flight.

"*Go*, Maureen. Get Dad. I'm sure it's nothing serious, but Dad will know what to do." Nellie looked at Annie and winked. Annie giggled back. Maureen was just the right side of full-blown panic.

"I'm really sick, Nell," Annie said pathetically.

"I know. Don't worry. We'll take you to the doctor and see what he says. Could you drink a little pop?"

Annie nodded weakly. Shortly after Nellie returned, they heard Mr. McGowan's footsteps on the stairs. Moving fast, he blustered into the room and surveyed the patient. Annie was still a funny color, and Mr. McGowan decided to take her to the emergency room for a "quick look." The girls fluttered about, getting her ready.

Four hours later they returned home to find

the two sisters waiting up. Their anxious inquiries were met with reassurance from their father.

"She'll be fine," he said breezily. "The doctor said it is a relapse of the mononucleosis she had last year. She's been burning the candle at both ends and needs a lot of rest." He summarized the situation quickly. "What she needs now is to get to bed."

"Did they check her for a brain tumor, Dad?" Maureen asked. Mr. McGowan rolled his eyes. "Maureen, she doesn't have a brain tumor. Headaches come with mono. That's all it is. Now, help your sister up to bed and everyone get some sleep."

Annie awoke the next day feeling wonderful. She lay in bed for a moment and discovered she was ravenously hungry. She began to get out of bed and nearly knocked heads with Maureen, leaning over the top bunk.

"How are you feeling today?" Maureen asked in concern.

"Actually, Maureen, I feel great. I'm starving, and I skipped dinner last night so I think I need to eat." Annie stretched.

"Annie, I have to ask you something. Promise me you won't get mad." Maureen looked extremely nervous.

"Go ahead, Maureen. What is it?"

"Okay. But remember you promised." Maureen paused and chose her words with care. "Are you sleeping with Kevin?"

Annie stared at her blankly. "*What*?" she asked,

in the time-honored tradition of obtaining time to think.

"I know it's ridiculous," Maureen said in relief. Annie's response had negated her suspicions. "I wanted to make sure you weren't pregnant or anything. Sorry I brought it up. It's just the way you fainted made me wonder . . ." She slid out of the upper bunk bed and began to dress. "I feel like pancakes. Do you want some?"

Annie groped for an appropriate response. "Uh, sure. If you're making them. . . ." Maureen departed, leaving Annie wrapped in shock. Surely she was not pregnant. It could not be possible. One little time. Annie reeled at the thought. It seemed like seconds before she heard Maureen shouting that breakfast was ready. Annie collected herself and went down to eat.

Chapter Two

The next two weeks were the longest in Annie's short life. She waited for good news. Kevin called her at least twice a day. Desperately seeking a reprieve, Annie went to the library. She found a book about the female body and read the chapter on pregnancy. It did not look good. Her symptoms were fairly typical. Flipping farther, she spotted a chapter on something called hysterical pregnancy. She vaguely tried to imagine any other kind. Yes, she decided, this must be what I have. A hysterical pregnancy. She giggled at the thought.

"Well, it sounds good to me," Kevin said doubtfully. "How long do these things last? I mean, you can't just stay hysterically pregnant for the rest of your life. Can you?"

Annie sighed. "I don't know, Kevin. At some point we are going to have to see a doctor and get a test done."

Kevin's voice held the suggestion of panic that had become so familiar to Annie these last couple of weeks. "What doctor? Annie, they'll tell your dad. We can't let anyone find out about this."

Annie suppressed a rolling wave of irritation. "Kevin, this situation is not going to stay stagnant. From what I've observed about pregnant women, they tend to expand horribly. Do you get it? We can't keep this a secret much longer." She eyed him suspiciously. She was tired of his "me first" attitude. His selfishness made her feel bitter.

"Let's give it another week, okay? I'm sure it's the hysterical thing." Kevin was constantly fidgeting with his keys these days, and Annie resisted the urge to snatch them away and throw them out of the car window. They were parked around the corner from her house. Kevin told her he absolutely could not face her father.

"I have a great idea. Let's drive downtown and forget the whole thing," Kevin suggested. "We'll get a six-pack and go to the lakeshore. C'mon, let's do it," he said persuasively.

"Can't drink," she said shortly. "Bad for the baby." Startled, they exchanged looks of mutual horror. It was the first time the possibility of a baby had been verbalized. "Oh, Kevin . . ." Annie began.

Kevin started to laugh. "This is a nightmare. Yes, indeed. You're going to have to trust me on this. We need a little bit of fun. Going crazy is not going to change anything, so we might as well go get some beer instead." Kevin was acting strangely, and Annie looked at him through narrowed eyes. "Junior will have to cope while Mom—that's you, Annie—and Dad—that would be me—go and get drunk. Are you ready, Mom?" Noticing Annie's accusing eyes, Kevin continued, "Annie, I know what you're thinking. Why is he so upset? I realize that you're the one who is pregnant, hysterical or otherwise, but I'm not going to abandon you. Therefore, I am also pregnant. I realize you get to do the really fun stuff, like actually deliver the baby, but my life is going to change a hell of a lot, too. Add to that the guilt about what I've done to you and the feeling in my stomach about what Grandpa"—at this he paused for a nervous chuckle—"is going to say, and I have to admit I am feeling a little . . . tense. Unless there is a miracle, things are going to get a lot worse before they get any better. Let's go have some fun. Okay?"

Annie felt guilty. Grudgingly conceding that this would affect him, too, she decided to stop punishing him. "Let's do it, Kevin. You're absolutely right. Let's go have some fun." Annie smiled as Kevin sighed in relief.

Two hours later he watched helplessly as Annie vomited into a garbage can. "I guess you're right, Annie," he said as they waited for her shaking to pass. "Can you find a doctor who doesn't know you?"

"I'm going to tell Maureen," Annie said with finality. "She goes to a female doctor somewhere in the suburbs. Maybe I can see her." Pale and sick, Annie felt empty. No longer afraid, she just wanted the waiting to be over. Stealing a glance at Kevin, she correctly speculated that he felt the same way.

"Try to make it for a Saturday, and I'll take you," Kevin said without expression. "What will they have to do?"

"According to the book, they'll test my urine. I guess they'll also do some kind of examination.

That's the part I dread," she said.

"Let's get it over with. Sorry you got sick."

Annie patted his arm in a distracted manner. "It wasn't your fault. I'm getting used to throwing up. It's not too bad. It was a good idea to try to have some fun, Kevin, but I think I'd like to go home now."

A week later they were waiting in the car outside a doctor's office. Kevin refused to go in and would not be budged. "I can't believe you're going to make me go in there alone."

"Annie, I can't go in there. Sorry. I'll be waiting right here for you." Kevin looked ashamed, and Annie could have kicked him.

"I wish *I* could wait here," she said resentfully as she got out of the car. Kevin looked sick but said nothing.

After what seemed like an eternity, she walked back across the parking lot. Seeing Kevin trying to read her face, she shook her head noncommittally. After seating herself in the car, she put him out of his misery. "We have to wait until after four. They won't have the results of the test until then." Annie looked white. "Take me home, Kevin."

"Was it awful?" he asked as he pulled into traffic.

"Yes," Annie said shortly.

"What did she say?" Kevin persisted.

"She said my uterus is consistent with a six-week pregnancy. She also said there could be reasons for that other than pregnancy. She asked me what my intentions were if the test is positive. Apparently

26

she is required by law to ask."

"What did you tell her?" Kevin asked.

"I said 'I guess I'll have a baby.' What else could I say?"

Annie was on the verge of breaking down, and Kevin stopped asking questions. Reaching over, he grabbed her hand and kissed it. "I'll call you at four fifteen and see what the verdict is. Then we'll go for a walk or drive or something tonight. Okay?" He spoke gently, but Annie noticed that his hands were clammy.

"Fine," she agreed tersely.

At four ten, Annie dialed the number to the clinic. A woman's voice answered and transferred the call to the doctor. "Miss McGowan?" Annie recognized the doctor's voice.

Trying to ignore the nausea, Annie answered, "Yes, it's me."

"Your test was positive. You're pregnant." Hearing no response, she continued. "You'll need to begin taking prenatal vitamins and come back in one month. Do you want me to call in a prescription for the vitamins?"

"Uhm, no. Not today." Annie could not concentrate and clutched the phone. "Thank you," she said shortly, and hung up. Reeling, she wandered up the stairs to her room and crawled into bed. She ignored the ringing telephone. Kevin would have to wait. She couldn't move. She heard a voice yelling up the stairs telling her that she had a phone call. Annie heaved herself out of bed and went down to destroy any lingering hope of Kevin's. Her news was met with repeated "Shit, shit, shit" on his end, and Annie ended the conversation agreeing to call him later. Finding her way back to bed, Annie fell into a deep and dreamless sleep.

Hours later Annie awoke to Maureen's concerned face staring at her from the side of the bed.

"I'm pregnant," Annie said.

Maureen's face contorted. "What!"

"I can't wait until someone says 'Congratulations.'"

"Give me a break," Maureen said with passion. "Who gets to tell Dad?"

"I thought I'd leave that to you and Nellie," Annie said in a dead voice. "I don't want to be in the same state when he hears." Annie noted absently that she felt no real emotion. She would have been happy to lie in her bed until she died. "I'm going back to sleep. If Kevin calls, tell him I'll talk to him tomorrow. Okay?"

Maureen looked at her in concern. "Sorry, Annie. I don't mean to be nasty. It's just such a shock. It will all work out somehow. I mean, this has happened before, you know. I have a few friends . . . " She trailed off after observing Annie's look of disinterest. "I'll come up and check on you in a few hours." With that she turned off the light and left the room. Annie rolled over in relief and went back to sleep. She would handle everything tomorrow.

● ● ●

The following weeks passed in a blur of horrors. Emotional meetings were held with the sisters. It was decided that Maureen would clear the house and Nellie would do the honors. Annie expressed little concern, and Maureen worried that Annie was having a nervous breakdown. Nellie said Maureen was overreacting. After speaking to Annie privately, she told Maureen that Annie was in shock.

The day Nellie told her father, Annie stayed at Rene's. She wanted to give him time to react. Nellie blessedly refrained from comment when Annie asked how he had taken it. She said he was a little shocked but would be fine in time. Annie's first meeting with him was uneventful. He greeted her casually and reminded her of the need to eat properly. He also told her that she would need to get to confession immediately. Annie groaned inwardly. Was it a sin to be pregnant? Mr. McGowan asked her one question and never uttered another word of reproach: "Annie, how did this happen?"

"Dad, I don't know," she responded, legitimately perplexed.

Maureen burst out laughing. "Well, usually—"

"Shut up, Maureen," Annie and her father replied in unison.

"All right. Never mind," Mr. McGowan continued. "You'll have to make some decisions. The first priority is, of course, confession. I'll take you up there this afternoon."

"Uh, thanks. Dad," Annie stammered. "I'd prefer to go myself."

"I don't want you going alone, Annie." He seemed worried. "You might get upset. Maureen, you go with her. Pop in there yourself while you're at it."

"Remember the motto, Dad," Maureen responded cheerfully. "Mind your own soul. I'm old enough to know when I need to go to confession. I will happily go with you, though, Annie. If the priest starts yelling at you, I'll rip open his door and scream 'FIRE!'"

"Oh, I'm sure he'll just say '*Shit*,'" Annie said tiredly.

"*Annie*," Mr. McGowan scolded. "Of course, he won't say that. Please do not swear in this house."

"Right, Annie," Maureen responded. "Only Dad is allowed to swear in the house. We have to go outside to swear."

Mr. McGowan drifted into the kitchen, and Maureen hissed to Annie. "'Don't know?' I can't believe you said that." She began to giggle. "Did you really think he was going to buy that? Was this, like, the Immaculate Conception?" She paused for a second and said with great gravity, "Just who is that baby you're carrying?"

Annie burst out laughing. "Shut up, Maureen. What was I supposed to say? 'We did it in the family tent?' Leave me alone. You wait outside the church. You'll make me laugh if you come in."

Later that day Annie and Maureen walked to St. Malachy's. Maureen made outrageous jokes the whole way, and Annie was beginning to get a stomach cramp from laughing.

"I definitely think you should use the Immaculate Conception defense, Annie," Maureen said brightly. "Really give him something to think about. Tell him you don't know how it happened but you suspect divine intervention."

"Maureen, if you don't shut up I am going throw up on the sidewalk," Annie threatened. She had to be serious enough to go into the confessional. "I mean it. I feel like throwing up."

Maureen immediately stopped joking as Annie knew she would. Vomiting threats were taken seriously these days. Annie left Maureen outside and entered the church. Her anxiety lessened as she observed the short line. She hoped to be last.

Annie's turn came quickly. She slid onto the kneeler and closed the door. She could vaguely hear the mumbling of the penitent on the other side and began to hum quietly. It was not polite to listen to someone else's confession. Alone with a crucifix in the darkened cubbyhole, Annie fought off the urge to cry.

The priest slid back the screen and began. Annie made short work of the preliminaries. Getting right to the meat of the problem, she said, "Father, I'm not sure I needed to come again, but my dad wanted me to. I had sex with my boyfriend. I confessed that a couple of months ago, but I just found out that I'm pregnant. Anyway, here I am."

"I see," said the priest quietly.

Annie appreciated his response as the first neutral reaction she had gotten to date. Encouraged, she continued, "I am not considering an abortion or anything." Did she hear him sigh in relief? "I am going to have the baby, but I haven't gotten any further than that." They both remained silent for a moment. Stifling a sob, Annie began again. "Father, what bothers me most is the poor baby. It's so horrible that everyone thinks he or she is a tragedy. I know it sounds absurd, but I want this baby. I feel so sorry for it. I would rather not be pregnant, but it's too late for that. I guess I can't expect anyone to be happy, but do they have to be so depressed? If a baby is conceived out of a marriage, is the baby a mistake?" Annie stopped and waited.

"There is no such thing as a baby that is a mistake. I think you are a wonderful person. Let's start with that." Annie began to cry in earnest. "It probably feels very good to cry, and you should do that a lot," he said kindly. "I want to tell you a few things. Okay?"

"Okay." Annie tried to stop sniffling.

"At the beginning of time God created us. All of us. He took a lot of time because He decided there would be a lot of people. He loved each one of us as though each were the only one He had created. Soon you are going to be a mother. Then you will understand God's love in a special way. You already do, don't you?"

"Yes, Father," she replied solemnly.

"Okay. So each soul was created. He knew each soul intimately. He carefully thought about when each soul should be born. At the beginning of time He created the soul of your little baby. He also decided when would be the perfect time to send that precious, innocent soul down to earth. He carefully looked around at all of the souls and decided you were the only one that could be the mother of this baby. He left nothing to chance. He knew this sin would be committed. He loves you like you are His only child. He thought, 'How can I make something wonderful come from something my little angel should not have done?' This baby is no accident, my dear. Your baby was created by God at the beginning of time and has some very special work to do in this world. Work that only he or she will be able to accomplish. Your baby is no mistake. There is no such thing."

He continued, "Your baby is a precious gift to our world. For your penance I want you to thank God every day for this child. Thank Him for His mercy and thank Him for His constant love. It may be that you decide to give this baby up for adoption. Even if you do, remember that you'll be a mother for eternity. God will let you know what is best. Never be afraid of what people think of you. God knows you better than anyone else. He's filled with joy today because you've accepted the gift of this child. That's all that matters. Is there anything else you want to talk about? You've told your parents?"

"Yes. Everything is okay. I'm not going to get

thrown out or anything."

"Good. I want you to call the rectory and ask them for the number to Catholic Charities. They can help you to look at all of your options." He hesitated. "Do you want to tell me your first name?"

"Yes, Father. It's Annie."

"Okay, Annie. I am going to ask God every day to protect you and your child. He'll take special care of you. Incidentally, are you clear on the rules regarding premarital sex? It doesn't become okay because you're pregnant."

Annie laughed shortly. "I know, Father. I don't know how to thank you. I feel happy. Thank you, Father."

"Thank *you*, Annie. You're a brave and courageous girl. Go in peace."

Annie stumbled out of the confessional. She kneeled down and said her penance. "Thank you, God, for my little baby," she prayed over and over. Her heart felt lighter than it had in two months. The worst was over. Everyone who mattered had been told except for the nuns at school. The priest did not think she was horrible. On the contrary, he thought her baby was a good thing. "A precious gift," he had called it. Annie smiled to herself. "Thank you, God, for my little baby," she prayed again. Cleansing tears burned her eyelids. She stayed and prayed for thirty minutes. The priest said that it only mattered what God thought. If Annie only worried about what God thought, her worries were over. God loved her. Of this she was certain. The rest could be dealt with.

With a light heart she skipped out into the sunshine to meet Maureen. "I was just coming in after you," Maureen said grimly.

Annie laughed easily. It felt good to laugh. "Maureen, he said my baby was a precious gift to the world." She did not feel anxious anymore, and her laughter was free of the underlying hysteria.

"Tell me you're joking." Maureen grabbed her arm. "You didn't use the Immaculate Conception defense, did you?"

The intense look on Maureen's face made Annie laugh harder. "But you told me to, Maureen." Maureen's horror forced Annie to relent. "Of course not, you goof. I told him the truth, and he said I am not bad and that the baby is a gift. This baby is not a mistake."

"Annie, of course you're not bad. No worse than the rest of us who never got caught." Maureen looked worried. "Annie, the baby will be the most adored little monster in the city of Chicago. Can you imagine? We'll spoil the child rotten." Seeing Annie's smile, she continued. "If you decide to keep this baby, we'll all help you. Nellie and I did not want to talk about the baby in case it upset you."

"I can understand that," Annie said emphatically. "I've been acting kind of weird. I feel better now. I think everything is going to be okay." She smiled at her sister.

"Of course, it will be," Maureen answered with gusto. "What else can it be? Life has to work out. It doesn't just stop because things get horrible for a while. How's your stomach?"

Annie stopped. After a moment she pronounced it sound. "My stomach is good. Let's get lunch."

With light hearts the sisters sought out hamburgers.

While Annie wrestled with her family's reactions, Kevin faced his own struggles. He agreed to tell his mother on the same day Annie went to confession. She waited in vain for his call. Lacking the courage to call him, she waited until the following day. At two o'clock in the afternoon, he called and asked her to meet him around the corner.

"I'm glad to see you're still alive," she began as she got into the car. "How did it go?"

Kevin looked uncertain. "Well, okay, I guess. She didn't say much. She gave me two pills to make me sleep, and I went to bed."

"She must have said something, Kevin," Annie said slowly. "What did your dad say?"

"Nothing. My mom says we're not going to tell him. She says he'll have a fit. We're not going to tell anyone." Kevin looked slightly defensive.

"Kevin," Annie began patiently, "I can understand her wish to avoid a scene, but don't you think he is bound to find out? What about your brother? Won't it be worse if they don't hear it from you?"

"Just because you want to tell the whole world does not mean that we have to."

"Pardon me?" Annie asked in disbelief. "My

family would eventually have guessed. Contrary to what you might think, Kevin, I don't want to be the poster girl for teenage pregnancies. How could I have not told my dad?"

Kevin's face turned red, and he began to shout. "People don't have to know, Annie. My mother said she would pay for an abortion. I told her you did not want that, and she said to tell you anyway. She said you should not have told your father."

Annie stared at him, white-faced. "Gee, Kevin, I can certainly see why you think she is so cool. Her solution is to chop your baby into pieces." Annie looked out of the window. She felt like a mist surrounded her head. Somehow, it had turned into a nightmare again. "Kevin, would you agree to an abortion? I'm just curious."

Hesitating a moment, Kevin looked like he was about to cry. "No, Annie. If you don't want that then neither do I. She also said you could go away to a home for unwed mothers. You could stay there until you have the baby, then give it up for adoption. No one would have to know that way either."

"Well, all I can say is thank God she's not my mother," Annie said with feeling. "For not saying much she sure had plenty of great ideas. What's with the obsession not to tell anyone? Her son looks like a big stud. I'm the one who looks like a tramp, Kevin. Good thing your mother has no daughters. She'd put a scarlet letter on their chests and make them jump off the nearest cliff." Annie was more upset than she knew. She had not expected his family to be happy but had hoped for compassion.

"Annie, I don't want to talk about this anymore," Kevin said, putting his arms across his chest.

"Neither do I. Should we talk about the weather? No. Let's talk about football." Annie was not calming down. The more she thought about it the angrier she became.

"Calm down." Kevin raised his voice. "I've had enough of this shit. Don't blame my mother. I admit she was out of line about the abortion thing, but I made it clear we were not considering it. Shut your mouth and listen for a minute. I have to ask you a question." Kevin paused for a breath. He had been pointing his finger in Annie's face.

"Well," Annie said, taking a deep breath, "as much as I would love to hear what you want to ask me, Kevin, I'm afraid I have to leave. Go talk to your mother like that." Annie pulled open the door and started to get out. She felt her head jerked back into the car and slammed against the headrest.

"Let go of me," she said between clenched teeth.

"Shut up, Annie. I asked you to shut your mouth and listen, and you are going to shut your mouth and listen." Kevin had all of the hair on the left side of her head in his hand. Her head was being pressed into the headrest, and Annie could feel her hair being pulled out.

"Kevin, you're hurting me," she said in a level voice. He looked like a madman, and Annie knew she somehow had to get away. Her heart was pounding in her chest. Kevin's face was contorted in rage, and she had the fleeting impression that he wanted to kill her.

Still holding her by the hair, he repeated, "Listen to me. I'm going to ask you a question and you're going to tell me the truth. Do you understand? The truth. Are you listening?"

Annie did not hesitate. "I'll tell you whatever you want, but let go of my hair."

"Just so you know, Annie, if you try to get out of this car I'm going to fucking kill you. Do you understand?"

Annie was about to start shouting in outrage. Looking into his eyes, she thought the better of it. She would have to get him off guard and make her escape. She nodded her head. Resisting the urge to glance around for help, she looked directly into Kevin's eyes. "What's your question?"

"What happened with Harold?" Kevin watched her intently.

Legitimately bewildered, she continued to stare. "What?"

"You heard me, Annie. What happened with Harold? Don't lie to me, because it won't work. I know exactly what happened. I just want to see if you have the guts to admit it."

Annie frantically searched for a response. What happened with Harold? She thought back. Nothing happened with Harold. Where had this come from? Mental pictures flitted through her head. What had Kevin heard? There had been nothing to hear.

"Kevin, I have no idea what you're talking

about. Nothing happened with Harold. You do mean Harold from the campground, don't you?"

Out of nowhere she felt Kevin's hand around her throat. His face was right up against hers, and he began to tighten his hand. "Tell the truth, Annie, or I swear I'll choke you. What the fuck did you do with Harold?"

Annie could not speak. She could not breathe. Frantically she clawed at his hand in an attempt to open her airway. Kevin continued to tighten his grip around her neck. She heard sounds coming from her throat and thought about death. Suddenly she was released, and Kevin moved his face back a few inches. Choking, Annie groped instinctively for the door handle. Kevin chuckled. Pulling her hand back, he said, "I don't think so, Miss Intelligence. Do I have to tell you again that you're not getting out of this car until you tell me the truth? You catch your breath and try again. I want to know exactly what happened with Harold. Every little detail." Annie continued to choke while attempting to take breaths. She resisted the urge to attack him, realizing finally that she was completely at his mercy. "That's it," he said. "Get comfortable and start to tell the truth, if you're capable of it."

Looking at him with hatred, she began. Her voice was hoarse as she told him exactly what had happened with Harold. She included every tiny detail she could think of. Harold walked over to them. He began to talk. He got them a drink. He protested when they got up to leave. He came up to their campfire. Annie left nothing out. Finishing the story, she stared levelly at Kevin. "Any questions?"

"Just one, Smarty," Kevin began. "Did you really think I was stupid? I've waited for over two months for you to tell me. When we got to the campground, we met Patty. She told us you had just left. She also told us you had been down there the whole night. I arrive and there you are acting so innocent up by your own little fire. You acted like you had been there all night. Didn't you?"

"Kevin, I acted like nothing. I told you we met Harold down by their fire. I did not lie about anything." Annie began to cry. "Why are you doing this to me?" Her body began to react, and she began to shake. "What is your problem? If you had questions, why didn't you ask me then? Two months later you come at me like the Gestapo?" Her breath came in gasps. "Do you realize you could have killed me?"

Kevin finally began to look upset. "Annie, I'm afraid I had no choice. You did not tell me the truth, and I had to know. My mother asked me if I am absolutely certain I am the father of this baby." A look of horror came over Annie's face. "I told her yes. I told her I was pretty sure you had never been with anyone else. You're sneaky, but you're not that bad." Annie stared. "Annie, don't get mad at her. She's looking out for me. I told her you weren't like that. I'm sorry I had to get rough with you, but you have to understand that I must know the truth. If we're going to get married, you'll have to get used to telling me everything. Don't be all mad. I didn't hurt you."

Annie looked around her as if to assure herself she was not dreaming. "Sneaky?" she said out loud. "Married?" she whispered to herself. Noticing Kevin groping on the dashboard, she opened the door and literally fell out in one move. He reached over to grab her foot, and Annie kicked at his hand as hard as she could. Rolling over, she landed on her knees and stood up. Kevin was leaning over, looking out at her through the open door.

"You look pretty funny rolling around in the dirt. You're acting like a nut, Annie," he said quietly. "Get back in the car."

Annie glared at him. She was safe now. A few yards from her house, she would have at least a ten-foot head start on him. "You are out of your mind," she said slowly. She was beginning to feel an emotion pushing itself up from her stomach. She paused briefly to identify it. Rage. That was it. "Kevin, listen carefully. I want you to tell me the truth. Are you willing to go screw yourself? Because that's what I want you to do." She mimicked his voice. "It's important that you tell the truth now." With that she turned to leave. She heard him calling her name, but she never paused.

Annie stumbled through her house to her bedroom. The mirror confirmed what she knew. Red welts rose up from her neck and throat. "Oh, God. Oh, God," she said over and over. Her eyes appeared too large for her small white face. Her hands still shook, but the ugliest sensation was in her stomach. Within fifteen minutes she would be vomiting. Sitting shakily down on the bed, she put her head in her hands. "Ouch." Her head hurt. Annie moved her hand gently over the left side of her head and came away with a handful of hair. Rolling onto her side, she lay down on the bed. Great gulping sobs racked her as she rolled over again. The left side of her hip was too sore to lie on. She guessed it had happened when she dropped out of the car.

Images popped into her head uninvited . . . Kevin's face when he was choking her . . . the view out the front window when he had her head pressed against the headrest . . . the way he had looked when she was lying on the ground. Annie could not imagine what had happened to Kevin to make him act this way. If only she was near his size, she could have fought back. Annie shuddered and was grateful no one was home. Rolling out the other side of the bed, she made the inevitable trip into the bathroom.

Chapter Three

After the nausea passed, Annie returned to her room. She still shook uncontrollably but no longer mumbled. She had been hysterical. Calming herself, she tried to think. "He's out of his mind," she said aloud. It would have made some sense if he had caught her with another man. But to bring up something that had happened over two months ago?

Had Kevin somehow read her thoughts? How could he know she had liked Harold? Annie gave herself a mental shake and took a deep breath. That was not possible. Even if Kevin sensed something, he would realize all she had to do was break up with him and go out with Harold. Annie wished bitterly now that she had. Then she remembered the pregnancy. So much for Harold, she thought in dismay. Annie was surprised at the brutality of her thoughts. She envisioned Kevin being beat up. Oh, how she longed to be bigger! Annie decided she would have nothing to do with Kevin. She wondered if he would try to contact her. Surely not. She thought about his marriage comment and began to laugh. Maybe Kevin had been proposing. The thought made her laugh even harder. *I'm losing my mind*, she thought wildly. Clamping down the hysteria again, Annie knelt down on the floor next to her bed. "Thank you, God, for my beautiful baby," she prayed. Pausing for a moment, she continued, "God, will you get Kevin for me? Have someone beat him up." Feeling embarrassed, she amended the request. "Sorry, God. I'll try to forgive him later. Right now I'm too mad. But I can't marry him."

Certain that God understood, Annie got into bed with the intention of taking a nap. Her breath still came quickly, but most of the shaking had passed. Footsteps on the stairs prompted her to turn to her sore left side and face the wall. Conversation was out of the question. She sensed the person coming closer. She remained still, and whoever it was left the room. Annie guessed it was Nellie. Maureen would have asked if she was sleeping. For the next two hours Annie lay in her bed and thought. Prior to this afternoon, she had assumed Kevin would be in the picture. It was a whole new ball game now.

Rolling onto her not-so-sore side, Annie pondered further. For some reason, Kevin was becoming a monster. He said it was her fault. Maureen said she had a smart mouth. Everyone said she had a smart mouth. Was this why Kevin had lost it? Annie thought about the whole Harold thing. She desperately played the first night of that momentous weekend through her head. She hadn't done anything too bad. Maybe she should not have been by their fire at all. Maybe she should have walked away when Harold approached them. It had seemed harmless enough then, but Annie did remember feeling guilty. She would like to run it by Maureen, naturally omitting the choking part. Annie felt humiliated. She thought about herself rolling around in the dirt. How mortifying. Thank God nobody had seen her.

Annie continued to mull it all over. Maybe his mother was the culprit. Imagine asking Kevin if he was certain he was the father. Her face flushed all over again. That had made Kevin violent. Annie seethed with rage. How nice of Mrs. Griffin to pay for an abortion. Or find her a nice unwed mothers' home. Annie considered the concept. Why not send Kevin? He obviously could not bear the embarrassment. Mrs. Griffin could go, too, Annie thought wickedly. She noticed the ache of loneliness in her stomach and began to cry again. The one thing Annie had counted on was Kevin. He was gone now. She was in this alone, and the thought pulled a thick blanket of depression down over her.

The sound of dinner preparations caused Annie to lift her head. The mirror was not her friend. The welts had developed even more, and Annie noticed fingerprint marks on the left side of her neck. Feeling herself slipping into hysteria again, she took some breaths and searched for a high-necked shirt. She was tired of crying. She was also starving. Her desire to eat overcame emotional needs, and Annie went downstairs. Their father was not home tonight, thank God, and Nellie was making pizzas.

"Hi, Annie," Maureen greeted her. "Hungry?"

"Starving. When will they be ready?"

Nellie and Maureen stopped.

"What's the matter with your voice?" Nellie asked.

"I don't know." Annie averted her gaze. She sat down at the kitchen table and looked out the window. "I must be getting a cold or something."

"Annie, it's not even September," Maureen noted. "You look awful."

The telephone rang, and Maureen grabbed it. Turning to Annie, she said, "It's Kevin."

Annie felt her stomach lurch. "Let's see," she said slowly. "What should we tell him? I know. Tell him to go to hell."

"Annie," Nellie said reproachfully. Maureen's jaw dropped.

"I'm serious, Maureen," Annie said with a rising voice. "Tell him not to call here. I don't want to talk to him."

Maureen was holding the phone against her chest so Kevin could not hear their conversation. After a moment she lifted the receiver to her mouth and said sweetly, "Kevin? Annie is not feeling well right now. Can she call you later?" Looking at Annie, she said, "He says it's really important."

Annie slammed her hand on the table. Rising, she grabbed the phone from Maureen and shouted into the mouthpiece, "Stay away from me, you fucking lunatic." After banging the telephone down, she sat gingerly at the table. She was sore.

Glancing up, she realized her sisters were stunned. Nellie in particular was frozen.

"You'd better tell us what happened with the fucking lunatic," Maureen said quietly. "Did he finally tell his family?"

"Well, he told his mother," Annie answered. "She took it well, I think. She told him he could not tell his father or brother, but she is willing to pay for the abortion." The girls were motionless.

"She was willing to concede I might not want to do that, so she also suggested I find a nice unwed mothers' home. Nobody would have to find out," Annie continued bitterly. "The goal seems to be secrecy."

"That bitch," Maureen blurted out.

"Stop swearing," Nellie implored. "It's not going to help anything. What else did she say, Annie?"

"Nothing. Oh, yes, she did ask Kevin if he was sure it was his baby."

"That bitch!" Nellie said violently. "You two have been inseparable for years."

"Nel," Maureen said sweetly, "foul language is not helping anything." Nellie looked white, and Maureen continued, "Let's call her and tell her we're going to name the baby after her. We'll distribute flyers at all the masses."

The telephone rang again, startling them all. Maureen grabbed it impatiently. After answering she said, "Kevin, did you hear what she said? Which part of 'Stay away from me, you fucking lunatic' was unclear?" Hanging up, Maureen sent Annie an apologetic look and started to laugh. "Are you mad?"

"No," Annie replied. "I don't want to talk to him. I don't care if you're mean this time."

"Wait a minute," Nellie said reasonably. "Kevin can't help what his mother does. Can he, Annie?"

"Well he can certainly control what he tells Annie," Maureen argued. "Why hurt her like that? Honestly, Nellie, the hell with him."

"That's not all," Annie offered. She felt compelled to tell them something despite her need to keep the violence a secret. "He accused me of doing something with a guy named Harold the weekend we went camping. He said I was a sneaky liar. He screamed at me, and he would not let me out of the car." Looking at their appalled faces, she stopped.

"Was this the camping trip he crashed?" Maureen asked quietly.

"Yes." Annie told them the whole story, excluding only the scene in the tent. They knew about that anyway. "What kills me is that he has not said a word about it for nearly three months. Today he pretended to have some top secret information. He really scared me."

"Well," Nellie said roundly, "I just hope he has the sense to stay away from this house. If he comes near here, I'll call the police."

Annie and Maureen groaned. "Nellie, don't be irrational," Maureen pleaded. "Annie, he does sound frightening. I agree that you should stay away from him. Do you think you can?"

"Does she think she can?" Nellie sputtered. "She

has no choice. Don't even put his name on the birth certificate. He'll come after the baby."

"Put Harold's name on the birth certificate," Maureen suggested with an evil glint in her eyes.

Annie and Maureen burst out laughing. "You're burning the pizzas, Nel," observed Annie.

The conversation continued through dinner. Eileen, their youngest sister, was out with Mr. McGowan, and Danny, their brother, was off working out of state. It was decided that Annie would not answer the phone. Their father would be told only that Annie and Kevin had fought. Annie felt better afterward. She was still depressed, but at least the girls knew about it. She had also called Rene.

"Did you and Kevin have a fight?" Rene asked bluntly.

"How did you know?" Annie asked in surprise.

"He called me, Annie," Rene related. "He was very upset and said your family was blaming him. He went on to say he had to see you. I'm supposed to call you and talk you into meeting him. He does sound upset, Annie, and I think he was crying. He also said he was acting upset because he was so disturbed at his mother's reaction."

"Rene, I can't believe he called you," Annie began. "Did he also tell you that he called me a liar and a sneak for what I did with Harold?"

"Harold who?"

"Campground Harold. Do you remember? Out of the blue Kevin attacked me for lying about Harold. He said your sister Patty told him we were down by their fire all night." Annie paused for a breath.

Rene sounded uncertain. "Did anything happen with Harold I didn't know about?"

"Of course not," Annie chided. "When would something have happened? I was with you the whole time, Rene. What's the matter with you?"

"I'm sorry, Annie, but what could Kevin possibly have been mad about? That you were talking to him? It doesn't make any sense. I mean . . . this was months ago. Are you sure there was not something else?"

"Rene, I don't want to talk about this. Kevin is crazy, and I am not going to talk to him. Tell him that. Okay?"

"Sure. Annie, is there anything I can do? Do you want me to come over?" Rene sounded concerned, but Annie knew her friend could not begin to understand the situation.

"Thanks, but no," she answered kindly. "I'm all right, Rene. I'm going to bed. I'll talk to you tomorrow. Do you want to pick me up for school?" Tomorrow was their first day of school, and Annie had to tell her advisor about the pregnancy. She was not looking forward to it.

"Yes. I'll be there by eight. Is there anything else you want me to tell Kevin?"

"No. Nothing. I'll talk to you later." She hung up and, after telling her sisters about the phone call, went to bed. It had been a long day.

Sometime during the night, Annie heard

Maureen slide out from her bed. Tiptoeing over to the window, her sister studied the darkness.

"What are you doing?" Annie asked.

"Didn't you hear that?" Maureen queried. "Someone threw something at the window. I have a feeling it's Kevin. What do you want me to do?"

"Oh, my God. Maureen, he's nuts. Tell him I'm sleeping and he should go away." Annie sat up and pulled the blankets around her neck. Feeling the bruises, she started to cry.

"Don't cry, Annie. I'll get rid of him." Maureen opened the window. "Go away, Kevin. She doesn't want to see you." Maureen was using a stage whisper. "I said go away. No. She's not coming out. I mean it. Call tomorrow and see if she wants to talk." Turning to her sister, she said, "He looks upset. I hope he has the sense to go away quietly. Let's wait a few minutes." Seeing Annie's white face, she remarked, "He can't break in here, Annie. Don't look so scared." At that moment they heard another *ping* on the window. Hearing quick footsteps from down the hall, they exchanged looks of dismay. "Here she comes," Maureen said as Nellie burst into the room.

"Is it him?" Nellie asked tensely. "I heard you talking to someone. I left my window open in case he pulled this. Don't worry, Annie. I'll handle this." Sticking her head out of the window, Nellie yelled down. "You better leave right now, Kevin Griffin, or I'll call the police. It's too bad your grandmother did not have an abortion. Tell that to your mother." Maureen and Annie were speechless. "No," she responded to his request to talk to Annie for one second. "Annie does not want to talk to you ever again!" With that she grabbed a hairbrush from the dresser and threw it out at him.

"Stop her, Maureen," Annie beseeched.

"Nellie," Maureen said, struggling with mirth. "Come in and close the window. I think he got the message."

Just then they heard Mr. McGowan's roar from downstairs. "What is going on up there?" The girls froze. No one answered. "Nellie? What are you doing shouting out your window? Whose grandmother had an abortion? Answer me."

"Sorry, Dad," Nellie called feebly. "We were just talking."

"Talking to whom? The whole city? Go to bed and close the window."

"Okay, Dad. Sorry." The three girls looked at each other for a moment and burst out laughing. Five minutes elapsed, and still they struggled for control. Mr. McGowan yelled up again. *"Be quiet!"*

Quieting, Maureen wiped her eyes. Looking at Nellie, she said incredulously, "Your grandmother should have had an abortion? Nellie you're as loony as he is. I can't believe you threw a brush at him." Annie groaned and put her head on her pillow. Then they all began laughing again.

"It's not funny." Annie winced. "Do you think he'll come back?"

"Are you feeling sorry for him?" Maureen asked.

Annie shook her head. "I would understand if you did. He looked so pathetic standing out there in the yard."

"Annie, do not back down this time," Nellie beseeched. "He has been mean before, and you always back down. He thinks he can get away with anything."

"Let's go to sleep," Annie suggested. The last thing she wanted was a conversation. Nellie left the room, and they got back into their beds. Annie heard Maureen giggling in her bed, and she started laughing again. "It's too horrible, Maureen. It's like a bad movie."

"I know it is. Nellie's out of control. I hope she doesn't call his mother or anything." Hearing Annie's gasp of horror, Maureen promised, "I won't let her, Annie."

Sleep was a long time coming to Annie. She wondered what Kevin would have said. He had nearly killed her. Annie's thoughts turned around and around until she finally fell into an exhausted sleep.

The interview with Annie's advisor did not go as well as she had hoped. The sister told her that the best solution would be for Annie to get her diploma by correspondence. The school did not have a distinct policy on the subject of pregnancy, but normally the girls were encouraged to stay at home and take classes through the mail. Annie maintained that she wanted her diploma from St. Therese's. After much discussion, it was decided that Annie would remain in school.

"Okay, then," the nun replied. "Let me talk to the principal. Stop in and see me tomorrow morning."

"I will, Sister. Thank you." Annie left and took a deep breath. Going off in search of Rene, she was relieved they would not throw her out. She was a bad example for the younger girls, and the thought made her ashamed. Still, she reasoned, it was better they see the result in all its figure-smashing beauty. Annie sighed when she realized that, once again, she was ravenously hungry.

Once Annie found Rene the two of them ambled slowly toward Rene's car. Deciding to go out for lunch, they discussed restaurants and opted for the cheapest one. They were settled in the car when Annie noticed an envelope stuck to the passenger-side window. She reached out and grabbed it. It was clearly marked "Annie."

"Rene, it's from him," she said with a shaking voice. "He was here." Annie dropped the envelope on the seat as if it were hot. "You open it."

"Are you sure you want me to?" Rene craned her neck, looking around the parking lot. "How did he find my car in this lot? He must really be on the edge. Doesn't he have school today?"

"No." Annie moaned. "They start tomorrow. He came over last night and threw rocks at the window. I didn't talk to him."

"I think you'll have to talk to him eventually," Rene stated. "It's good to give yourself some time away, but he's obviously frantic. See what he says," she urged, indicating the envelope.

Annie opened it and quickly read its contents. "He loves me and is sorry for the fight. He did not sleep at all, and he feels like he wants to die. If I give him another chance, he promises he will never be rude to me again." Annie looked at Rene dully. "Basically, he wants me to make him feel better."

"You're being a little hard on him, aren't you?" Rene asked hesitantly. "I'm not his greatest fan, but this has been a big shock for him, too." Seeing Annie's crestfallen face, she hastened to add, "It's nothing to what you're going through, but he does love you. Also, Annie, he has never acted like he was going to bail out on you. Quite the contrary. Many guys would. He sounds rational."

Annie sighed. "Rene, I may talk to him tomorrow. Right now I don't want to see him." Annie put her hands to her throat and gently felt the bruises. Starting to cry again, she said, "Can you take me home? I'm not hungry anymore."

Rene looked contrite. "I'm sorry, Annie. I'm not sticking up for him. It's just that I hate to see you break up with him now when you need him. Please don't cry. Let's get lunch, and we'll eat in the car. I'm buying."

The next day Annie was informed she was welcome to stay in school. If at any time Annie chose to stop, she could finish the year by correspondence. Annie was to meet with her advisor once a week to make sure everything was going well. She was also informed that the principal's door was always open if she felt the need to talk. Grateful, Annie noticed the irony. Most girls were complaining that they had to come to school. Annie was now thanking her lucky stars she was being allowed to stay. The thought made her feel older.

Mr. McGowan's delight was pathetic. Annie could not bear to talk to him these days. He always treated her as though she was about to cry. She did cry a lot, but everyone annoyed her. She answered his inquiries about Kevin briefly, and he did not pry. Her sisters must have warned him to leave her alone.

Nellie was going back to school, and Annie would miss her. Thank heaven Maureen would be around. Eileen had been told and was delighted at becoming an aunt.

Annie wrote Kevin a brief letter explaining that she was not willing to talk to him for one month. If he loved her as much as he claimed, he would respect her wishes. He stopped calling. Consequently, Annie was given time to think. She did little else these days. The situation dragged on. The vomiting had stopped. Annie now felt nearly normal and sometimes speculated that there had been a mistake. Her new doctor burst that bubble. She was progressing normally. Mostly she felt lonely. She missed Kevin more and more.

Kevin made the papers twice for football. He was having a spectacular year. She did not allow herself to think about his mother. She realized with sadness that Mrs. Griffin could at least have called to see how she was feeling. Annie wondered if the Griffins discussed her at all. She managed her emotions by shoving them away. Only then could she keep the tears at bay. Time limped by, and Annie slept whenever she could.

The first of October was a Saturday. Rainy and cold, the weather did little to encourage her to get up. Annie stayed in bed as long as her hunger allowed. Finally, she wrapped herself in a robe and dragged down the stairs in search of food. The doorbell rang, and she groaned. Nobody else was home. Annie waited, hoping the caller would leave. The bell rang again. With a snort of disgust, she opened the door. Kevin stood nervously on the porch.

Chapter Four

"What are you doing here?" she asked bluntly. Kevin never came to the door. Annie mentally cursed herself for coming downstairs in her pajamas. She cursed herself again for caring.

Kevin looked nervous but determined. "You said to wait one month. I waited. It has been the longest month in my whole life." Annie shrugged. "Please hear me out. I wanted to respect your wishes. I wanted you to know that I will do whatever you want." With that, Kevin cleared his throat nervously. "Will you please talk to me?"

Annie sifted through conflicting emotions. He looked terrific. He also seemed calm. She narrowed her eyes. "I'm not getting into a car with you."

Kevin winced. "After the last time, I don't blame you. Do you want to go for a walk?"

"I have to get dressed and eat. You can wait here and watch television." Seeing the apprehensive look on his face, she wondered whether to inform him that her father was out for the day. She decided to let him suffer. Grabbing an apple, she went up to dress.

In the safety of her room, Annie attempted to organize her thoughts. Kevin looked sorry. That was a good sign. She had missed him terribly, there was no question about that. Annie did not want to be alone. That was for sure. On the other hand, she could not tolerate his behavior. He had been hateful and frightening. Annie reminded herself that she had actually believed he might kill her. She must hold on to that during their conversation. She was afraid of him.

"I'm ready," she said lightly as she walked back into the living room.

Kevin looked relieved. "Let's get going. How about a walk to the park?"

"Fine," she responded briefly.

Outside, Kevin began the conversation. "Annie, I want to start by saying I am sorry about the fight in the car. I was out of line. I will never be pushy with you again."

Halting abruptly, Annie looked up at him. "Pushy? You were more than out of line, Kevin. You could have killed me. Do you realize that?"

"I don't blame you for being upset. I was obnoxious. But, Annie, I think you might be exaggerating a little bit."

"Kevin, if you think I'm exaggerating, I have nothing else to say." With that, she turned to walk away. He grabbed her arm. "Let go of my arm or I'll scream," she said through clenched teeth.

Appalled, Kevin released her. "Annie, I'm sorry. I didn't realize how upset you were. I never meant to hurt you."

Annie was astounded. "Kevin, you choked me. What was it you meant to do when you put your hands around my throat and squeezed?"

"I was half out of my mind that day," he explained emotionally. "I'm sorry. Can we talk about the future?"

Annie composed herself. "Kevin, I cannot plan a future with you. What if you get mad because I have a male doctor? What if you decide I'm flirting with the bus driver?" It was Kevin's turn to roll his eyes. "Your reaction to Harold was way out of control. Is there anything else you're waiting for me to 'tell the truth' about? I'll never know, will I?"

Kevin's face had turned ashen. "Annie, you were talking to Harold." Seeing her look of rage, he continued quickly, "I'm not saying there was anything wrong with that. I'm just stating a fact. You have told me before that you could not stand my jealousy. Give me a break here, Annie. Didn't I change? I think the Harold thing was just a reaction to the stress. I thought I was going to crack up before I told my mom. Do you know how hard that was? It was a hundred times worse for you. But hear me out. You didn't tell me you were down by the fire that whole night. I'm just explaining how I felt. I never said anything to you because I did not want you to think that I was getting jealous again. I tried to work on that. Didn't I?"

"Yes," she conceded. "Until this thing you were doing pretty well."

"Doesn't that mean I can do it again? There is so much at stake here. I will do anything not to lose you. Especially now. You need me, Annie. Don't push me away." Kevin tried to take her into his arms.

"I don't know." Annie pulled back and crossed her arms. "I was afraid of you that day. I really thought you were going to kill me. I don't think I could live like that." Annie blinked her eyes hard.

"Let me explain why I get so jealous," Kevin said intently. Reaching out to her, he grabbed her hand. "Let's sit on the grass for a minute. You look white." Annie was indeed white. She had the impression that her whole life was riding on this conversation. She allowed Kevin to pull her down to the damp grass.

"You are the best thing that has ever happened to me," he began. He took both of her hands gently into his own. "You know that, Annie. But I want to tell you again. I love you more than I ever thought possible. I thought about you constantly last month. I thought about what I would do if you broke up with me. For a second I thought I might be relieved. I'm just telling you my true feelings, so don't get mad," he cautioned. Seeing that she understood, he continued. "I figured I would go away to college. No one would know anything. I could start a new life and forget it." Annie kept her expression neutral. "There was only one problem. I could not be happy without you. Never. Besides, now we are going to have a baby. That blows my mind. I have trouble picturing the baby, but I know it's coming. I get jealous because the thought of you with another guy makes me want to die. I know you're too good for me." At this point, Annie groaned. "I know you hate when I say that, but it's true, Annie. You're smart and pretty, and people love you. You could have any guy you wanted."

"Not anymore, Kevin," she said blandly.

"Well, that's a good thing because you have me," he said simply. The look of innocent love in his eyes made Annie smile.

"Kevin, I want to believe everything you're saying. I really do." She paused to choose her words carefully. "I guess the problem is, I have to know you'll never lay a hand on me again. How can I know that?"

"I'm telling you right now," Kevin promised solemnly. "I've lived with my father long enough to know that I will never, ever be like him. I wouldn't put you through that, Annie. I do have a temper. I admit that. But you're not perfect either. The fault is not always mine." He looked at her hesitantly. "Admit it."

"I never said I was perfect, Kevin," she said slowly. "The fact remains that you are not afraid of me. I was afraid of you in the car. Everything else can be worked out but that."

"Well, I just worked it out. I promise you I will never lay a hand on you," he said, raising his hand as if to take an oath. "I promise you I will try to control my jealousy even though I'm going to have the most beautiful girl in the world as my wife. We've always said we would get married. How is that?"

Annie smiled in spite of herself. "I guess it's okay. One thing, though, Kevin. If you ever hurt me like that again, it's over. Do you understand?"

"I understand." Kevin spoke gravely. "I hate that you feel you have to threaten me . . . but, whatever it takes. Now, can we talk about the future?"

"Sure." Annie's spirits lifted. "What new horrors are in store for us?"

"A little optimism, please, or haven't you been reading the papers?"

Annie laughed aloud. "Yes, I know you are a superstar. Trust you to get in the papers to annoy me."

"I had to do something to make sure you were thinking of me." He grinned. "We'll get married after graduation. Hopefully, I'll get a huge scholarship, and we'll go off to college and live happily ever after. I've talked to a few scouts, Annie. There's no question that I'll do good. I like playing again. Now I've got a reason. Motivation helps. It will all work out."

Annie sighed. "I hope you're right. What did your father say about the baby?"

Kevin looked uncomfortable. "We didn't tell him. My mother says not to. I can't go against her wishes. I live in terror that he's going to hear. What can I do? You want to hear something strange, Annie?" She nodded. "My mother has not brought it up once since the first night. I asked her when we were going to tell my father, and she shook her head. She has never mentioned it again."

The look of genuine uncertainty on his face softened Annie's response. "That's bizarre," she said sympathetically. "It's like she's ignoring the whole thing." He nodded his head in agreement. "I suppose telling him on your own is out of the question?"

"No way. She'd kill me. Not to mention what he would do. I guess I'll just wait and see. I'm eighteen years old. I'll be nineteen when we graduate. What can they do? We're going away." He looked cheerful all of a sudden. "Won't it be great?"

"I hope so, Kevin. We'll be pretty broke for the first couple of years. I suppose I could get a part-time job after school."

"Let's worry about all of that later," he said persuasively. "It's enough that we're back together. I feel better. Do you?"

"Yes," she answered truthfully. "I'm still worried, though."

"Well, don't be. We have at least five months to worry, so let's just feel better now. Okay?" He looked so boyish that Annie smiled.

"Okay."

"Oh, by the way," Kevin added, "I think this belongs to you." He pulled a hairbrush from his jacket and handed it to Annie. It took Annie a moment to place it. Then she burst out laughing. Kevin joined her.

Feeling refreshed, Annie wiped her eyes. "Nellie gets a little carried away. Sorry about that."

"You're telling me." Kevin chuckled. "She hit me in the head with it. Then your dad started yelling, and I figured it was time to go." They laughed again. "Things aren't so bad, Annie. At least we can still laugh. This could work out well. . . . "

• • •

The pregnancy lasted an eternity. Annie faithfully attended school. She concealed her condition until nearly her seventh month. After that, she stopped trying. She learned to ignore the stares. Most of her classmates scrupulously avoided looking at her midsection. She was grateful. Her emotions were in a constant state of flux. Countless books on pregnancy persuaded Annie that moodiness was normal. It seemed unfair. Pregnancy was tough enough for women without fending off daily crying jags.

She watched Kevin breeze through his senior year. Bitterness threatened to overwhelm her, and she repeatedly reminded herself that Kevin was doing his best. His car had broken down in November. Kevin's parents drove him to sporting events, and he took the bus to school. Annie suspected Mrs. Griffin of preventing Kevin from seeing her. Kevin agreed but felt his hands were tied.

Kevin had not seen Mr. McGowan since the pregnancy was announced. Never entirely comfortable with Annie's father, Kevin now seemed especially nervous whenever Annie talked about him. The result was that they seldom saw each other. Once in a while he walked over, and Annie dutifully met him at the corner. For the most part there was nowhere to go. Kevin practiced and played so often that he rarely had free time. By Christmas, she was seeing him only once every two or three weeks.

Time crept by. Annie was not due until the first

week in February. The girls prepared for the baby. Annie had copied the list of necessities from one of the baby books and could not rest easily until every item was accounted for. Over the holidays, her sisters had a baby shower for her. Friends and relatives were supportive, but their kindness did nothing to ease Annie's self-consciousness. The shower, however, did net her quite a few of the baby things needed to complete the list.

"We achieved our goal, Annie," Maureen said with satisfaction as she rose from the floor the day after the shower.

Annie surveyed the baby items with a tired air. Their bedroom looked like a department store. "It would have been less traumatic to rob a convenience store."

"Oh, come on, Annie. It was fun," Maureen shot back. "Aren't these sleepers adorable? And look at this snowsuit! The baby will look beautiful in these."

"If it ever decides to come. Maureen, I swear I sometimes get this feeling that it's just a tumor or something." A powerful kick under her ribs forced her to grab her side. "Sorry, Baby. I guess I offended you. Thanks, Maureen. Everything is beautiful. I'm just sick of being pregnant."

Maureen looked at her compassionately. "I can only imagine. You look so big, Annie. But the doctor says you are right on schedule."

"What does he know?"

"More than us. Cheer up and we'll order a pizza."

At that moment the phone rang. Annie lumbered over to answer it.

"If it's Kevin, tell him you'll call him back after we order our pizza. Otherwise it'll never get here."

It was Kevin, and Annie promised to call him right back. Once she ordered the pizza she dialed his number.

"Hello," he answered in a hushed voice.

"Why are you whispering?"

"I don't want my father to know I'm on the telephone. I'm supposed to be downstairs going through the college letters."

"I see," Annie responded. "Do any appeal to you, Kevin?"

"Yes, there's a couple where I could be competitive," he said. "And they look like nice places. But what's the point in talking to them if I can't tell them I want to bring a wife and baby?"

"Kevin, you simply have to tell your dad. This is ridiculous. What does he say when you refuse to meet with these coaches?"

"He doesn't get it. He asked me yesterday if I was a moron."

"Nice," she commented dryly.

"Yeah, isn't it? I talked to my mom again, and she said she didn't want to talk about it. Annie, I cannot eat. My stomach has knots in it."

"Kevin, I know it's hard. But just blurt it out at the dinner table. What's the worst that can happen? He'll get mad and yell? He does that anyway. You can't go on this way."

Kevin's voice hardened. "You think I don't know that, Annie? Do you think I'm a moron, too? I just told you. My mother won't let me."

At that moment Annie heard someone come into the room and speak to Kevin.

"My mom wants to know when you are going to have the baby," Kevin said, somewhat surprised.

"She remembered?" Annie said sarcastically. "Ask her why she cares all of a sudden."

Kevin paused. "Soon, Mom. Annie said she hopes it's soon." After his mother left the room Kevin scolded her. "It won't help to be rude. She's only trying to be nice."

Annie held the phone in disbelief. "Kevin, the woman has ignored me for seven months. She has done everything in her power to prevent you from seeing me. She brings it up for the first time and you want me to be polite?" Annie tried to control the outrage in her voice. "Kevin, I think you should consider the possibility that I will never talk to that woman again."

An ugly fight followed. Annie tearfully told Maureen she would never speak to either Kevin *or* his mother again.

"It won't be a problem, though," Annie said from her bed, between bites of pizza. "I'll probably die in childbirth. The baby is never going to come. The doctor is a jerk. The nurses are mean, and I know they'll all be rude to me when I have the baby." Maureen listened, wide-eyed. Annie continued, "I think there is something wrong with the baby,

Maureen. They're just not telling me because they don't want me to know. That's how they are."

"I'm sure that's not true," Maureen said nervously. Dealing with this kind of hysterical outburst was a job for Nellie, who was not around. After calming Annie down, Maureen called Mrs. Nolan. The McGowan girls baby-sat for the Nolans, and Mrs. Nolan had been supportive throughout Annie's pregnancy.

Mrs. Nolan arrived in minutes, and Maureen gratefully sent her up to Annie's room. She and Annie talked for two hours. They would have continued but for Mr. Nolan, who phoned to say he could no longer control their children. Afterward, Annie felt like a new person. Everyone thought there would be something wrong with her baby. Nearly everyone hated her mother-in-law at some point. Mrs. Nolan promised Annie the baby would be fine. She also promised to be at the hospital and personally force the doctor to behave. She said the problem with doctors was that they were mostly men. They treated pregnancy like a mechanical process and ignored the emotional upheavals. Annie vowed to become an obstetrician and help every pregnant woman in the world.

Along with her words of wisdom, Mrs. Nolan brought a strawberry shortcake. Annie pitied Mr. Nolan, who would obviously be getting a late dinner, minus the dessert. She ate half of the cake in bed while perusing her newest infant care book. Maureen brought up a half gallon of milk, which

Annie swigged from the carton.

"Are you coming to the hospital with me, Maureen?" Annie asked her sister.

"Of course I'm coming," Maureen said, a little too emphatically. "I would not miss it for the world. I'm hoping your water breaks and I can do an emergency home delivery." Annie laughed appreciatively. "Just kidding. I've read the procedure about three hundred times. But I would never recover from the grossness. Nellie says I have to go with you and that she'll kill me if I throw up or faint. She says I have to overcome my selfish squeamishness and act like an adult. So there you are, Annie. I'm your girl."

"Mrs. Nolan said she was coming, too. That won't hurt your feelings, will it?" Annie said with trepidation.

Maureen nearly fell over with relief. "Of course not. Great idea. I can be the one who smokes cigars in the waiting room. I'll bring you in pizza or whatever you want."

Annie smiled in understanding. "You're a trooper, Maureen. I know how much you hate this kind of thing. We'll spare you as much grossness as possible." Glad to have settled that, they talked animatedly about the baby. There was no consensus on the name. They decided to reserve judgment until after they got a look at the baby.

That night Kevin called to clear the air. Annie was amazed. Normally, he ignored her for weeks after a fight. She thought with optimism that maybe he was growing up. He said this was not the time to fight. He could not bear the thought of Annie being upset. He understood she was probably feeling emotional, and they would not talk about his mother until things were calmer. He assured Annie that he loved her and that everything would be all right. Annie wondered if he had read chapter 10 of her baby book. It was the first time Kevin had taken responsibility for an argument. Annie did not retract one comment about his mother. But, in the interest of peace, she let it be.

Her due date came and went. The doctor explained that a due date was only an estimate. Women routinely delivered late. Annie thought she was going to explode. It was difficult to walk, and she dared not stray far from a bathroom. Everyone around her was nervous. Maureen in particular watched her every facial expression.

Maureen was working downtown these days. She had taken off a semester from school to decide on her major. To date, nothing appealed. Consequently, Annie's sister was now a receptionist in a law firm and immensely enjoyed the regular income. She worried incessantly that she would be at work when Annie went into labor. Every morning she asked Annie how she felt. Annie knew that if she confessed to the smallest of pains, Maureen would stay home. Annie noticed cramps all of the time. She had long since stopped timing them because they were never regular. For the most part, she ignored them.

On this particular day, the cramps seemed to have tapered off. Annie assured Maureen that today was not the day and waved her off to work. She lay in bed, idly listening to the morning sounds of the kitchen. Annie decided to take a bath. With a sigh she began the process of exiting the bed. It took some time these days. She stood up and noticed she was all wet. *Aha!* she thought. *Is it clear, colorless, and odorless?* Annie correctly guessed her water had finally burst. She held her stomach in excitement. Glancing in the mirror, she noticed how swollen and blotchy her face had become. Pregnancy played hell with a person's looks.

Because of her extensive reading, she knew that labor could be hours away. It did look like quite a bit of water, but that could be deceiving. Annie had a morbid dread of going to the hospital and being sent home. She would take no chances. Lumbering down the stairs, she met Mr. McGowan coming up.

"How are you feeling?" he asked with his customary I'm-not-worried-about-a-thing look.

"Pretty good, Dad, but things might be starting," Annie answered hesitantly. "I'm going to call the doctor and see what he says. He'll probably tell me to go back to bed and quit complaining. Are you going out somewhere?"

"I don't have to," he answered quickly. "Are you having pains?" His I'm-not-worried-about-a-thing look had become even more pronounced.

"Not really. I just feel kind of funny."

"Well, your mother did this quite often, Annie. She said no matter how many children she had, it was impossible to know exactly when labor started. Give him a call and see what he says. I'll stick around."

Annie called the doctor. He agreed that her water had probably broken. He was going to be at the hospital all day, so it worked out well for him. *I'm so relieved,* Annie thought sarcastically. He told Annie to come right in. Drumming up her nerve, Annie asked if she could stay home until she began having regular contractions. The doctor sighed. Mrs. Nolan had reminded Annie that she was paying him to provide a service. The doctor agreed to let her wait a couple of hours as long as someone stayed with her.

"He said not to worry for a while," Annie told her father. "Go ahead and go out," she urged him. "I'll be fine."

"Well, if the doctor thinks you're okay . . . " her father said uncertainly. "I'll only be gone an hour or so."

Annie waved him off and wandered through the house. Everything was in order. The baby would be sharing Annie's room for the time being. Maureen was going to take Nellie's room. Annie thought that she would miss Maureen. A sudden realization hit her. After today, things would never be the same. She would never share a room with one of her sisters again. Annie began to cry. She wished she could reach Kevin. Feeling a good solid contraction, Annie decided to call Mrs. Nolan and put her on notice. Annie often wondered what she would have done without Mrs. Nolan these last few months. *This is probably what mothers do if you have one*, she thought.

Mrs. Nolan answered on the first ring. She was more excited than Annie. She had a baby-sitter on standby and would call her. Annie cautioned her that it could be several more hours. Mrs. Nolan did not think so. Picking up her sense of urgency, Annie decided to time the contractions. Yikes! Seven minutes apart. They hurt, but not too badly. She went up to her bedroom. Almost immediately she heard her father come back.

"How are you feeling?" he asked quickly. "I think maybe we should run you over. Your mother always said they would not send you home if you were overdue." Mr. McGowan was beginning to perspire. The phone rang, and he sighed. "Maybe that's the doctor. I'll be right back." She heard him on the telephone and listened while he made his way back up the stairs. "That was Mrs. Nolan. She's in a bit of a state, Annie. She's only been through this a few times, so she's not as calm as we are." Annie smiled at him. He did not look calm. "Anyway, she says you should go right now. Your mother always went right in if her water broke." Annie knew she had no choice. If she waited any longer there would be two patients.

"Okay, Dad," she said, heaving herself out of

bed. "I'll be down in a minute." She paused. "I really don't want to go, though."

"I can imagine," he said with mingled sympathy and relief. "Your mother always said it was like falling off a cliff. Once you were pushed there was no way back. Just think, Annie." His voice lightened. "Sometime today we'll have a new member of the family. That's a wonderful thing."

Annie wondered if her mother had ever wanted to push him off a cliff.

"Mrs. Nolan wanted to come and get you, but I told her I would drive you over. She'll meet us there."

"Fine," Annie said shortly. "Let's go. I'll probably be in labor until next week. Shouldn't we wait a little longer?"

Three hours later, Annie's baby girl was born. Annie had timed it well. By the time she got there she was too far gone for any preparation. Later, Annie wondered that women did not die from the pain. She was overwhelmed by it. She asked for a Caesarian at least ten times, but the doctor only laughed. He was discussing hybrid tomatoes with the nurse at the time. Annie wanted to kill him. At the very least, she would find out where he lived and destroy his garden. She would have told him so but was fighting her way through another contraction. When it was over, she had come to her senses. The doctor held all the cards when it came to pain relief. She would have to cultivate him. She wanted to kill all of those people who wrote the baby books, too. How dare they talk about "discomfort" when referring to childbirth? She resolved to write her own book. In the future, girls would know exactly what was in store for them. There would be no such thing as premarital sex after Annie's book hit the stands. Postmarital either, come to think of it. It all came to the same painful resolution. Labor.

When the pain finally came to an end, Annie saw a small face looking up at her. The same books that equated discomfort with labor said that babies looked messy and strange directly after birth. They were wrong again. A miraculously perfect little person stared intelligently at her mother. Annie asked the doctor and nurses if they had ever seen such a perfect little girl. To their credit, they all said no. Annie looked down at her doctor, busily stitching, and wondered why she had ever disliked him. The nurses were benevolent. Mrs. Nolan had to be led from the room. Annie assumed she had gone to tell Mr. McGowan the news. The nurse took the baby away for tests.

Eventually they moved Annie to the recovery room. Almost immediately, she was bored. Annie rang the nurse, who patiently informed her that the baby was being cleaned and weighed. Annie repeated that she wanted her baby immediately. A newborn baby needed her mother. The nurse said kindly that she would walk over and see if they had finished with her. Moments later she came in with an impossibly small bundle. Annie gently lifted the blanket off the child's face. Snuggling the tiny girl's body against her own, she fell into a sound sleep.

"Annie," she heard a voice say. Opening her eyes, she looked around for Maureen.

"Maureen, why are you all wet?"

"I didn't wait for a cab," Maureen answered shortly. "It was raining. I ran from the train." Her eyes were red, and Annie wondered if she had been crying. "I'm so sorry I wasn't here, Annie," she began. "Dad called me and said you were in the delivery room . . ." A funny look came over her face. "Did you have the baby?"

Laughing delightedly, Annie nodded her head. "Look. She's the most beautiful baby in the entire world, Maureen."

"It's a girl?" Maureen asked. Annie nodded, and Maureen began to cry. "Nellie will kill me, but I think I might faint."

Annie sat up in bed. "You'll be okay. It is pretty shocking, I know." Annie spoke in a comforting voice.

A wan-looking woman paused in the doorway. She was evidently walking the halls and had stopped to get her breath. "When are you due?" Maureen asked sweetly.

The woman smiled briefly. "I had my baby yesterday."

Maureen looked appalled. "Oh. I'm sure that's why you look so good. I mean . . . for just having had a baby. . . ." The woman moved on, and Annie burst out laughing. Maureen sputtered, "How embarrassing. The poor woman. She looked like she was still pregnant." Then she, too, burst out laughing.

Maureen held the baby for over an hour and started crying again when the nurse took her back. Annie rested contentedly. This was without a doubt the happiest day of her life. She noticed in surprise that she did not care about anything. Maureen had called Mrs. Griffin and coldly relayed the news. Annie knew Kevin would come as soon as he heard.

"Her name is Mary," Annie said, softly drifting off to sleep.

Chapter Five

The birth of their daughter cemented Annie and Kevin. Later, when Annie tried to reconstruct the chain of events leading to Kevin's arrest, she would start with the hospital. It was as if someone had pushed a fast forward button on her life. The only constant in the blur of activity was the baby. A squirming bundle of humanity that required constant feeding and changing, she consumed Annie's focus. Somewhere in Annie's baby books there should have been a small paragraph. It should have read, "In six months you will feel somewhat normal. Reserve all major decisions until then."

On the evening of Mary's birth, Kevin blew into the hospital room. Annie watched him as he held his daughter for the first time. Anything short of absolute devotion would have disappointed. A rush of emotions flushed his face. She was satisfied. Kevin had not understood before. Annie speculated that fathers grasped the enormity of the occasion only after they saw their baby. Lying back, she gave him a peaceful smile.

Kevin began talking in a firm voice. Tomorrow he would take the day off from school. His father must be told immediately. Kevin planned to sift through his scholarship offers and make calls. Annie let his words flow over her like a soothing balm. For the first time in her life she was content to let someone else take charge. Thirty minutes after visiting hours were over, the nurse forced Kevin to leave.

For the next few days, Annie was kept busy. The phone rang, and flowers arrived hourly. She felt like a queen. Rene came bearing gifts. After briefly admiring the baby, she prattled on about the senior prom. Feigning interest, Annie found it hard to believe that somewhere there was a world where girls worried about prom dresses. She felt lonely. Trying to imagine herself in Rene's shoes, she felt like crying. She would not trade her baby for all of the proms in the world. Still, prom dresses were not frightening. Motherhood was. Once again, sleep proved elusive.

Maureen arrived bright and early the following morning. They were going home. Annie felt strange entering the house. She left as a girl and returned as a mother. Annie had just finished feeding the baby for what seemed like the hundredth time when Maureen called her to the phone.

"Hello," she answered impatiently. A new mother did not have time for phone calls.

"Annie, it's me," Kevin said. His voice sounded light.

"Did something good happen?" she asked.

"Annie, he knows."

Kevin sounded so happy that she felt tears sting her eyes.

"My mom told him and he knows. He's not mad. He's happy. I mean, he's real excited about the baby. He can't wait to see her."

"I'm so glad, Kevin," she said warmly. "You must be so relieved." Annie tried to grab some diapers that had to be folded but the cord would not reach.

"Oh, Annie, you have no idea. Listen, I'll be over in a few minutes. He wants you to bring her over right now. Can you believe it?"

Annie's relief turned to irritation. "No, Kevin, I cannot believe it. I can't bring the baby out in this cold. It might kill her. He'll have to wait. Besides, I'm so sore I can barely walk. Remember the stitches? Well, they're still there."

He sounded disappointed. "Well, I'll be over in a little while to see you both."

They hung up, and Annie marvelled that Kevin was no longer concerned about coming to the house. If she ever had a spare moment again, she would think about that.

Moments later Mary's latest round of breastfeeding was interrupted by another phone call. This time it was Mrs. Griffin.

"Annie, we cannot possibly wait to see this baby. I'll pick you up. Don't be silly about the cold. If the baby doesn't have a snowsuit I'll buy her one. We can't wait one more second to see our little granddaughter."

"Well," Annie replied flatly, "the hospital keeps liberal visiting hours."

"Oh, you know how hectic things get these days. I'll be right over."

Annie was left holding the telephone in disbelief. Mr. McGowan came in and admired little Mary while Annie apprised him of the situation.

"Pack her up, Annie, and go over," he advised.

"Dad," Annie retorted, "this woman has ignored me for months. All of a sudden they tell him and because he's happy she wants to be friends? Screw her!"

"Language, Annie," he remonstrated as he let the baby grip his hand. "These people are going to be your in-laws if you marry Kevin. Now, I know they're not perfect. But neither are we. Kevin loves them. You have to rise above your feelings and do this, even if you don't like her."

"Dad," she complained, "there seems to be a lot of sacrificing involved here."

"You're not kidding, Annie. Motherhood is a long, slow martyrdom. But it's worth every bit of it, isn't it, Miss Tiny Angel?" He was off, cooing at the baby, and Annie knew she'd get no sense out of him. Mary loved the sound of her grandfather's voice, and Annie gave a deep and violent sigh as she traipsed upstairs.

One month later, Kevin and Annie were married. A small reception was held at the McGowans'. The elder Mrs. Griffin wore a black pantsuit and a forced smile. The McGowan sisters made searing jokes until Annie begged them to behave. The day passed in a blur. Annie worried about the baby. Mary cried a lot and seemed to be in constant pain. Annie felt certain that Mary suffered from an elusive disease that had so far escaped diagnosis. Mrs. Nolan said the baby was gassy.

Their weekend honeymoon plans made Annie nervous. Mrs. Nolan had agreed to take the baby. Annie trusted her experience, but vague feelings of foreboding engulfed her. Mary would die before she returned. She was sure of it. The last month had been grueling. The baby slept only two hours at a time. She constantly wanted to eat. Annie seldom got any rest and had dark rings under her eyes. Despite Mrs. Nolan's constant reassurance, Annie was sure that she was doing something wrong. The books said that babies should go four hours between feedings. Unfortunately, Mary could not read the books, and Annie staggered through each day like a robot, wondering when she would collapse.

Toward the end of the party, Kevin persuaded her to get ready to leave. She handed Mary over tearfully. In the car, she emotionally informed her husband that she would not get a minute's peace with worrying about their daughter. Seconds later, he gently shook her awake. They were at the Hilton. Annie managed a tranquil smile. Her honeymoon was one continuous nap. Whenever she awakened, Kevin called for room service. He waved off her apologies. She needed the sleep, and he loved cable television. They were both happy.

• • •

The blur continued after the wedding. Mrs. Nolan watched Mary while Annie finished school. Kevin eventually moved his clothes over to the McGowans'. Mr. Griffin took over the scholarship quest and spent long hours negotiating details. Shortly before graduation, he presented them with their options.

Kevin, Annie, and Mr. Griffin sat at the Griffin kitchen table. Three schools met their criteria. They were looking for a full scholarship for Kevin, along with housing for the family and a stipend for food. Also considered was the best athletic possibility for Kevin. The schools were in three different states, and Mr. Griffin had arranged the offers in three piles.

Glancing down at the papers, Kevin responded immediately. "Texas. We'll go to Texas."

Much discussion followed, but Kevin remained adamant. They would go as far as possible. Annie realized with dismay that she had no say in the matter. Kevin politely informed her that the decision was made.

Bristling, Annie asked her husband to clarify which decisions would be joint. Kevin said that, as the man of the family, he would listen to her opinions but ultimately was entitled to make the final call. A long, tense conversation resulted in guidelines, set by Kevin. She was informed that she could make most decisions about the baby and the household. Fearing a full-scale battle, Annie backed down.

It got her thinking. Kevin was wonderful in

many ways. He was faithful, devoted, and responsible. He was also a male chauvinist. Marriage was supposed to be challenging, but Annie was stung at just how sticky it could get. Kevin had a temper. That was no secret. But it was not triggered by just the jealousy issue anymore. A myriad of topics could now plunge them into war.

The subject of Annie's academic future also proved tricky. Kevin said little. Mr. McGowan brought it up daily. While Annie's first responsibility was to her new family, she should apply for scholarships in her own right. Annie instinctively knew that if she pushed now she would slam into another brick wall with Kevin. Promising her father she would investigate the issue further, she bided her time.

The last months at home were bittersweet for Annie. Everything was changing. Maureen was going back to school. Maureen and Nellie were saving for a trip to Europe, and Annie tried not to envy them. Nellie had one more year of school to go, and Eileen was working away at grammar school. Danny was still gone. Occasionally, he called or sent a postcard. Unable to attend their wedding, he promised to surface in the next few months.

Rene would attend school with Nellie, downstate. She frequently stopped by the McGowans', usually to consult with Nellie. Sometimes Annie wished that she had not gotten married. The thought made her feel guilty. She asked Kevin if he ever felt sad at what they were missing. Kevin said sweetly that he figured they were getting it both ways. They got to go away and be together. Mary was a bonus. This reassured Annie. She would hate to think that Kevin had regrets.

Much too quickly, it was time to go. Mr. Griffin was driving them to school with a trailer attached to the car. Three days of packing brought Annie to the strange realization that everything they owned fit in a tiny box.

Annie sat on her front porch on the eve of their departure. Her thoughts were heavy and desolate. Hearing the creak of the screen door, she glanced up to see Kevin.

"The baby's asleep," he said quietly. "I think she'll be fine in the car, don't you?"

Annie shrugged. Twenty-four hours of driving would be unpleasant no matter how good the baby was.

"Are you scared, Annie?" he asked gently. When she remained silent, he continued, "I wouldn't blame you. But I think we'll love it there."

Laying her hand in his, Annie smiled at him. There was nothing he could say to console her about leaving her family. With an ache in her heart, Annie realized that growing up was painful. She understood, yet again, why she was too young to be married with a child. Stifling a deep sigh, she vowed for the millionth time not to let her age affect Mary negatively.

Her reverie was broken by Kevin's departure. He was turning in early. Annie considered her situation. The mothering part was not the problem. Books, advice, and common sense were readily available. It was the marriage part that gave her cause for concern. Kevin was unpredictable. His anger flared unexpectedly. Mrs. Nolan had explained that men were different. Regardless of how many centuries elapsed, they retained some elements of the caveman. Annie had listened intently. It made sense.

Annie asked her about the power imbalance. Kevin obviously felt justified in taking complete control. Mrs. Nolan had looked blank. Pressed for examples, Annie related their conversation about the Texas Decision, as she dubbed it. Mrs. Nolan was thoughtful. Annie stated further that Kevin retained strict control of their money. He knew where every penny was spent. Mrs. Nolan suggested that Annie tell Kevin to lighten up a bit. The older woman suggested that Kevin's youth was the culprit. He was overcompensating. It would certainly wear off once Kevin got comfortable with his new responsibilities.

Annie hoped so. As it stood, she felt she had traded her father in for a younger version. At least her father had blind spots and a sense of humor. She rebuked herself. Kevin was not all bad. He was still hysterically funny, and he truly loved her. Her father said it was amazing how quickly Kevin had assumed responsibility for his little family. Adjustments were necessary, Annie reasoned. Some would be rocky.

She stared at the trailer. At least she would have her things. Plenty of books had been packed, and no one could take away Annie's reading. The thought cheered her. She would find a library right away. Surely there were buses in Texas. The Griffins would have no car. Kevin's had long since traveled its last mile. Annie felt her spirits rise. The baby could be taken anywhere. They did have a stroller, and Annie did not fear being alone. Her inherent sense of adventure asserted itself. It could be great. Annie resolved to be optimistic and cheerful. Kevin deserved at least that.

Twelve hours later they were on their way. Annie did not cry until she saw her father wipe his eyes. The car, driven by Mr. Griffin, pulled away from her house with Mr. McGowan and her sisters waving good-bye. Too choked up to speak, Annie glanced down at Mary, sleeping in her car seat. She shut out any further thoughts as she sped toward her new life.

Chapter Six

The road stretched on forever. Conversation did not flow freely in the car, and Annie was grateful when Mary woke up and demanded a bottle. Somewhere north of Memphis, Annie persuaded Kevin's father to give her a turn at the wheel. The tension quickly became unbearable. Mr. Griffin loudly insisted that Annie was not using her rearview mirror properly. Annie always looked behind to check her blind spot. Her father-in-law maintained that if a driver was looking behind, no one was driving the car. He reminded Annie that she could not be looking at scenery while she was operating a motor vehicle. Annie argued back briefly, then closed her mouth. A period of silence ensued.

Another few miles disappeared behind them. Annie was just letting herself feel the exhilaration of the open highway when she heard her navigator grunt. She suppressed an exasperated sigh.

"Did you grunt?" she asked.

"Pardon me?"

Annie grinned wickedly to herself. The Griffins never said anything openly.

"I thought maybe you had some more advice for me."

Mr. Griffin spoke considerately. "Well, now that

you mention it . . . the front end of the car is wobbling. Can you see it?"

Frowning, Annie made a show of concentration. "No, I can't. If I'm staring at the front end of the car . . . who is driving the car? I'm on the highway now. This is a motor vehicle. I really can't be looking around at the scenery."

Mr. Griffin began to laugh. "You may be pretty sharp, Annie. But this is power steering. You're jerking the steering wheel back and forth, and the front of the car is wobbling. This is not a go-cart. You don't need to steer it back and forth." He spoke with humor in his voice, and Annie was not offended. "Just take it nice and steady. See what I mean? Now it's not wobbling."

"It was never wobbling. Kevin, did you feel it wobbling?" Annie cast behind her.

"Kevin, look up here," Mr. Griffin requested impatiently. "It's wobbling again. Women can't drive. All they can do with a car is aim it."

Kevin concentrated on the front of the car. He remained silent. Annie was beginning to lose patience herself, and toyed with the idea of aiming at a tree. After a tense minute limped by, she said lightly, "Your wife has been driving for years, Mr. Griffin."

"Not correctly. I would never let her on the highway. It's not safe to let bad drivers on the highway."

"Are you implying that I am a bad driver?" Annie asked shortly.

"Annie, that's enough." Kevin spoke sharply. "Hold the wheel steady and the car won't wobble. You're probably not used to power steering."

"Kevin, do you think my dad drives a tractor around the city? We have power steering. I'll tell you what," she said bluntly as she put on her directional. "Rather than give us all an ulcer, I'll let you professionals handle the driving." Annie spotted a rest area. "I'll just aim for the toilets." When the car was parked, she grabbed her purse and got out. She took herself to the bathroom to smoke a cigarette.

Moments later, Kevin poked his head in the door. "Are you mad, Annie?"

"What do you think?" Annie asked hotly. "What a bunch of baloney! I was driving fine. He just doesn't want anyone else to drive."

Kevin shifted uncomfortably. "I told you he was a pain in the neck. Stop arguing with him." Kevin spoke sharply. "I don't want a stomachache over this, dammit. Get in the car and keep your mouth shut."

Annie frowned. "Keep my mouth shut? That's a nice thing to say. I'll certainly try. Has it ever occurred to any of you that the reason he gets away with so much is because you keep your mouths shut?" Annie ground her cigarette out on the floor and stalked past him. Turning briefly she retorted, "Don't talk to me like that, Kevin Griffin." She strode back to the car and climbed into the backseat. "I'm safely in the back now, Mr. Griffin."

"Okay," the older man said pleasantly as he moved over in the seat. Kevin got in on the passenger side. "Why don't we let you pick the restaurant for dinner, Annie? What do you have a taste for?"

Annie wanted to kick the back of both of their seats. Seeing Kevin's pleading look, she took the olive branch. "I don't care. I love Italian."

"Italian it will be," Mr. Griffin said magnanimously. "How is the baby, Annie?"

"Fine. She'll sleep for at least another hour, I think."

"You're a wonderful little mother, I must say. That's the nicest baby I've ever seen. You take such good care of her." Annie softened in spite of herself. She was always grateful when someone said she was doing a good job. Annie hoped she was a good mother. She certainly tried hard. She glanced up and met Kevin's eyes. He winked at her and smiled. She made a fist at him, then smiled. A trip like this was bound to be tough. Awkward, too. Annie did not want to think about all of them in one hotel room. Surely they would get two rooms. She cursed herself for not making that clear to Kevin before they left. Any more tension and she would begin to say horrible things. Some people giggled when they were tense. Annie made smart comments. *God help us all if we have to sleep together*, she thought grimly.

Annie spent the rest of the day comfortably nestled in the backseat. She insisted on two motel rooms, claiming she would feel terrible if the baby kept Mr. Griffin up all night. After a look of alarm, he quickly agreed and insisted on paying for both rooms. Annie had to keep from chuckling as she unpacked the baby's things. It was very awkward traveling with a baby on formula. Annie had splurged and bought eight-ounce ready-to-feed bottles with disposable nipples. At fifty cents a bottle, they were not cheap. And Annie felt quite rich every time she screwed on a nipple and threw out its predecessor. Kevin said it was wasteful. He had wanted to bring a cooler and make bottles as they were needed. Annie had stood firm on this, though. She told Kevin that if he was not willing to spend the extra ten dollars, he could sit in the back with the baby. He had uncharacteristically backed down. *Ha*, she thought. *Maybe that's the way. Inconvenience him a little.*

She also had a long talk with her husband in the privacy of their room. Annie waited until he was relaxed. She then sweetly broached the subject of arguments. She agreed with Kevin that disagreements were inevitable. She wondered aloud if there was anything they could do to keep fights from getting ugly.

Kevin thought about it for a moment. "If you could stop yourself from making smart comments, it would help a lot."

Annie took her time answering. She had read an article on communication in a woman's magazine that said you should listen first and deal with your partner's statements. She was also supposed to reflect on his feelings. Almost as fun as psychology class.

"Does it make you feel minimized when I say something sarcastic?" she asked with great seriousness.

Kevin looked at her warily. "No. I'm not sure what being minimized feels like. The opposite of maximized, I would think. Hmm. Problem is, I don't know what that means either. I do know it pisses me off when you talk back."

Annie bit back an explosive reaction to the term "talk back."

Turning to face him, she said kindly, "Kevin. Do you love me?"

He answered without hesitation. "Yes, I do, Annie. You know that."

"Well, I love you, too. And I don't want us to be at each other's throats. I know we're young, but we don't have to be miserable. Everyone in the world thinks our marriage is doomed because of our age. Wouldn't it be nice to prove them all wrong?" Annie paused. "I know that's not the most important thing. The most important thing is that we make each other happy. I want you to be happy, Kevin. You deserve it more than anyone I know. Help me out here. I can't stand it when you tell me to keep my mouth shut. It's insulting. I know you don't want to hurt my feelings, but it does."

Kevin looked at her for a moment and then pulled her down onto the bed with him.

"Kevin," she protested. "The baby is awake."

Mary was indeed awake. Annie had her resting on a blanket on the floor.

"Annie, I just want to hold you for a minute," he said in a thick voice. "You're so good. I'm sorry I said that to you. I don't even think about things like that. Does it really bother you?" Annie nodded her head from against his chest. "Then I won't talk like that anymore. I want you to be happy more than anything. We'll have a wonderful marriage. I promise. Okay?"

"Okay," she said with relief.

Kevin rose up on one elbow. "Just one thing, Annie," he said gravely. "Don't start maximizing me, okay?"

Annie made an attempt to punch him in his chest. Kevin laughingly pulled her down on top of him. "What was that all about?"

Laughing back, Annie spoke lightheartedly. "I'm trying to communicate with you, Kevin. If you must know, I was attempting to reflect your feelings back to you so you'd know that I heard you."

"Are you going deaf? Why wouldn't you hear me?" he said playfully. "What the hell are you talking about, Annie?"

He was joking, but Annie noticed he looked a little nervous. "Oh, Kevin, I read an article on communication, and I was trying it out." Annie was embarrassed and added defiantly, "I hate the way we fight, and I thought maybe if we could learn how to talk with each other better, we wouldn't fight so badly. Honestly, Kevin. What's the harm in trying to be as good as we can?"

"Nothing, Annie," he responded contritely. "I think it's wonderful. It's a little strange that every time something goes wrong, my wife runs to the library. But that's a good thing. Just explain things to me and I'll try to learn, too. Okay?"

Annie hugged him hard. She thought confidently that they could work out any problems as long as they could talk them out without fighting. They would have to practice. She realized it was not fair to blame Kevin's temper for everything. She, too, had a temper. Annie would try hard to control herself. She thought that the article had done one thing for them. Instead of attacking Kevin for being mean, she had opened the door for a discussion. Maybe there was something to it after all. Feeling pleased with herself, she organized the room while Kevin showered. Mary smiled up at her from the floor.

After their discussion, it was easy to be kind to Mr. Griffin. As good as his word, he had found an Italian restaurant. Mary was actually cranky forcing Kevin and Annie to take turns eating their dinners.

Annie could barely wait until she turned twenty. For some reason she was sure that at twenty she would feel confident. It sounded old. Like an adult. "Yes," she would respond, "I'm in my twenties." People asked her if Mary was her little sister. Annie hated that. "My goodness, no," she would respond in her most adult voice. It was embarrassing. She did not even look eighteen. She looked more like fifteen. Yes, it was difficult. She had taken to wearing makeup to look older. It did not really help, though. She looked like a girl with makeup on. Mrs. Nolan had promised her that she would be quite happy about her youthful appearance in a few short years. Annie could not wait.

Toward the end of the second day, the Griffins' car blew through Texarkana. Entering Texas gave Annie a strange feeling in the pit of her stomach.

"Is that a cactus?" she asked aloud.

"It sure is, Annie," Mr. Griffin responded enthusiastically. "This state is like a different country altogether." With that, he launched into an educational monologue on the characteristics of Texas. Apparently, even driving was different here. Vast distances stretched between cities; speed limits were not enforced. It was acceptable to come right up behind someone. Nothing personal, Annie thought. Also, Mr. Griffin had been told that wildlife posed a significant hazard to drivers. During dusk and darkness it was not safe to drive without a "spotter." A spotter was kind of like a navigator whose job was to watch the road intently for deer or other large animals. Hitting a deer could kill someone driving at a high rate of speed.

Guns were legal in Texas but could not be concealed. According to Mr. Griffin, everyone owned guns. He pointed out a number of pickup trucks with stocked gun racks. Annie was impressed. She asked why they felt the need to be armed. Kevin's father reckoned it would be handy to have a gun in the event you struck an animal. Annie made a face. No wonder they needed spotters. She reminded Kevin to keep his eyes open. She hoped there were not a lot of accidental shootings.

As if reading her mind, Mr. Griffin launched into another discussion about boys' being taught to handle guns. A deep respect for weapons was instilled in young boys. That same respect prevented the irresponsible handling of guns. Mr. Griffin speculated that the number of accidental shootings in Texas was lower than in places where boys were not familiarized with their fathers' guns. Annie wondered if she was a feminist. Being around this man could certainly start a girl thinking about it. He went on to say Texas was the kind of place that respected a man's right to behave like a man. Laws were tough. Responsibility came with those rights, and violators were not mollycoddled like they were up north. Annie had heard this from her father. He said that Texas knew how to deal with criminals. It all sounded very masculine.

Down into the heart of the state they traveled. It was midnight when they arrived in the small college town that was to be home. Exhausted, they spilled into one motel room. Annie felt twinges of embarrassment at the close quarters but soon fell into a dreamless sleep. The following morning she awoke to Kevin pulling the covers from her.

"Get up, Annie," he commanded. "My dad is down in the restaurant. We have to pack up and go meet him."

"How's Mary?" Annie answered sleepily, peering over at the makeshift bed near the bathroom.

"Fine. I'll get her up and dressed. Get in the shower, Gorgeous."

Two hours later they pulled up in front of their new home. A series of six buildings with eight apartments each comprised the married housing. Flush with the west side of the campus, these buildings did not look like university issue. With old red-brick and white trim, they looked downright stately. Annie was delighted. Kevin explained that the other married housing units were like small boxes. There was a long waiting list for these, but because Kevin was an athlete, the Griffins had been prioritized. Kevin could not hide his smile as they inspected their new home.

"Why didn't you tell me how nice they were?" she chided him.

"I wanted it to be a surprise, Annie. I know how worried you've been about coming so far. I figured it would be something nice at the end of it." He checked to see where his father was. Looking out their third-floor window, he spotted his father unstrapping the baby from her car seat. He ushered Annie out into the hallway. Swooping her into his arms, he carried her across the threshold. "Now it's official."

Annie smiled. "You're very sweet. Now, put me down and go unpack my stuff. We have to get started."

Kevin came up with the first box. His father

followed him in with the baby on one arm and her diaper bag on the other.

"Look who everyone forgot," he cooed. "She was down there by herself, and she's very put out." Annie looked at Mr. Griffin affectionately. How could she dislike anyone who adored her baby so much? "If you'll take this princess, Annie, I'll go find a store. Do you need anything for the baby?"

"No," she answered sweetly. "I'll get diapers and formula later. Tomorrow I'll do a big shop for groceries." Annie mused out loud. "Kevin, can you get the baby's bouncy seat on your next trip up?" Kevin nodded cheerfully.

Annie walked Mary around their new home. It was lovely. Annie thought the third floor was just fine. She liked the height, and the view was impressive. Gazing out at the sky, she wondered why it seemed so vast. Shaking off her reverie, Annie got down to business. This was a one-bedroom unit. When Mary got bigger they would need two bedrooms, but for now it was fine. A good-size dining room merged into a large living room. The kitchen was spacious. Muted green tile gave it an old-fashioned feel, which Annie loved immediately. Two large windows overlooked the back porch and the rest of the apartments. Noticing little houses in the yard, Annie watched as a young woman carried laundry inside. Carting laundry up and down would be no picnic, but Annie shrugged. You could not have everything,

Depositing Mary into her seat, Annie put her

in a sunny spot with a bottle. Opening the first crate, she talked to the baby as she worked. A beautiful white cloth-covered container came out of the first box. Annie grinned in delight. This was the crucifix that the nuns had given her as a wedding present. Its early appearance was a good omen, and Annie ceremoniously hung it on the wall.

That evening Kevin and Annie rested in their first home. It was only eight, but already they were sprawled out on the bed. Mary was asleep in her crib in the dining room. Annie was not certain she would keep her there, but for now it seemed convenient. Mary still slept through anything. According to the books, it was best to have babies out of the parents' room as early as possible.

Mr. Griffin insisted on staying in a motel room for his three-night visit. He said a young couple needed their privacy, and Annie heartily agreed. He was due over early in the morning to take Kevin around the campus. Annie was going to persuade him to take her grocery shopping first. That way she could try out her new kitchen. She also needed a whole list of things from a department store. Why had it never occurred to her that they would need hangers, scissors, and a silverware organizer for the drawer? In unpacking alone she had come up with a list of twenty-two items. She fervently hoped Kevin would not come shopping with her. He was apt to scrutinize every purchase. Annie did not want to have to defend her right to buy a dish towel for the counter.

She rolled over and propped herself up on one elbow. Kevin was looking through a course catalog, and Annie watched him jealously. College would be liberating after high school. Imagine looking through a book and choosing the classes you wanted. Kevin told her it was not quite that easy. For the first two years you had to retake things like English, history, and speech. Annie did not care. You actually got to pick the times and days you wanted to attend school. She mentally resolved to see an admissions counselor as quickly as possible.

Glancing up at the large double windows in their bedroom, she frowned. She had a bag of cast-off drapes and curtains from Mrs. Nolan and her mother-in-law. She hoped she would find a set to fit. The kitchen window would be no problem. Blinds were already in place. Annie loved the clean look of the white blinds against the green walls. The apartment was so airy when it was empty, and Annie determined to preserve some of that look. She did not want clutter. Back at the McGowans', her little family had been crammed into one room, and Annie had felt like a hopeless slob. There was simply too much stuff for one room. Seeing their possessions spread around the large apartment had shown her that. Here there was room for everything.

"Do you want something to drink?" she asked Kevin.

"Sure. Thanks."

Annie really wanted an excuse to wander into her kitchen. What luxury to have your own refrigerator! Opening the door, she admired the clean shelves. A case of soda was snug against an open can of formula. It was as if the two items were nervous in that large space.

"Tomorrow you will have plenty of company," she promised them out loud. Feeling embarrassed, she grabbed two cans of soda and quickly closed the door. Opening a wall cabinet, she ran her hand along the shelf paper. The lower cabinets had not been done, and Annie reached over to her list and added thumbtacks. She remembered how embarrassed she had been when Mrs. Griffin handed her two rolls of shelving paper in a store in Chicago. She felt her face burn all over again. "Is it wallpaper?" she had asked. Annie had hoped so, because she did have an opinion on wallpaper. Her father said it was crazy to stick paper on a perfectly good wall. Mrs. Griffin had rolled her eyes as if searching for patience, and Annie wanted to hit her. Feeling tears burning her eyes, she had walked away.

Mrs. Griffin often asked Annie questions she could not answer. One day she asked her if she was going to get a separate beater for her potatoes. Annie was totally nonplused. Mrs. Griffin smiled at the two neighbor women who were there for coffee. They smiled back sympathetically as if to say, "What can you do with such inexperience?" Annie had flushed that time, too. Taking the bait, she'd asked why she'd need a separate beater for potatoes. At the McGowans' they used a manual beater for everything. They did not own an electric mixer. They had at one time, but Eileen had taken the attachments into the yard and they had never been seen again. According to these ladies, a woman wanted a separate mixer for cake mixes because the one for the potatoes should only be used for potatoes. Annie had replied that she would mash the potatoes by hand, thus eliminating the need for a specialized appliance. The women had chuckled. Annie was informed that Kevin liked his potatoes very creamy. Annie had replied that she liked hers baked.

Kevin adored his mother, and Annie truly wanted to be friends. She felt her own mother's absence keenly these days. Mrs. Nolan was the closest thing to a mother she had. Annie always thanked God for Mrs. Nolan. Mrs. Nolan also thought Kevin's mother was a witch and supported Annie on everything.

Mrs. Griffin had wanted to come on the drive to Texas. Blessedly, Mr. Griffin forced her to stay home. He promised to bring her in October for a game. Annie had been tremendously relieved. The last thing she needed was Mrs. Griffin's superior presence while she attempted to get her home up and running. Annie leaned against her counter in her own kitchen and daydreamed. When Mrs. Griffin came in October, she would be ready. She would go to the library and get out books on entertaining. Things with floral centerpieces and candles.

Annie would make an elegant dinner. A glance into the dining room burst Annie's pleasant daydream. They had a small round white table with two dilapidated red restaurant chairs. Hmm. Maybe a book on Japanese dining. Annie laughed out loud as she pictured Kevin's parents trying to sit on cushions on the floor. Hearing Kevin call to her from the bedroom, she poured the soda into two of her beautiful new glasses. They were clear with large pink flowers. Annie thought them the height of elegance.

Ambling through the dining room, she glanced at Mary. How peaceful babies looked when they rested. Glancing up at the crucifix, Annie held back a gasp. A large, hairy spider about the size of a silver dollar was perched on the top. She bit back a scream and put the glasses down on the table. She had seen pictures of tarantulas. This spider was without a doubt related to the family. The intruder was directly over the crib, and Annie hesitated to move fast for fear of startling it onto the baby. She overcame her panic long enough to pull the crib away from the wall. Reaching in, she grabbed the sleeping child.

Kevin was already off the bed. "Why did you get her up?" he asked in surprise.

Annie quickly sent him into the dining room. He came back with an equally disturbed look on his face. "Give me a shoe," he said grimly. Annie was close to tears. "Kevin, you can't throw a shoe at the crucifix."

"Don't be a nut. How else am I going to get the damn thing down?"

"Kevin, I mean it. Do not throw that shoe at the cross. It's like throwing it at Jesus." Annie was pale and shaking by this time. "Should I take the baby and get out?"

"Calm down! It's only a spider. It'll go away on its own."

Annie clutched his arm. "Kevin, I swear to you, if you let it go away, I will never sleep a night in this apartment. I mean it. Mary could have been killed. We can't watch her forever." Mary chose this moment to begin a vocal protest.

Kevin looked uncertain. "Okay. Put the baby down and come with me. I'll try to scare it off the cross."

Annie quickly put a blanket down on the floor and deposited the screaming infant on it. Following Kevin into the dining room, she held his arm. "Keep your body between the wall and the bedroom in case he goes for the baby."

Shaking her off, he yelled, "Shut up, Annie. You're freaking me out." Kevin threw the shoe at the wall directly below the crucifix. Both of them screamed and ran back into the bedroom as the spider jumped from the crucifix to the wall. Bursting into laughter, Kevin prepared himself for a second assault.

"Go, Kevin," she said weakly. "Go kill it. It's not on the crucifix anymore."

"Did you see it jump?" he asked in disbelief. "Annie, I don't want to go out there."

Annie remained adamant. "I won't stay here unless I see that thing's dead body. Go smash it quickly before it has a chance to jump again. I'm sorry. I truly cannot go out there."

"Okay. But if it kills me, you're going to feel pretty bad. Should I do it with the shoe?"

"No. Use a book." Annie handed him a telephone book from the closet floor. "Do it quick, Kevin. Is it a tarantula?"

"It sure looks like one. Kiss me for the last time, my darling!" he said dramatically. Reaching into his pocket, he pulled out a jawbreaker. "If they take you alive, eat this."

Annie pushed him away. "Hurry *up*, Kevin. It's not funny." After he tiptoed out of the room, Annie stuffed a towel against the floor underneath the door. What if it bit him? Laying Mary on the bed, Annie patted her back. Mary immediately went back to sleep. Listening at the door, Annie refrained from asking for a progress report. She did not want to startle it. Suddenly she heard Kevin give a loud shout. She opened the door just in time to admit his flying body.

"Did you get it?" she asked imperiously. Kevin was rubbing his hands all over his arms and legs.

"Gross! Gross!" he repeated.

"What's gross?" Annie asked again. "Did you kill it?"

"I think so, Annie. Go look at the phone book

and see if it's smashed."

"I don't want to, Kevin."

"Too bad, Annie. I had to kill it. You go see if it's dead. That's fair."

"Kevin, you're the man of the house. Isn't this your job?"

"Don't change the subject. C'mon. Go check."

Annie went out and confirmed the kill. She made Kevin carry the whole telephone book out to the garbage. She also insisted on bringing the baby's crib into their bedroom. Kevin thought this irrational. Annie did not even pause. Better that Mary be emotionally damaged by sharing a room with her parents than dead from a poisonous spider bite.

Annie lay in bed with her eyes wide open that night. It was a bad omen, and she knew it.

Chapter Seven

All too soon, Mr. Griffin departed for the long ride back to Chicago. Annie held Mary tightly as they watched him pull away. She was startled at the burning prick of tears in her eyes. This was her last connection to her father and sisters. She thought sadly that the Griffins' car would be parked a few blocks away from her family. Irrationally, she envied it. She chanced a look at Kevin. Annie momentarily imagined it was her father pulling away.

"Come on." She shifted Mary and grabbed his hand. "I'll make you a grilled cheese, and we'll go for a walk. You can show me the campus."

Kevin smiled down at her and nodded. "We'll walk to the store and get a *TV Guide*. Can you believe we get free cable?"

Thus cheered, they began their life together.

Initially, all was good. Kevin attended school every morning until noon. He came home for lunch, then went to practice until five thirty. Annie had dinner ready for him at six. They spent their evenings companionably watching movies or playing Scrabble. The game was not begun until the baby slept. Annie popped corn and made lemonade.

Soda was expensive and reserved for special occasions.

Kevin liked school and loved sports. Much of their conversation revolved around his performance and chances of playing. He was a bright individual, and the classes came easily to him. Annie was glad to see him adjusting.

Obtaining groceries presented a problem. The coach arranged for a player to drive Annie to the grocery store on Saturday mornings. But often she needed provisions during the week. Regardless of how completely she made her list, a critical item was forgotten. Annie cheerfully packed Mary into the stroller and walked the two miles but was limited in how much she could carry home. Also, bad weather sometimes prevented these trips. Kevin was not interested, repeatedly reminding his wife that it was her dilemma. Annie usually managed but sometimes had to buy milk and bread at the convenience store. Kevin was strongly opposed to this because milk there was fifty cents higher. It was a problem.

Annie spent her days tidying the house and minding Mary. She loved having her own home. Cleaning and laundry could be dealt with by ten-thirty in the morning. Mary was still a good baby, and Annie had no problem getting her work done. It was only in the afternoons that time dragged. Afternoons were open for exploring, and Annie noticed how spread out everything seemed. She grudgingly conceded that Texans had all the room in the world. But it was tough on people without cars. Public transportation was limited to an erratic bus service that actually varied its route as far as Annie could tell.

Only poor people rode buses. Most were Mexicans, and Annie liked them. She thought the mothers very affectionate. Anyway, they were poor like her.

She found the public library and obtained a card. It was downtown, about six miles from campus. Kevin told her to use the college library. Someone told him that a "bad element" rode the buses. Annie laughed out loud, picturing the Mexican mothers with their children. Besides, she could not take books out of the college library unless Kevin was present, plus everyone stared if Mary so much as yawned. Annie loved the little library in town. Her Friday trip for books immediately became a bright spot in her week.

Another highlight was her daily trip to the student center to check the mailbox. Sometimes she browsed in the adjacent bookstore. Once she splurged and bought a notebook for $1.50. It had a beautiful cover with the school logo on every page. Surprisingly, Kevin did not get mad. The Griffins had little money, and Kevin tended to get angry if Annie wasted any.

Letters from home were the ultimate highlight of any day. Eileen wrote religiously. Annie's younger sister's letters were filled with breezy eleven-year-old nonsense. They came in tubes disguised as Tootsie Rolls or in little boxes with Mickey Mouse labels. Invariably, something for Annie, sometimes a piece of gum or stickers that smelled like strawberries, was tucked inside. Once there were four leaves from the McGowans' lilac tree, wrapped in plastic wrap and mounted on construction paper. Eileen called them bookmarks. Annie placed these treasures in an honored place on the refrigerator.

Nellie wrote occasional missives with anecdotes about her own college life. Maureen proved to be the correspondent extraordinaire. Filled with local gossip, her letters were racy and fun. She was still outrageous, and sometimes Annie kept these letters from Kevin. They tended to substantiate everything Kevin hated about females. Working in a bar was great fun for Maureen. Still steady with Mr. Wonderful, she made enough money to support herself as she finished college. Because she dealt with liquor salesmen, she received every piece of promotional material offered. Kevin said they would never have to buy T-shirts with Maureen around. Yes, packages from home delighted Annie.

Letters from Danny came once in a blue moon. His mail had a foreign look and bore stamps from places like India and Africa. He was struggling with monsoon season somewhere. He would soon be in New Orleans and promised to drive up to see them. Annie could hardly wait.

One day Annie marshaled her courage and visited the admissions office. She chose a time when Mary was sleepy and would nap in the stroller. An enthusiastic counselor promised Annie that financial aid would be available. Additionally, the campus sponsored a day-care center where Mary could be deposited while Annie attended classes. The school made every effort to assist mothers in obtaining an education. Annie felt certain that Kevin would not be pleased. She would have to broach it carefully. Finding a quiet bench, she worked steadily until the forms were completed. The counselor told her to look for a response in six weeks.

Annie thought fast on the way home. Kevin's initial complaint would be financial. The best approach was to leave it be until the letter arrived. If she did not land a scholarship, she would keep quiet. If she did, the financial argument would be moot.

It *was* possible that Kevin would be supportive. Sighing deeply, she quickened her pace. She would have to get dinner in the oven quickly. Tonight was a special night. Maureen was calling. Annie was allowed to use the phone only once a month. Kevin had worked out the rate and determined that it was too expensive to call Chicago except in emergencies.

Kevin's bossiness disturbed his wife. They could not afford extras. That was a given. The Griffins were living on a fixed income. But he treated Annie like a child. A bad child. Annie read several books on marriage. When she was honest, she knew they had problems. Communication was difficult. Most disagreements escalated into fights. But the books said every marriage had rocky episodes, and Annie struggled to find the correct method of dealing with conflict.

Kevin was moody. If he was in a bad mood, Annie kept quiet. She could not ask him what was wrong. It made him mad. She had to be careful, too, about reading. Kevin did not like her reading. He accused her of ignoring him. Annie tried postponing her book time until he went to bed. Then he said it was rude not to come to bed with him. Kevin seemed to want sex every night. Annie could go to bed, then get up and read. Unfortunately, that, too, offended him. Annie controlled her anger and matched her reading time to Kevin's studying. So far this had solved the problem. Annie knew she gave in too much, but every book stressed compromise. The problem was, she could not remember a situation where Kevin did the compromising.

Pushing the troubling thoughts from her mind, Annie parked the stroller and carried the baby up the stairs. Within ten minutes dinner was cooking and the house was tidy. Kevin came home in a mood. He stayed quiet through dinner. Annie tried gently to feel him out. Something was obviously bothering him. She hoped he would not ruin her phone call. Annie quickly cleared the table and put the baby to bed. Kevin hunched over his books silently. The tension was so thick, Annie wondered why the walls did not blow out.

Finally, she cracked. "Is something bothering you?"

Rage rushed out at her like water from a burst

dam. Kevin accused her of complaining. He said Annie was destroying them by her selfishness. Practice and school were draining. All he got when he came home were complaints about how hard it was to get a few groceries.

Annie listened. She knew from experience that the real issue was yet to be revealed.

Annie embarrassed him by taking the bus with the baby. The college library was not good enough for her. She had to haul the poor baby all the way downtown on a dirty bus. A good mother would not expose her child to such danger.

At this, Annie exploded. "I'm a bad mother for taking my child on a bus? Why don't you admit you want me locked in the closet?"

Kevin shoved her against the wall and screamed, "That shows what a selfish bitch you are. Being a wife and mother isn't enough." He berated her for thirty minutes. With a sinking heart, Annie heard the phone ring. She made a move to answer it but was blocked.

"Don't even think about it." He sneered.

Once again, Annie knew fear. She remembered this Kevin. She remembered him from the front seat of his car. When he finally quieted down, Annie marched into the bedroom and closed the door. Mercifully, Mary still slept. Throwing herself onto the bed, Annie began to cry. The bedroom door burst open. An enraged Kevin grabbed her by the arm. Dragging her off the bed, he pulled her into the living room and threw her onto the couch.

"Listen up, Annie," he shouted. Kevin emphasized his words by jabbing his finger into Annie's chest. "No more waltzing around campus with the baby. No more buying dollar-fifty notebooks at the bookstore. You're not in college. Your job is here with the baby. Do you understand?"

Annie's voice shook with emotion. "Waltzing around campus?"

Kevin's laugh was ugly. "Don't talk back to me," he threatened. "*Do you understand?*" His right hand shot out and punched the wall above her face. Annie covered her head and waited. "Stupid bitch!" he swore. "What? You think I'm going to hit you? Knock it off, Annie. Quit playing the martyr. Why don't you tell me what you were doing over by the business building?"

Annie looked up and saw hatred in his eyes. Someone had seen her by the business building. If she tried to explain now, she'd get hurt.

"How dare you talk to me like this!" she retorted furiously. "I walk around campus every day. Sometimes I go one way, sometimes I go another. I was also waltzing around by the fine arts building. Yesterday I tangoed by the gym." Seeing his face, she hastened to add, "If the baby gets cranky, I walk. So what?"

"So maybe you should tell me so I don't look like a fool when someone says they saw you." Kevin took a deep breath. He lowered his hands to his side. "It looks like my wife is out sneaking around."

"Sneaking around?" she repeated, legitimately

puzzled. "Kevin, I swear, I'm not being smart. What do you mean by 'sneaking around'?"

"Annie," he said patiently, "if a husband doesn't know where his wife is, she's sneaking. You never told me you went walking to these places. That means you were sneaking."

Annie shook her head in disbelief.

"Are you serious?"

He was getting mad again, and she decided not to push. Kevin sat down next to her. Taking her face in his hands, he gazed at her without speaking. Annie resisted the urge to slap his hands away.

"What's really going on, Kevin?"

"Annie," he whispered, "you act so innocent. You forget. I know you. I know how you can be."

A knot twisted in Annie's stomach. "How can I be, Kevin?"

"Do you think I've forgotten about Harold?"

Annie's eyes widened in disbelief.

"Do you think I'm stupid?" he whispered.

Annie resisted the urge to replay the Harold incident yet again.

Kevin continued. "I forgave you, Annie, but I did not forget. I love you more than anything. But I can't trust you. You lie."

The rest of the argument passed in a blur. Three hours later, Annie still sat like a wooden doll. She longed for bed. She attempted to persuade Kevin she was trustworthy. It was futile. Emotionally drained, she stopped caring. Finally he wound down, and they went to bed. Kevin drifted off immediately. Annie stared into the darkness for hours. She must have gone to sleep at some point, because her eyes opened to sunlight.

Lying on her side, Annie let her mind dance through last night's argument. Was she a sneak? She did not think so. She had applied for the scholarship in a secretive manner. But Kevin would have forbidden her had she asked permission. Did that make her sneaky? At any rate, the deed was done. If he thought she was sneaky yesterday, wait until he found out she had applied for school. There was a million-dollar question here, and Annie wrestled with it. Did Kevin think Annie was sneaky because of her methods? Or were her methods the result of Kevin's controlling behavior? It was the chicken-or-the-egg problem.

Her mind flitted to the "waltzing around campus" item. How could walking be wrong? Annie would understand if she was seen with a strange man. It never occurred to her that Kevin needed a re-enactment of her every action. Could it be embarrassing when people saw her somewhere? She supposed. The bottom line was that Kevin did not trust her. And all because of Harold. Annie tried to recall what Harold looked like. Poor innocent Harold. With one conversation he had dashed any chance of happiness for Annie. Mary, too. And Kevin, for that matter.

Annie rejected such simplistic reasoning. *Nothing happened*, her mind screamed. She quickly skipped away from that old line of thought. The

Harold scenario was like a book that had been read too many times. The ending never changed.

Kevin had also said she complained too much. Wasn't that part of marriage? Kevin certainly shared his frustrations. Annie wished she had thought of that last night. Kevin talked at length about practice and school. She realized then that there existed an enormous double standard in their relationship.

For a moment, reality shifted. The arguments were too confusing. She felt like Alice in Wonderland. *Kevin should be happy that I'm trying to make a life here*, she thought bitterly.

Instead, he calls me sneaky and selfish. Annie remembered something else said last night. He'd said that she was lucky that he married her at all. Annie acknowledged the truth in this. Many men would have fled. *I wish he had*, she thought darkly. *I wish I had never gotten pregnant*, she added. She thought of little Mary and nearly drowned in guilt. Annie began to cry. She was as bad as Kevin said.

Rising quietly, she went to the bathroom to wash her face. *I'm a good mother*, she thought defiantly. Taking rides on the bus did not hurt Mary. Annie looked in the mirror. Dark circles ringed her eyes. She wondered how to act. It was Saturday. Unfortunately, Kevin would be around all day. He sometimes accompanied her to the grocery store. Annie prayed he would stay home.

Wandering into the living room, she froze. There was a hole in the living room wall. Hastily, she covered it with a picture. Thinking of the neighbors, her face burned with shame. They must have heard every word of the fight. Annie would have to avoid them. *Too bad*, she thought wistfully. Kevin had said there was another married football player from Chicago in their building. Maybe his wife would be a friend.

Annie opened the blinds and let the harsh sunshine stream through. Squinting at the light, she tried to shift the lonely ache in the pit of her stomach. It was a constant presence these days. She wanted to go home. What if she called and asked her father to send an airline ticket? He would, she knew. She could be home by Monday. For a glorious moment, it seemed like a miracle. Imagine being in her own bed! Annie dismissed the idea. Her father would be worried. He would be disappointed. He would ask what the problem was. Annie did not know herself what the problem was. A failed marriage within a year equaled total disgrace. No. Annie was not going home. That meant she was trapped. Trapped in a bad marriage, she thought dramatically. No wonder there were so many country western songs.

Okay, she mused, *I'm stuck. So is Kevin. We can either be miserable or make it work. I can't abandon my husband at the first sign of trouble. I promised to love, honor, and obey. What on earth was I thinking? Anyway, there's no point whining because it's not perfect. We can always see a marriage counselor*. Annie's eyes opened wide. Why hadn't she thought of that before? There was hope after all. Couples had fights. That was nothing new.

As for the present, should she be mad today? Conciliatory? Gone waltzing? She giggled at this.

Annie heard the baby begin to stir. The bed creaked. Kevin began cooing to Mary. Every morning he reached over and pulled the baby into bed. Hearing him talk softly, Annie felt her heart melt. He loved his daughter. He loved his wife, too, and Annie knew it. She resolved to try to patch things up. From now on she would tell him every single detail. If she dropped a quarter, she would tell him she bent down on Third Street. Annie would make him trust her. A small niggling voice reminded Annie that she had tried this before. Slapping it away, she told herself she had not tried hard enough.

With a false air of briskness, she entered the bedroom. Kevin continued playing with the baby.

"Annie, I'm sorry I got so mad last night," he offered.

"Well," she answered thoughtfully, "you did get carried away. I think we need to talk things out, Kevin. If something bothers you, tell me right away." She searched for words. "I don't mean to complain."

Kevin was facing the wall. His voice was muffled. "You're not complaining, Annie. You're just talking to me. I'm a jerk. Sorry." Annie sat down on the bed and rolled him over on his back. He looked sheepish. "Don't panic and think we've got a bad marriage," he pleaded. "I'll lighten up. I promise. How would you like to go out with that other couple tonight?"

Annie felt her spirits surge. "I'd love it, Kevin.

But what about the baby?"

"They have a baby, too," he said lightly. "They're just like us, only with rich parents and a car. They said to bring Mary. They invited us for dinner."

"Kevin, why didn't you tell me?" Annie chided. "What should we bring? I'll make a dessert." Her mind leaped ahead. "Thank God I'm going to the grocery store. Should we bring wine?"

Kevin laughed out loud. "Relax. I just found out yesterday, and we weren't exactly talking last night." He considered. "I'd say bring beer. Nobody our age drinks wine. He also said you could go to the store with his wife during the week."

They talked for a while longer. "I wonder if they go to mass." A sore spot with Annie was her inability to get to church.

"I didn't ask and don't you." Kevin spoke firmly. "It's none of our business. Do you hate me?"

"No." Annie tried to be honest. "I don't like you when you're mean, though. And you called me a bitch."

"I don't know why you stay with me, Annie," he responded contritely. "You're too good for me. It won't happen again, but please don't do things without telling me. Okay?"

"I won't, Kevin. Let's get dressed. We're getting picked up in half an hour, and Mary has to be fed."

Scooping up the baby, Annie felt dampness. "You're a wet little peanut, aren't you?" she said affectionately. Mary smiled and grabbed for Annie's nose. "And starving, too, I'll bet." Mary gurgled in joy. Pausing, Annie glanced down at Kevin and smiled.

"I love you, Annie. More than anything."

"I know, Kevin. Don't look so serious. I'm not going to die or anything. Just don't maximize me, okay?" He laughed appreciatively at their inside joke and began to get up. The day was starting better than Annie had dared hope.

Throughout the day, Annie's mood fluctuated violently. One minute, hope and optimism soothed her. Then, waves of anxiety assaulted. Concentration was difficult. Grocery shopping took forever. Repeatedly, Annie assured herself that Kevin was not mad. The fight was over. But every few minutes, her mind presented a brutal flash of last night's argument. There was a hole in the wall. That message was clear. *Next time it will be my face*, she thought, frightened. Maybe it had been a dream. A nightmare. She would check the wall later. *No*, her brain insisted.

Kevin had dragged her from the bedroom into the living room and called her a bitch. Right now he was pushing the cart ahead of her. He looked relaxed and happy. Mary was chuckling at her dad's funny faces. Annie stared after them, lost in thought. Surely she was overreacting. Pushing up her sleeve, she studied her arm. An angry welt was darkening. *Thank God*, she thought. *I'm not crazy.* The bruise was tangible. Wasn't that better than Kevin's verbal assaults? Yanking down her sleeve, she looked around furtively. Her thoughts raced. She could say she'd banged her arm on the railing of the stairs. Sadly, she realized that nobody cared. She told herself this was a good thing. Imagine the humiliation of someone finding out! A vision of the neighbors slid into her head, causing her face to heat up. Still, Annie allowed for the possibility that the neighbors had not been home.

Consoled, she allowed herself to feel normal. Things were as they seemed. An attractive young wife and mother was shopping on a Saturday morning. Her handsome husband amused their beautiful baby so Mom could concentrate on the respectable task of organizing their nourishment. *All we lack are a couple of singing bluebirds*, she thought wildly. Bending over to scrutinize a box of rice, she noticed there was something wrong with her throat. Ah, yes, a scream was trying to escape. She snatched a box of rice and clutched it. If she flew at Kevin from behind, she could choke him. Annie stood helplessly, certain she was losing her mind. A cold hand squeezed her heart. Mental illness. People would feel sorry for Kevin. His wife had gone around the bend. She was too young, they would say. She couldn't cope. It would be the ultimate form of control. "No," she blurted out loud. Frightened, she struggled for control. She could not be found talking to a box of rice in the dry goods aisle. Annie giggled. Ragged nerves turned the giggle into a stream of laughter. A shopping cart awkwardly nosed around the corner. Kevin and Mary eyed her in concern, causing Annie to laugh louder.

"Annie," Kevin whispered, "what the hell is the matter with you?" Annie stopped laughing and looked at him brightly. "I guess I'm so fucking happy I can't help it. Oops. Bad word choice." The appalled look on Kevin's face increased her mirth.

"Get a grip, Annie! You're acting like a head case. The coach's wife is by the frozen foods. She wants to meet you." Kevin's face was wary.

"Am I scaring you?" Annie queried gleefully. "How does it feel, you big jerk?" She took a breath and stopped laughing. "Just kidding, Kevin. I'm a little punchy." She began to walk past him and paused. "Incidentally, don't ever call me a head case, you bastard."

Reshelving the rice, she stalked away. *Screw him*, she thought. *Maybe I'll carry the rice box with me and tell it everything*. Annie laughed a little less hysterically as the insanity drifted off. Kevin charged after her with the cart.

"What's the matter with you, Annie?" he said shakily.

Annie shook her head to clear it. "Sorry, Kevin. I'm okay now. Where is the wife?" Brushing her long hair back from her face, she forced a smile. "Honestly, I'm fine."

Kevin bent down and kissed her on the forehead. "You're upset about last night," he said flatly. "It's my fault. I'm sorry, Annie. We'll talk about it at home. Believe me, it won't happen again." He spoke with quiet confidence. "I am the luckiest guy in the world to be married to you. I'm not going to blow it. I promise."

Annie sighed. "I'm not trying to make you feel guilty, Kevin. But your temper is out of control." Kevin pulled her close and held her. "I'm sorry, Annie."

"Newlyweds!" sang out a woman's voice. Mrs. Nelson, the coach's wife, appeared. "Only newlyweds hug in the grocery store." Kevin and Annie smiled in embarrassment. "Hello," she continued. "I'm Andrea Nelson. You must be Annie."

Annie extended her hand. The three made small talk while Mary desperately attempted to climb out of the cart. Babies were effective icebreakers, and Annie took stock of the older woman with darting looks. Dressed tastefully, Mrs. Nelson had a feminine drawl and wore a hairstyle that managed to look chic and simple. After telling the Griffins to expect a dinner invitation, she drifted to the checkout.

Inexplicably, Annie felt cheered by the conversation. Mrs. Nelson had treated her respectfully. She had admired Mary and told her that great things were expected from Annie's academic future.

Annie grilled Kevin. "What did she mean about my academic future, Kevin?"

"Probably that she heard you were smart," Kevin bragged. "I told the coach your SAT test scores." Looking down at Annie, he grinned. "Actually, I compared you to Einstein. Coach said you should apply for a scholarship. I told him you were too busy with the baby. Maybe later. Would you like that?"

Annie frowned. This was the time to tell him. Right here in the cereal aisle. But she could not get the words out. Something held her back. They would have a serious talk, and she would tell him then. It would have to be soon. Kevin would be on good behavior for a while after last night. The thought jolted Annie. Was this really so predictable? The apologies, the promises, the loving consideration? *Well*, Annie thought roundly, *he's not going to do it again. I'll be very clear about what I'll tolerate in the future.*

"I sure would like to think about it, Kevin," she admitted. He smiled down at her. Life slid back into focus.

That evening Annie prepared scrupulously for their dinner out. A whipped cream pie graced the middle shelf of the refrigerator. Mary's best pajamas were washed and folded neatly. Annie sensed Kevin's tension. Social situations made him uncomfortable, and he made her promise they could leave directly after dinner. Cheerfully, she agreed. The prospect of a short night was not disturbing. Any night at all was welcome.

The evening was a success. Greg and Darlene Kemp were friendly and welcoming. Darlene had short brown hair and looked as though she was having trouble taking off the baby weight. Greg was similar to Kevin. Big and handsome. The couples had quite a bit in common, and the conversation flowed. A perceivable difference, as Kevin had pointed out, was their obvious financial comfort. The Kemp apartment was nicely furnished, and Darlene wore expensive clothes. She served a chicken casserole and complained that Texans had never heard of pork roasts. Annie could not imagine buying *any* roast on the Griffin budget. The Kemps came from Evanston, a northern suburb of Chicago. Annie listened with pleasure to the familiar accent. She had not realized until now that she missed it.

Both babies slept, giving the mothers time to talk during cleanup. Darlene also disliked her mother-in-law. The Kemps, too, had arguments. Darlene volunteered this information as though it were completely natural. Annie listened intently. *Maybe we're not doing so badly after all*, she thought. Darlene commented on Kevin's obvious affection for Annie. The young woman actually sighed. Greg was not demonstrative. Darlene said Annie was lucky.

The pie was served in the living room. Both Darlene and her husband praised the confection. Gratified, Annie caught Kevin's wink. Inevitably, the subject of school came up. Darlene was determined to begin after Christmas, and Annie watched in amazement as the couple bantered. They laughed while exchanging pretend barbs. *How wonderful*, thought Annie. Here they are disagreeing, and nobody is shouting. She glanced furtively at Kevin. Maybe he would learn something.

Two hours after dessert, Annie and Kevin departed. Walking home in the warm darkness, Annie quizzed her husband.

"Did you like them?" she asked neutrally. She knew better than to act too enthusiastic.

"I sure did, Annie. Did you?"

"Yes," she responded. "Darlene is nice. At home I don't know that we would have been friends. But I liked her."

"Greg is nice," Kevin said slowly. "But I know what you mean. I probably would not have hung out with him at home. Darlene sounds like a feminist, don't you think?"

Annie groaned inwardly. "I did not get that, Kevin. She wants to go to school. That's all. I actually kind of agree with her. As long as we're here, we might as well get two diplomas. Right?"

"Annie," Kevin said sternly, "if you want to go to school, that's fine. But first you have to come up with the money. And what about the baby? I'm not going to watch her. I have to study. For now, I don't see how it could work."

"I think it could, Kevin," Annie said pensively. She had to tell him. Annie opened her mouth.

"Anyway," Kevin continued, "I liked Darlene, but I sure am glad that you don't talk to me like that. Kind of bossy, wasn't she?"

"They were just playing, Kevin," she retorted. "Greg didn't mind. He was enjoying it."

"What else could he do?" Kevin asked. "She was embarrassing him. Don't get too close to her, Annie. She's a bit much."

Annie arched her eyebrows. "Surely you are not in charge of who my friends will be."

"I don't care who your friends are. Just don't get like Darlene. The pie was great, Mrs. Griffin. I certainly married a good cook."

"Thank you." She hated being called Mrs. Griffin. It reminded her of her mother-in-law. Annie shuddered. Kevin's parents had blessedly postponed their visit until after Christmas.

Kevin reached for the baby as they mounted the stairs. Like babies everywhere, Mary was portable. Annie went ahead and opened the door. She turned on the television while Kevin put Mary to bed. The Kemps had told them that WGN from Chicago came on their cable after midnight. It was mostly old movies at that time, but the commercials were entertaining. Used car dealers hawked their wares in harsh Chicago accents. Annie remarked to Kevin that people watching from around the country probably thought all Chicagoans spoke that way. Kevin said that people thought of Chicago as Gangster Town. They had a good laugh.

"Annie," Kevin called from the kitchen. "Where is the phone bill?"

"On the counter," she answered.

"I looked there. Find it now," he ordered. "I'm going to pay bills in the morning, and I want them together."

Annie sighed. Rummaging through the kitchen, she found everything but the phone bill. It was gone. She searched drawers, cabinets, even the top of the refrigerator. "Kevin, are you sure you don't have it? I can't put my hands on it."

"Annie, I just told you I do not have it."

"It's one o'clock in the morning," Annie said. "I'll find it tomorrow."

Turning off the television, they went to bed. Annie was exhausted. As she drifted into sleep, she reviewed her list of worries. They had not discussed the fight. They would have to talk about it tomorrow. There was something else. Oh, yes, the phone bill. Surely it would turn up. The real problem was the scholarship application. Kevin would have to be told.

Chapter Eight

They never did find the telephone bill. The issue
snowballed, resulting in Annie's loss of mailbox
privileges. Kevin said this was not the first piece of
mail she'd misplaced. How was he supposed to keep
things in order if Annie lost correspondence? Annie
spent Sunday searching while Kevin berated her.
Finally, Annie went downstairs to the garbage bin.
Kevin followed her down and said she was an
embarrassment.

Shortly before dinner, Kevin implemented the
silent treatment and took his books into the dining
room to study. Annie struggled with her anger. She
was pulling the drawers out when the phone rang.
Maureen was calling with a neighborhood update.
Annie cut her off and apprised her of the missing
phone bill. Maureen informed Annie that people
occasionally lost mail. One simply called the phone
company for a replacement. Or you paid an estimate and caught it up later. Cheered, Annie hung
up and shared the information with Kevin. Mistake.

First, he accused Annie of telling her family their
problems. Next, he said that maybe the McGowans
did business that way, but the Griffins were more
responsible. Annie retorted that Maureen had
hardly encouraged them to head for the border.

There was simply no reason to make a world event out of a piece of misplaced mail.

Kevin exploded. "You hit the nail on the head," he screamed. "Everyone should be like your family. No one should worry about anything. Let's make a joke and be done with it." Annie remained quiet. Kevin was waving his arms furiously. It was time to back down. "Your father is no Einstein, you know, Annie."

Annie rose from her chair. "That's true," she replied icily. "Nevertheless, he's more successful than your father will ever be."

At that Kevin threw a stack of books against the wall. Annie walked over and picked up the now screaming baby. "Just so you know, Kevin. Start anything, and it will be the last time. Think about that."

Annie walked into the bedroom and closed the door gently behind her. Inside, she comforted Mary. Cursing herself for not leaving the apartment, she tried to stop shaking. Annie promised herself two things. One: The talk about Kevin's violence would come today. Two: She would not put herself in this situation again.

Eventually, Kevin began to move around in the dining room. So far so good. His movements were unhurried and calm. He knocked on the bedroom door.

"Can I come in?"

"Are you rational?" Annie countered.

"Perfectly."

"Then come in and we'll talk."

Kevin sat down next to her on the bed and sighed. "I don't know what to say. Tell me one thing. Are you planning on leaving me?"

Annie resisted the urge to qualify her next statement. "I meant what I said. What don't you understand?"

"So you're going to leave?"

"No. But if you touch me again, I won't stay." Annie noted his look of misery and hardened her heart. "Why is it okay for you to say whatever you like? Then, when I respond, you lose it. I've had it, Kevin. What horrible thing did I do wrong today?"

Kevin avoided her direct stare and tried to shift Mary. The child had climbed up on his leg and was beating her little fists against his thighs for attention.

"Annie, we'll talk later, when the princess is in bed. I can't concentrate while she is trying to play with me."

Annie swooped the baby into her arms. "I'll put her down for a nap," she said crisply. "We can talk in the front room."

Annie went into the kitchen and prepared a bottle. She lay Mary in her crib. The child's face immediately registered protest. It was not nap time, and she knew it. Annie swiftly put the bottle in her mouth and watched as her little eyes began to close. Annie softly shut the door and went into the living room.

Sitting down on the floor by the window, Annie watched Kevin lower himself into the recliner. He reminded her of a man facing execution.

"So," he began, "what do you want?"

Annie let her breath out and checked her response. "Kevin, what do you think I want?"

"I haven't got the slightest idea," he retorted. "You're mad because I insulted your father?"

"No," she replied patiently. "That was mean, but you got it right back. Why did you slam all the books into the wall? Were you trying to scare me?"

"No," Kevin said angrily. "I was pissed off. I'm trying to run a household here, and you're losing mail. Then you go and tell your sister the whole story. She acts like I'm a big loser. She's got all the answers in the world. What's the big deal? I threw a few books." Kevin was talking defensively, but he looked frightened. Annie instinctively knew she had a shot at making her point. She spoke carefully.

"Kevin, I'm sorry if that's how it seemed. That's not how it was intended. You have a right to keep household things private. Is that what you mean?"

"You're damn right it is," he sputtered self-righteously. "Every time I make a mistake, it gets blasted all over the south side of Chicago."

"What are you talking about?" Annie asked, flabbergasted.

"You tell them everything," he accused. "I need to know that what happens in this house is between us. How would you like it if I told my friends you lose everything? Or that you don't always keep the house clean?"

"Now what are you talking about?" she asked

in dismay. "When isn't the house clean?" A feeling of defeat suffocated her. She frantically shrugged it off. "Kevin, maybe I better go first so we don't get off track. We're talking about this." Bitterly, she pulled up the sleeve of her sweatshirt. A large bruise colored her upper arm. Annie rose abruptly. She pulled the picture from the wall, displaying a large hole. "And this." Taking a few steps into the dining room, she kicked the books. "And these. Kevin, if you want the house cleaner, then tell me. But for right now stick to the goddamned subject. You promised you would never do this. I can't stand it, Kevin. You tell me I'm crazy. Do you want to know something? Living like this would make anyone crazy." She took a deep breath. "I'm not finished, Kevin. I truly believe that our problems can be worked out. I'm willing to go a long way in compromising. But I am not compromising with your temper."

"Are you finished now?" he asked calmly.

"Yes I am."

"I think my wife is a little upset here," he joked. "Is it that time of the month?"

Annie stared at him in disbelief. "Kevin, if you dare make a joke of this, I swear I'll kill you."

"Threatening to kill me?" Kevin said with a wave of his arm. "Annie, listen to yourself. I know you don't like it when I say you're crazy, but admit it. You get a little scary at times." Kevin was looking kind and compassionate. Annie resisted the urge to slap him.

"Answer the question," she demanded. "What

are you going to do about it?"

Rising slowly, he put his arms out to her. She stood firm. Kevin turned to face the window. It was possible he would lose his temper, but Annie was unafraid. She was too mad. *Marriage is painful*, she thought coldly. *So is love*.

"Kevin," she said, softening a little, "just so we're clear. I love you very much. I would never *want* to leave you. But I can't be happy if I'm afraid of you."

Kevin nodded his head. Startled, she realized he was fighting tears. She closed the distance between them and put her arms around him from behind.

"Annie, will you help me?" Kevin said as he turned to her. "I don't want to be like my father. I won't lose my temper anymore. I promise."

Kevin and Annie now spoke with humble simplicity. They loved each other. They had everything that mattered in the world. Annie told him about the scholarship application. He was proud of her. He actually said that. She told him how afraid she had been for him to find out. He shook his head in disgust. He said he was really out of control if his wife was afraid to tell him things. The phone bill situation made him feel like he was failing. He wanted to be a good husband and father, but it was scary sometimes. Annie could not believe her ears. She sputtered that she was often afraid she would not be a good wife and mother. Kevin was astounded. He said she always did everything right. That was part of the reason he felt inadequate. Annie promised to mess things up once in a while.

They laughed. They had sex. They woke the baby up and went out for hamburgers. They had never done that. Kevin said he needed to lighten up about money. He promised that he would try very hard. Annie felt happier than she had in months. Her friend was back. Surely they would have smooth sailing now.

The next day she went to check the mailbox and discovered that he had stolen her key.

Annie stood staring at the key chain in her hand. She and Mary were in the student center. She looked down at her daughter, nestled snugly in the stroller. "What should I do, Mary?" she asked the baby. "He must have taken it."

Annie scrutinized the ring. It was a Dewars Scotch key chain, courtesy of Maureen, and quite sturdy. The key could not have fallen off. Annie instinctively knew that Kevin had gone along with her last night because he'd had no choice. He would get her in other ways. Taking her key. Further restricting her freedom. Annie smiled absently in response to the baby's chatter. Was she paranoid? Kevin was her husband, for heaven's sake. Surely he was not plotting against her. Annie's forehead creased in concentration. She would obviously have to confront him. The thought made her sag wearily against the wall. Annie realized that she needed to talk to someone. A professional.

Walking briskly, she made it home in minutes. Annie put a record on the stereo. Music was becoming very important to her. It reminded her of who she used to be. As she tidied up the house, she felt tears begin to sting her eyes. To keep from getting emotional, she pulled the baby's walker into the kitchen as she prepared dinner. She sang every song to Mary with exaggerated faces and movements. Before long they were both laughing.

Annie screamed when Kevin poked his head around the kitchen corner. He was always so quiet when he came in. He startled her every time.

"Dammit, Kevin," she swore. "If you keep doing that, I'm going to deadbolt the door and make you knock." Leaning against the pantry door, she held her hand over her heart. "How was your day?"

"It's not my fault you're half deaf. Do you want me to blow a horn when I come in?" Kevin spoke shortly. He was not in a good mood. "My day was fine. Why is the stereo up so loud? I thought you had a boyfriend over."

"No. Just me and my dancing partner. Say hi to Daddy," Annie instructed. Mary grinned up at Kevin and put out her arms. He picked her up and swung her in the air. The baby laughed in delight. "Mary is having a very happy day today, Kevin. But I'm not." At that instant Annie knew how she would handle the situation. "Hand it over, Mister. Give me the key."

Kevin casually opened up the fridge and grabbed the lemonade. Reaching for a glass, he shrugged his shoulders. "What are you talking about?"

Annie felt her stomach tighten. "Give me back my mailbox key, please."

He reached down and picked up the baby again. Looking at Annie, he said quietly, "Annie, don't make an issue out of this. I'm tired of fighting with you. You keep losing mail. That's the fact. From now on I'll get the mail and bring it home. I'll keep the bills and give you any letters. What's the big deal?"

The afternoon sun glinted off his brown hair. Annie squinted against the light in an effort to marshal her thoughts. She was not crazy; Kevin was sinister. If she fought about her right to have a key, he would say she was a feminist. If she confessed her suspicion that he would keep her mail, he would call her paranoid. If she said that she preferred to read her letters first, he would accuse her of trying to hide something. Possibly love letters from Harold. Lifting her chin, Annie stared him right in the eye.

"Give it back."

"No," he said flatly. "In order to avoid any further fights about bills, I'm getting the mail. That's final, Annie. Get over it. What's for dinner?"

"Someday you'll be sorry we went this way, Kevin." With that she turned back to the stove. "Pork chops."

Weeks passed. Annie asked every day if anything had come for her. Every day he said no. One night he took the garbage out and met Greg Kemp in the yard. Annie watched the two men talking. Still looking, she grabbed Kevin's folders and started searching. In the back of the last folder was a letter from Maureen. There was also one from Danny. Both had been opened. Annie replaced them and restacked the pile. Next, she ran into the bathroom and locked the door. Turning the water on hot, she stripped frantically and poured bubbles. She would have to account for her red face.

By the time Kevin started banging on the bathroom door, she was immersed in a sea of bubbles within a virtual sauna. Her eyes were dry.

"What the hell are you doing with the door locked?"

"Taking a bath." She leaned forward and unlocked the door. Settling back into the bubbles, she leaned her head back and closed her eyes.

"Wake up, Annie," Kevin demanded. "Since when do you lock the door?"

Annie answered slowly, as if groggy. "Since my husband started disappearing with the garbage. Anyone could walk in here." She paused. "Where did you go?"

"I was talking with Greg. They want us to come over for dinner tomorrow."

"No, Kevin," she said sharply. "Tell them to come here. We should have asked them sooner."

Kevin sat down on the toilet and stared at her. "What's the big deal?" Annie opened her eyes and glared at him. It was crucial that he not know she had found the letters. She needed time to think.

Annie redirected her indignation. "Do they

think I'm incapable of cooking a dinner?" she snapped. "They can come here or forget it." She closed her eyes and sank back into the bubbles.

She heard Kevin sigh. "Kind of sensitive, aren't we?" Annie ignored him. "Okay. I'll tell them to come tomorrow." When Annie again failed to respond, he left. She opened her eyes and saw that he had left the door open. She lurched forward and slammed it. He did not come back.

Kevin was insecure. Annie knew that. She had excused his continual bad behavior because of it. At some point, though, he was responsible. She thought hard. He was doing a burn over the college application. It had to be that. He could not find a reason to condemn the action so he was doing nasty things he perceived as safe. It was very important to Kevin that he not look like a nut. He had to appear reasonable and controlled. Annie shuddered. He wanted to cut her off from her family. That was probably why they were here in Texas instead of at a midwestern campus. She knew that now. No phone calls. Now he wanted to cut off the letters. Annie's relaxed body belied the furious activity of her mind.

She was smarter than him. He could not change that. There was no way he could take her mind away. Annie took a deep breath and submerged. She stayed under as long as she could hold her breath. Blowing up through the surface, she took deep gulps of air. She was thinking like a lunatic. This was her husband. Why would he want to cut her off from her family? Annie wondered if he could get to her head. Drive her crazy. The ultimate control.

All right, she mused intently. If she was crazy, she must be paranoid. Kevin had gotten the letters and forgotten to give them to her. After all, she had stopped asking him. This was an oversight, blown grossly out of proportion. He was not diabolical. He was Kevin. Annie shook her head at her silliness.

"Kevin," she called.

Kevin poked his head playfully in the door. "Yes, my little Sybil. What is it?"

Annie smiled easily. "Sorry, Kevin, did you get any mail for me?"

His expression did not change. "No. Nothing."

Annie watched him with a pleasant expression on her face. She would bide her time. A thought popped into her head. Why not get a replacement key? What the hell? Apparently their marriage was destined to be sneaky. She would check the box during the day before he got there. At least she would know how far he was going.

"Kevin," she continued, "I've been thinking. I'm going to get a job during the Christmas rush. The department stores are hiring part-time help. It'll be a few extra dollars. What do you think?"

Kevin frowned. "Get it out of your head. No wife of mine is going to work in some department store."

He backed out and closed the door.

Oh, yes, I am, Annie thought grimly.

Chapter Nine

The next day, Darlene called to say that the Kemps would not be coming to dinner. Their little boy had an ear infection. Annie was gracious and extended the invitation to the following Saturday. Darlene informed Annie that a mandatory team dinner was scheduled for Saturday. The wives were also expected to attend.

Annie was nonplused. Kevin had not mentioned it. Darlene suggested that he had forgotten. She begged Annie to come so she would have someone "normal" to talk to. Both girls laughed out loud.

"I really can't think of anyone I could get to baby-sit," Annie hedged.

Undeterred, Darlene said breezily, "I'm using one of the neighbor girls. They live below us. Their mother is in school full-time, and the two girls are in high school. They're both good. Do you want me to call the sister for you?"

Annie's mind raced. It was risky, not talking about it with Kevin first. The thought of another confrontation was unbearable. At the same time, surely Kevin had meant to mention the dinner.

"Darlene, that would be great. How much do we have to pay them?"

"Well, if we're gone four hours I would say

about ten dollars. That way they'll come back when you ask them." Darlene sounded quite efficient. "I usually buy them soda and snacks, too. I'll call her now and call you back."

Annie sat looking at the phone. Ten dollars. He would have a fit. Moments later the phone rang. Darlene had made the arrangements.

Annie hung up and stared. Kevin was at practice. Mary was sleeping. If she was going to make the call, this was the time.

Much thought had gone into this phone call. On the last visit to Mary's doctor, Annie had noticed a sign on the wall. It gave a hotline number for people in violent relationships. She had heard the term "battered women." Luckily, she did not have to worry about that. Kevin was not abusive. Still, Annie needed to talk to a counselor, and maybe they could tell her where to get one. She had looked up the past phone bills. Local calls did not show up. It was safe to call from home.

Before dialing, she ran to the window, just to make sure. This was paranoia. Kevin was not due home for another two hours. He had never missed a practice yet. Not even part of a practice. Kevin played with the flu and sore muscles. Discipline. That was the name of the game. He was doing very well, and it looked as if he would be playing in the upcoming game. He explained to Annie that for a freshman that was exceptional.

Sitting herself down at the desk, she dialed

quickly. "Women's Services Center," drawled a soft female voice.

Annie informed her that she needed information about counseling. After a brief pause the woman asked patiently, "What kind of counseling?"

"Well"—Annie spoke in a rush—"actually, it's kind of marriage counseling except that I don't think my husband will go. So I guess just counseling for me."

"Are you having marital problems?"

"Not really," Annie said nervously. "Just some adjustment problems. Maybe communication problems. Things like that."

"I see. Did you know that this is an information center for abused women? We have many services that might help you."

"Oh, no," Annie answered hastily. "We don't have *those* kinds of problems. My husband is not abusive. He's just a little insecure. I am doing something wrong, and I don't know what it is. I thought maybe a counselor could help me figure it out."

"Certainly," the woman agreed. "It's important to know when you need to talk to someone."

Annie was beginning to like this person.

"Would you like to come in and talk with one of our counselors?"

"God, no," Annie blurted. "I'm sorry. But he'd have a fit if he thought I was going somewhere like that. Is there a place that does regular counseling? Like . . . a regular place?"

"Sure." The woman was not offended. She gave Annie the number of a community services center that offered counseling on a sliding scale. She promised Annie it would be inexpensive. She made Annie promise to ask for a girl named Caroline. Annie agreed. Business taken care of, Annie was loathe to let go of this warm voice. There was a pause.

"What's your name?" Annie asked.

"Dana. Do you mind if I ask your first name?"

"No. I guess not. Is this place confidential?"

"Yes," Dana answered. "Everything you tell me is confidential. I would not ask you for your last name unless you were coming in. Even then, we wouldn't need it. It's just nice to have something to call you."

"I understand." Annie tried not to sound paranoid. "My name is Annie. As long as we're talking, can I ask you a couple of questions? Do you have a minute?"

"I sure do, Annie. My job is to answer the phones, and they're dead quiet. What kind of questions?"

"Well, what kinds of things do these abusers do? Do they beat up their wives?"

"That's part of it." Dana was speaking slowly, as though carefully phrasing her sentences. "But there's a lot more to it. It's a combination of emotional and physical abuse. Mostly, it revolves around the abuser having control of his partner."

"Oh," Annie said in relief. "My husband is not like that at all."

"Annie, I'd like to send you some written information so you could learn more about it. Can I mail it to you?"

"God, no. He took my mailbox key. I'm not allowed to get the mail anymore."

"I see."

"It was my fault," Annie hastened to assure her. "I lose all the mail. Actually, I only lost one little phone bill. I didn't even lose it. It was on the counter. I remember because it had cranberry juice on it. It just disappeared. So now he thinks I lose all of the mail. He has my letters in his folder, and he's telling me they never came."

"It doesn't sound very nice. Annie, do you work?"

"No. He won't let me. It would help if there was a little more money."

"I can certainly understand that," Dana answered placidly. "Annie, would it be okay if I had a counselor call you tonight? Just to talk things over and make sure you get to the right person."

"No, Dana. Not while he's home. I'll end up trying to explain, and it will start a fight. He's touchy. If he thought I was talking to a women's organization, he'd kill me "

"What do you mean, kill you?"

Annie laughed a bit too hard. "Sorry. Wrong thing to say to a battered women's counselor. I only meant he'd get mad."

"What kinds of things does he do when he gets mad, Annie?"

"Oh, let me think. Nothing much. He yells a lot. Calls me names. If he's really mad, he might punch the wall or push me around or something. Nothing abusive. Just nasty."

"How many times have you had bruises after a fight?"

Off guard, Annie answered casually, "A couple of times. One time he nearly strangled me. But that was a long time ago. Lately, just bruises on my arms. Nothing major. He's gotten a lot better about his temper. But I think it's getting bad again."

"Sounds scary," Dana offered calmly.

"That's what bothers me the most." Annie was speaking quickly now. "I hate being afraid every time we get into a fight. It's not fair. Nothing around here is fair. He says it's my fault. There's a million reasons why it's my fault. Some of them make sense, but some of them are absolutely insane. I'd be embarrassed to tell you."

"Is he jealous a lot?"

Annie was stunned. "Yes, he is. He's terribly jealous. Why do you ask?"

"Just wondering. Can he be loving and sweet one minute and be a monster the next?"

"Yes. That's what drives me crazy."

"Annie, there is a profile for this type of person. They tend to be jealous and possessive. They are also controlling. They act like they want to know where you are every minute. Another issue is trust. Abusers will accuse their partners of lying. To avoid arguments, partners stop telling the abuser things.

These instances are then used to prove that the wife is untrustworthy. In other words, you're damned if you do and damned if you don't. Women in these relationships say it feels like walking on eggshells. There's much more to it than I can tell you over the phone. Are you okay, Annie?"

Annie was clutching the phone. "Yes," she answered in a small voice. "I'm a little shaken up. You're describing my husband exactly."

"I know, Annie. I'm sorry. I don't want to upset you, but it's important that you know the facts so you can keep yourself safe. Do you think you're in danger right now?"

"No, of course not. He's not even home. He's not like this all the time, you know." Annie was getting angry for some reason.

"I know he's not mean all the time, Annie," the counselor answered compassionately. "If he was, you'd never have married him. I'm sure he can be very loving and sweet. I do think that it's important to look at the signs or symptoms in your home. When you told me he takes your mail and he would not allow you to work, it sounded a bit familiar. Most marriages are not like this, Annie."

Annie sighed deeply. "It's not supposed to be this way, is it?"

"No, Annie. It's not."

"Okay. I'll call Caroline and make an appointment. It's a start. Do abusers get better if they get counseling?"

"When they admit they have a problem, they

can get better. Usually, though, abusers are so busy blaming everyone else that they don't admit they have a problem. Some do, though. Annie, I want you to remember if you ever feel you're in danger, call. If you're ever in immediate danger, call the police. Okay?"

"Geez. It's not that bad. Dana, I can't thank you enough. Can I call you again if I think of any more questions?"

"Annie, you can call anytime you want. One more thing. This type of behavior usually gets more frequent and severe. It gets worse. It's important that you know that. Stay safe."

"Yes. Thank you. Good-bye." Annie glanced at the clock. She had been on for over an hour. Feeling guilty, she jumped up and pulled meat out of the fridge. It was chicken. Should she bake it or fry it? She stood in the kitchen. A decision was not forthcoming. Kevin sounded like one of those abuser guys. Call the police? Thankfully, Kevin was not that bad. Annie longed to call Maureen. For a second she considered it. This was certainly an emergency, but not the kind she could explain to Kevin. She stood holding the chicken for another ten minutes. Hearing the baby wake, she jumped again. She stared at the chicken in her hands. It was too late for baking. Fried it would be. She set it down and went to get Mary up.

After dinner, Annie apprised Kevin of the arrangements for Saturday night. He grunted from his textbook.

"Is that okay with you?"

"Fine. We can't make a habit of baby-sitters, but once in a while it's necessary."

"Kevin, why didn't you mention this party to me?" she asked in a neutral voice. "It was a little embarrassing to hear it from Darlene."

"Now you know how I feel when I hear my wife is over at the business building. It's no big deal. I forgot."

Just like the letters, she thought.

Yes, Dana had gotten to her. Kevin was nice when Annie was doing exactly what he told her to. But really. Imagine telling her to call the police? She would talk to another counselor. In the meantime there was nothing to do but act normal.

Chapter Ten

Annie did not call the counselor that week. Later, she would marvel at her ability to live in the present. They called it denial. Kevin was sweet and affectionate. He finally gave her Danny's letter, along with two from Eileen. Danny wrote that he would be in Chicago for Christmas.

Annie sighed as she read that. She knew there was no way they could afford to go. It would be different if they had a car. Flying was out of the question.

Annie asked Kevin if there was any sign of her scholarship application. He said no. He did give her another letter from Eileen, leading her to believe he was no longer withholding mail. Annie forgot to get a replacement key. She speculated that Kevin had adjusted to the idea of his wife attending school. The worst was over.

On this note she prepared for the party on Saturday night.

The baby-sitter arrived on schedule. Annie had written down all pertinent information on the memo pad by the phone.

Greg and Darlene had offered to pick them up, but Kevin preferred to walk. That suited Annie. Smiling up at Kevin, she reached for his hand.

"It's nice to be going out to dinner, Kevin."

"There's nothing like a free meal," he agreed. "Annie, don't talk too much tonight. Okay?"

"What do you mean?" she said in a hurt voice. "Do I talk too much?"

"No," he answered. "It's just that I don't know these people well, and I don't want to be all chummy with them. You know?"

"I wasn't going to invite them all over to see our wedding album," she chided. "Honestly, Kevin. What a thing to say. Do you want me to say anything at all?"

"Don't get all bitchy. I just don't want you to be a social butterfly."

Annie remained quiet. Did she usually talk too much? She was a social person. But people liked it when you made conversation. Still, she would try not to say too much tonight.

Their silent walk ended at the campus center. The dinner was being held in a large room downstairs. Annie quickly spied Darlene and led Kevin over to the table. The Kemps had saved two seats.

"We were right to dress up," she whispered to Darlene.

"Thank God," Darlene agreed. "Greg is tense for some reason. Look at him." She inclined her head. Greg did indeed look as nervous as Kevin.

"Don't feel bad," Annie whispered. "Kevin told me not to talk too much."

With that, the girls burst out laughing. They kept their heads together until it was time for the

155

presentations. Darlene made faces, and Annie giggled. It was almost like being with Rene.

There was a lanky boy at their table who looked miserable. Darlene informed Annie that he was from Wisconsin. He had never been away from home and was desperately homesick. Annie leaned over and asked Kevin about him.

"The poor kid can barely get through practice," Kevin confirmed. "He practically cried during the national anthem at the last game. It reminded him of home."

Annie looked horrified. "That's terrible, Kevin. Why don't you invite him over for dinner sometime? It must be horrible to be stuck in the dorm."

"Don't start, Annie," Kevin said shortly. "He'll live."

Annie watched the boy all through dinner. When Kevin and Greg got up to talk to the other players, she leaned over the table. "I'm Annie Griffin. I don't think we've met."

Looking surprised, the boy extended his hand. "I'm Tommy Gill. I've seen you walking with your baby."

"I do a lot of that," Annie replied with warm smile. "This is Darlene Kemp. Our husbands both play."

"Oh, I know who they are," he said enthusiastically. "I'm from southern Wisconsin."

"What part?" Annie asked. He told her in a wistful tone. She smiled in delight. The McGowans had spent many summers camping ten miles from his home. The boy was delighted. He became animated at once as they discussed his hometown.

"It's very small," Annie noted pleasantly.

"Yes," he agreed. "That's why I like it so much. There's so much to do." He went on to describe the winter activities he desperately longed for. "You can't even tell that time is passing here. The seasons don't change. It's weird."

Annie nodded her head. This had bothered her, too. What on earth would they do at Christmastime? They laughed at the thought. Darlene was listening happily. At that moment, Kevin and Greg walked back to the table.

"Kevin," Annie said excitedly, "Tommy's from near the campground we always went to." After receiving a blank look from her husband, she continued. "You remember. You met Rene and me there once. That's where he lives." Kevin looked even more blank. An embarrassed silence was settling upon the group. "I'm not making this up," she promised Tom. "Kevin was there once. My family went every summer."

"Let's go, Annie," Kevin said tersely.

Startled, she grabbed her purse. "So soon? Okay. I guess I'm ready."

Darlene, Greg, and Tom collectively tried to persuade them to stay. Kevin was adamant. They had a baby to think about, he reminded Annie. Annie's face flushed.

Annie tried to make her good-byes. It was not easy with Kevin fidgeting by the door. Walking quickly, she caught up with him in the vestibule.

"What's the big hurry?" she asked innocently. She knew what the problem was. Kevin was angry that she had talked to Tommy. Choosing to ignore the obvious, Annie made small talk for the first part of their journey home. Kevin did not respond. Eventually, Annie, too, lapsed into silence. She had a sick feeling in her stomach. Tommy was a nice guy. He was much more like Annie and Kevin than the Kemps. Annie knew she was in for trouble. She hoped Kevin would ignore her for a few days and be done with it.

As they mounted the steps in their building, she reminded him that he needed to escort the baby-sitter home. It was the right thing to do.

Annie greeted the sitter cheerfully. Kevin plopped down on the couch and stared at the television.

"Kevin, are you ready?" Annie asked nervously. "Can you walk Tina home?" Kevin ignored her. Tina was beginning to look uncomfortable.

"Mrs. Griffin, it's no problem. It's only across the yard. I can just run."

"Nonsense, Tina," Annie said briskly. "Kevin is apparently glued to the news. I'll walk over with you."

Returning, Annie fumed. It was one thing to be mad. She was used to that. But did he have to humiliate her? She decided not to broach the subject tonight. He looked too tense. Tomorrow she would let him have it. Entering the apartment, she went straight to the bathroom and dressed for bed.

Annie was brushing her teeth in the bathroom when she saw his face in the mirror behind her. She was turning to talk to him when she felt her head violently slammed forward.

The toothbrush speared the inside of her upper lip as the side of her face made contact with the medicine cabinet. Still facing the mirror, Annie looked down to see blood streaming onto her pretty green face towels.

Clutching her head, she grasped the sides of the sink. Another glimpse of his face prompted Annie to slither down and away from him. Viciously, he kneed her in the small of her back. A jolt of exquisite pain shot down her legs as she collapsed to the floor. She must have started screaming, because Kevin was kicking her, shouting for her to shut up. Annie closed her mouth and curled into a ball. The kicking stopped.

"Slut," Kevin said as he backed out of the room. Someone was pounding on the floor. It was coming from the front room. The downstairs neighbors, Annie thought gratefully. Kevin stormed around the living room, pounding back.

"Assholes!" he shouted loudly.

Annie was consumed with pain. It was not over. She knew that. Kevin would scream and shout for at least four hours before he would be able to sleep.

Annie scooted over to the tub and pulled herself up. Sitting, she took stock. It was excruciating to sit. She was bleeding heavily from the mouth. Grabbing a washcloth, she shoved it into her mouth and let it hang out. There was blood all over the sink, floor, and wall. Annie felt a pulsing on the left side of her head. Running her fingers across her face, she was relieved to see no signs of blood. It must all be coming from her mouth. From the sounds of things Kevin was back on the couch. Annie thought of Dana. She wondered what her chances were of reaching the phone. She would have to get to it and dial the operator, then at least shout for help before Kevin reached her. She shuddered.

Casting around for another plan, Annie decided to make for the back door. Down the stairs and over to . . . where? Somewhere with a phone where she could call the police. She tried to think realistically. Kevin was fast. He'd have her in no time. If she could get down just one floor she could bang on the neighbors' door. They thought she was a lunatic anyway. Surely they'd call the police. Annie's heart hammered thunderously in her chest. She thought of poor little Mary sleeping in the bedroom. She had to get the police.

Clenching her teeth, she pulled herself up against the sink. The mirror was a bit of a shock. Her left eye was swelling fast, and her upper lip looked like a harelip. Annie pulled the rag out. It was saturated. She let go of the sink. *Go!* she told herself. *Go!*

Annie glided silently out into the dining room. Kevin did not look up. With shaking hands she undid the lock on the back door. "Hey!" she heard him bellow. The lock gave just as she heard his first thunderous footfall. Annie was halfway down the stairs when he caught her by the back of her nightgown.

"Stupid bitch!" he muttered as he began to drag her back up the stairs.

"*Let me go!*" she screamed.

"Fuck you. You're a little slut, and you needed to be taught a lesson." He grabbed for a better grip on the back of her nightgown. Annie lurched away, half falling, half rolling down the stairs.

"*Help!* Help me!" she screamed as loudly as she could.

As Kevin struggled for another hold, the neighbors' back porch light went on. Kevin lifted her easily into his arms. With his hand across her mouth, he took the steps two at a time. In seconds they were back in the apartment and Annie was thrown onto the couch. She looked up at him defiantly.

"Get this through your head, Annie." Kevin's chest was heaving, but his voice was surprisingly gentle. His next words dashed any hope that he had calmed down. "I will kill you, yes, kill you dead, if you ever try to leave me again. Do you understand? You can try to hide, but I'll find you. When I do, you'll be sorry you were ever born."

"I'm already sorry," she snapped.

Kevin put his finger against her mouth. "Do you want to live? Don't talk. You are a trashy slut. If we had not left when we did, you would have been making out with Tommy Gill. I should have known better than to leave you alone with Darlene. Five minutes and you're acting just like her. Understand me, Annie. I won't tolerate this. Do I need to say it again?"

"'No.'' Maybe he would talk himself down. "I understand."

"Admit that you were attracted to Tommy," Kevin said kindly.

"I was not even remotely attracted to Tommy."

With lightning speed he slapped her across the top of the head.

"That's another problem you have." He sneered. "You're a liar. Next time I ask you a question, tell me the truth. I know that's hard for you. You're a deceitful little slut like your sister Maureen. I've been throwing her letters away. I don't want you reading about her sexual exploits."

"What sexual exploits?" Annie demanded. "Maureen has been steady with her boyfriend for years." She felt a wave of exhaustion. This would go on for hours.

At that moment they heard a knock on the front door. Neither moved. Kevin put his finger to his lips, indicating that she should remain quiet. Annie felt her spirits soar. The knock came again. Louder.

"Police. Open the door," said a deep male voice.

Annie remained expressionless. She looked up at Kevin. Leaning over, he whispered into her ear. "If you want to die tonight, tell them something." He spoke in a slow and measured voice. "I'll kill you.

Now go open up the door."

Kevin went to the farthest corner of the room and sat down. Annie slowly rose and opened the door. Her whole body was shaking. If she told them anything, he'd kill her. *Not if he's arrested*, she thought. But Annie knew that Kevin would not get life in prison for beating her up. He would eventually get out. And she believed him. He would kill her.

Two uniformed officers stood on the landing. They looked casual and relaxed. One was older, probably in his late forties. The other appeared to be in his mid-twenties.

"There was a report of a loud disturbance, ma'am," said the older one, taking charge. "What happened to your face?" Annie felt her composure slipping. She began taking gulping breaths as she tried to speak. They looked so calm and normal. Still holding the door, she felt Kevin come up behind her.

"Honey, ask them to come in," he said reproachfully. "Please come in, gentlemen. I have to apologize for my wife. We're having an argument, and she's a little upset. She fell coming up the stairs." Annie backed up as they entered the apartment. She felt as though she was in a bad movie. "Sorry about the noise," Kevin continued. "We were at a party and began to argue when we got home."

"What was the argument about?" asked the veteran officer. He was looking at Annie. A glance at Kevin told Annie that it was not safe to speak. She looked at the floor and shrugged her shoulders. "He got jealous."

The officer looked at Kevin. Kevin smiled sheepishly. "It's not one of my better qualities, I'm afraid. You see, when my wife has a few drinks, she gets a little friendly with other guys. And that's not one of her better qualities. I do tend to get bothered by it, though."

"You're a fucking liar, Kevin," Annie said emotionally.

"Hey, lady," the officer intervened, "that's no way to talk to your husband. Watch your mouth." Annie rolled her eyes. "Being a smartass is not going to help matters. Who was screaming for help on the back stairs?"

"That would have been me," Annie answered sarcastically. "Its not one of my better qualities, but when I have a few drinks, I scream for help on the back porch."

"Ma'am, you have a real problem with your mouth," the officer said in warning. "Now, we're here to help. Your mouthing off is not going to make it any smoother." He was pointing his finger at her. Annie resisted the urge to slap his hand away from her face. Her husband was trying to placate the man. Kevin was defending her!

"This is insane," Annie cried, sobbing now in earnest.

"Officer, again, I must apologize for my wife," Kevin appealed. "She's homesick and tired. She took a bad fall on the stairs, and it upset her. I'll admit, I lost my temper and started yelling. She ran down the back stairs in her nightgown. I got her back into the house as fast as I could, but it might have upset the neighbors." He had his hand on Annie's back, and he was attempting to comfort her. "It's all right, Annie. You go to bed now and let me talk to these guys."

Annie glanced up at the young officer He was looking at her intently. With a flash of understanding, Annie got it. He knew.

"Just a minute," the young man interrupted. "Ma'am, can I ask you a few more questions? That's a pretty bad split lip you've got there. Where did you fall?"

"On the front stairs there," Kevin answered quickly. "Right down on the first floor."

Annie remained silent. Kevin stood staring at her. She was not looking at him but could feel his gaze.

"Is that what happened?" the officer asked, looking directly at Annie. "I guess what I'm wondering is how you split your lip and bashed the side of your head at the same time. Seems a bit awkward. Know what I mean?" She nodded. "Unless someone is fibbing."

"Now hold on a minute," his partner intervened. "Married people have fights. That's not against the law. Young lady, did someone intentionally assault you and cause those injuries?" Annie was looking down at the floor. Then up at the ceiling. The older officer continued, "Because if they did, you could sign a complaint and that person would be hauled off to jail. He would sit there until a judge set his bail. He would have a permanent arrest record and all because his wife was flirting at a party. See what I mean?"

Annie walked away. She left Kevin talking. They were discussing sports, and of course they knew who Kevin was. They thought his chances looked pretty good this year. The older policeman told Kevin a joke about damn Yankees. The damn Yankees were the ones who never left Texas. He laughingly told Kevin that they had no problem with Yankee athletes, though. Kevin was most welcome in the Lone Star State.

Annie lay on her bed and wondered if this were real. She felt so powerless. At one point it was obvious that the younger guy was putting two and two together. But Annie had presumed the older one was in the dark. Until he told her she could have Kevin arrested. He knew, too. Right from the start. It was all right with him as long as Kevin kept it quiet. Annie figured she was lucky she had not been arrested on a noise ordinance for screaming on the back porch. She fumed. She wanted to kill Kevin. Not painfully. Just dead. But Kevin was not going to let her go. Ever. Even if she left him, he would come after her.

Hearing her name, she sat up in bed. Why did they not leave? They weren't going to do anything. She walked back out.

"Mrs. Griffin," the nice one said, "I've told your

husband, and I wanted to tell you, you probably need to have your mouth looked at. I'd guess you need a couple of stitches up there."

"Thank you, officer. I'll do that in the morning."

He gave her a compassionate smile. "You call us if anything makes you nervous, now. Ya hear? We work twenty-four hours, and we're as near as your phone. Understand, Mr. Griffin? We're as near as that telephone on the desk there."

"Sure," Kevin answered innocently. "Thanks for coming. Sorry for the trouble." He closed the door.

Turning toward Annie, he began, "See what you did, Annie. Now they've got my name. You're the biggest embarrassment a man ever had to live with. What the fuck were you thinking? Out in the yard in your nightgown." She leaned back against the wall in shock. "If you ever pull any shit like this again, you're in big trouble. Fucking nut! I don't know how I stand you."

Annie looked up at him. She started doing her usual replay of reality to assess her guilt. She stopped herself. This was not her fault. She had not even called the police. She had only tried to escape. She had done something terribly wrong in her early life, and God was punishing her. God wanted her to be stuck with Kevin for the rest of her life. She prayed, and nothing changed. Kevin was going on about how she would have to try a little harder not to flirt. It would not be hard. This was the last time he would take her out.

Annie tuned him out and continued to think. Did God hate her?

"*No!*" a voice shouted in her head. Annie was startled. Had the voice been real? She would have giggled, but Kevin might think she was not paying attention.

Does God want me to stay with Kevin until he kills me? She tossed it up as an experiment. "No," the voice said more quietly. Annie understood.

"You can't have my soul, Kevin," she interrupted.

"Pardon me?" Kevin asked in a startled voice.

"You heard me," Annie continued flatly. "No matter what you do to me, no matter how often you tell me what a loser I am, no matter how much you twist the truth, you cannot have my soul. So what do you want? Eventually you'll lose me. You know that, don't you?"

Kevin's face paled. "You're talking crazy again, Annie. Listen to yourself." He made no move to follow her as she walked into their room and climbed into bed.

Annie felt calm. Kevin could not destroy her. He could beat and humiliate her. He could even kill her. But he could never consume her. That was the nameless fear that was driving her crazy. That she would disappear altogether. No, she vowed. God did not want this for anyone. God would help her. *So long, Kevin Griffin*, she thought. *Somehow, some way, I'll escape*. Annie drifted into a dreamless sleep.

Chapter Eleven

The following day Annie ignored him. All day. It was Sunday, and there was nothing going on. Her left eye was swollen, and her lip was puffed out. Her back hurt. She was forever shifting to locate a comfortable position. The idea of anyone seeing her like this was unthinkable: she was housebound. Pale and upset, Kevin paced around like a caged bear. He walked into the kitchen while Annie was feeding the baby, and looked startled to see her face.

"Why do you make me do it, Annie?" he asked in a strangled voice.

Moving slowly like a robot, Annie pushed past him to get the milk. There was no struggle with depression. Like the tentacles of an octopus, she let it wrap coldly around her. Welcoming the dead heaviness, Annie found it muted the pain. For now, there was nothing worth feeling. Death did not frighten her. She longed for it. If not for Mary, she would be entertaining thoughts of suicide. She entertained them anyway. There were two items, however, firmly barring that option. One: Kevin might get his hands on Mary, permanently distorting Annie's innocent child. With the inherent conceit of every mother, Annie knew that nobody could love Mary as well as she. Two: suicide was a big sin.

Perhaps the biggest. Annie paused momentarily. Was it worse than hurting someone else? Probably they were equal, she mused. She gave herself a mental shake. Wrong was wrong. She was stuck on earth with Kevin. *Not for long*, she promised herself.

Kevin wrestled with guilt. She sensed it. In a vastly detached way, Annie pitied her husband. The only plight worse than her own would be Kevin's. She shuddered. How tragic to live Kevin's warped and bitter existence. She realized that emotionally she had written him out of her life. Tomorrow she would rethink the marriage thing. It was over. There was no pleasing Kevin, and she might die trying. Her mind lurched backward, reviewing Kevin's accusations.

Even mentally she lacked the strength to defend herself. *Well*, she thought, *there's only one thing for it. I'll accept full responsibility. It can be all my fault, just so it ends*. The thought freed her. What had he called her? Spoiled? Annie thought hard. Could she live with that? She was spoiled and sneaky. Yes. She nodded grimly to herself. Spoiled and sneaky was okay. She would be spoiled and sneaky by herself, thus sparing all men from her badness. She would be Jack the Ripper, too, if it enabled her to exit the cruel charade that was her marriage.

Later, toward evening, Annie sat sprawled on the bedroom floor with Mary. The contents of the toy box lay strewn about, lending a hurtful cheeriness to the room. Annie heard the couch shift. Kevin had been staring at the television for the last few hours, trying to act normal. Now he opened the door and stood behind her. Annie concentrated on the puzzle in front of her. Children's puzzles were therapeutic. Unlike life, everything fit.

"I'll get my own dinner if you want," he said uncertainly. To her silence he added, "Do you want anything?"

Annie shook her head. *Fall over dead in the kitchen, please*, she mentally requested. *What are the odds?* Surely somewhere in the world a nasty man had fallen dead in his kitchen. Annie thought dejectedly that Kevin was fairly safe working with the butter knife he would certainly use to make a peanut butter sandwich. She shook her head again to scatter the badness. Mary gamely began shaking her head. Annie smiled in spite of herself. Something struck her. She was going to abandon Kevin, no doubt about it. But there was something she could do for him. She could spare Mary. Annie would shield his daughter. Maybe later in life Kevin would understand and thank her.

Mary pushed a book in her face. *Green Eggs and Ham*. Annie sighed deeply and began to read. Sam I Am was kind of like Kevin. Relentless. Galloping through the story, Annie began to use first mad, then pleading voices. Mary laughed in delight. The little pixie face watched Annie's intently for the next change of expression. In spite of herself, Annie came to life. She laughed out loud at the end. On the heels of laughter, tears rushed down. Like sentinels, they had waited steadfastly, knowing their time would come.

She remembered the voice from last night. Real or not, Annie clutched at it. Whoever it was had said no. God did not want this for her. Yes, it was a big mess, but who better than God to clean it up? God did not care if she was rotten. He was looking for faith, Annie knew. Blessedly, she had that. Following that thought, Annie realized that her current risk was that of falling into despair. That would tie His hands. She had to hope, trust, and parachute out of the crashing plane that was her marriage. An unsettling issue popped into her head.

What about the forgiveness thing? Hmm. Surely she could forgive Kevin from a safe distance. Like . . . thousands of miles. Annie resolved to pray for Kevin every day. But she had to leave. Lately she had found herself thinking violent, hate-filled thoughts. Enough of that. From now on she would think good, hopeful thoughts. What about the lies? Annie pondered deeply. In order to escape, and she finally understood she would be fleeing for her life, she had to deceive. The question hung in the air as she waited for last night's voice. Nothing. She would take that as a thumbs-up. The shortest distance and all that.

Breathing deeply, she gave Mary a genuine smile. She felt cleansed and peaceful. Odds were she would survive this day. Tomorrow she would take action.

• • •

Monday morning, Kevin went off to school as usual. A sickly gray color suffused his face. He looked scared. Annie, on the other hand, was serene. She could hardly wait for him to leave so she could call the counselor. Ignoring his good-bye, she watched through the window as he headed for school. He walked slowly with his head down. Annie beat back feelings of pity.

Popping Mary into the high chair, Annie steadily spooned fruit into the child. Cheerios came next. That would buy Annie twenty minutes. It was too risky to call Chicago. One expression of sympathy would toss her over the edge. Nervous breakdowns were an unaffordable luxury.

Dialing the number, she asked for Caroline. A woman's voice told her that Caroline was in session and would call her back. Annie thought quickly. Finally, she requested that Caroline call back before noon. She stressed that it would not be safe to call after that. The woman sounded perplexed. Annie said it again, the same way. She thanked the woman for her help and hung up. At this stage, Annie did not mind offending Kevin. She did, however, need time to think before any more head-on collisions.

Putting on some music, she cleaned house. Mary began to bellow from the high chair, so she picked her up. The baby's clothes were out on the table, and Annie gently laid her down for a change. Her diaper was dirty. Looking at her speckled bottom, Annie decided to pop her into the sink for a quick bath. She didn't have a full-blown rash, but Annie knew it could become one if it was not kept clean. The pediatrician in Chicago had told Annie that the best prevention against diaper rash was a clean bottom. One bad rash had made a believer of Annie, and she silently prayed that the counselor would not call back just yet. Poor little Mary was loudly indignant at a bath that was tantamount to a dunking. Annie wrapped her in a towel and with one hand made her a bottle of juice.

Annie took a large mixing bowl from the cabinet and filled it with assorted goodies. Placing it on the couch, she helped Mary into a standing position. Mary was just starting to "cruise," as the experts called it. This meant she was pulling herself up on furniture and walking from piece to piece. Watching her for a moment, Annie decided that *cruise* was much too smooth a word. *Lurch* better described the infant's method of travel. Annie sighed. Mary would be walking in no time. Another shower of grief fell down upon her. How sad that Kevin would not watch this beautiful child grow up. Again Annie disciplined her thoughts. Feeling manic, she started to clean with a vengeance. At exactly ten o'clock the phone rang.

It was Caroline. Annie briefly told her that she had spoken with Dana, who had recommended her. Caroline told Annie that she did not have any openings at this time. Annie was silent. This contingency had never occurred to her. Caroline asked her what kind of situation she was in at the moment.

"Uh, I'm not really sure myself," she said, groping for words.

"Are you having marital problems?" Caroline probed gently.

"The police would think so," Annie began hesitantly. "I don't want to start crying. I'm trying to think of a way to say this."

"Well, Annie," Caroline said definitively, "the best way I know is straight out. What's going on?"

"We had a fight the other night." Annie paused. "I lost. I have a bad bruise over my left eye, and I think I should have gotten stitches in my lip but I had no way to get there. He would not have let me go anyway. I also have bruises all over the backs of my thighs and on my back. He was kicking me. I think I need to leave, but he's going to kill me if I do. I'm not sure what I want to do right now. . . . I feel like it's time I did something." Annie was about to continue when she heard the counselor start to say something.

"Pardon me," Annie said politely.

"Go ahead, what were you going to say?" Caroline waited.

Annie took another deep breath. "As bad as that sounds, I have one bigger problem. I think I'm losing my mind. I mean, I'm really frightened I might be going nuts."

Caroline burst out laughing. "Annie, I'm sorry. Let me tell you why I'm laughing. You sound like a perfectly sane person to me. It's just that if you told me you felt emotionally great, I might be worried.

175

If you feel like you're going crazy, that's good. It means you're normal. Anyone in your shoes would be losing it right now. Can you get over here at twelve?"

"Can you see me?" Annie asked in delight.

"Sure. I can see you during lunch," Caroline said cheerfully. "Will you be able to get here? Where is your husband right now?"

"He's at school and then at practice. He is an athlete and would never miss a practice. I can take the bus, but I'll have to bring my baby. Is that okay?"

"Sure," Caroline responded easily. "We love babies. I might even be able to scare up a baby-sitter for her. I'll see you at noon, Annie."

Annie hung up the phone and sat with her hand on it. She had done it. No asking Kevin. No fighting about it for six months. She was packing up Mary and going to a counselor. Just making the arrangements made her feel stronger. She was over eighteen and would do what she wanted. Kevin could not control everything. This would all be great except for two things. One: She still loved Kevin. Two: He would kill her if she tried to leave. Shrugging her shoulders, Annie began to get ready. It was a pretty good day, and you couldn't have everything. Within fifteen minutes, she and Mary were heading to the bus stop.

Annie gave the bus driver the address, and he dropped her off right at the door. She realized with a start that the clue to where she was headed was probably the black eye and split lip. She kept forgetting that she looked like a prizefighter. She remembered being dragged back into the apartment in her nightgown. Her face flushed every time she thought of it.

After giving the receptionist her name, she sat down. The stroller folded up, but Annie could not decide whether to take Mary out yet. Decisions were impossible these days. Little ones like this. She mulled it over until she heard a woman's voice call her name. Standing up, she turned and saw a woman who appeared to be in her thirties by the receptionist's desk.

"Caroline?" Annie said uncertainly.

"Yes, in the flesh," the woman answered. "Who is this darling little thing?"

Annie smiled proudly. "This is Mary. Say hello, Mary."

Caroline bent down and took the child's hand. Mary immediately began a long story in baby dialect. Annie chuckled. Mary was usually shy around strangers. Caroline listened seriously and made appropriate responses. "She's wonderful," she exclaimed. "Whatever she's telling me is extremely important." Standing up, she extended her hand. "I'm Caroline Martin. You must be Annie." Annie shook her hand and nodded. She liked this woman immediately. "Come on back to my office. One of the girls is going to hang out with Mary in the playroom if it's okay with you. That will give you a bit of a break so we can talk."

Annie followed her down a hallway to a small room filled with toys. A young girl about Annie's age was hurriedly eating a sandwich.

"Sue," Caroline introduced them, "this is Annie and her daughter, Mary. Mary has some important things to say today so I don't think you'll have any problems."

Sue abandoned her sandwich and smiled at Annie. "Great. We'll play in here. Don't hurry. If I need you, I know where to find you."

"Thank you so much," Annie said. "There is a bottle of juice in the diaper bag if she gets cranky. And she's just been changed so she'll be all right until I get back. I'll just back out so she doesn't see me going." Sue nodded. She was already squatted down in front of the stroller with a stuffed porpoise.

Caroline led Annie to another small office in the same hallway and motioned her in.

Annie settled into a comfortable chair and looked around. The room had a good feel to it. The walls were painted a light mauve, and two country landscapes graced the windowless wall. Their colors blended nicely with the mauve and added to the general serenity of the room. Caroline seated herself across from Annie and smiled.

"Have you ever been to a counselor before?"

"No," Annie answered shyly. "This is the first time."

"Well, then"—Caroline crossed her legs and became businesslike—"there are a couple of things

I'd like to fill you in on first." With that she launched into an explanation of confidentiality. Annie listened with one ear. The other ear was enjoying the melodic sound of Caroline's voice. She was not originally from West Texas. That was clear. There seemed to be a bit of Eastern Seaboard behind the light drawl. The confidentiality was comforting, though. Apparently, Caroline would never tell anyone what Annie said. They would have to torture or subpoena her first. Even then she would not tell unless Annie signed a release of information. Also, there was a sliding scale fee arrangement, which meant that if Annie had no money, she did not have to pay. Annie explained that Kevin dealt with the money and she did not have much extra with her today. Caroline waved it off. She said they would deal with that down the road.

Caroline went on to talk about scheduling. She was booked at this time. That meant that initially Annie's appointment time might shift every week. Annie studied her as she spoke. Caroline was very attractive. Taller than Annie, she was thin. Svelte, Maureen would have said. She wore an abundance of light gold jewelry that made constant tinkling noises as she moved her arms and hands. And her head. Feathery gold earrings brushed against her shoulders as her head moved. She passed over a form to read and sign. Annie noticed her hands. Her nails were beautifully manicured and polished in the same mauve shade as the office walls. Her hands, too, were graceful. Annie self-consciously made fists. She had not thought to look at her fingernails in a while. Indeed, it struck her that she barely combed her hair these days. Everything about this woman suggested grace and dignity.

After signing several forms, Annie leaned back in her chair. Caroline shoved the papers haphazardly into a file folder and also sat back.

"Annie, normally I would get to know you slowly. We would talk about your family life as a child and things like that." Caroline leaned forward and studied Annie intently. "Quite frankly, we don't have time for that. I don't like the look of your face. Let's talk about your husband. Can you tell me what's going on?"

Annie looked down at the floor. She had not even begun to speak, and she was choking up. A warm sympathetic voice was too much. It had been so long since there was someone who seemed to really care about her. Tears began to stream into her lap, and she watched them land on her clenched hands. A box of Kleenex appeared on her lap, and she held it like it was a lifeline.

"I'm sorry."

"Don't apologize. People cry a lot in here," Caroline answered calmly. "Take your time, Annie. I'd guess you've got some pretty good reasons to feel sad."

Annie cried even harder. Caroline waited patiently. After a few minutes Annie felt herself winding down. It felt so good to cry. Kevin became enraged if she cried at home, so she seldom did.

She had forgotten what a relief it was to express pain.

"I'm losing my mind," she whispered.

"What makes you think that?" Caroline said noncommittally.

"I can't think straight anymore," Annie began. The words flowed freely. "I could not decide in the waiting room whether or not to take Mary out of the stroller. I dwell on little decisions for hours." Annie finally looked up. "Also, I'm having bad thoughts." She waited. So did Caroline. The room was still. "My husband says I'm crazy. Sometimes I want to kill him, and I can actually picture myself doing it. I never would," she hastened to add. "But what kind of person daydreams constantly about her husband's death?"

Caroline looked at her steadily. "The kind of person who is very pissed off and frightened."

"I'm not mad at him," Annie said wonderingly. "I mean, of course, I am sometimes. Most of the time I just don't understand why he gets so mad at me. I wanted my marriage to work."

"Is it over?"

"I don't know." Annie frowned. "I think he might kill me." With that she burst out laughing. "Sorry," she said, embarrassed. "See what I mean? I'm behaving like a lunatic."

"Why did you laugh?"

"Did it sound absurd to you?" Annie asked. "I just said I'm not sure if I want to end my marriage. In the next sentence I said my husband might kill me." Annie began to take big gulps of air. "I'm going crazy, Caroline." She sobbed. "How can I not be sure if I want a divorce? He's going to kill me. I thought he would kill me the other night. I can barely sit on this chair, my legs hurt so bad. I think he did something to my back. It's hurting all of the time. I ran out of our apartment in my nightgown screaming for help. What's wrong with me?" Annie's breaths were still coming in gasps, but she was not sobbing. She desperately needed answers. Wrapping her arms around herself, she stopped and waited. "Do you think I'm crazy?"

"Not at all," came the certain response. "I think you're stressed to the breaking point and scared to death. Add to that confusion and loneliness, and I'd say you were pretty much coping the same way any woman would in your circumstances." Caroline paused and stared at Annie until their gazes locked. "Annie, I'm going to tell you a secret. Are you listening?" Annie nodded. "There is nothing wrong with you. Let me repeat that. From what I've seen so far, and what I know about domestic violence, I'd say you were perfectly normal. You're not crazy. Not even a little."

Annie put her head in her hands and cried again. This time she rocked back and forth in her chair. A few minutes passed before she even attempted to pull herself together. It was like a huge burden had been miraculously raised from her shoulders. She was not crazy. She had never really thought so. Annie's self-esteem suddenly poked up from some buried place. She felt a shred of dignity rising in her chest and actually sat up straighter because of it.

"Thank you, Caroline." Annie spoke gently. Her head was clearing a little. She told Caroline about the fight on Saturday. She left out nothing. Caroline was unshakable. What a relief to tell all of these horrible things and have her look back at you with an intelligent and calm expression. Annie understood that she could tell Caroline everything. Her heart felt connected to the world again. The dirty, ugly secrets were in the open, and this diminished their power. When she finished, she looked at Caroline with quiet anticipation.

"Okay, Annie. Let me try to explain what is going on in your marriage." Caroline leaned forward, and her jewelry tinkled happily. Even ugly things could not disturb this woman's air of serenity. "First of all, let me say that you are an intelligent and courageous woman." Annie's eyes welled up again. "You probably don't realize how brave you are. You asked me if you were crazy because you ran out in your nightgown. I would have to say no. You made a gutsy attempt to save your life. He could have killed you. You do know that, don't you?" Annie nodded uncertainly.

"Annie, let me put it this way. When he slammed you into the mirror, he could have killed you. You've just told me how big he is. He apparently is not exercising self-control. He could have crippled you when he kneed you in the back. From now on I want you to practice looking at this clearly. The reality is this: Whether or not he intends to, and you've told me he has threatened to kill you, you could end up dead. So if he chokes you just a little and squeezes too hard, the result is a body bag for Mary's mommy."

A frown had settled deeply into Annie's perfectly still face. She shook her head. Fearful that Caroline might mistake her action, she said quickly, "I don't mean I don't understand. It's just that I want you to continue. I'll think about how horrible that is later. Please keep explaining."

"Okay. This is not easy stuff for you to hear. I want to give you a sheet of information. Men who behave this way, people call them abusers, have a certain set of characteristics. A profile, if you will. I want you to look it over and see if any of it sounds familiar."

With that, she handed Annie a sheet of paper. On top was the heading PROFILE OF A BATTERER. Annie winced. Surely Kevin was not someone who could be called a batterer. It sounded awful. She began to read through the sheet. By the time she was on the fourth one, she could feel the color draining from her face.

PROFILE OF A BATTERER
- *Jealous/possessive*
- *Tries to isolate partner*
- *Tries to control partner, often financially as well as emotionally*

- *Jekyll and Hyde personalities*
- *Explosive temper*
- *Low self-esteem*
- *Blamer*
- *Projects own faults onto partner; tells partner it is all her fault*
- *Verbal assault/emotional abuse in addition to physical abuse*
- *Generational*
- *Possibly comes from violent family*
- *More violent when partner is pregnant*
- *Denies beatings and minimizes their severity*
- *May have other problems with the law*
- *Violence runs in a cycle. Tension building is followed by abusive incident followed by honeymoon phase. Honeymoon phase is characterized by the following behaviors: apologizes; sends flowers; cries; promises anything, including things like stopping alcohol or drug use, attending counseling, vacations, attending church; and promises to never hit partner again. Often becomes very involved with the children during this phase and attempts to be very supportive of his partner.*
- *Does whatever it takes to get his partner back; the cycle repeats itself over and over again*

Annie stared at Caroline in disbelief. "This is Kevin. Almost exactly. I don't get it. Is it something they can't control?"

Caroline was gentle but firm. "Annie, look at it this way. When he hits you, he acts like he's out of control. Right?" Annie nodded. "He pretends that you make him so crazy that he cannot help it. Right?" She nodded again. "Does he ever get really mad at anyone else?"

That was easy. "Yes. He can't stand his coach. He absolutely hates a couple of the guys on the team. They make him crazy. He'll come home and throw things he's so mad."

"Does he ever hit any of them?"

"No. Of course not. He'd get kicked off the team if he did."

Caroline compassionately continued. "That's my point. He hits you because he can get away with it. He makes a choice to be violent. It's not something that's out of control for him. When the police came, he was completely calm and polite. Minutes before, he had hit you in the head. If they had not come, he might have killed you. You said yourself he was escalating. Kevin knows exactly what he's doing. It's a power thing. When he feels like he's not controlling you as much as he'd like, he uses violence to bring you around. Get it?"

Annie was pale but deadly calm. "Caroline, that's so manipulative." She searched for words. "It's . . . it's diabolical. So if there was a consequence, he would not hit me either?"

"Something like that. Sweetheart, he's very dangerous. You should remember that tonight when he brings you flowers. I promise you this: It's not over. Kevin is not going to help you pack and wish

186

you well. Most women who are killed are killed when they try to leave the abuser. I can't stress that enough, Annie."

Annie was bewildered. "This is too much. That son of a bitch had me thinking it was all my fault. Caroline, I want to kill him again. Why are they most dangerous when you try to leave?"

"Because they can't lose you. That represents the ultimate loss of control. They often say they'd rather kill you than see you with another man."

Annie nodded. That sounded exactly like something Kevin would say. Emotions swirled around her, and she squeezed her eyes shut. Annie felt her head falling into her lap. Suddenly she felt a strong hand on her arm accompanied by the sound of lilting bells.

"Hold on, Annie." Caroline's voice was confident. "You can handle this. You knew all of this anyway. I just put some words on it for you. Nice and slow," she coaxed evenly. Annie began to relax. "It's a lot of information, but we had to move quickly. You're a smart girl. You can cope with this, and I'm going to help you. You're not alone anymore. Don't think I don't understand how you're feeling. Can you sit up?" Annie had her head down in her lap. The dizziness was passing. "I'm going for ice water. Will you be okay for a minute?"

"Yes. I'll be fine." Annie heard her voice and was reassured. It sounded normal. The feeling of faintness was passing. No more denial. The truth was right in her face, and it demanded action.

Caroline tried to persuade her to see a doctor. Annie declined. She had neither insurance nor money. A doctor would order X rays. Additionally, Annie did not have transportation. She finally stopped making excuses. The truth was she did not have the energy to deal with the obstacles. She needed every spare ounce of strength to absorb what she had been told.

Caroline also tried to persuade her to go back to Chicago. Another negative response. Annie was going to finish this in Texas. Annie had heard about jurisdiction on a talk show. If she ran out of state with the baby, Kevin could file for divorce in her absence and get custody. Caroline confirmed that jurisdiction could be a wild card. At any rate, the Griffin budget would not accommodate attorney fees right now. That was a problem in itself.

"Your head is probably swimming, Annie," Caroline said with a worried look.

"No," Annie responded emphatically. "I feel better than I have in ages. Don't worry about me, Caroline. I'm taking it all in. I'll be fine now that I know what I'm dealing with. It's just a matter of sorting everything out in my head and making some decisions."

Caroline insisted they make a safety plan. That was a series of actions Annie would take in the event things looked like they might get out of hand again. She was to put all important papers in one place, along with the bankbook and some spare money.

Annie had no idea where she would get this spare money, but get it she would. She agreed to come back to see Caroline on Thursday. Three days away. As she walked out the door, she paused.

Turning, she said, "Why did Dana tell me to see you?"

Caroline smiled sweetly. "Someday I'll tell you, Annie. Now, stay alive so you get to hear."

Chapter Twelve

Annie pushed the stroller out into the harsh Texas sunshine and squinted. She felt disoriented. Something huge had just happened. In the ninety minutes she had spent with Caroline, all dreams were dashed. Like children's bubbles, they had popped and evaporated. Some instinct told her she should feel liberated. Annie just felt weary.

She squinted again. She really must buy a pair of cheap sunglasses. She tried to decide what to do with herself. After a quick inventory of her pockets, she fished out five dollars. Enough for a counter lunch at the local diner. Annie was not hungry, but knew she should be. The diner was a comforting destination.

Caroline had told Annie that domestic violence was common. Annie's mind rebelled against the facts. How could this type of terror be common? Impulsively, she had vowed to Caroline to help every battered woman she encountered for the rest of her life. Caroline had nodded, setting off a round of tinkling. "That's pretty much the way it works, Honey," she had said affectionately.

Annie pulled out a pack of cigarettes and rebelliously lit one on the street. Kevin said she could not afford to smoke. Annie heartily agreed. She knew she should quit. At the same time, she wanted to smoke right now. She was also about to blow five dollars for lunch. She no longer feared having to account for the money. Indeed, Annie noticed that she no longer feared Kevin. Physically, of course, he was scary. But Annie knew something. Kevin would not hit her in the next few days. He was on good behavior. She shuddered. It was frighteningly predictable. If she bought the abuser explanation, and she did, Kevin would be violent again. But not for a while. As long as he thought she was staying, she should be safe.

In a matter of minutes, she arrived at the diner and stubbed her cigarette out on the pavement. Mary napped soundly in the stroller. Annie selected the last seat at the lunch counter and wedged Mary's stroller between her own seat and the adjacent stool. This would ensure privacy. Ordering a BLT, fries, and a Coke, she settled in to think. Her thoughts were disorderly. Kevin fit the profile. According to Caroline, the possibility of a spontaneous and miraculous change was remote. Therefore, she had to leave. Period.

She felt tears approaching and pushed them back. Her lunch provided a welcome diversion, and Annie ate as if starved. Everything tasted delicious. Even the pickle and the parsley garnish. Sated, she sat back and lit another cigarette. Caroline said she would have to take it one step at a time. She would need financial help. That meant a phone call to Chicago. What about the mailbox key? The money would have to be wired. She would ask her dad how much he could part with. He would say it depended on how much she needed. A few hundred ought to be enough initially while she decided on a plan. Caroline said they would work on that Thursday, after Annie had some time to think.

Realistically, she should go back to Chicago. Why was that thought so terrible? Because Kevin would follow. She knew it. Scholarship be damned, he would chase her back and create havoc there. For some reason, Kevin felt he had certain entitlements to her. Annie would have to explain the whole disaster to her family. How much would they understand about domestic violence? Well, the girls would get it. She thought of Maureen's reaction and cringed. At best it would be more ugliness. At worst, bloodshed. Her father would be mystified. Annie remembered seeing a news program about a man who had beaten his wife to death with a bat. Mr. McGowan had shaken his head in bewilderment. "Why would anyone want to hurt his wife?" he had wondered. Clueless. It was beyond his comprehension, and Annie would crack up if she had to persuade everyone that Kevin was the culprit. He was an expert at appearing innocent. By the end of it, he would have her locked up in a psychiatric ward. She would have to work things out here.

Caroline would help her. Annie thanked God for Caroline. Heaving herself up off her stool, she checked the time. Kevin would be home at five. It was nearly four already. Annie decided to go home and make dinner. She did not have to talk to him, but it would help her stay sane if she did something normal. Also, she was worried about him. He looked strained and sick. How bizarre that she could hate him so much and feel so sorry for him. It was a maternal feeling. She was going to hurt him badly when she left. He would condemn her for years. Maybe forever. Nevertheless, leave him she would. Strangely, it was a relief that he had assaulted her on Saturday. Because of that she had taken steps.

The bus ride was soothing. Mary continued to sleep, and the bus driver actually put the bus in park and lifted the stroller up the stairs for Annie. Leaning back against the seat, Annie sent up a brief prayer. She would need guidance. The open window invited a soft breeze, and Annie let it caress her face sweetly. The answer to her prayer? Someone up there was comforting her. The thought made her smile.

A hand clamped down on her shoulder, and Annie jumped. Soft brown eyes looked down at her. Mexican mom. She had her own infant on her hip and needed the stroller moved. Annie apologized in Spanish and shifted the wheels to grant passage. The woman smiled and then frowned. Reaching down, she moved one finger softly along Annie's bruised eye. Making a fist, she uttered what sounded like a Spanish oath. Annie stared at her pleasantly. What was she talking about? Two other Mexican women on the bus behind them burst out laughing. Annie looked at her in bewilderment. Making a motion with her hand, the woman made clutching, twisting motions in the air at about groin level. Annie got it and burst out laughing. These women knew about domestic violence. *Ha*, she thought. She was less alone than she thought.

Home at last, Annie parked the stroller and climbed the stairs. Mary was happily groggy. Opening the front door, Annie paused. She heard the scrape of a chair, and Kevin rounded the corner.

"Annie, where have you been?" he blurted out in a tortured voice. His face was gray except for red blotches. Alarmed, Annie set the baby down.

"What's wrong? Did someone die?"

"What?" Kevin sounded perplexed. "What are you talking about? I thought you left me."

With that, he turned sharply and went into the bedroom, closing the door behind him. Annie gave a huge sigh and closed the front door. Carrying Mary into the kitchen, she stopped dead in her tracks.

There were the flowers. Twelve red roses. Kevin had never bought flowers. Not even when the baby was born. What was next on Caroline's list? Annie felt the urge to giggle. She consoled herself with the thought that this was anxiety created by a highly emotional situation. Now, what should she do with the grieving abuser? Batterer? Dr. Jekyll? Mr. Hyde? This was not funny, and Annie had to be serious. He sounded like he was in anguish. Should she remind him about the ban on tears? Annie decided to start dinner and give him privacy. A mean and nagging voice suggested that his tears were manipulative. Ignoring it, she opened the freezer for meat.

Mary was standing against the bedroom door, banging it. She wanted her daddy. Annie closed the fridge and picked up the roses. She did own a vase. Mrs. Nolan had sent her flowers in the hospital, and they had come in a beautiful glass vase. Annie could not believe at the time that it was hers to keep.

A paper fell to the floor from under the flowers. Mail. Any mail at all seemed contraband, and Annie picked it up with a guilty glance toward the bedroom. Mary was yodeling now. The envelope was addressed to Annie. It had been opened, and Annie quickly read the letter. Her heart surged. Mrs. Annie Griffin was hereby informed that based on past academic achievements and current financial need, she was awarded a full scholarship. In effect for the spring semester, she would need to apply again next year. There was also a housing stipend for $200 per month, based on the fact that they had a child. It would start in January.

She leaned against the counter. Dear God, she was finally going to school. With a racing heart she headed for the bedroom. With her hand on the knob she stopped. The door opened. Kevin bent down to grab Mary so she would not fall into the bedroom. He looked up at Annie with a sorrowful face.

"Congratulations. I knew you'd get it."

Annie smiled in spite of herself. "When did it

come? Kevin, this means I can go to school."

"Are you going to leave me?" he asked quietly. "I would not hold it against you. I've been worse than terrible." Swallowing heavily, he looked down at her sadly. "All I've ever wanted was for you to be happy. If you would be happier away from me, Annie, then go. I'll be here if you want to come back."

He put out his hand and stroked her bruised eye. Annie's heart was once again twisting and turning. This was not Dr. Jekyll or Mr. Hyde. It was not the Abuser. Or even the Batterer. It was Kevin Griffin. Her childhood friend. The only one in the world who knew how terribly she still missed her mother. She let her head fall forward onto his chest.

"Kevin, Kevin." She moaned. "I don't know what to do. I can't handle you anymore. I saw a counselor today."

He stroked her hair gently. "I know, Annie. I'm a little confused myself. How can I hurt you like that when I love you so much? I don't mean to, you know."

Mary began to protest indignantly at being left out of the family hug. Kevin reached down and picked her up. She pulled at his nose and smiled. What was happening? Annie had been so sure in Caroline's office. Now, she felt her resolve slipping.

"Annie, you don't owe me a thing," Kevin began. "But in spite of that, will you please talk to me?"

"Kevin, I'm exhausted. I really am. Do we have to do this tonight?" Annie could not talk to him until she had a chance to decide. The scholarship and stipend threw a whole different slant onto the picture. With a job and a little help from the campus nursery, she might have a crack at this.

"That's fine," he said gently. "How about I go out and get us some hamburgers? Could you eat?"

He was so humble. It was hard to see him like this. "That's great. I'll get the house organized."

He was not out the door five minutes before Annie was on the telephone. "Maureen?" she demanded. "Call me right back."

Seconds later the phone rang. "You're not going to believe this," Annie started. She told her about the scholarship. She knew that her father would be ecstatic, and she wanted him to know right away. Luckily, he was not at home. Annie did not want to talk to him until she made some decisions. Maureen was excited but not surprised. Annie wondered how everyone could have so much faith in her. She told Maureen things were not going well with Kevin. She kept quiet about the fight and the counselor. Instead she said they were considering marriage counseling. Maureen was appalled. Annie ended the conversation with a promise to keep her posted.

Hanging up, Annie went to attend to the roses. She found a small envelope attached to the ribbon. Her mailbox key was taped to a small florist card. "Congratulations! I wish I was worthy of you," read the card. Annie did not know whether to cry or rip it up. The lack of self-esteem revolted her. Was that number six? The damned abuser list kept popping into her head. Shaking it off, she arranged the flowers in Mrs. Nolan's vase. She placed them on the table and lifted Mary up for a better view. How lovely they looked. Annie felt sorrow coming back. What a happy day this should be in their little household! She glanced up at the crucifix. Maybe there would be a miracle. God could do it. But even He had to contend with Kevin's free will. How wonderful if Kevin was that one in a thousand who decided to change.

Annie forced herself to be realistic. She felt a headache coming on and made a firm decision not to think about it any more today. It was too much.

Kevin came home with dinner, and they ate. Pleasant interactions drew a shutter down over the large issues looming between them. Kevin was polite and attentive. He made the lemonade and poured glasses. He brought Annie a napkin. He cleaned the baby and took her down from her high chair.

Annie's emotions continued to fluctuate. On one hand, she was touched. He was trying so hard. On the other hand, she felt anger. Why did he act like this only when he thought she was going to leave? After the baby was put to bed, he joined her in the living room. Annie was staring blankly at the television.

"Did you get out of practice early today?"

Kevin averted his eyes. "No. I skipped it."

"You skipped it? With the big game next Saturday? Can you do that?"

"I don't care, Annie. I came home for lunch, and you were gone." He met her gaze. "I don't give a shit about playing. It all means nothing if I don't have you. I thought you left me. I sat here trying to decide if I should kill myself."

Annie gasped. "Kevin. How can you say that?" Changing her tone, she continued. "Are you serious?"

Kevin looked out the window again. "Annie, if you leave me, I don't want to live. I thought about it and thought about it. We've always known that I need you more than you need me. I have no desire to live if you're not with me." Kevin was matter of fact. He looked at Annie with naked honesty, and she chose her words carefully.

"Kevin, I can't believe I'm hearing this. You're talking about suicide?"

With that, he put his head down into his hands. "I'm sorry. I shouldn't have told you. It'd be better if it just happened."

Annie knelt down in front of him. "That's never the answer. Kevin, do you hear yourself? Even if we don't get along, you're still Mary's father. Can you imagine me telling her someday that her daddy killed himself?" Annie forced him to look at her. "It's going to be all right. You're doing well in school. You're only a freshman and you're playing on Varsity. What do you want? We're doing the best we can, Kevin. Go easy. I don't know anyone who has tried harder than you have. Except maybe me." He laughed shortly with her.

"Then why does my wife want to leave me?"

Annie spoke without emotion. "I never said I wanted to leave you." Frowning, she continued. "It's just that I can't live with your temper. You could have killed me the other night."

Kevin looked down again. "I would never have killed you, Annie. You're exaggerating."

"Well, Kevin, let me put it this way—I'm not sure I'm willing to take that chance. You know what I mean?"

She rose and turned away from him. Was she exaggerating? What had she really suffered? A couple of bruises. A bloody lip. Maybe she was overreacting. Maybe Caroline was overreacting. If it were not for that stupid profile, she might be able to convince herself. As it was, Kevin was too typical to pretend this was not happening. Annie sighed deeply once again. What a relief it would be to pretend it had never happened. She got the scholarship. Things would get better.

"Annie"—Kevin interrupted her thoughts—"you mentioned marriage counseling once. What about that? I'm game if you are. I mean, what the hell? I will honestly do whatever it takes to keep you." He waited. She remained silent. "C'mon. We've got to try everything before we throw in the towel, don't we? Annie, do you know how much I love you?" She nodded with her back to him. "Then you must know I'll do anything in my power. Counseling might help. You said yourself I had problems with the way I grew up. Give me one last chance. I'm begging you."

"Don't beg me, Kevin," she snapped irritably. "All I want is to be safe in my own home. And to be treated like an adult." She felt her temper beginning to rise. "By the way, thank you for the mailbox key. That's the kind of stuff I'm talking about. How dare you take away my key? And I want to get a job, Kevin. We need the money. You never stop talking about how broke we are, yet you forbid me to work. Where is the sense in that?" She paused for a breath. "While I'm at it, how dare you accuse me of flirting with that poor homesick boy at the dinner! All I did was talk to him. Your jealousy is not my problem, Kevin." Annie heaved herself onto the couch. "Remember, you wanted to talk about this, not me. I'm not a dog on a leash, and I swear I will never be treated like that again."

Kevin was now sitting directly across from her. He had listened patiently to everything she said. Annie actually felt pretty good. This was how it was supposed to be, she marveled. If you were mad at your husband, you should be able to tell him. Normally she was afraid to.

"Are you finished, Mrs. Griffin?"

"I don't know. If anything else comes to mind, I'll let you know."

"Well. Regarding the mailbox key. You're right. I was wrong. I was simply reacting to my panic at not handling the bills properly. It won't happen again." Annie inclined her head but said nothing. The key was the least of their problems. "Regarding your getting a job. Go ahead. It can probably be worked out if you tell them you can work evenings and weekends. The money would be extremely helpful— and you're right, I'm not the boss." Annie nodded but still said nothing. "About my jealousy. I have no defense except that I'm married to an extremely attractive and outgoing wife. I'm not very confident, and I feel like you'll fall for someone else. That's my problem. I agree. I think the answer is to go out more so I get used to our being around other people, including other men. You were just being nice at the dinner, and I'm sorry. I was a real jerk. It won't happen again." Annie remained quiet. "I think I've covered all of our problems. Have I left out anything?"

"Just one thing. What about the fact that you nearly killed me on Saturday? What are we doing about that?"

"It won't happen again. I promise." Annie rolled her eyes. "Annie, give me a break. I'm promising the moon for a reason. I am going to get used to the idea that you're going to school and working. I can't keep you in the house. I understand that. I'm giving on everything I possibly can. I'm not going to hurt you again because I know you'll leave. You're going to have to trust me on this. Okay?"

Annie rose and again knelt in front of him. "Kevin, how resentful are you going to be if I start school and get a job? You say these things now, but will it last? Last time we had a talk like this you took my mailbox key the very next morning. Why should

I believe you?" She thought quickly and made a decision. She summarized the discussion she'd had with Caroline. Including the profile. Kevin looked undisturbed.

"Kevin, doesn't it bother you that the profile fits you to a T?"

"No it does not, Annie." He frowned as he searched for words. "That fits every husband. Every husband gets jealous. Every person in the world has low self-esteem if you get close enough to know them. Show me a person who is the same personality all of the time. You're certainly not. What does that make you? Dr. Jekyll and Mrs. Hyde? Think about it, Annie. You have a temper, too, and you know it. Who started yelling five minutes ago? It was not me. Did I go psycho and hit you? No. I figured it was your turn to get things off your chest. I've been a jerk, I agree. But I'm not some battering abuser nut. I'm just a guy who got married a little young and is trying to make it work."

Annie was quiet. Inside she was reeling. She had been so sure . . . but maybe Kevin was right. Annie certainly was not perfect. She had never pretended to be. At the same time, something was terribly wrong.

"Kevin, what about the control thing? Say what you like, but that was true. You try to control me all of the time."

"Annie," he began patiently, "are we in a marriage or not? Look around you. Every spouse tries to control his partner. Yes, I try to control you. But don't you try to control me? You're always telling me how much to drink or not to drink. You're full of orders about how you want the towels folded and where to put my clothes. That's just marriage. Now, you're probably thinking those are harmless little things. You're right. I'm willing to agree that I did try to stop you from getting a job. But it didn't work. It's that simple. I tried. You balked. You're getting a job. Honey, I don't think this is as big a deal as you're making it out to be. I adore you, Annie. I'm not going to make you unhappy. I promise."

Annie stared at him with narrowed eyes. He was doing it again. He was waving a magic wand, and everything was going away. It was scary. What about the agony of the last two days? Had she dreamed it?

"Kevin," she persisted, "I'm not trying to be rude, but this has all happened before. Remember? You promised not to hurt me before, and I got hurt again. You're making my head spin, but I'm not going to let go of that."

Kevin rose slowly and came over to where she was sitting. Looking up at him, she thought again how big he was. Right now he was benign. Saturday he had been deadly. That's what she had to hold on to.

Now he knelt down in front of her. "Annie, whatever you think, I'm not letting go of that either. That cannot happen again. I know that, and I agree. Will you hear me out on something?" She nodded her head warily. "I think that a large part of the problem is communication. Apparently, we don't do it well. It's not a huge problem, but it is a problem. If we could talk more about our feelings, I would not explode."

"Let me get this straight, Kevin," she said levelly. "You beat the shit out of me because you can't express your feelings?"

Kevin let out a deep sigh. "That's exactly what I'm talking about, Annie. You get sarcastic whenever I try to make a point. I can't compete with you verbally. So I shout you down." He looked at her sheepishly. "I think we have gotten into some bad habits. If we saw a marriage counselor, maybe he could teach us how to communicate. It's always been a problem for us. Am I right?"

Annie nodded her head reluctantly. It was all true. She would have liked to argue that she was sarcastic because it was her only defense. He shouted her down before she ever got sarcastic. Another puzzling case of the chicken or the egg.

"I don't know," she mused. "You really think we won't have these huge fights if we learn to communicate?"

He looked at her appealingly. "All I can say is I'm willing to give it my best shot. If I need to change, I'll change. Will you?"

"You know I will, Kevin," she said heatedly. "I just don't want to be the one doing all of the changing." She reached for his hand, and he kissed her fingers. "Okay. I'll call this counselor and see if she can see us this week."

"Uhm. Don't get me wrong here, Annie," he hedged. Seeing her eyes narrow, he added quickly. "I would prefer to see a man. That's all. This lady is probably very nice, but she's your counselor. You know? Let's see someone objective. That's all I ask."

"Fine," she agreed. Kevin had made so many concessions, she could not very well object to this little thing.

Annie rose the next morning with a heavy, hung-over feeling. Snatches of disturbing dreams flitted through her mind as she groggily commenced her morning routine. Kevin was loving and gentle. Despite this, Annie could not shake the feeling that, once again, she had been had.

After the breakfast was cleared, she called Caroline. She pensively tapped a pencil on the table, waiting for the return call. One thing was certain. If she was going to get a job, she must do it quickly, before Kevin changed his mind. She decided to walk up to the closest department store later that day and get an application. They were looking for Christmas help now.

Caroline called and listened carefully as Annie described last evening's conversation. Annie heard her counselor sigh. Caroline cautioned Annie that Kevin was nice because he wanted to be. He could just as easily decide to be abusive. She also said marriage counseling could be downright dangerous in situations like this. With a feeling of helplessness, Annie told Caroline about the suicide threats. Caroline was quiet for a moment.

"Annie, what if I told you that suicide threats by abusers were common?"

Annie sputtered. "You mean it's a form of manipulation."

"Well, yes. Sort of." Caroline spoke in a measured voice. "That's not to say that they don't mean it, of course. You should never ignore a suicide threat. But abusers will do whatever it takes to gain your sympathy and make you stay. Another thing I want to add. Annie, when Kevin is suicidal, he is very dangerous. He thinks you're staying now, so he may be calm. But if he gets the idea you're leaving coupled with his suicidal thoughts . . . he would be extremely dangerous. Let me say this clearly— it would be so serious, I would encourage you to go into hiding."

"Caroline, you're scaring the hell out of me."

"Good. I'm trying to. Annie, I know that what Kevin is doing is typical. But it's important for you to know, too. Your decision to stay or go is your choice. I'll be here no matter what you do. You're not going to wear me out."

"Thank you," Annie said humbly. "I feel like I have to give it a last shot. He was so sincere, Caroline. I think he meant what he said. He's going to try. How can I walk out without giving him the chance?"

"I understand completely, Annie," Caroline said warmly. "Let me give you a number for the organization that does marriage counseling. They're the same group only in a different building. It's the same sliding scale, so don't worry about money. Call me next week and let me know how you're doing. Okay?"

"I will. Thank you, Caroline."

Annie called and made an appointment for Thursday with a male counselor named Charles. She also left a message for the baby-sitter, then loaded up the baby for the walk to the store. Thank God, she had not told Maureen or her father she was leaving. It would be too embarrassing to call back and say she had decided to stay. One could not be too careful about marital problems. Annie could forgive but knew her family might not.

She tried to look on the bright side. Kevin might change. She was going to school and looking for a job. She was getting everything she wanted. An instinct told her that she had gained a little ground but remained on the same smoking battlefield. Annie cleared her mind and focused on the present. She was not the same girl who had walked into Caroline's office. She was ready to fight if necessary. She thought back to Kevin's explanation of the profile. Was it possible that all marriages had these struggles? *No*, she thought grimly. *Not like this.* Annie had never actually known anyone who had gotten beaten up by her husband. *But*, said the voice, *how would you know? How many people know that I'm getting beaten up?* Outside of Caroline and the police . . . nobody. Possibly the neighbors, but Annie refused to think about them. It was too humiliating.

She arrived at the store and requested an

application. The girl at the service desk was friendly and told Annie to fill it out right away. The manager was scheduling interviews that very week. Annie thanked her for the tip and filled out the form. Handing it back, she thanked the woman again. The young girl winked and put Annie's application on the top of a pile. Annie smiled and left.

Walking home, she detected a slight mood lift. A job meant freedom. And a paycheck. Annie spent the whole walk home telling Mary how she would spend the money. There was also the stipend. Of course, that would go to Kevin for bills. Regardless, more money would be coming in. Surely the tension would ease.

Chapter Thirteen

Annie landed a job in the camera and jewelry department. She also accepted her scholarship and registered for school. Kevin was being as supportive as possible, and Annie felt her suspicions waning.

Marriage counseling was a disappointment. Kevin ridiculed Charles but otherwise seemed comfortable. Annie was, of course, grateful they were going at all. The problem was, they were not talking about what Annie considered the real issues. Certainly communication skills merited discussion. But Charles and Kevin treated the sessions as though it were the only problem. Annie asked Kevin when they were going to talk about the violence. Kevin got offended and accused her of trying to embarrass him. He remained adamant. Annie was forbidden to bring up violence or suicide. When pressed, Kevin stated that if Annie stayed with him, he would not take his life.

Feeling blackmailed, she bided her time.

Kevin's big game went well, and he received quite a bit of press. Annie dutifully clipped the articles and sent copies to her mother-in-law. The local television station interviewed Kevin at practice, so Annie called the station for a copy. For five dollars they made her a tape.

Kevin cooperated with Annie's work schedule. He got home from practice, and she left for work. She had his dinner ready and the baby fed. The baby went down at seven, and then he studied. He grumbled, but Annie ignored him. College couples had to make sacrifices.

Work became Annie's salvation. It was a fifteen-minute walk to the store if she hurried. She worked from five-thirty until ten. The shift started at five, but the supervisor relented when Annie told him Kevin was an athlete. He, too, followed the progress of the college teams. Annie was competent and quick. She learned the differences in merchandise and took pride in her ability to assist customers. She felt good about herself again. Between earning money and looking forward to the start of her college education, life seemed promising. She was careful not to share her exuberance with Kevin. Instinctively, she knew that if she acted too happy Kevin would be threatened.

He always asked her if she worked with men. Annie told him to walk up and check. It was all women in her department. He snapped that he hardly felt the need to spy on her. In truth, there was a stockboy—or man, rather—who had taken a liking to Annie. Bill the stockboy, as she dubbed him, often stopped by to see if Annie needed anything from the back. He made jokes and flirted, but Annie kept her distance. When she was honest with herself, she admitted he made her feel pretty. That part seemed harmless.

She persuaded Kevin to let her keep her first paycheck for Christmas presents. During breaks she roamed the store in search of bargains. The baby would not require much. Annie had her eye on a beautiful set of blocks. That would be the big present. Annie would also pick up a couple of inexpensive items to wrap. She needed a big ball and maybe a push toy. Certainly there would be packages coming from Chicago. Babies did not know the difference, she told herself sensibly.

Kevin was a different story. There were all kinds of neat things to buy for him. He complained that he owned no tools. Annie knew full well that Kevin was not mechanically inclined. At the same time he could work a screwdriver, and they did not even own a hammer. She found just the thing: a starter tool kit. At twenty dollars, it was expensive. But Kevin needed to feel like the man of the house. Maybe this would help. She also got him socks and a sweater.

Annie wrapped the presents and hid them in the closet. Kevin was under strict instructions to keep away. Annie loved Christmas. It was magical, and she was determined that they enjoy their first Christmas alone together.

The Kemps were flying to Chicago for the holidays, and Annie tried not to be jealous. Their parents had prepaid two tickets, and the baby was free. Darlene searched for presents within their budget. Annie suggested tins of cookies. The tins were on sale at her store, and she picked up ten for her friend. They did not see much of each other these days, but

Darlene did stop in the store one evening for a visit. Bill the stockboy chose that moment to make an appearance with a Coke for Annie. Darlene raised her eyebrows and smiled.

"Who is your friend?" she asked archly.

Annie shrugged her shoulders. "He's a stockboy. He's like that with everyone."

"He seems to like you, Annie," Darlene said conspiratorially.

"I think he might have a small crush on me," Annie acknowledged in spite of herself. "I barely speak to him, but he keeps coming back. The other night he asked if he could give me a ride home. Can you imagine?"

The girls giggled. Then Darlene sighed. "How fun, Annie! I'm sick of being at home. I would love to tell Greg that someone was flirting with me. Maybe it would wake him up a little."

Annie looked at her in amazement. "If I told Kevin that Bill was flirting with me, he'd beat him up. I can't believe you would tell Greg that."

"Greg wouldn't care. He'd say something like 'How fun for you.'" Annie looked astounded. "Seriously, Annie, Greg is not the jealous type. I wish he was. At least you know Kevin cares about you."

Annie shook her head. "I don't know, Darlene. I would rather know that Kevin trusted me."

Darlene looked impatient. "Well, of course he trusts you. What's not to trust? You never even go to a movie with me. Kevin should lighten up a little."

Annie bristled in spite of herself. "He tries, Darlene. He does. He's just insecure."

Darlene smiled. "The grass is always greener, they say. Call me tomorrow. I want you to taste my latest cookie creations. I'm thinking of putting them in my mother-in-law's tin." Both girls shuddered. Darlene's mother-in-law was an extraordinary baker, so that tin was important.

A customer coughed politely, signaling the end of their conversation.

"I'll see you tomorrow, Annie," Darlene said hurriedly. "Look out for Bill."

Annie smiled impishly. As she displayed cameras for her customer, she thought about Darlene. The young Mrs. Kemp was nice enough, but Annie did not trust her. She should not have said anything about Bill. Surely she would not tell Greg, who surely would not mention it to Kevin. Annie's stomach squeezed for a moment. Should she request that Darlene keep quiet? No, she decided. That was like entering into a conspiracy. Darlene would say nothing. Annie certainly would not if the situation were reversed. She was being paranoid. And so Annie put it from her mind.

Annie attended to her job duties. Cheerfully waiting on Christmas shoppers, she had no inkling that one brief conversation had jeopardized her very life.

Rain spattered Annie's face as she hurried home from work. It was Thursday. She was fifteen minutes late. A co-worker with romantic troubles had delayed her. Kevin got insecure if Annie was even a few minutes late. The thought of another fight prompted her to quicken her pace even more.

It was four days before Christmas. The temperature was in the sixties, which was helpful. Colored lights festooned the houses, and each street lamp sported either a snowman or a bell. *How silly*, Annie thought. The children here had never seen a snowman.

Hurrying up the stairs, she prayed Kevin would be in a good mood. Tension was rising, and a sixth sense told her that Kevin's good behavior was wearing thin. If she questioned him, he would say he could not be perfect all of the time. Annie's brow furrowed. Her marriage was complex at the best of times. Lately, she lived in fear of toppling into a hidden trap.

She paused on the landing. Voices came from her apartment. Annie opened the door and stepped in, and her eyes widened in delight. Her brother Danny was sitting at their kitchen table. Dropping her purse on the floor, she ran to him and was snatched up in a bear hug.

The three laughed and talked at once. "He just knocked on the door," Kevin said. Danny said he wanted it to be a surprise. He drove straight through from Chicago and had no idea what time he would arrive. If it had been any later, he would have gotten a hotel room. Annie scoffed at that. She said she could not believe she would be with family at

Christmas. Danny's smile vanished.

"I'm leaving in the morning, Annie," he said sadly.

"What?" she demanded. "You are not! You're staying for Christmas if I have to tie you down."

They all laughed merrily. Annie sat down at the table, and Kevin came around and took her jacket.

Annie smiled up at him. "I got stuck talking to Lorena in the parking lot," she explained. "Her boyfriend went back to Lubbock, and she's devastated."

Kevin rolled his eyes. Seconds later, he placed a mug of beer in front of Annie. "We're drinking, Mrs. Griffin."

"Fine by me," Annie said gaily. "I'll drink all night if Danny tells me he'll stay." Turning to her older brother, she beseeched, "Danny, rearrange whatever nonsense you've got planned." Pausing, her expression changed. "Hey, I thought you were staying in Chicago for Christmas. What *are* you doing here?"

Kevin and Danny burst out laughing. "Annie," Kevin scolded, "hush for a minute and let the man explain. He's trying to tell you."

They all laughed again, and Annie made a zipper motion across her mouth. "Speak."

Danny began to explain. He had intended to stay in Chicago until after the New Year. Unfortunately, a call had come in from his company a few days ago. Some kind of problem had arisen involving a boat accident. They needed a ship captain to fly over to Japan and bring a boat back to the United States. It was an emergency situation, and he did not like to turn them down.

Annie looked perplexed. "Are you flying from here?"

"No," he answered patiently. "I'll be flying from New Orleans. I have to stop by my apartment and take care of some business tomorrow."

Annie remained bewildered. "You mean you have to drive to New Orleans by tomorrow afternoon? That's ridiculous, Danny. There's no way you'll make it."

"Annie, darlin', I'm not driving to New Orleans. I have a reservation in the morning from your little airport. I'll be there in a little over an hour."

"Oh," she said in relief. "That sounds safer than racing across Texas." She frowned again. "What about your car? How are you going to get it home?"

Danny frowned. "I hadn't thought of that. Shit."

Kevin chuckled. "Annie, he's leaving his car with us. He drove it down here to give it to us."

Annie was delighted. "But we can't let you do that," she protested. "What will you have?"

Danny shrugged. "I'm buying another one, Annie. I hate to sell the Dodge because it's been so faithful. It has a lot of miles on it, but it's in great shape. The insurance has been paid for a year, oil's changed, title is all signed over, and she's yours. I'll be gone for at least two weeks on this trip. When I get back to New Orleans, my new car will be ready.

I planned on stopping here for a few days after Christmas, but the plans changed. It worked out great. All you have to do is drive me to the airport in the morning."

"Thank you, Danny," she said quietly. "It will mean a lot to us."

"Forget it," he said pleasantly. "Kevin, I'm thinking we need more beer. I have a feeling it's going to be a long night. Can you run up to the store for us?"

"I'm way ahead of you," Kevin said happily. Stepping out of the kitchen, he put his arms out. His coat was already on. "I'll be back in twenty minutes or so." Opening the door, he paused. "Wait a minute. Where are my car keys?"

They chuckled again. Laughter flowed so freely during a reunion. Danny tossed the keys over with a grin. "I'll never drive it again. Kind of sad."

"You're breaking my heart, Danny," Kevin jested. "Tell your sister what kind of car you're buying."

"I'm getting a new Corvette," Danny said matter-of-factly. "I've always wanted one, and I figure, why not? I've got the money."

"Well, I agree," Annie said vehemently. "If you want one you should have one, Mr. Money Bags." Kevin walked out, and they waved to him. "How come you're so rich all of a sudden?"

Danny abruptly changed the subject. "Annie, Kevin will be right back. I need to talk to you."

"What is it, Danny? What?" The bruise was now

so faint she thought it invisible.

"Forget it." Danny took a long drink and set down his beer. "Here's the deal. Maureen is worried about you. So is Nellie. And now, so am I. Why don't you come with me in the morning? We'll drive, and you can fly home from New Orleans. I've got the money."

Annie sputtered. "Danny, I don't . . . I can't just . . . What do you mean?"

Danny eyed her intently. "Do you want to tell me about it?"

Annie shook her head. He continued, "There's another option here. We could take the baby and leave tonight. Or you could come down to New Orleans and stay in my apartment until I get back."

"But why, Danny? What would I be doing there?" Annie said helplessly.

"Gee, I don't know Annie," he retorted. "Maybe hiding?"

"No." Annie shook her head vigorously. "We're seeing a counselor and trying to work things out. I have to give him this chance, Danny."

"I understand completely. Get me a piece of paper," he ordered as he pulled out his wallet. "Hurry. He'll be back any second."

Annie sprang out of her chair and went to the desk. Grabbing a memo pad, she handed it to Danny with a pen. He pulled a card out of his wallet and scribbled something on the paper. He handed it to Annie and reached back into his wallet again. "Get an envelope." Annie jumped up nervously again and grabbed an envelope out of the desk drawer. Danny pulled out a small stack of bills and placed them in the envelope. Reaching down, he added the piece of paper and sealed the envelope. "Go hide this where Kevin won't find it."

"Danny, I can't . . ." she began.

"Just do it, Annie. If you don't, I swear I'll take you and Mary with me in the morning."

Annie ran to the bedroom and looked around. Where wouldn't he look? She moved quietly so as not to wake the baby. Seeing the diaper bag, she made a decision. Annie placed the envelope between two diapers near the bottom. Back in the dining room, she eyed Danny quizzically.

"What's on the paper?"

Danny spoke fast. "A phone number. In New Orleans. His name is Buddy, and he's a good friend of mine. He's a tough guy, but you'd never know it to look at him. If you get nervous, give him a call. He can help you out with anything you need. There's five hundred dollars in the envelope. If you get into a spot and need more, call Buddy. I'm serious, Annie. If you think you might get hurt again, get the hell out of here. Okay?"

"Yes," Annie said miserably. "Thanks, Danny. I'll feel much better with the car and some money. He's not that bad."

"Annie," Danny said, "I like the guy. I used to anyway. Don't defend him. Nobody knows what goes on between two people. But I'm telling you this. There are guys who beat up on women just because they can. If he's one of them, and only you know the truth, then you have to leave him. You just do. Not just for your sake but for Mary's. Screw him, Annie. You don't owe him anything." Seeing her face, he lightened up. "We're here if you need us. Now, let's get another beer. You won't believe who Dad is dating."

By the time Kevin returned, they were in stitches at Mr. McGowan's latest romance. Their father was quite in demand and enjoying it immensely. It was three o'clock before they went to bed. Annie lay her head on the pillow contentedly. She had her emergency money.

At seven o'clock Annie opened her eyes to Mary's demands for breakfast. Her mind interrupted sleepy thoughts. Something wonderful had happened. In a flash, she remembered Danny, sleeping on the living room couch. She grabbed Mary from her crib and closed the bedroom door behind her.

"Do you want to see your Uncle Danny?" she asked the baby.

Mary smiled tranquilly. Annie loved her daughter in the mornings. Mary always woke up full of sunshine and happiness. It was too bad everyone could not wake up this way. Still holding the baby, Annie sat down on the coffee table.

"There he is, Mary," she cooed. "He drank too much last night. We might not be able to get him up."

A groan came from under the blankets. "Why

do you always get up so early, Annie?" moaned her older brother.

"Ask my daughter," Annie responded cheerfully. "Or don't you want to see the most intelligent child in Texas?"

Danny poked his head out. "She looks like a kid," he said in delight. "Hi, Mary. When did you grow up?" Mary gazed intently at the newcomer. "She's looking at me like I belong on a garbage dump."

"I know." Annie sighed. "Sometimes she does that with strangers. It takes her a while to warm up."

Danny sat up and put his arms out to the baby. Mary surveyed him even more skeptically. Raising her eyebrows, she looked away. Danny burst out laughing. "I'll be damned. She's too good for me. The way I feel right now, she's probably right. Do you have any aspirin in the house?"

"Yes. Exactly what time does your flight leave?"

"Ten. It's not going to be pretty."

Annie stood Mary against the coffee table and rose to get the aspirin. "You'll be fine. You need a hot shower and some breakfast. Then I'll run you out to the airport." She kept talking as she rummaged through the kitchen cabinets. Raising her voice an octave, she continued. "I can't believe you're abandoning me so fast. Only you would come for a thirteen-hour visit."

"Don't yell, Annie," he beseeched from the living room. "If I had it my way, I would be here at least a few days." He paused. "I think Mary would spit on me if she knew how."

Annie reentered the living room to see Mary still glaring malevolently at her uncle. Annie scolded her gently. "Mary, be nice."

"She's trying, Annie." Danny spoke woefully. "I think she knows things about me. You're a scary little princess. Aren't you, Mary?"

Mary launched into streams of laughter. Danny and Annie exchanged startled looks. "Annie, this is too much on a hangover." Danny chuckled. "Why is she laughing at me?"

"I don't know," Annie said, mystified. "I think she's playing with your head. Come on, Mary. Time for breakfast." Annie scooped her up affectionately. "Do you want to jump in the shower, Dan?"

"Yes. Good idea," Danny said briskly. "Do you have any tape? I'll need to fasten my head so it doesn't fall off when the water hits it."

Annie laughed and went to make Mary's breakfast. Within minutes she heard the water running. Seconds later, Kevin staggered out of the bedroom. Annie smiled and handed him the aspirin. "Danny's carrying his head under his arm. How does yours feel?" Kevin grunted and accepted the tablets. Annie hoped her husband was in a good mood. His bad moods were like cold showers.

"Did I hear you mention breakfast?"

That sounded friendly enough. "Yes. Give me a minute to get Mary fed, and I'll start ours. I'll make a feast." Studying him more closely, she added, "If you want to go back to bed for an hour, it's fine with me."

"No. Danny's leaving in a couple of hours. You can take him to the airport, and I'll stay here and nap with my little beauty queen." Kevin turned to Mary and began to play hide-and-seek with her spoon. "Do we have to see Herr Charles today?"

"He's not German, Kevin," Annie said impatiently. "Yes. We have a one o'clock appointment. We can actually drive."

"That's right," Kevin said without emotion. "We're just like rich folks now. Did you line up Tina to baby-sit?"

Annie nodded. Since Kevin was playing with the baby, she handed him a bowl of yogurt to feed her. He grimaced but pulled up a chair and began to shovel it in. Mary liked to feed herself, but the yogurt needed an adult.

Thirty minutes later, they sat down to a large breakfast. Afterward, Annie did not bother clearing. They remained at the table and talked. Clean and fed, Danny looked like a new person. You would never guess he had had a late night. At twenty-eight, he looked more like twenty. Kevin, on the other hand, looked a little wan.

"Do you want to shower before I leave to take Danny?" Annie asked him.

"I might as well wait until after I nap. I'm going to take Mary out in the yard." Kevin rose from the table and went off in search of clothes for the baby.

Annie held her seat. Kevin never dressed Mary, but he could certainly do it today. She was reluctant to miss even one minute with her brother.

Kevin congenially dressed the baby and took her outside. Annie cleared the table and started the dishes. Danny lounged on the counter and smoked cigarettes while she worked. Annie could not stop looking at him. It was hard to believe he was sitting here in her kitchen. They talked quickly, jumping from subject to subject. There was so much to say. He was delighted she was starting school and promised to return within the next few months for a proper visit. He said Nellie wanted to come to Texas for spring break.

"Don't tell her I told you," Danny said nervously. They exchanged a glance and began to laugh. How glorious to share a sense of humor! Annie had forgotten what fun could be had in a simple conversation. It was a family joke in the McGowan house. Everything was a secret, but every one knew everything. The McGowan family members often forgot what they were supposed to know. Many hilarious episodes were the result of botched attempts to surprise each other. They chattered on. In what seemed like minutes, it was time to go. On the way to the airport, Danny again introduced the subject of his friend.

"I'm thinking, Annie," he said casually. "Maybe Buddy should call and check in with you once in a while."

"Don't let him call me, Danny," Annie said

quickly. "I don't want Kevin getting all wild on me."

"Why would he get wild?" her brother demanded. "This guy is a friend of mine."

Annie shifted uncomfortably in the driver's seat. "He gets jealous, Dan. He'll accuse me of having an affair or something. Don't let the guy call me. It will make trouble."

Danny said nothing. Annie was driving and thought she would die of happiness. The airport was eight miles from the town, and she was flying along a two-lane highway.

"Danny, you have no idea how much this car is going to change my life. It's been horrible trying to get around."

"Yeah. You need a car all right," he agreed flatly. "This car is highway ready, Annie. You can drive it back to Chicago any time you want."

"I get it, Danny." Annie's affectionate smile took the sting from her words.

They hugged at the airport as Annie fought back tears. Being with Danny had reminded her of how terribly she missed her family. "Remember," he called back to her as he left. "Call Buddy for anything you need. Anything at all. One more thing. The girls put some presents and stuff in the trunk." He turned to leave and stopped again. "Merry Christmas, Annie."

Annie smiled. She was too choked up to speak. She cried on the way home. Danny was off to spend Christmas alone in a Japanese hotel. Would it have been better if she had not seen him at all? Not really. It was nice to know that life could bring such wonderful surprises. Also, being with him, even for a short time, had reminded Annie of who she was. For some reason she was losing her identity here. She cheered. In less than twenty-four hours she had acquired a car, a mysterious friend named Buddy, and $500 of emergency money in case Kevin got nasty again. Hardly a day for complaining.

Later, Annie and Kevin departed for their counseling session. Kevin was in a foul mood. Annie shot conversation openers at him but was largely ignored. Normally she agonized during Kevin's silent treatments. Today she felt aggravated. One would think Kevin would realize how sad she felt about Danny's leaving, she thought resentfully. He should be grateful they had a car. Instead he was stewing about something and acting as if Annie must be punished. She thought bitterly that he ruined every good event in their lives.

The session started off tensely. Charles asked how their communication exercises were going. Kevin was silent. Annie gave an innocuous answer. Charles asked Kevin if there was something bothering him. Kevin looked away, and Annie could have strangled him. She wanted to tell Charles this was all an act. This was Kevin's way of starting a fight out of nothing. She sat back in her chair and watched angrily as Charles tried to coax Kevin to discuss his feelings.

"Charles," she finally interrupted, "this is

Kevin's way of saying he is not pleased about something. He'll stay quiet until he explodes. After that, he'll tell us what's bothering him."

Kevin glared at her with hatred. It wouldn't be long, she knew.

Charles also stared at Annie. "Annie," he said sternly, "Kevin has admitted to us that he has difficulty expressing his feelings. It won't help to be unkind."

"I'm not being unkind," she replied. "I'm informing you that there is a pattern. I'm glad this is happening here instead of at home. Kevin," she said kindly, "tell me what's on your mind. If you're mad about something, this is the place to get it off your chest."

"Some things should be discussed privately," he snapped. "I can't believe you would want me to say certain things in front of Charles."

Charles looked intrigued. "Annie," he said professionally, "is there something you do not want Kevin to discuss in front of me?"

Annie kept her face blank. "I can't think what it would be." She turned to Kevin. "Say whatever you like."

Kevin's face reddened. Annie thought with trepidation that Charles had better be careful.

"Why don't you tell him what you were doing after work last night?" Kevin said angrily. Annie stared at him. Charles stared at her. In spite of herself, her face reddened. She probably looked guilty. "Don't start, Kevin. I was talking to Lorena about her boyfriend, and you know it. Why don't we tell Charles what I can't bring up?"

Kevin chuckled meanly. "Why don't we tell Charles about Harold?"

Charles remained quiet.

"Harold is a figment of your imagination, Kevin. But yes, I agree, we should tell our counselor about all of these things instead of hiding the dangerous problems." She addressed their counselor. "Charles, as you can see we have a serious trust issue. Kevin does not trust me. There is absolutely no basis for his constant jealously. He freely admits that. Yet he treats me like a tramp waiting to happen. These things have to be worked out, and we both know it."

Kevin gave Charles a beseeching look. "I think she's having an affair." Choking back a sob, he put his face in his hands.

Annie sputtered in rage. "You liar." She searched for words. "Kevin, you are either mentally ill or the most manipulative person I've ever met. Look at me," she demanded. He kept his head in his hands and shook his head.

Charles intervened. "Kevin," he said, gently touching Kevin's knee, "can you do something for me?" Kevin nodded, head in hands. "Can you look at Annie and tell her how you feel?" Kevin nodded again.

Kevin looked up dramatically. "You're tearing me apart, Annie."

Annie checked her temper. "How, Kevin? Tell me specifically how I'm tearing you apart."

"You know how. The constant flirting and fooling around. I can't take it anymore."

Annie rolled her eyes. Kevin jumped from his chair, pushing it back violently into the wall.

"Did you see that?" he demanded, looking at Charles. "Every time I tell her how I feel, she rolls her eyes at me. She constantly minimizes my feelings. I can't take it anymore." Choking back sobs, he fled the room.

Charles flew out after him. Annie heard him pleading with Kevin in the hallway. Kevin refused to come back and eventually stormed out of the building. Charles slowly came back into the room.

Annie gripped the sides of her chair. She was stunned. Charles, too, looked shaken. He also looked angry.

"It's not his fault," Annie said, instinctively defending her husband. "He had a lot of problems growing up."

"I don't think Kevin is the problem here, Annie," the counselor said coldly.

"Pardon me?"

"How can you be so insensitive?" Charles asked her. "The man was baring his soul to you, and you rolled your eyes. Are you having an affair?"

Annie was speechless. She sputtered for a few moments and then stopped. "Go to hell, Charles. You're as nutty as Kevin."

Annie rose to leave. Turning back, she added, "Kevin plays you like a violin. I've tried to tell you what's going on. The only thing that matters in this room is Kevin and his pretend feelings. Have you ever once asked Kevin to listen to my feelings? No. Because he fooled you, too. This is supposed to be marriage counseling. Kevin is a violent man. He scares me. If we had ever focused on my feelings, you might have found that out."

Charles looked at her in disbelief. "Are you certain you're not saying these things to justify some of your behaviors?"

Annie shook her head. "Charles, Kevin knows I'm not having an affair. He does live in fear that I'll find someone else. But he knows I'm not unfaithful. He was saying that for your benefit. He probably thought you were coming on to me or something." It was obvious that Charles did not believe her.

"You, Charles, are a lightweight. I just hope you didn't get me killed."

Chapter Fourteen

Annie closed the door on Herr Charles. She stood in the lobby uncertainly. *Naturally, Kevin has the keys and the car*, she thought resentfully. The car would be one more area of control for Kevin. Annie felt a fleeting moment of despair. She should have gone with Danny.

Taking a breath, Annie left the building. Kevin could ignore her until hell froze over. She would ignore him right back. That small voice told Annie that his silence would be the least of her problems. Annie decided to take the bull by the horns this time. If Kevin began to act violently, she would leave. She had the money. She had the car. She might even be home for Christmas. Annie smiled at the thought. Like submerging in a cold bath, the realization struck her that Kevin would never allow her to leave. She would have to escape.

Mulling it over, she began to walk down the street. Half a block later, the car screeched to a halt beside her. Kevin opened the door on her side.

"Get in," he barked.

"No thank you, Kevin," she retorted. "You just acted a beautiful scene back there. Now you want me to *get in*? Forget it!" Annie resumed walking.

Her back was to the car. She heard the door

slam and turned to see Kevin charging her. "Don't touch me, Kevin," she warned quickly. "I swore to you I would leave, and I meant it." Kevin stopped two feet from her. His face was contorted in rage. *He wants to kill me*, she thought wonderingly. *He really does.*

"Kevin, take some deep breaths. Let it pass. It's me. I'm not your enemy. I love you, and I'm here because I want to be."

Kevin turned abruptly and got back into the car. Annie stood on the sidewalk. If she had any sense, she would run. She knew that. But Mary was at home. So was the money. And Kevin had the car. Annie needed ten minutes in the house by herself. She also needed the car keys. Kevin must be placated for now. She approached the car.

"Are you calm?" she asked. Kevin nodded his head. "Am I safe to get in the car and go home with you, Kevin?" He nodded his head. Annie took a deep breath and held it. She could hardly make him sign a promissory note. Sending up a frantic prayer, she got in.

Kevin took off from the curb like the car had been launched. They nearly collided with a truck at the first intersection when he ran a red light. Annie held on to her seat belt and cursed herself for getting in.

"Kevin!" she shouted. "Slow down, dammit!"

He slammed on the brakes. Annie was braced but still hit her head on the dashboard. "Oh, God." She started to cry. "Why are you doing this to me?"

Kevin punched the seat next to her head. Annie put her hand on the door handle and began to shift her weight. Kevin lightly grabbed her hand and placed it in her lap.

"You're not getting out. And I'll tell you why. I'm not going to hurt you. You have me over a barrel, and you love it."

Annie looked him squarely in the eye. "What are we talking about, Kevin?"

"I can't lay a hand on you or you'll leave. Fine. I won't touch you. Even when you deserve it."

"What do I deserve, Kevin?" Annie shouted back. "Why do I deserve to get beat up?"

He spoke through gritted teeth. "Because God only knows what you were doing last night after work. Acting all sweet in front of your brother doesn't cut it. If Danny knew how you were, he would be disgusted."

"What, Kevin? What could I have done in the fifteen minutes between work and coming home to you?"

Kevin sighed and seemed to relax.

"Is it over, Kevin? Can we go home?"

Whenever he wanted to hurt her, he told her things about her family. He said they talked to him about her. He once said that Maureen had admitted Annie was a flirt. Annie assumed he was making it up. It hurt, though, and he knew it.

Kevin put the car in gear and began to drive. He was calmer now. Annie looked straight ahead. She hoped the worst was over. After a couple of miles she felt his hand on top of hers. Annie glanced over at him. He looked at her beseechingly.

"Annie, please don't be mad," he said quietly. "I'm sorry."

"You're always sorry, Kevin."

"How come you didn't come home right after work?" he asked in a passionate voice. "Just tell me the truth, and I won't get mad."

"I was talking to Lorena about her boyfriend. He left again, and she's upset."

"Fine. That's all I wanted to hear. Sorry." Pulling her hand up to his mouth, he kissed it gently. Annie tried not to cringe. He was repugnant to her. At the thought, she was awash in guilt. "Kevin," she said, "we want to have a nice Christmas. Right?"

"Absolutely."

"Let's not fight, then. Is it really over?"

"Yes, Annie," he said with finality. "I'm fine. I started feeling insecure seeing you have such a good time with Danny. You never laugh like that with me anymore. I think that's what started it."

"Kevin, Danny is my brother. You can't be jealous of him."

"Stupid," he agreed. "But wait a minute. I got mad and did not hurt you." He grinned at her. "See, I told you I would never hurt you again."

Annie smiled wanly back at him. He had nearly put her through the windshield. She peered into the future. Kevin would not hurt her physically anymore. That would be wonderful, of course, and he did deserve credit. He would, however, torment her emotionally. Depression sat down firmly on her lap. She wondered if he had controlled himself today only because they were in public. It was possible and did not bode well for the evening.

If the tantrum was indeed over, he would be nice for a couple of days. That ought to take them through Christmas. No more seeing Charles, though. Annie wanted to see Caroline. Looking at her watch, she saw it was nearly three. It was Friday. Christmas was on Wednesday. Caroline would probably not be in until Thursday. Annie felt the old ache of loneliness returning. Caroline was the only one who understood.

Kevin was stroking her hand, and Annie fought the urge to slap him. After a fight he had an intense need for reassurance. Conversely, Annie despised her husband after an argument. He fought dirty and then waved his magic wand. According to Kevin, once he apologized it was over. No matter what he had done, she was expected to forgive him immediately.

"Annie," Kevin said as they pulled into their parking lot. "I forgot to tell you. I'm going out tonight."

"Fine," she said in surprise. "Where are you going?"

"Any players who did not go home are getting together at a bar. Kind of an informal Christmas party. I'm going with Greg. The Kemps are not going home until tomorrow. You don't mind, do you?"

Annie tried not to be too enthusiastic. "Not at all. It will give me a chance to get ready for Christmas. I got a turkey for our Christmas dinner." Kevin smiled at her affectionately. "Kevin," Annie said suddenly, "we can go to mass on Christmas Day."

Kevin laughed. "We can go to mass every Sunday if you want. We have wheels, Annie." They both laughed, and Annie felt a little better. She would have the evening to herself. She would think about this fight and what it meant for the future. She was always glad to see Kevin getting out. She reasoned that the more he went out, the more he might relax about her getting out. So far it had not happened.

Annie got out of the car. "Are you coming in?"

Kevin remained in the driver's seat. "I think I'll take the car out for a ride. I need to do some Christmas shopping and cool down. You know?"

"I do realize that you controlled yourself today, Kevin. That was good."

He smiled sheepishly and waved. Annie climbed the stairs slowly. Mentally exhausted, she decided to call Caroline. She quickly paid the baby-sitter and saw her out. Mary was still napping, so Annie had peace. Without taking off her jacket, she dialed the number. For the first time she was put directly through to Caroline's office.

Annie told her about the fight. She told her about Danny's money and the car. She asked Caroline if it was terrible that she did not want to see Charles anymore.

"Not at all," came the clipped response. Annie

pictured Caroline and could almost hear the delicate tinkling of jewelry. "Honey, you get any more marriage counseling and you'll end up dead."

"That's how I feel," Annie said in relief. "Kevin uses it to manipulate me or something. I'm not sure what's happening, but it's not good."

"I agree, Annie," Caroline said calmly. "I'm in the office tomorrow. Why don't you come in and see me? Do you think you can get away?"

"I'll try," she said hesitantly. "I don't know if he'll let me. It might start everything up again."

"I understand," the counselor said easily. "I'm not busy, though, and I'll be here all day. Give me a call if you can swing it. Bring the baby. I'm a little worried about you. Are you sure he's over this last thing? Holidays are a dangerous time for women in your situation."

"Don't tell me that, Caroline," Annie said despondently. "I was just thinking in the car that the reason this whole thing happened was because he knows how excited I am about Christmas. He seems to ruin everything that makes me happy." Annie hesitated. "Caroline," she said in a small voice, "I think he wants to kill me. It sounds insane, but I saw it in his eyes."

"It does not sound insane, Annie. You know him better than anyone. I don't think you're safe there, Annie. That's my gut instinct." Caroline was speaking quickly, as though she were afraid to let Annie hang up. "Are you sure you won't consider leaving?"

Annie was staring out of the back window.

Letting her breath out, she realized she had been holding it.

"I'd have to get the car keys. Somehow I would have to get out of the house by myself. With Mary." Annie continued to think aloud. "You know what's weird, Caroline?"

"What's that?"

"Less than an hour ago I thought he was going to kill me. Then he kissed my hand and told me he was going to get me a Christmas present. Before that he told our counselor that I was having an affair and stormed out of the room. Then he drove like a maniac and nearly put me through the windshield. Now I'm sitting here, and I don't know if I should leave or not. I must be as nutty as him."

"It's tough, isn't it?" Caroline empathized.

"Yep. It sure is." Annie frowned in concentration. "Part of my problem is that I'm so tired. I can't decide what to make for dinner, never mind whether or not I should grab my child and run for my life. Am I blowing this out of proportion? He didn't hit me, Caroline."

"That's true, Annie. He controlled himself because he wanted to. Will he want to tonight when you're trapped in the apartment with him? He nearly killed you today. You said yourself that you could see that he wanted to kill you. That stuff does not just disappear, Annie. It's all there, waiting for the next trigger."

Annie sighed. "I can't leave him alone for Christmas, Caroline. It would be too mean. I think

I'll try to get through the holidays and then take stock. I think it's over. I really do. I can't stay with him. It's a matter of doing it as painlessly as possible."

"I see," Caroline said nonjudgmentally. "I know that it hurts a lot, Annie. It takes a lot of guts to get out of something like this. Will you do me a favor, Honey?"

"Sure. What?"

"Call me tomorrow and let me know how you're doing. Okay?"

Annie promised and hung up. She felt much better. Someone understood. Caroline wanted her to call the next day to make sure she was safe. It was a warm and comforting feeling. Annie wished she could sort out her feelings for Kevin as easily. In the last few hours they had run the gamut. Remembering she had missed a good bit of sleep the night before, she lay down on the couch. Even if Mary got up in ten minutes, she would have a rest.

She dozed fitfully. Thirty minutes later, Mary woke up. Annie entered the kitchen as though in a trance. Her mind jumped from idea to idea. Should she leave tonight? Logically, yes. Kevin's moods had been all over the board the last few days. If he left the car and rode with Greg tonight, she would have an opportunity. Annie decided she could drive to the nearest town and get a hotel room there. She resisted the urge to call home. There was nothing anyone could do right away. The explanations alone would exhaust her.

At five fifteen Kevin came in. He looked happy. Too happy. *He probably took out a life insurance policy on me*, Annie thought irrationally. He made a big production of hiding her present in the linen closet. Normally, Annie would have been excited. She loved presents. Tonight she felt morbid and depressed.

She threw together sloppy joes for dinner. Kevin raved about them. She made a point to talk about Christmas Day so he would not suspect she was considering escape. Kevin chattered. He thought it was great that they were spending the holiday alone. Annie smiled. She was going to love her present. Would Annie like to guess what it was? Annie thought she would fall over dead if she had to play this out much longer. Clothes? Jewelry? Kevin laughed too loudly. She wondered if the hangover was making him manic. She asked him if he felt tired. No. Just excited about going out tonight.

Annie cautioned him against drinking too much. She casually suggested that she let Greg drive so he would not have to worry about driving drunk. No way! he exclaimed. Part of the fun was driving his own car. That settled it. Annie felt relieved. She could decorate the house and go to bed. Everything would seem less sinister in the morning.

"Kevin, I'm going grocery shopping in the morning," she said cheerfully. "Why don't Mary and I let you sleep in? I'm going to try to catch mass as well."

Kevin poked his head around the corner of the kitchen. "I won't be out late, Annie. I'd love to go to mass in the morning." He smiled. He was talking too fast again. "Unless you're up to something and don't want me to go." This was said as if it were a joke, but Annie sensed the underlying threat.

"Not at all," she said breezily. "Your presents are all bought and wrapped." She smiled at him, deliberately misunderstanding. "I'm not spending another penny."

"Good. We can't afford it. I'm jumping in the shower."

Mary hung on her leg. Annie was preoccupied and opened the pots and pans cabinet. Mary eyed it steadily. Without warning she let go of Annie's leg and toddled over to it. Grabbing the top of the cabinet, she turned to Annie with a look of amazement on her face. Annie cheered and clapped. Mary gurgled in delight, rocking back and forth on her heels. She was walking. After much praise and kisses, Annie went back to the dishes. She wanted to weep. Another joyful milestone and she was too strung out to enjoy it. Kevin went into the shower happy. For all she knew he would come out with a gun. Maybe he had stopped for the gun after he got the insurance policy. Annie giggled. Kevin would not think it through that much. He would just kill her. While wiping the counters, Annie decided to call home tonight. She needed a dose of sanity. She found a lighter on the counter. Had it really been only this morning that Danny had sat there and laughed with her? Annie felt her eyes well up again.

At that moment Kevin came into the room.

"What's the matter?" he asked sharply.

She began to cry. "I'm homesick," she burst out. "I miss my sisters and Danny and my dad. And then we had the fight today and Mary started walking and it's all too much."

Blessedly, Kevin did not take offense. Annie usually did not bring up homesickness because it made him feel insecure. Tonight he was touched. "That's why you're acting so strangely. I knew something was wrong," he said as he took her in his arms. "I thought you were planning to leave me." He stroked her head soothingly. "It's okay, Annie. It's natural that you're homesick. I'm a little homesick myself. But we've got each other. And Mary." Kevin looked around. "Where is she, by the way?"

Annie's voice was muffled by Kevin's shirt front. "In the cabinet. She crawls inside to get the pots out."

"She's quiet anyway." Kevin continued to console her. "Annie, I'm sorry about today. I'm acting mean, and I know it. Maybe it's the holidays. I'm fine now. I want you to have a wonderful Christmas."

Annie nodded her head and let herself be comforted. Maybe he was right. A lot of people got strange around the holidays. He promised she could spend Christmas Day on the phone if she liked. Come to think of it, Annie should put the baby down tonight and call home. The hell with the bill, he said. He was going out, so Annie should also have a treat. Annie smiled genuinely. "Thanks, Kevin. I feel much better," she said honestly as she wiped her eyes. "I love you so much when you're like this."

A look of pain crossed his face. "I'm not like this often enough."

"You try your hardest, and I know that."

He pulled her to him again. "Would you rather I stayed in tonight?"

Annie thought about it. Kevin was on his best behavior, so she was safe. And if truth be told, she did not want to leave him. Not now. Not ever. She simply wanted him to be nice.

"No. You never get out. I'm okay." Thinking for a minute, she added, "But, Kevin, can you get home by eleven or so? I won't be able to sleep till you're home, and I don't want to be up late. Is that fair?"

"Absolutely. If I'm going to be later then ten, I'll call. Deal?"

"Deal."

He went to get his coat. Annie was playing peek-a-boo with Mary, who was still inside the bottom cabinets.

"Have a pleasant evening, Mrs. Griffin," Kevin said as he kissed her. "I left a little treat for you by the phone."

Annie raised her eyebrows and waved good-bye. She immediately walked over to the phone. There on the handset was a pack of cigarettes. She laughed out loud. This was his way of saying she could stop pretending. Annie raced to the back door and stepped out onto the porch. Kevin was getting into the car. "Thank you for my treat," she called down, laughing.

He looked up and grinned. Putting one hand across his chest, he bowed deeply. "Whatever it takes, my lady."

Annie inclined her head in a flirty manner. This was the Kevin she loved. She felt lighthearted and happy. Kevin could be lovely when he wanted to. Annie entered the house with renewed vigor. This was just the kind of pleasant evening she needed.

She filled the tub with a mountain of bubbles. Splashing with Mary consumed the better part of an hour, and it was after eight when she tucked her little one into bed. Annie dragged the presents out of the bedroom so she would not awaken the child later. Wrapped in a warm robe, she contemplated. Should she call home first or decorate the house? There was no tree yet. The Griffins were waiting until Christmas Eve in the hope that prices would be more favorable to their budget. She decided to decorate first.

Garland and ornaments were strewn on the floor. Working steadily, she soon transformed the little apartment. A small wreath and a Santa Claus hung on the doors. A bright garland held silver ornaments across the wall in the dining room. Chintzy but festive. She took great care in arranging the Nativity. An old lace drape folded in fourths covered the television set. It looked pretty, and she figured they could flip it back when they wanted to watch something. She smiled in satisfaction. A few strands of colored lights added the magical quality she had yearned for. This would cheer them up.

She was about to call when she remembered the box from home. Like a child, she ran into the hallway and opened the box. There were several small packages for Mary along with one marked for Kevin and Annie. Annie held the presents in her hands. Closing her eyes, she imagined her sisters wrapping them. A thought popped into her head, and she turned the presents over. Sure enough, they were fastened with electrical tape. Annie laughed in delight. The McGowan family never had any tape in the house. True to form, the girls had gone into Mr. McGowan's tools for the silver electrical tape.

Dropping the presents back into the box, she climbed up onto the counter and grabbed an ashtray. She was ready. For the next thirty minutes she chatted happily with her sisters. Eileen had sent a very special present. It was wrapped in Bambi paper but was for the whole family. Maureen was on a date, but Nellie filled her in on the local gossip. After thirty minutes had elapsed, Annie reluctantly told Nellie that she had to go.

Annie was still sitting at the table when the phone rang. It was Nellie. She figured they could talk for another thirty minutes on the McGowan phone bill. Annie laughed in delight and settled down for another long chat. Nellie said Mr. McGowan would be calling in the morning. And they would certainly call on Christmas Eve and Christmas Day. Nellie also informed her that Mr. McGowan had met Mrs. Griffin in the drugstore. The two parents agreed to split the difference from now on and fly the young family home for Christmas. That was good news. Next year she would be home. If she was still here at all. She dismissed the depressing thought and promised Nellie that she would stay home in the morning until her father called. Once again, they hung up.

Annie glanced at the clock. It was nearly nine thirty. Kevin would be home soon. Annie was anxious to fill him in on the news. She turned off the big lights and left only the Christmas lights on. The little apartment looked cozy and warm. Annie stretched out on the couch. Everything would work out, she promised herself. If she were looking on the bright side, she would note that Kevin had indeed controlled himself. Had he really wanted to kill her or was that her imagination? It was too late for those thoughts. She focused instead on the Kevin who had grinned up at her before he left.

She awoke with a start. Kevin was still not home, and Annie wandered groggily into the kitchen to check the time. It was midnight! Annie felt a squeeze in her stomach. If Kevin was still drinking, he would be very drunk. That was not good. Kevin got nasty when he got drunk. Also, why had he not called at ten? Especially after how sweetly he had left her.

The phone rang, nearly sending Annie through the roof. She grabbed it quickly before it could ring again and wake the baby.

"Annie," said a tense female voice, "it's Darlene. Were you sleeping?"

"No. I was just wondering where Kevin was,"

she answered honestly. "Is Greg home?"

"Actually, that's why I'm calling." Darlene was very upset. "I was up packing, you know, we're leaving tomorrow at five, and Greg came in. He's kind of loaded but not too bad."

Darlene had a tendency to run on, and Annie was impatient. "Where's Kevin?"

Darlene paused. "That's why I'm calling. Annie, you're going to kill me."

"Why, Darlene?"

"I'm so sorry. Greg and I had a fight the other night. He never gets jealous. He doesn't seem to care about me at all." Annie listened patiently. There was no hurrying this woman. "Anyway, I told him what you said about Kevin. I'm really sorry. I swear it never occurred to me for a minute that he would tell Kevin."

Annie's stomach was now in complete lockdown. She held it with one hand while she tried to get more information.

"Darlene, what did I say about Kevin?"

Annie heard Darlene take a breath. "That if he knew about Bill the stockboy he would beat him up."

Annie looked around the apartment frantically. "Oh, my God. Oh, God, Darlene, how could you? Tell me exactly what Greg told him. Quick! I have to get out of here!"

Darlene was crying. "Annie, what's wrong with Kevin? Greg said he was freaking out. I would not have called, only Greg made me. He said Kevin was going nuts in the parking lot of the bar. He finally took off in the car, driving like a maniac. Greg said I had to call and warn you. Who is Harold?"

"Harold?" Annie said in bewilderment. "What does Harold have to do with anything?"

"Kevin told Greg that you had an affair with some guy named Harold before you were married and that he suspected you had something going on at work." Darlene stopped talking long enough to give a large sniffle. "Do you, Annie?"

"Kevin is out of his mind. Tell me exactly what Greg said."

"He only said that there was some stockboy at work that liked you. He said it as a joke. They were talking about wives and stuff, and Greg was pretending to be mad at Kevin for making the rest of them look bad. He said this guy was flirting with you at work. I swear, Annie. That's all he could have told Kevin because that's all I told Greg."

"Darlene," Annie reminded her, "that's all there was to tell. When would I ever see this guy?"

Darlene's voice warmed. "That's what Greg tried to tell Kevin. Did you know that Kevin checks your pay stubs to make sure you're working when you say you are? Anyway, Greg tried to tell Kevin that it was impossible. He says he talked to him for over an hour, trying to calm him down, but Kevin was nuts. Annie, I'm so sorry." Darlene started to cry again. "I knew right after I told him I should not have. But he didn't think it was a big deal. Honestly. Greg thought the whole thing was a big joke until Kevin went crazy."

"I have to go, Darlene, " Annie said tensely. "He's going to kill me. I should get out of here."

"He'll get over it, Annie," Darlene said, trying to comfort her. "They get mad, but it blows over."

"You don't know Kevin," Annie said in despair. "I don't know what to do."

"Are you serious?" Darlene sounded scared. "You're not really thinking of leaving, are you?"

"Darlene, you don't understand. Kevin is going to kill me. I have to get out of here."

"Well, where are you going to go?"

"I don't know. Can I come to your apartment?"

"Oh, Annie," Darlene said sadly. "You know I'd love to help you. But I don't think Greg wants to get involved. Kevin really scared him. Is there somewhere else you can go?"

"Yes," Annie said coldly. "I'm sure I'll think of something."

Annie hung up the phone. Her hands were shaking violently. There would be no point explaining anything. This was as close as Kevin had ever gotten to hard evidence. Annie knew from experience that she could talk till the cows came home. She ran to the bedroom. Her breath was coming in shallow gulps. If he got home, she knew, she might die tonight. Pushing her hand into the diaper bag, she felt around for the money. She would grab the baby and call a cab. No. She could not even wait that long. She would get out of the apartment first. She could walk to the nearest gas station and call the cab from there. Annie frantically began to pull diapers from the bag. In desperation she turned the bag upside down and emptied it. A small piece of paper fell out. Annie held it close to her eyes. It was in Kevin's handwriting.

"Who is Buddy, and where did you get the money?"

A chill ran through her body. Annie dropped the paper like it was a snake. Kevin had her money.

"Oh, God. Help me, God," she muttered frantically. She opened her drawers and pulled out a pair of pants. Stripping off her bathrobe, she pulled up the pants. She needed shoes and a blanket for the baby. She would walk to the nearest street and flag down a car. Someone would take her to the police station, and she would call home from there. Her hands shook violently as she tore through the closet looking for shoes. She ended up with boots and jammed her feet into them.

Frantically, she searched for the baby's jacket. She would have to go without it. Annie ran to the crib and grabbed her tiny daughter. Wrapping the blanket snugly around the child, she cuddled her against her chest. She would not even bother with her purse.

She was two steps from the front door when she saw the knob turning.

Chapter Fifteen

Annie stopped breathing. Backing up, she headed for the kitchen door. Footsteps pounded behind her, but she never paused. She was halfway down the stairs when Kevin grabbed a handful of her hair.

Stopping dead in her tracks, Annie said softly, "Let me go, Kevin. You're drunk. I don't want to talk to you like this."

"Nice try, Annie," he said, turning her around by her hair. "Don't scream. Walk up the stairs."

"Kevin, let me go," Annie repeated calmly. She was holding the baby snugly to her chest. Her head was being pulled almost sideways but she did not complain. Instinctively, she knew two things: If she made any fast moves or reentered the apartment with him, she would die.

Kevin reeked of alcohol. Annie noted in dismay that the smell was not beer. More like whiskey. She would have to be more careful than she had ever been in her life.

"Up the stairs, slut. Quietly. If you scream I'll kill you and the baby. I don't want to live anymore anyway. Then we can all be together forever."

They were still on the stairs. Annie was in a quandary. He was pulling her steadily by her hair. She was afraid to fight with the baby in her arms.

They were on the third floor, and a fall could be fatal for Mary. She remembered Caroline saying something about suicide. Suicidal abusers were extremely dangerous. Annie doubted Kevin would kill himself sober. Drunk . . . there was no telling. He pushed her to the railing.

"Walk, Annie or you're both going over."

Kevin made the decision for her. She could not go over the railing with the baby. Her breaths came slowly. Each was separate. A lifetime long. Annie began to climb the stairs. Kevin stayed behind her with her hair in his hand. He had it right by the roots so she could barely move her neck.

"Kevin, don't do this. Let me go put the baby down, and we'll talk. I know you don't want to hurt me."

An ugly laugh exploded from him. "You wish I didn't want to hurt you. Frankly, Annie, the jig is up. Get your ass in the house, and we'll figure out what to do with you." Annie still did not move. "I mean it, Annie." Kevin twisted the handful of hair, and Annie sucked in her breath. "Move now, or I'll hurt the baby, too."

Annie entered the apartment. It would have been better if she had been lying on the couch when he arrived. Seeing her trying to escape had confirmed every bad thought in his head. She should have left this afternoon. She should have left with Danny. She should never have married him after the incident in the car when she was pregnant. She should have . . .

"Put the baby in the crib."

Annie went to the bedroom. Her whole body seemed suspended. This was a nightmare. Annie was experienced with nightmares. Normally she could wake herself up. She commanded herself to wake up. Nothing happened. Annie put Mary in her crib and gently covered her up. Mary opened her eyes briefly and smiled up at her mommy. "Pray for us, Mary," she whispered. The child closed her eyes peacefully.

Annie closed the door and stood in the hallway.

"Get me a glass," he commanded. There was a bottle of Jack Daniel's in front of him. Annie went into the kitchen. She toyed with the idea of a desperate lunge out the back door. Reading her thoughts, Kevin slurred, "If you're thinking of running again, let me promise you one thing. I'll kill Mary if you get away. Just so you know where we stand."

Annie had figured as much. This time she knew it was not safe to leave her child. She would have to hope he kept drinking and passed out. She would encourage him to drink. Annie got a large glass and put only two ice cubes in it. Placing it in front of him, she started to head for the living room. The fight must be kept away from the baby at all costs. Kevin rose and walked to the phone. He staggered slightly, and Annie was encouraged. Kevin could hold a great quantity of alcohol, but he was not accustomed to hard stuff. From the looks of the bottle, half empty, he'd had a sizable head start.

Reaching the desk, he picked up the phone. He smiled over at Annie and with an abrupt motion pulled it from the wall.

"Just in case you get in a chatty mood. Tonight you're going to talk to me." He threw the phone into the kitchen and sat back down. "Sit down here with me and talk. Tell me all about your stockboy. How many times did you fuck him?"

Annie walked over to the table and sat down. "You know I would never do that, Kevin."

"Wrong answer," he yelled. Reaching over, he knocked her out of the chair. Annie lay still on the floor. He pulled her up by her shirt and placed her back on the chair. "Let's try it again. How many times did you fuck him?" Annie remained silent. "*Answer me!*"

"I never touched him, and he never touched me."

Slam. Back on the floor. This time Annie's head hit the corner of the wall. She felt no pain. Only confusion. After he lifted her back onto the chair, she realized she was bleeding. Must be a cut on her head.

"Sloppy bitch." He sneered. "You're making a mess all over the table. Go get a towel."

Annie dutifully went into the bathroom and grabbed a towel. It was one of her guest towels. She used it anyway. She purposely did not glance in the mirror. She had no desire to see the look in her eyes.

Sitting back down at the table, she held the towel to her head.

"Poor pitiful Annie." He continued to sneer. "Stuck with a jerk like me. What did you ever do to deserve this? Miss Smarty Pants. Too bad I'm a little smarter than you, Annie. Right?" She remained silent. "*Answer me, bitch, or I'll rip your fucking heart out!*"

"Yes, Kevin," she said quietly. "You're smarter than me."

"You know it, Annie. Which is why you're in such trouble right now. You were going to leave today. Or tonight. That's why I took the car. You'll never get your hands on this car. Where you're going you won't need a car. You're going to burn in hell. Because that's where you belong. In hell. You should not be allowed to touch that child in there. Your hands are evil. What did you do to Bill with those hands? I can't stop wondering. Tell me what he looks like."

"Kevin, there is absolutely nothing between me and this guy. Let me tell you what happened. Okay? It's not as bad as you're imagining."

Kevin considered for a minute. "No. First we're going to open our Christmas presents. Go get them. I want to see what kind of presents my whoring little wife bought me."

"Kevin, let me just tell you—"

"*Lies? You want to tell me lies?*" Kevin was screaming. Lowering his voice, he continued. "Don't tell me one thing, Annie. Just for tonight, do exactly what I tell you. If you talk back or argue or piss me off in any way, I'm going to kill you. You know that.

If you want to stay alive . . . *Do what I fucking tell you!*" He paused for a large swallow of whiskey. "Go get my presents."

Annie went into the living room and got the presents. It was one thirty in the morning. He had been drinking for four hours. Annie wondered how long he could hold out. She did not care anymore. If he killed her, it would be over. She could rest. She thought sadly of Mary. If Kevin killed her, at least he could not get custody of Mary. Mary would go to the McGowans. They would take good care of her, Annie knew.

She deposited the presents in front of Kevin on the table. He ordered her to sit down. She did. He began a tirade about Christmas. It would have been wonderful if Annie had not ruined it. At two o'clock he opened his first present. The tool kit.

"How nice," he crooned in an ugly way. Taking each tool out of the plastic organizer, he threw them at her one by one. Annie covered her face as the metal tools bounced off her head. "Just perfect for throwing at sluts. Look on the package, Annie. What does it say?"

Annie glanced at the box. "Great for household chores."

Kevin hit her in the head with the box. "Wrong again. It says 'Just perfect for throwing at sluts.' You're so smart, but you can't read. You're going to flunk out of college. Read it again."

"Perfect for throwing at sluts," she intoned.

Kevin laughed uproariously. "That's better.

Maybe I'll let you live." Annie looked down at the table. She was unprepared for Kevin's blow to the front of her chest. She flew backward into the wall and then onto the floor. Her head struck the wall and the floor. Annie felt something snap in her wrist. She was stunned but still felt no pain. She lay on the floor, unable to rise. Kevin loomed above her. He kicked at her gently with his foot.

"Get up, Annie. I want to talk to you."

Annie could not move. She heard him from a distance. She knew she should get up before he got madder. For some reason her body would not respond. Suddenly she felt a brutal kick in her back. She curled up instinctively and covered her face. The kicking went on for what seemed like an eternity. Kevin was methodical. He worked his way from the back of her neck down to her feet. Annie remained curled up. The back of her body was preferable to her face and stomach.

Eons passed, and the kicking stopped. Annie lay still. She heard Kevin return to the table and fill his glass. He was breathing heavily and muttering to himself. Annie sensed his confusion. Somehow, she was mentally alert but remained still. Let him think he'd killed her. She thought of a possum and felt pity for the rancorous animal.

Kevin began to cry. She could not make out what he was saying. He repeated a sentence over and over. Whatever it was held no consolation for him, because he continued to cry and mumble.

Unaware of time passing, Annie remained on

the floor. Hazy thoughts clouded her mind. She pictured the Christmas tree in the McGowan living room. One by one, Annie identified the ornaments. There was the fat snowman lit from inside. There was always an argument over whether or not to use a colored light. The little snowman. No light necessary. A homemade ornament boasted a picture of Nellie in the middle. This was the result of a Girl Scout craft. How it had survived so many years was a mystery. Annie continued to mentally scan the tree. Too much tinsel. The girls could never agree on when to stop. When their mother was alive, she had set limits.

Under the tree was a white sheet strewn artfully by Maureen. The Nativity was displayed there with its own strand of white lights. There was no real theme to this tree, Annie discovered. Pink balls jockeyed for position with red balls. They all hated the pink balls, but for some reason they never disappeared. Only the nice ornaments broke or vanished. Why was that? Annie wondered. It was the same with sunglasses and socks. You could not lose the obnoxious ones. Annie allowed her mind to reenter the Griffin household. Kevin was quiet. Was he sleeping?

"Bitch," she heard him mutter.

His voice was terrifically slurred. Annie opened her eyes a slit. There was blood. Lots of it. The tiny act of opening her eyes awakened the rest of her body. Annie was hurting.

Hearing the scrape of his chair, she closed her

eyes again. She sensed him standing over her.

"Are you dead, Annie? Did I kill you?" Kevin was jabbing her mouth with his foot. "Are you faking? I'm not calling an ambulance. Get up."

Annie remained motionless.

"*Get up, I said!*"

With that, he kicked her in the mouth. Annie shouted out loud and covered her head. She could hear Kevin's ugly laugh. A feeling of rage engulfed her. *Let him kill me*, she thought. *Either way. But I'm not going to die like a dog.* Annie rolled into a sitting position with her back against the wall. She spit to clear the blood. Grabbing the leg of an overturned chair, she tried to hoist herself into a sitting position. A spear of pain shot up her left arm. Her hand was not working. The agony made her scream.

"*Die, Kevin,*" she shouted. "Die slowly! Kill me, too. I don't care. You're not hurting me because I don't care anymore. If I die, I won't have to be with you."

Kevin backed around the table and sat down again. He never took his eyes off her. Annie held her left arm in her right hand and stared at him. She no longer felt any fear. Just hatred.

"You think you're so powerful because you can throw me around." She paused for breath. Breathing was painful for some reason. "You're not, Kevin. Only bullies and cowards beat up people who can't fight back. It means nothing. Kill me if you want. It won't change a thing."

Kevin drained his glass, and Annie walked past

him into the living room. It was five o'clock. There was no sign of the sun yet. If she could stay alive for another couple of hours, something would happen. Surely daylight would end this torment.

Annie lay down gently and closed her eyes. She did not dare enter the bedroom because she knew it was not over. He was still awake. At all costs she had to keep the fight away from Mary. Hearing him get up again, she suppressed a cry.

Kevin lowered himself heavily to the floor near her. He was still drinking but had dispatched with the glass. Annie noticed that less than a fourth of the bottle remained.

"Annie"—he spoke heavily—"in spite of your brave little speech, this is far from over. I need more information before I decide if I'm going to let you live. Who is Buddy, and why is he giving you money? Are you getting paid for fucking?"

Annie considered. There was no real course of action that would protect her. From what she had seen in the past, she was going to get assaulted no matter what she did. Fighting back? That just delighted him. Attempts at self-defense justified his abuse. The trick was to stay alive. Annie realized at that moment that she had absolutely no control over her life.

"Buddy is a friend of Danny's. I have never met him or spoken with him. Danny gave me the money in case we ever had an emergency. He gave me Buddy's number because Buddy works in the same company. He said if there was a family emergency, like if someone died, we should call Buddy and he would know where to reach Danny. It's as simple as that."

Kevin stared at her through bleary eyes. An ugly smirk twisted his face. "You're such a good liar, Annie. I almost believe you. Were you surprised when you discovered I had found your hiding spot?"

"Yes, I was." Annie kept her tone matter-of-fact in spite of the hysteria that was lurking beneath her conscious thinking. "I was surprised that you did not mention it to me. If I had found that much money, I would have gone right to you for an explanation. It was meant to be a surprise, Kevin. That's all there is to that."

Kevin chuckled harshly. "Well, if I was a stupid man, I would have let you know I found it. But I thought of something better." He leaned forward awkwardly and put his face right up to hers. "I know you've been planning to abandon me. What a surprise if you had no money when the time came! No money. No Buddy. I'm smarter than you'll ever be," he said, complacently leaning back. He took another swig and pondered. "I'm trying to decide what to do with you. If I let you live, you'll leave. Maybe not tomorrow. But someday. I can't watch you forever. I would like to have sex with you one more time, though. Let's have sex, Annie. Want to?"

"Kevin, I'm hurt. Leave me alone. Tomorrow I'll do whatever you want. And I'm not going to leave you. If you promise not to drink anymore, I won't leave you. We'll be okay." Annie was fighting for her life, and she knew it. Kevin was a powder keg. Any breath by Annie could be the match that ignited him. He momentarily closed his eyes. Annie kept talking softly, trying to lull him to sleep. She was still reclining and would have preferred to sit up but knew better. Any movement at all could disturb him. She saw his hand relax. The bottle dropped onto his lap. No response. Annie watched him intently for what seemed like an eternity. At last she sat up. She did not try to be quiet. Better to be acting naturally if he opened his eyes. She sighed noisily. Still no response.

She rose painfully and began to walk toward the back door. Annie was inches from freedom when she sensed him behind her. She flinched as he grabbed her neck but felt no emotions. She had tried. That's all she could ask of herself. Kevin squeezed her throat and turned her to face him.

"Last chance, bitch. I was testing you."

The full force of Kevin's rage exploded as he choked her violently. Annie remembered little after that. At one point she thought she was dead. But that was only a respite. Kevin was preparing to rape her.

The sun was well up when she knew consciousness. She was lying on the kitchen floor. Something was holding her feet down, and she kicked it. Kevin's head bounced off her legs. Annie wondered if he was dead. Hearing him snore, she realized he had finally passed out. The bottle of whiskey lay empty beside him.

Annie Griffin felt void of emotion. She rose slowly and checked for injuries. Hard to say. There was more blood on the kitchen floor, but that could have been from her head wound. Head wounds tended to bleed a lot. Her legs were sore, but they seemed to be supporting her. That was a good thing. She would need to walk out of the apartment. Annie stood and stepped over Kevin. She unlocked the door and hesitated. There was something she was forgetting. Glancing down, she realized she was naked. She should probably get some clothes. Annie again stepped over her husband and walked to the bedroom. Mary was there. Annie had forgotten about Mary, too.

Good thing I need clothes, she thought. Annie dressed herself in a fog. Later she would look at the green sweat pants paired with a silk sweater and wonder who had picked her clothes. Right now she moved like a robot. Simple tasks. She could handle them.

Dressed, she grabbed Mary with her right hand. The left one was giving her trouble. Annie lifted the baby and held her firmly against her chest. Mary was beginning to rouse, but Annie ignored her. These were important tasks that needed to be done, and she could not risk being derailed. If her mind did not concentrate, it would shut down completely. She realized that she was in shock. What a good thing this shock was. It helped you to get important jobs done when you needed to.

Stepping over her husband again, Annie left the apartment. Pausing on the landing, she turned around. She had forgotten something important. Returning, she adjusted the baby's weight and found Kevin's pants. Reaching in, she took his wallet and opened it. There was her money and Buddy's number. She also grabbed the car keys. Annie knew she could not drive now. Later she might want to.

She started down the stairs. No hand on her back this time. Kevin would sleep at least four hours. Annie crossed the yard and knocked on Darlene's door. She waited patiently while the Kemps woke up. Mary was trying to peek out from under the blanket, but Annie would not let her. If she looked at her daughter, she would fall apart. The door finally opened. Annie ignored Darlene's gasp of horror.

"Take the baby, Darlene. Greg needs to take me to the hospital." Darlene stepped back and held the door for Annie, hand still over her mouth. "I know you're leaving this afternoon," Annie continued in a dull voice. "If you can watch her for a couple of hours . . . I think my arm is broken. It won't take them long."

Her last memory was of Mary being lifted gently from her arms. Darlene was crying. Annie remembered that. Greg was white. She remembered that, too.

Chapter Sixteen

Annie lay parked in a hallway, waiting for an X-ray technician. Not a word had passed her lips since she was helped into the Kemps' car. There was nothing to say. The examining doctor ordered pictures of her left arm and her chest, along with her head, neck, and spine. In reply to his queries, Annie shook her head. If she tried to talk, she would lose her mind. By staying silent and concentrating very hard, she was able to stay sane.

"Annie, you're obviously traumatized," the doctor said compassionately. "You don't have to talk until you're ready. I just want to let you know what I'm doing." With that he explained his findings. He told her she was going for X rays and they would talk again. Annie nodded her head and pulled the sheet up closer around her neck. "I'm not giving you anything for pain yet," he continued. "I have to make sure you've had no concussion. Do you understand what I'm saying?"

Looking him directly in the eye, Annie nodded her head. She tried to say something, but her voice was too hoarse. Everything hurt so badly. "Sorry," she managed to mutter. She sounded like a man and looked at him in alarm.

He lay his hand on her leg gently. "Were you

choked, Annie?" After her affirmative nod, he added, "That's why your voice is hoarse. It will come back, but I do need to get some pictures of your neck. Your friend Greg tells me that your husband probably did this. Is that correct?"

Annie lowered her head into the pillow on her lap. He was going to make her crazy. Annie resolved to keep her head in the pillow until he left. The hand patted her leg again. It felt good. Safe and comforting.

"No more talking now," he said placidly. "I just wanted to make sure you were with us mentally. It's common to feel a kind of detachment. It's called shock. Perfectly normal. I just did not want to confuse it for a concussion. I am calling the police, Annie. It's something I have to do with this level of injury. For right now, lie back and let's see what the pictures say. You're going to be fine. I promise."

She lay back on the gurney and stared at the ceiling. The nurses came and wheeled her down the hallway, where she was parked.

The technician disturbed her reverie. After what seemed like a hundred shots, he parked her back in the hallway. Eventually someone pushed her back to the small examining area. Rolling onto her side, Annie wondered what would become of her. Poor little Mary was stuck with the Kemps, who were leaving for Chicago in a couple of hours.

Suddenly there was a timid knock on the door. Annie rolled over painfully but did not respond. Hospital personnel did not knock. Three more timid knocks, and the door opened slowly. Herr Charles poked his head around the door.

"Annie," he said fearfully, "your friend Greg told the nurse that you were in counseling, and they called me. What happened?" Herr Charles's glasses were slipping down his nose, and he nervously pushed them back up. He kept the door open and had one foot in the hallway. Annie felt hatred in the pit of her stomach. An internal prompter told her that Charles was not to blame for this. Kevin was the guilty party. Annie ignored the prompter and found her voice.

"Charles, I think he's communicating better now," she said icily. Her voice was hoarse, startling them both. Annie continued anyway. "I told you, didn't I? I just want you to admit that I told you and you ignored me."

Clutching the door, Charles groped for words. "I'm sorry . . . I had no idea . . . you must know that I would never have—"

"You ignored me, Charles. You were so impressed with Kevin's athletic ability that you ignored me. I have nothing to say to you."

After more apologies, the door closed quietly. *So much for Herr Charles*, Annie thought wickedly. *No more feeling guilty*, she admonished herself. Being nice would get her killed. Thinking about Kevin's Christmas had landed her in the hospital. Annie decided then and there that she would get a divorce. Right here in Texas. According to Caroline, Texas had jurisdiction. Fine. She would finish it here and take her scholarship. He had hit her for the last time.

Annie felt a wave of rage at Charles. He was despicable. And unprofessional. At that moment there was another knock on the door.

"Come in," she commanded hoarsely.

A young police officer opened the door gently and stepped inside. Annie recognized him. He had responded to the call by the neighbors last month. "Hello," he said politely. "I'm here to ask you a few questions. The doctor is concerned that someone did this to you." Annie nodded her head. "My name is Officer Grady. Let's see"—he began looking down at a piece of paper in his hand—"your name is Anne Griffin. Is that correct?"

"Yes," Annie said. This was the most humiliating experience in her life. She wondered how long it would take.

"Your name sounds familiar," he said with a puzzled look on his face. "Have I met you before?"

Annie sighed. "Yes, Officer. You met me last month when my neighbors called you to our house. My husband and I had had a fight." He looked blank. "We live on campus, and my husband is an athlete. His name is Kevin Griffin."

Recognition dawned in the young man's eyes, quickly followed by disbelief. "What happened to you?" he asked in alarm. "I'm sorry I didn't recognize you, but your face . . . You don't look the same," he hastily added. "Let me start again." He smiled, and Annie felt a little less embarrassed. He seemed like a regular guy. Kind of like Danny, who was forever saying stupid things and then regretting them.

"May I call you Anne?" he asked politely.

"Annie. Yes, please."

"I feel pretty sure your husband did this. Is that true?"

Annie kept her face immobile. "What if he had? What would happen?"

"Well," the officer began with an impatient motion of his hand, "a lot of things could happen. He should be locked up, first of all. He apparently tried to kill you, from what I can see," he stated, indicating the brace around Annie's throat.

"Someone choked me until I lost consciousness," she said flatly.

"Okay, Annie. That's what I'm talking about. Whoever did this needs to be arrested and charged. All you need to do is tell me what happened and agree to sign a complaint against him. Nothing would make me happier than to lock up your All-Star husband."

"If it were my husband that did it and I signed this complaint, how long would he stay in jail?"

"Well, that's hard to say. He would have a bond hearing, and the judge would set a bond. Then he would have the opportunity to bail himself out. He would have to have the money, of course." Officer Grady looked uncomfortable. "He would probably be out before his trial."

"He'll kill me if I do."

"We'll give you a restraining order that keeps him away from you," he added quickly. "Then when he comes near you, we can arrest him. You can't let him get away with this, Annie."

"I'm not letting him get away with anything," she said. "He does not ask my permission before he attacks me. Why didn't you arrest him at my house? You guys asked me right in front of him if he had hit me. What was I supposed to say? He told me before I opened the door that night he'd kill me if I told you anything. He will." Annie looked down at her hands as the young man shifted his feet. "You just admitted he'll bond right out. I'm not sure what to do. Somehow I have to file for divorce."

Officer Grady looked up quickly. "That's the spirit!" he exclaimed. "It's hard for us to intervene when couples are living together. I'm going to go over and talk to him right now. See if he admits anything." He noticed the fear in Annie's eyes and made her a promise. "I'll tell him you refused to talk. Don't you have a baby?"

Annie explained that she had left the baby with neighbors who were leaving town. She told him she had to be home before four to get Mary.

"Annie," he said calmly, "I'm no doctor, but I can't see you being released before tomorrow. They have not even set your wrist yet."

"Is it broken?" she asked in surprise.

"According to the doctor, it is. You also are going to need stitches in two spots in your head. Can someone else watch your baby for now?"

"There's no one," she said despondently. "I have no family here."

The officer cleared his throat and made motions to leave. "Let's take it one step at a time. I have to go talk to your husband. What you need to do now is get treated. I'll be back in a couple of hours to talk to you again. Annie, please think about signing a complaint. I think it's the right thing to do." He smiled and left.

Annie lay back again. Her mind was working quickly. Part of her wanted desperately to sign the complaint. The other part of her mind argued it would be too dangerous. *He might kill me anyway*, she thought in despair. Annie closed her eyes in exhaustion. A restraining order was only a piece of paper. She could hardly picture Kevin being deterred by a piece of paper. Still . . . it might help to have some consequences. Annie was still wrestling with her dilemma when she heard yet another knock on the door.

"Come in," she growled in her new voice. As the door opened, Annie heard a low tinkle. "Caroline?"

"It's me," came her voice. A beautifully manicured finger was held up inside the door. "One sec, Annie. I'm talking to the policeman."

Annie felt herself beginning to cry. Just the sound of her counselor's sympathetic voice set her off. If there was one person in the state of Texas who cared about her, it was Caroline. Annie lay back and listened as she spoke to the officer.

"I certainly appreciate that, Officer, but I'm

not clear. Why can't you put him in custody immediately?" Annie could not hear the officer's words, just Caroline's. "Do you usually have a victim's testimony at a murder trial? No. Of course, you don't. The victim here is obviously too injured to deal with these issues." Apparently, the officer agreed to talk to her later. "Thank you, Officer. I'll look forward to that."

Caroline stepped into the room. Looking at Annie, she gasped. "Oh, Annie . . . I'm so sorry. I knew you were in danger."

Annie sat up gingerly and held out her arms. Caroline stepped closer and lightly held her. Annie cried and sputtered gibberish for at least ten minutes before they separated. On observing Caroline's equally weepy state, she began to cry again. How wonderful that someone cared enough to cry for her.

"They want me to sign a complaint, Caroline," Annie said fearfully. "He'll kill me if I do."

"Sweetheart, it looks to me like he's going to kill you anyway. If you sign a complaint, at least you'll have a restraining order and he'll know he'll be arrested. Also, sometimes they'll put him out of the house. Have you thought about that? Where are you going to go if he is still at home?"

Annie frowned. "I guess I just assumed that after this . . . he would leave."

Caroline pulled up the only chair in the spartan cubicle. "Honey, let's talk reality here. I know these guys better than you might think. Right now you're thinking that this thing he did is so bad, he'll have to admit he's a scumbag and give you anything you want. Is that right?" Annie nodded her head wonderingly. Caroline's perception never failed to amaze her.

"I'm here to tell you that it's not going to happen. Any remorse he might feel is going to be thrown in the trash as soon as that nice police officer knocks on his door. These guys are out for number one. Period. I know they talk a good line about worshiping and adoring you, but, ultimately, someone who gives a damn about you does not attempt to prevent you from breathing, which, from the looks of your throat and the neck brace, Kevin did. Are you with me?" Annie nodded, and Caroline took a deep breath.

"If I'm correct, he is right now explaining to Officer Grady that most of your injuries were either self-inflicted, accidental, or the result of his having to restrain you from doing a Highland Fling in the courtyard naked. Get my picture? He's not going to take responsibility for this. True to form, he is going to blame you and your imaginary boy-friends. He may say you're mentally ill. Or a drug addict. Or maybe an alcoholic. Whatever. What he will not say is that he is abusive and has hopes that eventually he will have the opportunity to destroy you. Wake up, Annie. You're lucky to be alive. Where is the baby?"

Annie was reeling. The abrupt change of subject left her confused. "Mary? Uhm, she's at the Kemps', but they're leaving for Chicago. I have to pick her up. What time is it?"

Glancing down at a delicate jeweled wristwatch, Caroline frowned. "It's after twelve. What time are they leaving?"

"Four or five. I'm not sure. Caroline, I have to get the baby. I can't stay here." Annie's voice was beginning to crack. "There's no one to watch her."

"I know." Caroline was pensive. "Let me go talk to the doctor."

Smiling comfortably, she left the room. Moments later she reappeared. "Annie, he says that the soonest you will be released is tomorrow morning. You've got a broken rib, a broken wrist, they're about to come in and stitch your head, and he's worried about internal injuries in your neck and throat. You're not going anywhere, Honey." Annie sighed and lay back down.

Caroline continued, "Would you trust me with Mary? It's completely unprofessional, but I don't see any options. Rules were made to be broken and all of that." Seeing the hopeful expression on Annie's face, she continued cheerfully, "She'll fit right in with my monsters. I have a portable crib . . . you're not nursing or anything . . . that's the solution. I'll take her to my house until tomorrow or whenever you get out. It'll be our little secret." She smiled warmly.

"Caroline, what will your husband say?" Annie spoke hesitantly.

The older woman smiled confidently. "Don't worry about him. He'll ask me first if I'm crazy and second if she's hungry. He's not a problem, Annie."

"What a wonderful marriage you must have," Annie said sadly.

"It is wonderful. And you can have one just as wonderful someday. Marriage is the greatest, Annie. Trust me. All men are not like Kevin."

Annie gave her a wan smile. A thought occurred to her, and she sat up again. "Caroline, when is Christmas?"

"Tomorrow is Christmas eve. Why?"

"You can't have Mary on Christmas Eve. It will ruin your holiday."

Caroline gave a snort of disgust. "Don't be absurd, Annie. I would not have offered if it was a problem. Let's take it one step at a time." She paused momentarily. "When Charles called me, I was sure you were dead. Thank God, you're okay."

"Charles called you? What did he say?" Annie was curious. "How did he know to call you?"

"We work for the same agency, Annie. Remember, I told you? Just different buildings. He knew that I was seeing you initially and that you switched to marriage counseling. He's extremely upset."

"He ought to be, Caroline. Do you know what he said?" Annie felt her face beginning to flush. In her opinion, horsewhipping was too good for Herr Charles.

"I can only imagine," said Caroline with resignation. "Don't be too hard on him, Annie. He feels terrible, and I agree that he should. But like many counselors, he knows nothing about domestic violence. He'll learn now."

Annie lay back to rest. Caroline patted her hand absently and opened a book. She told Annie she would wait for the officer to return so they could develop a safety plan. Annie was humbly grateful for her presence. Caroline made everything seem normal. Annie contemplated that Caroline was like a mother. God must be substituting people for the mother He had taken.

She must have slept, because she awoke to find herself alone. "Caroline," she cried out.

The door opened immediately, and the hand entered. "I'm here, Annie. I'm just talking to Officer Grady."

Annie heard the quiet voices. Caroline sounded tense. Officer Grady sounded apologetic. After a few minutes, they entered.

The young man smiled at Annie briefly and began to speak.

"Well, I spoke with your husband, Annie. He denies assaulting you." He sighed and seemed to measure his next words. "He says you were out drinking and came home like that."

Annie sat bolt upright and then winced at the pain in her back. "That's a lie!" she said with clenched teeth. "I was home all night. Ask the Kemps. He's lying."

Caroline intervened. "We all know that, Annie. We all know Kevin did this to you. Officer Grady is just telling you what Kevin is saying."

Officer Grady smiled gratefully at Caroline and continued. "I was very stern with him, and he's definitely scared. I told him that you were not talking yet, but we hoped you would speak to us soon."

Annie interrupted him. "He's going to come here and try to get me. I'm not safe here."

"No, he is not." The policeman walked to the side of Annie's bed and put his hand over hers. "Annie, if I thought he was going to hurt you again today, I would have arrested him. He's shaken up. He knows he's in big trouble."

Annie stammered for words. "Was he . . . did he ask how I was doing?"

Silence fell, and Annie lowered her head. "You mean to tell me he did not even ask if I was okay?"

"No." The man spoke slowly. "He said he was fed up with your drinking and infidelity. He has the baby and says that you are not welcome to come back."

Turning feebly to Caroline, Annie gasped. Caroline quickly put her arms around her and spoke reassuringly. "This is what they do, Annie. I told you. This is not at all uncommon. He's taking the offensive. Officer Grady understands all this, and he believes you. The problem we have is the baby."

Annie sat back and dried her eyes roughly. "What about the baby? Go get her. He's a monster."

Officer Grady sighed and spoke patiently. "Annie, I don't have the right to take the baby from him. Technically, he is the father and has every right to her, with you in the hospital and all. I respect your feelings on this, but there's nothing we can do unless you sign a complaint. Then we can get a court order."

"Caroline," she asked weakly, "is this true?"

"Hold on, Annie," said Caroline efficiently. Annie knew the look on her face. Caroline was so ladylike that Annie suspected people underestimated her. "It's true that Mr. Griffin has every right to this child. Annie certainly would be the first to agree with that. He has not been accused of molesting or injuring the child in any way." She paused and turned to Annie. "Do you think that Mary is safe with him for the night?"

Annie nodded her head affirmatively. Kevin would not hurt Mary sober. Also, if he was blaming Annie, he was not dangerous. Based on what he had told the police officer, Annie knew that he would be playing the role of father of the year.

Caroline continued. "It's obvious to both of us, Officer Grady, that Annie is the undisputed victim. Do you agree?" He nodded his head vigorously. "Now, Annie has not decided to sign a complaint yet. We need a temporary plan to get us all through the holidays safely. Right?" she queried. He again nodded enthusiastically.

Annie nearly chuckled. Caroline was reeling him in.

"Well, then, what needs to happen is that Kevin has to leave the home tomorrow and give Annie the baby."

He still watched her, but now looked blank.

"Yes," he said thoughtfully, "that's the best solution, all right. But how can we make him do that? I mean, without a court order."

Caroline smiled brightly. "Well, I was thinking that you could go over and persuade him to leave. You know . . . talk him into it. Let him know that after Christmas he can talk to a judge but that usually in these circumstances this is how it's done. Tell him that it's not fair and you think he should talk to an attorney after the holidays, but for now he needs to surrender the baby tomorrow and find another place to stay. What do you think?"

He stared at her intently for a moment and then started to chuckle. "You want me to go over there and bully him. Don't you?"

Caroline smiled serenely. Annie looked hopeful.

"W-e-e-l-l, I sure do see your point. It seems like the fairest solution. We can't have Annie here in a motel, with injuries and all, worried about her baby for Christmas." He paused and glanced at Annie. "Is that what you want, Annie?"

"Yes," she said fervently. "I am going home tomorrow whether they like it or not. And I don't mind him seeing Mary. But I don't have anywhere else to go, and he does. He has a lot of friends here. I just need to figure out a way to pay for an attorney so I can file for divorce."

"I understand," he said gently. "Let me run back over there and see if I can shake him up a little."

Smiling, he picked up his hat from the chair and turned to Caroline. "You missed your calling, ma'am. You should have been a used car salesman."

Caroline smiled sweetly at him. "You're wonderful," she said admiringly. "And I'm not just saying that."

He grinned again and left. Annie turned to Caroline, and they discussed the situation. Shortly the nurse arrived with an ominous tray of instruments.

"Stitches," she said briefly. "You can stay if you want," she said politely to Caroline.

"Thank you . . . no." Caroline looked squeamish. "I need to go make some calls." Turning to Annie, she said, "I'll be back when you're finished. And then I'll stay until our Sir Galahad comes back. We'll have this sorted out in no time."

Annie waved to her and steeled herself for the needle. She had never had stitches.

Fifteen sutures later, the doctor agreed to give Annie a shot for the pain. Annie sent the nurse for Caroline. She needed to take care of business first. When Caroline entered with the long-suffering Officer Grady, she looked ebullient.

"It's all worked out," she said. "Tomorrow you will probably be released by eleven. Kevin has agreed to stay at a friend's, the ones who left town, and he'll turn the baby over to you when you get home." Caroline's face turned serious for a moment. "Officer Grady told him he would need to find a friend to hand Mary off so you don't have to see him." Annie smiled at the officer gratefully, and he looked solemn.

"There's only one stipulation here, Annie," Grady began. "He is determined that he have the baby for Christmas. I did not want to rock the boat, so I agreed. You're not going to be feeling much better anyway. That way you can rest."

Annie nodded wearily. "That's fine. Christmas is nothing to me now." Looking into his compassionate eyes, she asked, "Will he have a friend pick her up and drop her off on Christmas Day?"

"Absolutely! I told him he can have no contact with you at all until we finish investigating the case." Grimly, the young man continued. "Kevin is like a long-tailed cat in a room full of rocking chairs right now. You don't have to worry about him for the next few days. You and I will talk again after the holidays. Get some rest." Nodding briefly to Caroline, he turned to leave. "One more thing," he said at the door. "Annie, you're going to need a new connector cord for your phone. Somehow the last one was broken. Kevin said the baby must have done it. I'd advise you to get that in the morning." With a reassuring wink, he departed. Both women sighed.

"Well," Caroline said briskly, "not perfect, but better than I dared to hope." She moved over to Annie's bedside. "At least Kevin has been temporarily neutralized."

"I hope so," Annie said quietly.

"You need rest. Now. You've dealt with too much in the last twenty-four hours. Anything else you're worried about before I leave?"

Annie frowned in concentration. "I don't think so. I have money to take a cab home in the morning. Where do I get a phone cord?"

Caroline waved her hand. "Oh, I'll pick that up tonight and drop it off to you. Are you sure you don't want to call your family?"

"*No!*" Annie said vehemently. "There is nothing they can do. I don't want my father flying down here on Christmas Eve. It would just make everything more complex." Annie glanced at Caroline pleadingly. "You do understand, don't you?"

"Yes, Annie, I do," was the reply. "You're desperately trying to retain some control. And you're doing fine." Smiling affectionately, Caroline put a hand on her arm. "I'll send the nurse in with the shot."

Annie lay back and listened to Caroline's jewelry as she walked down the hallway. She waited for the nurse. The pain was everywhere. Apparently the shock was wearing off, because her head and wrist were throbbing. It hurt to breathe in. The doctor said that a hairline fracture of one of her ribs was to blame. It would heal on its own. The wrist would be set in the morning, when some of the swelling had gone down. For now it was immobilized. The stitches had been awful, and Annie shuddered, remembering. The nurse came in and administered a shot, which she said was Demerol. Almost immediately, a peaceful warmth spread through Annie's body.

It was not so bad, she mused. Many people got divorced. But Mary would be from a broken home. Annie grimaced at the mental image of a house cracked in two. It was better than being dead. She felt her body slip into an even deeper level of relaxation. What a wonderful shot! If she was honest with herself, she would admit she was relieved. "I'm relieved," she said to herself out loud. "I wonder why?" Just before sleep overtook her, she understood. She was relieved because it was finally over. At last Annie McGowan would be free.

The radio was playing Christmas carols the next evening. Annie sat alone at her kitchen table with the telephone in front of her. She desperately wanted to call home. Mary had been asleep for over an hour. Annie rose finally and pulled the plug on the radio. The mere act of turning the switch was not enough. The joyful melodies forced too stark a contrast to her present mood.

Making her decision, she dialed quickly. She would act normal.

"Hello," came Maureen's breezy voice.

Annie swallowed hard. "Maureen?"

"Who is this? Annie?"

"It's me," she said tearfully. "My voice is messed up. How is everyone?"

"Fine, fine," Maureen said impatiently. "Where have you been? Dad was trying to get you yesterday, and Nellie and I have been calling and calling. What's the matter?"

Annie discarded her resolution and gave in to the tears.

"S-sorry," she stammered. "I'm homesick, I guess."

Maureen's voice hardened. "You tell me exactly what's going on right this minute, Annie. I mean it. We got a letter from Danny that said he thought we should talk to you about coming home. Why did he say that? Is Kevin being mean?"

"Oh, Maureen, I don't know where to start." The tears would not stop now, and Annie talked through them. "The last few days have been awful."

"It sounds like it," Maureen said with uncharacteristic calmness. "Start by telling me where you were yesterday."

"I'll tell you, Maureen, if you promise not to scream and yell. And you have to promise not to tell anyone. Not Dad or Nellie or anyone. Promise?"

Silence echoed over the thousand miles separating them.

"It's bad, isn't it?"

"Yes, it's pretty bad." Annie collected herself. "But I have it mostly worked out. I don't want anyone to know until after Christmas. Do you promise?"

"Annie," Maureen said in a frustrated voice, "I guess I'll have to or you won't tell me. I promise. But if it's bad I'm going to tell them right after Christmas."

"Well, between the two of us we'll have to figure

out how much to tell Dad."

"Stop it, Annie! What's happening down there?"

Annie took a deep breath and began. "Yesterday I was at the hospital. In summary, Maureen, Kevin . . . he came home drunk and kind of attacked me."

"*Kind of?*" Maureen exclaimed. "You had to go to the hospital? What's wrong with you?"

"Are you going to stay calm? Really, Maureen, I can't take it if you get upset. I'm kind of shaky myself right now."

Maureen lowered her voice. "Sorry. What was hurt?"

"Well, I have a broken wrist, a broken rib, and I had fifteen stitches in my head." She ignored the gasp and continued. "They gave me a neck brace because my neck is sprained. Other than that, I'm just bruised."

"Oh, my God!" Maureen was starting to cry. "I'm sorry, Annie." Her voice changed. "Where is the baby? Did he hurt the baby?"

Annie sensed the panic in her sister's voice and rolled her eyes. Just as she had suspected. She would now have to comfort Maureen. "Maureen, the baby is fine. And I'm fine, too. Just sore. And I wish it wasn't Christmas, and I wish I was home." With that, she started to cry again.

Maureen shelved her own emotions. "Annie," she said calmly, "do you want to come home tomorrow?"

"I can't." Annie sniffled. "I look terrible. Dad

would have a fit if he saw me like this. I have to take care of things here, and I don't want to waste the money."

"Give me a break, Annie," Maureen said impatiently. "We'll prepay the ticket at this end."

"Who is going to pay it?"

"Dad, of course. He's loaded, Annie. He just acts poor." Both girls laughed. "I want to kill Kevin. He's such an asshole."

"Oh, God, don't start. Not now. I agree, but if I get started on that I might never stop. I knew he was getting weird, and I was going to leave. Danny left me money . . . I just kind of never actually did it. I should have, I know."

"Well, for God's sake, don't blame yourself. It's a wonder you're speaking at all." Maureen sounded perplexed. "Why did he do it?"

"He thought I was having a fling with the stockboy at work."

"Are you?" she asked incredulously.

"Don't be a jerk, Maureen. Of course not."

"Sorry." Her sister was immediately contrite. "It's just that I don't get it. Why does he always think you're going to have an affair? You're not even a flirt. He would have killed me a long time ago."

"He's a lunatic," Annie said wearily. She was too tired to get into it.

"I told you, Annie," Maureen said stoutly. "Remember I told you he was a Psycho Boy years ago? Tell me what to do."

They talked for another hour. Annie explained

her game plan, and Maureen argued. She wanted Annie to pack up and come home immediately. Right after she signed a complaint. Annie explained that she would have to clear things up first. Officer Grady agreed with Caroline that if Annie took Mary out of state without a court order, it could blow up in her face. Kevin could file in her absence and get custody. At best it would be a few weeks before she could leave. Maureen was all for telling their father immediately, but Annie was loath to spoil his holiday. There was nothing he could do, and Annie was not sure she would tell him at all. Annie felt that Nellie, too, was prone to overreaction but in a more dangerous way. Nellie would promise anything to get the information and then immediately call the Griffins and anyone else she considered at fault.

After agreeing to speak to the rest of the family the next morning, Annie hung up. She felt better. It was comforting that someone in her family knew what was happening. She glanced at the clock. It was only nine, but she was exhausted. She wished she could go to bed but felt sure she would lie awake all night. She had slept well in the hospital. Promptly at eleven this morning, Officer Grady had arrived. He said he was driving by and wondered if she needed a ride. Tears welled up in Annie's eyes at this thoughtfulness. She had thanked him and accepted. The officer waited with her until Kevin's teammate ran across the courtyard with the baby. His presence was sending a message, Grady said.

For the tenth time, Annie checked the doors. They were all locked and chained. She had soup cans stacked against both entries. At least if he broke through, she would have some warning.

In spite of her precautions, she was not overly concerned. Kevin was playing a role now. He would not take any chance at being branded a criminal. Image was important to him. For all he knew, he could be charged with a felony at any time. No. He would not dare approach her until he felt safe.

Annie arranged Mary's presents in the living room. There was no tree. Luckily, Mary was too young to notice. The other presents were shoved into the linen closet. Kevin had cleaned up. Checking his drawer, she noticed he had taken his clothes.

With a deep sigh, she went into the kitchen and found the bottle of painkillers. She filled a glass with water and tried to open the container. It was childproof. "Annie-proof," she noted aloud. Try as she might, she could not get the top to release. The arrows were lined up properly, but still it stuck. Annie felt tears of frustration in her eyes and swore out loud. She leaned against the counter and took a break. After several deep breaths she tried again. Still no progress. Muttering severely, she opened the junk drawer and pulled out Kevin's new hammer. "Perfect for throwing at bastards," she said out loud. A flood of memories overcame her, and she viciously smashed the pill vial. It shattered. Pieces of plastic and pills shot off in every direction.

Crouching down, she began to pick up the debris. She speculated fearfully that even one of the pills might kill a baby. Quickly, she tried to sweep the mess into a pile. Crouching low, she looked under the refrigerator. Sure enough, there was a tablet. Stretching her hand out did not work. She could not get to it. Annie collapsed onto the floor. Her whole body was sore, and she had reawakened the pain in her rib by straining.

She gave in to the sobs and slowly pulled herself into a sitting position against the stove. Hugging her legs, she lowered her head onto her knees and cried loudly. "I hate him," she repeated over and over again. When the worst had passed, she looked around her angrily. Reaching up, she felt for the hammer on the counter. Wincing with pain, she grasped it and hurled it with all her might. It made a satisfactory bang on impact. It also made a sizable dent in the cabinet. *Ha!* she thought. *Keep the security deposit.* Remembering one of her conversations with Caroline, she tried to decide if she was redirecting or misdirecting her anger. The cabinet was really innocent. Yes, she thought, it's also inanimate and therefore an appropriate target for redirection of anger. Now, if she had thrown the hammer at the doctor, that would be displaced or misdirected hostility. Whatever. Inappropriate. That's what Kevin was, she decided. Inappropriately hostile. A nice clinical term. She would put that on the divorce petition. Her grounds would be inappropriate hostility on the part of the husband toward the wife.

She sighed and looked around her. "Merry Christmas, Annie," she said sarcastically. That made her laugh out loud. "I'm having a Christmas Pity Party." Annie decided she was too tired to attend her own pity party. She got a knife out of the drawer without getting up. She quickly swiped it under the refrigerator and recovered the tablet. Rising carefully, she grabbed the broom and swept up the mess. She looked around and remembered sadly how much she had loved her little kitchen. Now she thought, *This is where he choked me*, or, *He hit me over there*. She swallowed the prescribed tablets, turned off the light, and went to bed. Certain of insomnia, she reached under the mattress for her flashlight so she could read. She lay back to rest for a moment and almost immediately fell into a deep, dreamless sleep.

Chapter Seventeen

Sunlight streamed through the bedroom window on Christmas morning. Annie opened her eyes and looked to Mary's crib. Mary, too, had just opened her eyes, and gave her mom a sleepy baby smile. Annie smiled back. She wondered if there was ever a thing so precious as the morning smile of a sleepy child. They were alone in the apartment. There was no Kevin giving her a stomachache. Just clear morning light and an innocent baby.

"Merry Christmas, little Mary," Annie said.

Mary pulled her covers over her head playfully. She peek-a-booed Annie and laughed in delight when Annie put her head right next to the bars to startle her.

"Let's go see what Santa brought you," Annie said, reaching into the crib. Carrying her daughter into the living room, she marveled that life could be so pleasant. Caroline had told her about this. She said it was not difficult to raise a child alone after an abusive relationship. Problems seemed minimal when the constant stress and fear were eliminated. Annie felt something like relief wash over her. Right now all she had to worry about was having fun with her little girl.

Mary rapidly tore paper from the gifts. Once

the actual gift was uncovered, the child lost interest and reached impatiently for the next. Annie told her she was missing the point. Mary was unconcerned.

"Good thing I did not spend a lot of money on you, Miss Paper Puller," she said with mock severity. "I could have wrapped up the silverware."

Annie left Mary playing in the debris and made breakfast. In minutes, Mary came toddling in to check the progress. Annie hoisted her into the high chair with her good arm. The cast seemed as if it weighed a hundred pounds, but the doctor said in a few days she would not know she was wearing it. So much the better. Kevin was sending his emissary for Mary at ten. If Annie thought about it, she would get depressed. Caroline had informed her that her moods would fluctuate wildly. Annie had been advised to exult in the positive and wait out the negative. Wise advice, and Annie resolved to follow it strictly. It was time for exulting.

"Do you want to sing Christmas carols, Mary?" she asked.

Mary gave her a polite wave and continued to eat the oatmeal and pears that Annie fed her.

"We'd better not," Annie mused. "That would be pushing it."

Mary nodded sagely.

Annie continued. "This Christmas is a blow off, Mary. Let's talk about what we want to do with Christmas Future. Usually we'll have a big tree. It'll have lights and ornaments and tinsel." Mary smiled agreeably.

"At night before you go to bed, we'll read our story in the front room with only the Christmas lights on, and everything will seem so cozy. You'll love it.

"We might go live in the mountains somewhere. I wonder where there are some mountains," Annie mused. "We simply cannot celebrate Christmas without snow. Right?"

Mary shook her head vigorously. "You're the smartest baby I ever met. You won't mind growing up without Daddy. You can still see him, and—honestly, Honey—he's kind of a nut."

Mary looked very solemn.

"Sorry, I know he's your dad, and I do like him. It's just that he wants to kill me. You know?" Mary burst into unexpected peals of laughter. Annie joined in.

"Wacky, isn't it? Who would want to kill a nice girl like me?

"Do you want to wear a frilly Christmas dress today? Your sinister granny sent it. She hates me, too. Good thing you like me." Mary largely ignored her and concentrated on her breakfast. "I'll put your pretty dress on and send a comfortable outfit. Mary, please understand that the only reason I'm sending you with him is to keep peace. I'm pretending it's not Christmas, and I want you to do the same. Next Christmas will be better." Mary hurled her spoon at the wall.

"I take it you're finished, Princess." Annie gingerly removed her from the high chair and took her right to the sink. She prepared the bath, and awkwardly stripped the child. Her neck was hurting, and she knew she should be wearing the brace. She promised herself she'd put it on as soon as Mary left.

After rinsing the baby, she set her down to run naked. It was Mary's favorite pastime. Annie collected the elements of Mary's Christmas apparel while listening to the wild ripping of paper.

After handing Mary off with a loaded diaper bag, Annie sat back to take stock. Were movies playing on Christmas? She'd need a long, preferably tragic, film. That would require a trip to the store for the paper. That would require getting dressed. Annie pondered. Maybe all this activity should be preceded by a little rest. Her rib was painful, and her neck felt terrible. Annie put the brace on and took a pain pill. Grabbing her latest book, she propped herself up in bed. She reminded herself that she had often longed for this type of solitude. Luckily, the book was a Gothic mystery. Annie read with relish an account of the heroine's rapidly deteriorating plight. Someone was trying to kill her, too. Annie speculated that she was more fortunate than this poor girl. Annie at least knew who the enemy was.

She must have dozed, because she opened her eyes with a start. The light had a late feel, and Annie went in to check the clock. It was nearly three o'clock. Perfect. She had killed three hours or so. She dressed as rapidly as her injuries would allow. Annie noticed more bruises coming out but ignored them. For some reason she did not want to see the marks. She looked in the mirror only briefly to ensure that her hair was properly fixed. A small section had been shaved, and Annie had a hard time covering the bald spot.

An hour later she was comfortably ensconced in a dark theater with two other unfortunates. A haggard-looking theater attendant sold the tickets, took the tickets, and distributed popcorn to his three holiday guests. The movie was long, tragic, and pretty much uneventful. Annie thought she was bored but regretted the closing credits. Walking out, she checked the time. Christmas was almost over, thank God.

Driving home, she thought about last Christmas. She had been told to concentrate on positive thoughts. *It could be worse*, she thought. *I could be stuck back in last year and have to live this year all over again.* She shuddered. That was kind of a positive thought, and she commended herself. She decided that everyone should spend one Christmas alone. It was good for the soul. Never again would Christmas seem as important. It was only another day. Lots of people were alone on Christmas. At least four that she knew of in this town. The poor old man in the movie had blown his nose throughout the whole film. Annie thought sadly that he needed to beef up his denial reserve. It was working great for her.

Realizing she was ravenous, she looked for an open restaurant. No luck. Even the convenience stores were now closed. Annie thought mournfully that she would have to find something at home. That would be challenging since she had not been shopping in days. She sighed. Depressed people should never allow themselves to get hungry, she thought. It made everything seem worse. Coping mechanisms melted in the face of hunger. She would go home and call Chicago.

As she walked up the stairs to her apartment, Annie noticed a package outside her door. *It's probably a bomb from Kevin*, she thought, only half jokingly. No. There was a letter taped to the top. Annie opened the letter and read, "Merry Christmas from Ted and Cindy Grady." The policeman? He was the only Grady she knew. Annie opened the door and put the bag down on the table. Tears were starting, and she felt her denial dissipating. Inside the large bag was a plate piled with turkey, potatoes, and everything else. Another wrapped plate held three desserts. Annie opened the wrapping of what appeared to be a present. Inside was an expensive bottle of bubble bath with matching lotion. Annie sat down at the table and cried for their goodness. Someone close by wished her well, and it tore the veil off her terrible loneliness. The policeman, a total stranger to her, had gone home and told his wife.

What a truly wonderful woman she must be, Annie thought tearfully. She's never even met me. Something about the present touched her as well.

The whole thing was unnecessary, but even if she had felt compelled to make a gesture, Mrs. Grady did not have to send such an expensive item. Then in a flash Annie knew that Cindy Grady had wrapped one of her own gifts. The thought made her cry harder. How good people were, she thought. Someday, she promised herself tearfully, someday she would return their kindness.

After eating the delicious dinner, Annie took a beautiful bubble bath with her exquisite gift. She used it sparingly and vowed to say a prayer for Cindy Grady every time she looked at the bottles. After a tearful soak, Annie felt peaceful and relaxed. Strong enough to call home.

Annie dialed the phone and in seconds heard Mr. McGowan's gruff voice. "Hello," he said imperiously. Annie laughed out loud. He always answered as though the caller was terribly invasive even dialing his number.

"Merry Christmas, Dad," she said brightly.

"Annie, is that you? Merry Christmas!" He sounded cheerful. "How's my little Mary?"

"She's fine, Dad," Annie said truthfully. "How is everyone there?"

"Fine. We're all fine. What are you doing tomorrow, Annie?"

"Nothing. Why?"

"Can you pick me up at the airport at eleven forty-five?" Annie's mouth dropped open. She remained silent. "If not, I can easily get a cab. Do they have taxis there?"

"Uh, yes . . . taxis? Uh, yes, I suppose they do." Annie caught her breath. "Did you talk to Maureen, Dad?"

"Maureen should be horsewhipped for not telling me you were in trouble before this. Don't be mad at her—she started crying at the dinner table, and Nellie got it out of her. Would you rather I drove down with a trailer to bring your things home?"

Annie clutched the table and searched for the right words. Her father was calm and logical. It was clear in his mind, Annie knew. If one of his children got into trouble, that child needed to come home. He could not begin to understand the complexity.

Misreading her silence, he continued. "Don't tell me you're thinking of staying with that ape. I spoke to Father Tom."

Annie cringed. Father Tom was their uncle and a priest.

"He said these things happen. You can get an annulment. Now, the Holy Father doesn't like these annulments, so we'll need to work fast, while we can still get one in this country. It can all be worked out."

Finding her voice, Annie suppressed hysterical giggling. She pictured herself being marched first to confession, that was a given, just on the off chance she was in any way responsible, and then straight to the Tribunal, where Mr. McGowan would demand immediate satisfaction.

"Dad," she said hesitantly, "it's not that simple."

"What are you talking about? Maureen said he hurt your neck."

"Well," she began patiently, "Texas has jurisdiction over the marriage. I'll need to get divorced here first."

"Nonsense," he replied quickly. "I'll put a call in to Harry. He'll sort it out."

Annie cringed again. Harry was Mr. McGowan's attorney and dear friend.

She realized what she was up against and spoke firmly. "Dad, you cannot come here tomorrow. It's just not a good time. Really. There is nothing you can do, and I'm just fine. You cannot come."

She heard a deep sigh. "Annie, what can I do? Now, I made a reservation, and it's all set—"

"Dad," she interrupted him. "Send Maureen. Could you send Maureen?"

He paused. "I could . . . sure . . . I can, but don't you want me?"

Annie rolled her eyes. *Give me the words*, she prayed. "Of course I do, Dad, but not right now," she implored. "It would be great to have Maureen, though. Would that be okay?"

"Yes," he responded firmly. "If you want goofy Maureen, then you shall have her. Tomorrow at eleven forty-five. Is there anything else I can do? Do you want some money?"

"Not yet, Dad," she replied in blissful relief. "I'll see how much an attorney will cost and let you know. Okay?"

"Okay, Sweetheart. Merry Christmas. Here's Maureen now."

Maureen came on the line sounding tense. "Are you furious?"

Annie laughed out loud. "Maureen, I could kill you. Is he really upset?"

"He was like a raging bull, but he calmed down after he talked to Father Tom. Now he's busy making plans. Father Tom told him to bring you right home and end the whole thing quickly."

"Did he really tell him that?"

Maureen lowered her voice. "Yes, Annie. He also said that once a husband was violent, they were violent again. He told Dad to get you a lawyer and get you 'the hell out of it.'"

"He's probably right. What's Nellie's take on the whole thing?"

"I'll let her tell you herself. She's pulling the phone away . . . Annie, I'll see you tomorrow. I'll have to tell work it's a family emergency. I have to go to Texas and find my sister a new husband."

Annie laughed again and listened to the scuffle at the other end.

"Annie?" came Nellie's authoritative voice. "I told you he was a pig. Thank God, you're getting out now. You can be in school here in three weeks, and Mrs. Nolan will mind the baby."

"Nellie," Annie beseeched, "don't tell anyone yet. I don't know what I'm going to do, but I'm pretty sure I'll stay here for at least this semester. I have the scholarship."

"Why, that's nonsense. Dad will pay your tuition here, and you can live at home. I always knew it wasn't safe to send you so far off."

"Nellie"—Annie again searched for words—"he's not all bad. He's a good father, you know."

"Don't defend Kevin Griffin to me," her oldest sister said stoutly. "I only hope those barbarians in Texas have the sense to lock him up."

Annie basked in the family support. Nellie said that if Annie did choose to stay, as unwise as Nellie thought that was, then she, Nellie, would come down right after Maureen. She felt sure Kevin would respond to her threats. Annie chuckled and promised to talk about it later. Mr. McGowan signed off with the command that Annie tell Kevin not to bother her. Annie giggled. "I will, Dad."

The doorbell rang, and Annie said quick good-byes. Mary was home, sleepy and soggy. Annie changed her with a light heart. She kept chuckling as bits of the conversation floated through her memory. Mary fell asleep promptly, and Annie lay in bed with a book. The soup cans were back in place, and she felt lonely and scared. Suddenly, she remembered. In a little more than twelve hours, Maureen would be here. The thought made her laugh out loud, and she fell asleep happy.

On Monday morning Annie cleaned the apartment as quickly as her injuries allowed. Despite the recent tragedy, Annie was a woman preparing her home for a visit from her sister. By ten thirty she looked around in satisfaction. If she moved fast, she could run through the grocery store on the way to the airport.

She was just grabbing her purse when the phone rang. Annie answered it quickly. A male voice with a deep Texas drawl introduced himself. "This is Judge Dan Wilkes, from down at the county courthouse. I'm sitting here with Ted Grady."

Annie's stomach tightened. "Yes?"

"Well, I'll get right to the point, Mrs. Griffin. Ted is darn worried about you. He seems to think we need to look real close at what your husband might get up to in the future. Now, ma'am, I'll be honest with you. I don't like to interfere in families. And I don't like wasting anyone's time. Mostly in these types of cases, the woman says she wants to sign complaints and then drops the charges. Wastes everyone's time. See what I mean?"

Annie was not certain if she was being supported or reprimanded. "Yes, I can see where that would be . . . um, a problem."

"Good. Now, I looked over the report and I'll tell you frankly, I don't like the sound of these injuries. Seems to me that Kester needs to be smartened up. These athletes think they can do anything they want. You come on down here and sign these complaints. I think Kester needs to be talking with a man instead of picking on a little lady. See what I mean?"

"Yes." Annie thought frantically. "I'm very grateful, sir, both to you and to Officer Grady. The only problem is . . . you see . . . my husband tends to get angry. If I did sign complaints against him, I'm afraid he would hurt me."

The older man's voice became impatient. "Well, that's the whole damn reason I'm doing this. Grady here thinks he's dangerous. He says you're a nice lady. A smart lady. Ma'am, let me explain this a different way. If you don't sign complaints, and he keeps bothering you, maybe even hurts you, there's not a damned thing I can do about it. If he comes and takes your little one tonight . . . well . . . let's just say he has that legal right. If you get down here and sign these complaints, I'll personally issue a restraining order. I will also personally explain to him how we treat ladies in West Texas. The order will give you the home for now, if that's what you want, and talk about how we need Sport to behave in the future. Annie, are you listening?"

"Yes, I am, very carefully."

"Good. Ma'am, there is nothing we can do unless you sign this. Then the next time he bothers you, Grady here can scoop him right up. He needs to be taught a lesson. Don't worry about him coming after you. I'll scare the pants right off him. Okay?"

"Okay," she said shortly. What else could she say? He made sense. Annie thought briefly of Caroline. This would make her day.

"Now," said the judge with satisfaction, "I told Grady you'd understand a little horse sense. You come on down here this morning."

"Well, I can't come right now, Judge. I have to

pick up my sister at the airport at noon."

"Her sister is coming in today, Grady," she heard him say. "That's just fine. Grady was real worried with you being all alone and all. Come on down with your sister then, say about one?"

"That would be fine, Judge."

She hung up and put her purse back on the table. She had not realized she was still clutching it. Her hands were shaking. Kevin would kill her. It would have to be a mighty big scare to calm him down, she thought, unconsciously lapsing into the judge's dialect. One thing he said had turned her around. The threat of Kevin's trying to take Mary was valid. Annie knew that Kevin would try whatever would hurt her most. Mary was the next logical target. She thought of Kevin in jail and winced. He would never forgive her, and he would blame her all the way down the line. So what? Annie thought rebelliously. He had nearly killed her. She glanced down at Mary, who was trying to remove her little shoes. There were no options. Annie took a deep breath and reached down to grab Mary with her good hand. She would see what Maureen had to say.

"I don't see where the decision is, Annie," Maureen said easily. The girls drove down the highway from the small airport. "Have you ever asked Kevin not to beat you up?"

"Of course," she answered.

"Well, I guess he's not listening, then. This judge makes sense. Kevin's not going to lie down for this.

Think about it, Annie. There's a pattern here. Kevin always acts really nice after he's been nasty. You might get suckered in again. This way, there's not much chance of him talking you out of a divorce. If your luck holds, he won't be talking to you at all." Maureen paused. "Do you want to get divorced?"

Annie paused. "Maureen, I would love so much to be free of this whole thing. It's a nightmare. Yes, I do want to get out."

"There's your answer, Annie. You sign complaints, and I think you'll get the divorce."

"That's true," Annie responded thoughtfully. "If I sign, we won't reconcile. He'd never forgive me. I'm going to do it. Kevin never listened to me in his life. If I thought he'd leave me alone, I would not do this, Maureen."

"I know, Annie, I know," Maureen confirmed. "He took away your choices. Think of it that way. Kevin tied your hands."

That was a good way to look at it, Annie pondered. He had tied her hands by his last assault. Also, his version to Officer Grady had been absurd, slanderous, and very telling. Kevin was not remorseful. He was dead set on avoiding consequences. She set her jaw and drove with purpose now. It was the only thing to do.

"Annie, this child is so smart looking. And beautiful," Maureen said, reverting to gushing over her niece. "Why is she stuck in that awkward seat?"

Mary was sitting in an infant seat that was secured in the back by the seat belt. "I don't have a proper car seat. I have to get one."

"Well, we'll stop and buy one today," said the doting aunt in baby talk. "Is that what you want, Mary? A fancy new car seat? We'll go shopping right after Mommy signs your daddy's arrest warrant. Then we'll all feel like celebrating. Won't we, Pretty Girl?"

"Maureen," Annie scolded. "That's not funny."

"She's smiling, Annie," Maureen continued. "Mary thinks it's funny. She's such a smart little girl! Aren't you, Mary?"

Annie glanced in the rearview mirror. Mary was indeed lapping it up. "You're speaking her language, Maureen. She loves to be admired."

It was wonderful to have someone around who adored her little one, and Annie could not help smiling.

They arrived at the courthouse promptly at one. Maureen stayed outside with Mary while Annie went in. The judge was waiting for her and said that Officer Grady had promised to stop back by if he could. It was all very quick. Annie raised her right hand and swore to tell the truth right there in the judge's chambers. He had already prepared the order. Kester (Kevin, she had been forced to correct him, much to her mortification) was ordered to stay away from the apartment and Annie. The petitioner, that was Annie, was awarded temporary custody of their daughter, and Kevin could not harass her in any way.

Sitting back in the plush leather chair, Annie

glanced up at the judge after reading the order through. He was in his fifties, she guessed. Gray-haired, he looked very stern. Annie smiled tentatively at him, and his whole face suddenly wrinkled. His eyes nearly disappeared, and Annie thought him the most handsome man she had ever met.

"You're a nice lady, Mrs. Griffin," he said kindly. "There are plenty of good men out there who would be lucky to call you their wife. Remember that. A leopard does not change its spots, and I don't think any man who is capable of treating his wife like Kevin treated you is worth having."

"Thank you, Judge." Annie struggled with her emotions. She was very raw these days. The slightest kindness set off an emotional firestorm. Collecting herself, she asked, "What if he wants visitation?"

The judge leaned back in his chair and considered. "Well, I'm not inclined to grant him visitation just yet. We'll see how he behaves at the bond hearing." He watched Annie closely and said, "I'm going to issue a warrant, you know. That way we can serve this order on him in person. I'll tell him if he behaves like a gentleman for a couple of months, we'll consider visitation. How does that sound?"

"Yes, okay, I guess that's fine." Kevin was going to be arrested. Annie was at a loss and turned in relief when Officer Grady walked in.

"Hi, Ted," the judge said congenially. "Mrs. Griffin is all ready to go. We didn't need you at all."

They all smiled, and Annie rose to leave.

"Thank you, Judge," she said humbly.

"Thank Ted here, ma'am. He bothered me until I called you. Now, you leave this business to us and have a nice visit with your sister."

Annie smiled and backed out. Ted Grady gave her a warm and reassuring wink. "I'll follow you out, Annie."

Annie walked quickly down the cavernous, cool hallway of the County Building. She stepped with relief into the bright light. Maureen was chasing an ecstatic Mary around the lawn of the building.

"Maureen," she whispered as she approached them, "get off the grass. I'm sure you're not supposed to be on the grass."

Maureen looked unabashed. Annie thought wistfully how relaxed and pretty Maureen looked. "Oh, who cares, Annie. She loves it." Mary took off in a determined toddler trot, and Maureen took off after her. Glancing around, Annie saw Officer Grady approaching her.

"Thank you so much for the Christmas dinner, Officer," she said.

He waved his hand in dismissal. "Glad you enjoyed it. You're doing the right thing, Annie. I know it's probably not easy for you. Is that your sister?" Annie followed his gaze to Maureen, who was coming back with Mary on her shoulders.

"Yes," Annie said, smiling. "She just got here." As Maureen drew closer, Annie made the introductions. Maureen was charming and in seconds had the officer smiling and chuckling. He walked them over to the car and promised to contact Annie when Kevin was arrested and served.

The girls got into the car. Maureen waved again at Officer Grady and turned to Annie. "He's gorgeous," she said in raptures. "I love how he talks. Did you hear him say 'Y'all'? He's like something out of a western movie. Annie, do you have an impossible crush on him?"

Annie laughed out loud in spite of herself. "He's very married. In fact, his wife sent me Christmas dinner and a present." She paused. "But yes, isn't he handsome?"

"They sent you dinner and a present?" Maureen was wide-eyed. "Oh, Annie, I could cry. That was so nice. Was this the absolute, most horrible Christmas you ever had?" Without waiting for an answer, she continued. "If it's any consolation, we were all miserable, too. I mean, the thought of you here by yourself, and I didn't even tell them all that he did. . . . Annie, I can't believe how you look. I mean, I didn't say anything at the airport because I don't want to upset you. But honestly! Do you want my honest opinion?"

Annie looked at her sister ruefully. "I'm sure it's coming."

"I think he's nuts. I mean certifiable. He nearly killed you. I have a week to work on you, but I might as well start now. You should come home. I'm afraid of what he might do."

Annie rolled down her window and let the cool air blow through her hair. "We have all week, Maureen. Let's go to lunch. Are you hungry?"

Maureen smiled and took the message. "Starved. Dad gave me loads of money so let's go get something expensive. He figured we'd need a good few bucks to sort out your Disastrous Marriage." The girls laughed uproariously. It did not take much. With high spirits they set out to spend some of their father's money.

Within the hour they were seated at a trendy restaurant on the outskirts of the city. Mary was perched in a high chair with Maureen's purse in front of her. Sifting through the contents would keep the child happy until the food arrived. Maureen stared in amazement at the quart glass of iced tea that was placed in front of her.

"Do they really expect me to drink all of this?"

"All that and more," Annie said brightly. "They'll be around with the pitcher to refill it within minutes. People here consume quantities of this stuff."

"Why are they all so slow, then?" Maureen asked with a glint in her eye. "If I drink half of this, I'll be flying out of my pants from the caffeine. You'd think they'd be moving a little faster."

Annie laughed appreciatively. Maureen had such a fresh outlook on Texas life. "Just think what they'd be like without it."

"True." She grinned. "Do any of them drink pop?"

"They call it soda, and yes, but not as much as tea. Tell me what's new at home," Annie said. "Is Dad dating anyone?"

Maureen would not be sidestepped. "First we

have to talk about you. I was sent here for a reason. My mission: Bring you and the baby home. I have seven days to complete this mission, along with about five hundred dollars. I am to use any tactics and accept no resistance. Dad says never mind the divorce. You can get it in Illinois, but you'll have to wait a while. You can come home now and start school locally. He said to tell you the first two years don't mean much anyway. It's where you graduate from that counts. What do you think? It would be nice if you agreed now and let me relax for the rest of the week."

Annie chuckled with her but shook her head. "Maureen, if I go home, none of this will be resolved. He'll eventually follow me and make my life hell. Can you see Dad dealing with this?" She indicated the neck brace. "He's too old for this kind of stress. I have a shot here. I have a life. Now I've got the car, the scholarship, and the college nursery for Mary. I might need a job or someone to watch her while I work. I don't know. I haven't gotten that far. But I do know this." She lowered her voice. "Kevin is out of control. Can you imagine him coming to Dad's house? He might kill him or something. He's way out there, Maureen, and he doesn't think he's doing anything wrong. He thinks I deserve it. Imagine what I'll deserve for getting him arrested?"

Her brow creased in concentration, Maureen replied thoughtfully, "I disagree with one point. Kevin knows what he's doing is wrong or he would not be denying it. He's not bothering you now.

Right? That's because he knows he's in trouble. As long as you have this criminal charge pending, he'll stay away. Also, why would he tell the cop that you're a slut who drinks too much? To make himself look good. He's like a dog covering his misdeed." Annie wrinkled her face distastefully. "That shows that he knows he's guilty. What a psycho, Annie! Was he like this every day?"

Annie told her everything. Maureen was a sympathetic listener, and two hours flew by. Finally, Mary would not be pacified any longer. The girls paid the bill and departed. A ringing telephone greeted them at the apartment. It was Nellie, calling to inform them that Kevin was back in Chicago.

Chapter Eighteen

Annie clutched the phone. "What do you mean he's in Chicago?"

Nellie was succinct. "Apparently, he can no longer tolerate your roving eye. According to his evil mother, he's beside himself. You are stressing him out, and he needs a separation. He feels just sick about leaving Mary, but you pushed him beyond endurance." Nellie took a breath, then continued. "She called here to say that maybe Dad could talk some sense into you."

"Bastard!" Annie swore vehemently. "He's such a liar, Nellie."

Maureen was taking the baby's jacket off. "What? Why is he a liar?"

Annie ignored Maureen and demanded clarification. "First of all, Nellie, what is he doing in Chicago?"

Nellie's voice was dripping with ridicule. "His mother was beside herself when she heard about the separation. They're all pretty much beside themselves over there. She thought it would do Kevin good to get home and take stock."

"Did Dad—"

Nellie cut her off. "Of course not, Annie. I told her truthfully that Dad was also beside himself and that he had no desire to talk about any of this until your injuries healed."

"You didn't," Annie gasped.

"Yes, I did." Nellie was furious. "I didn't sugar-coat anything. I told her that her mind was remarkably uncluttered by facts. Apparently, Kevin left out the parts about the pending criminal charges and the hospital. She knows now. She said that in the circumstances Kevin could be forgiven for getting a little irate."

"Oh, dear God," Annie said weakly. "Do you see what I mean, Nellie? He's vicious. He'll slander me all over the city."

Maureen demanded answers. "He's slandering you all over Chicago? Damn! I'm in the wrong city. What did the mother-in-law tell Dad?"

Annie told Nellie to hold on and briefly brought Maureen up-to-date. Maureen's opinion was simple. "So what? Tell Nellie to calm down." Annie stared at her without comprehension. "Annie, let them say what they want. This is war. The truth is, Kevin is going to meet a couple of sheriffs when he does get back. Let the mother explain that away. Let it go, Annie. You don't have to convince anyone you're doing the right thing."

Nellie heard Maureen's advice. She, too, calmed down. "She's right, Annie. We're overreacting. Let the Griffins do what they want with Kevin. The real issue is getting you home alive."

"Okay, Nell," Annie said sadly. "I guess you're right. What about Dad?"

Nellie snorted in disgust. "I can handle things at this end. Mrs. Griffin will have to go through me to get to Dad, and that's not going to happen. Annie, what did Maureen mean about sheriffs?"

Annie handed the phone to Maureen. Too exhausted for additional explanations, she took Mary in for her nap. After a quick diaper change, she put Mary in her crib and lay down on the bed. Her mind was reeling. How terrible that she and Kevin were reduced to this. She heard Maureen laughing in the dining room and smiled. She decided not to cry. It would wear her out. She would see Caroline tomorrow and make sense of it all.

The next day Annie did have a good cry. Sitting in Caroline's office, she held a piece of paper in her hand. On it was written a name in flowery handwriting.

"She's a good lawyer and a dear friend," Caroline explained. "She'll take your case for free. She calls it pro bono. You have to see her tomorrow in her office, and she'll draw up the papers. There's a filing fee, but she thinks she can get it waived. What do you think?"

Annie was weepy. "I don't know. I'm incredibly grateful." She frowned in tearful concentration. "My dad could give me some money, Caroline, and I have some put aside."

Caroline waved a graceful hand. "Keep it. You're going to need every penny. She *wants* to do this, Annie. She does one case for free each year.

When I told her about you, she jumped right at it. She also defends battered women."

"Why would they need defending?" Annie asked perplexed.

"Well, Honey," Caroline explained, "it's not uncommon for a battered woman to defend herself and end up killing him. Many times she feels that the only way out is to kill him while he is sleeping. Or else she's protecting her children. It happens. Then she's charged with murder or attempted murder. I could tell you stories . . . but let's concentrate on you. Are you feeling ambivalent about getting a divorce?"

"Yes," Annie said, no longer surprised that Caroline could read her mind. "Isn't that bizarre?"

"Not at all. What specifically is bothering you?"

"It's going to sound strange. On the one hand, I often thought about Kevin dying. It seemed like that would be the only escape. In some ways it still does. I would lie in bed and imagine he had a car accident. Or a heart attack. And then I would feel so guilty. How horrible that a woman would actually want her husband to die. I also thought about killing him. Caroline, I didn't tell you everything that happened that night. There was something else that he did."

Caroline's pained expression suggested to Annie that she had an idea. "Do you want to tell me now?"

"He raped me," Annie said flatly. "He's my husband, right? I did have sex with him on a regular basis. So how come it's destroying me?" With that she burst into sobs and could no longer continue.

The box of Kleenex appeared. Caroline said nothing. "I'm going crazy, Caroline. I wanted to kill him that night. I wanted to kill him when he was passed out on the floor with no pants on. If there was a gun in the house I might have." Her sobs continued. "Here's the really sick part. I'm not sure I want to divorce him. I'm going to because it's the right thing to do. But part of me misses him. I miss being a family. I miss the idea that Mary's father is asleep in the next room while I'm cooking dinner, that someone is around who cares as much about Mary as I do. And he does, Caroline. I know he does. It doesn't mean he's a well-adjusted father. I know that, too. But he does love her, and I miss sharing that with him."

Annie gave up and collapsed into tears. Caroline sat, peacefully solemn. After the storm passed, Annie raised her eyes. "I think I'll stop crying now. I'm wasting time."

"You're not wasting time, Annie," Caroline said grimly. "This is what this time is about."

"I get through the days," Annie said, bewildered. "But it's like I'm bobbing around in a sea of denial. There's this horror hanging over my head, but if I looked at it all the time I'd go around the bend. You know?"

"Yes, I do," Caroline said levelly. "What is this thing hanging over your head? Specifically? Close your eyes and turn around. See what it is."

Annie closed her eyes. She squinted as tears

struggled to come through. "It's Kevin with the mean face."

"What mean face?"

"The face he had when he was beating me up."

"Okay. I take it you're afraid of that face."

"Terrified. I hate that face. I want to kill him, Caroline. So why do I miss him?"

"Because he has been a major part of your life for seven years. Of course, you miss him. It's perfectly normal. Annie, have you ever had a tooth pulled?" Annie nodded. "After the dentist pulls it, you're relieved. Right?" Annie again concurred. "Well, how many times does your tongue run itself over the spot where the tooth was? Ten? Twenty? More like a hundred times a day. Just because it was hurting you does not mean you don't notice it's gone and miss it. It leaves a gap, Annie. It's going to take a while. As time goes by, you don't miss it as much. But it does take time. Now, should you have kept the tooth? Of course not. It was causing you pain and might have made you very sick, even killed you. Pulling the tooth was the right decision. But it's going to hurt."

"I take it Kevin is the tooth in this analogy?" Annie said with a grin.

They burst into laughter. "Yes," Caroline confirmed. "He's the tooth. The infected molar." Again they laughed. "Nobody can make you ready, Annie. It's up to you. Don't feel guilty because you miss Kevin. He's your husband. Part of you is going to feel loyalty for him after he's arrested. What you have to remember is that Kevin is getting arrested because he committed a crime. You are getting divorced because Kevin is abusive. Yes, I agree he probably loves Mary. But not enough to let Mary's mother live in peace. You're going to have to fight for every ounce of peace, Annie. Backing down will only prolong the agony." Caroline changed gears. "Do you want to talk about the sexual attack?"

"No," Annie said. "Not at all. Maybe someday, but not for a while. It was the most horrible thing that's ever happened to me. I have to remember that every time I feel sorry for Kevin. Or I think I miss him. He's a dog, Caroline, and part of me hates him."

They discussed details for the rest of the session. Annie asked Caroline to read into the future and predict Kevin's next move. Caroline said she would be surprised if Kevin bowed out gracefully. She warned Annie not to expect cooperation. That was why the criminal charges were so critical. The restraining order hinged on them.

Annie left feeling tired but clear-sighted.

Within twenty-four hours, Annie signed another document listing her as the petitioner. *Griffin* vs. *Griffin* asked the court to grant Anne Griffin a divorce on the grounds of irreconcilable differences. The attorney, Madeline Freeman, a dark-haired woman in a severely tailored suit, informed Annie that the petition would be kept simple. In these cases, she said, the less there was to argue about the better. Her primary concern was Annie's safety, which was currently being monitored by the criminal court's restraining order. She explained that her objective was a speedy divorce.

Annie nervously explained that Kevin could have anything as long as he left her alone.

The attorney interrupted her, "Sure, sure . . . I know. No offense, Annie, but it's best to trust me on this. I'm asking that you maintain the residence. Where are you going to go with a baby? The respondent is also being asked to pay your hospital bills, along with child support at a rate to be determined by the court. You'll, of course, retain full custody with reasonable visitation granted. These are not big requests."

"Kevin is going to be furious," Annie interjected nervously.

Her lawyer looked up. "Don't you get it, Annie? A sudden wind change will aggravate Kevin Griffin. He's not exactly going to be pleased about the arrest warrant either. We're throwing in the divorce papers, too, while we've got the restraining order."

Madeline Freeman took Polaroid snaps of Annie's injuries and asked Annie to sign a release of information so she could access the medical records. The photos would be available to the prosecutor's office in the unlikely event that the case went to trial. Annie wondered aloud why her case was not likely to go to trial.

The attorney frowned. "You've got medical

reports and pictures. He'll have to plead guilty. He'll lose a trial."

This news consoled Annie immensely. "He's going to say terrible things about me if he can."

Madeline did look up now. "Annie, they all threaten to do that. The only relevant issue at trial will be if the jury or judge believes beyond a reasonable doubt that Kevin Griffin committed the crime he's been accused of. Kevin's allegations that you're sleeping with the chess team . . . or whatever he's saying . . . are not relevant."

Annie smiled at this. Thirty minutes later, she was back in the car heading for home. While stopped at a light, she began to cry. Events were moving too quickly. One week ago she had hurried home from work. Her biggest problem was whether or not Kevin would be angry because she was late. Seven days later, she had a car, she had been raped and assaulted, had been admitted to a hospital, had charged her husband with battery, had celebrated Christmas, and had two visitors from home. Oh yes, she reminded herself, and had filed for divorce.

The light changed. She accelerated, still sniffling. Feelings of loneliness dogged her, and she admitted to herself that she missed Kevin. After a firm mental shake, she forced herself to be realistic. She had been lonely with Kevin, too. And she had been afraid. Caroline's advice was to take it one step at a time. Annie was supposed to relinquish the things she could not immediately control. Like worries about the future.

Later she and Maureen lay sprawled across the living room floor with Mary. Annie filled her sister in on the details. She was officially getting divorced. How sad it was that Kevin would find out from a stranger.

"What else can you do, Annie?" Maureen asked reasonably. "He's not going to take it well no matter how you wrap it. Let him fracture the sheriff's ribs."

Annie nodded absently. "I know. I know. There's probably not a good way to break this kind of news. Besides, Maureen, what does he expect me to do? He doesn't like me. He wants to kill me. Does he think I'm a moron? I have to leave him."

"Of course you do," Maureen said sympathetically. "Annie, he's done this before. I mean, who are we kidding? Kevin's always been kind of abusive. You could never go out unless Kevin was there. That's not right. You know that yourself."

"I know, Maureen," Annie said ruefully. "It was never normal. But who would have guessed he'd get this bad? He was nice in many ways. He loves me so much." Maureen rolled her eyes, and Annie exclaimed, "He does, Maureen! I know he does. It's twisted. But part of me thinks he loves me a lot. He doesn't know how to love, that's the problem."

"Any more of his love and you'll end up dead, little girl," Maureen predicted darkly. "Dad is going to kill me if you don't come home with me. So I've thought of a solution. Why don't I take Mary as a peace offering? You've got a lot of things to take care of. You're pale, Annie. You need to get better.

You also need to start school and make arrangements for Mary. Let me take her home, and Nellie will bring her back. It'll give you a break."

Surprising herself, Annie agreed. "I know I should argue, but frankly, Maureen, it's a great idea. I would love two weeks to get sorted out. It would simplify things. Do you think she'll be okay without me?"

Maureen was stroking Mary's hair. Mary had crawled into her lap and was lying quietly. The child gazed at her aunt with worshipful eyes. "I kind of think so, Annie."

The girls both laughed. Annie shook off pangs of guilt. Mary adored her aunt. Maureen was full of treats and fun. Annie thought remorsefully that she had not been a very good mother lately. *How could I be?* she defended herself. Hardening her heart, she nodded. Mary would be better off away from her emotional mother right now. Annie would take care of business and prepare a life for them both.

The remainder of the week passed pleasantly. The sisters took Mary for long drives in her fancy new car seat. On New Year's Eve, they shared a bottle of wine and watched TV. Annie wondered with an ache where Kevin was celebrating. Maureen was lighthearted, though, and Annie was much better for spending time with her. They were just toasting the New Year when the phone rang. Nellie was calling with a full report.

"Kevin's mother called today," she began. "She asked me to inform you that Kevin will be moving in with one of the guys on the team. She also said in view of the circumstances it would be best if you moved back here."

Annie bristled. "Did she really? She has a lot of nerve."

Maureen was immediately frustrated. "Who? Who has a lot of nerve?"

"I think she's amazing, Annie," Nellie agreed. "She said since you already tried counseling, there was no point delaying matters."

Nellie paused, and Annie was alert. "What else?"

"Well, she said Kevin does not want a divorce. In spite of the way you've acted, he hopes to work things out. He'll only stay with this guy until you come around."

"I knew it," Annie said quickly. "He's told her horrible things, but he does not want a divorce?" She took a deep breath. "At least he's got somewhere to stay."

Nellie brightened. "I've got good news, too. You're losing Maureen on Monday, but guess who's coming to see you on Tuesday?"

"Oh, no." Annie moaned. "Not Dad."

"Annie," Nellie chided. "You're rotten. No. Not your loving father who is worried sick about you. Danny is blowing your way again. I told him it would be extremely rude to come and stay for less than twenty-four hours. He agreed. Apparently he's staying from Monday until Wednesday. He's driving up from New Orleans in some fancy new car he bought. He has to go right back, of course, and can't come here. But at least you'll have another visitor."

Annie smiled. She felt tears of gratitude in her eyes. How lucky she was to have family. "That's great, Nel. I'll be glad to see him."

"*See who?*" demanded Maureen.

"I hear her, Annie," Nellie said cheerfully, referring to Maureen. "I won't keep you. Don't worry about Mary. We're all delighted she's coming. We'll call you every night if you want."

"Thanks, Nellie," Annie said. With that, she handed the phone to the impatient Maureen. Plopping down on the couch, she thought hard. Danny was coming for a reason.

"You have to learn to shoot, Annie," Danny said impatiently. "I like Kevin as much as I like anyone. But he does not like you. One might suggest that Kevin hates you. We've been over this before. If you want to stay, you need protection."

Annie sighed. They were sitting at her kitchen table. Maureen and Mary had departed yesterday. Danny had arrived today and characteristically was getting right to the point.

"I'm not disagreeing with you," she said thoughtfully. "I just wonder if I could shoot it."

"Think back a few days," her brother said dryly. "Would you have used it the night he pulled this?" He looked pointedly at the cast.

Annie concentrated. "Yes," she said firmly after a pause. "I thought he was going to kill me. I would have shot him."

"Of course, you would have," said her brother in satisfaction. "Now, I'll take a short nap, and then we'll find a field or something."

"Okay, Danny," Annie said affectionately. "Go ahead and take my bed." Danny had departed New Orleans at two o'clock the previous morning and made record time. On Friday he would leave the country again. Deep disappointment had lined his face on hearing that Kevin was out of state. Annie could not help but wonder what his intentions had been.

A stillness settled over the tidy apartment. Annie relished the quiet and sat down on the couch to think. According to Nellie's intelligence, Kevin would be back in town by Thursday night. He had practice on Friday. Once he was arrested, anything could happen. He would be served with the restraining order. That should spell out the rules to him. Annie considered her husband for a moment. She shook her head negatively to the empty room. Kevin would not respect the rules forever. And paper would not stop him. Yes, she would take the gun. If only to scare him.

The sun slipped toward the horizon, softening the rough beauty of the cactus field. Annie shifted her weight in an effort to frighten away the rattle-snakes she was certain lurked underfoot.

"Do you have any antivenom in your death bag, Danny?" she asked her older brother.

He replied lightly, "No. But not to worry. We

can amputate any affected area with a little whiskey and a pocketknife. Now pay attention. Guns are no joke." He muttered sternly as he unpacked a black leather bag. Annie sighed and tried to concentrate.

"This is a .22-caliber Ruger. It has a clip and is semiautomatic. It's a small weapon but should bring down a big man if you aim it right." He glanced down at his younger sister.

"Okay," she summarized. "The clip holds the bullets, which are rounds. Depending on my mood, I can shoot once or seven times. What if I miss, and he's really mad? Can I shoot over my shoulder while I'm climbing out of the window?"

Danny frowned. "Stop messing around. Do you want to die? I can't stay with you, and he's coming back. You said yourself he might kill you next time. Concentrate, Annie! This may come down to him or you." Danny's manner softened his tone. "You're a sitting duck. If you insist on staying, you have to learn to use the gun."

Annie met his gaze directly. "What if I kill him, Danny?"

"Then our problems are solved, and we'll throw a party," he said gaily. "C'mon. Pay attention." He gingerly turned the gun over in his hand and continued his instructions. "This is the safety. When the safety is on, the gun won't fire. Click it off with your finger, and she's ready. Always click the safety on when you're finished. I cannot stress this enough. Whenever you even look at the gun, check the safety. Guns are not bad, Annie, people are. You have to be serious about guns. They can save your life or get you killed. Take it. Let's try one."

He gently handed the gun to his sister. She felt the weight of the weapon in her hand and began to put her finger on the trigger.

"Safety!" he barked. "Check the safety!"

Startled, she jumped back and nearly dropped the gun.

"Dammit, Danny. You scared me to death. I hope whoever I'm shooting has the courtesy to keep quiet."

"Take it nice and easy until you're comfortable handling it."

She carefully turned the gun and checked the safety. "Safety is on," she said lightly. "Life as we know it may continue."

"Let me show you how to aim," Danny said, resuming his lesson. "Another crucial point: Never point a gun at anything you do not intend to shoot. And never, never shoot at anything you don't intend to kill. I don't care if it's a squirt gun. Guns go off, especially in shaky hands like yours. Are you ready? Raise the gun and aim." He pointed to the cactus targeted for destruction. "That's your bad guy. Aim a little low. This gun has a kick."

"What's a kick?"

"When you fire, the gun jumps up a little. If you're aiming for the chest, shoot a little lower." In response to her look of bewilderment, he added, "Have you ever seen a shotgun fired in a western movie? The gun jumps up when she fires. That's why you aim a bit lower. Another important point about aiming: Always aim at the biggest part of a person's body. That's the middle. Let's assume you want to hit the bad guy in the chest. Aim a little lower, and you have a snowball's chance in hell of actually hitting him. Understand?"

"Implicitly. If I aim for his genitals I'll connect somewhere near the light fixture." She smiled widely.

"Shoot the damn thing," he said, rolling his eyes. "You'll see what I mean."

Annie aimed the gun with her good hand and braced it with her cast. Closing her left eye, she carefully squeezed the trigger. *BOOM*. The gun went off with no apparent damage to the prickly target. "Whew!" she said, letting herself breathe. "I see what you mean. The cactuses in West Texas are safe from the likes of me."

"*Cacti* is the plural form of *cactus*," Danny observed dryly. "Not bad, Annie. You didn't faint or anything. Let's try it again."

The lesson continued for two hours. With the light nearly gone, Danny cleared up the debris. Annie looked around the field and sighed.

"How did I end up in Texas shooting at *cacti*, Danny?"

"You married the wrong guy, kiddo," he said simply. "It's nothing to be ashamed of. People marry maniacs every day. That's why they get guns and divorces."

"Guns stink, Danny," Annie said with feeling.

"Maybe if I prayed more, this would not have happened."

"Guns and rosaries, Annie. We need them both. I always carry holy water, and I usually have a gun. C'mon, let's get out of here before the snakes come out. We'll go get a beer. I hear there's a blizzard in Chicago."

They dumped their gear in the car and headed back onto the ranch road. Annie gunned the accelerator and glanced back at the dust clouds trailing them. She let her thoughts wander. Was she really capable of killing Kevin?

Chapter Nineteen

On Friday evening, Annie waded through bills. Under Caroline's direction, she tackled concrete tasks involving her future. While writing checks and addressing envelopes, she began to feel capable. The helplessness that had paralyzed her was lifting. That afternoon she had opened a checking account in her name. A small deposit satisfied the account manager. Annie was reluctant to put all of her money where she lacked immediate access to it. There was no telling when she might get in her car and abandon Texas. She resolved to have the car filled with gas and cash ready at all times. She likened it to wearing a parachute in a plane. Odds were against having to use it, but if you needed it, you needed it.

She was just getting up to stretch when the phone rang. She jumped and looked at it uneasily. Kevin would definitely be back in town by now.

"Hello," she answered with a confident voice.

"Annie? It's Darlene. How *are* you?"

"Hi, Darlene," she answered cautiously. "How was your trip?"

"Fine, fine," Darlene said impatiently. "I felt so bad leaving you like that. Are you feeling better? Greg said you had some broken bones."

"Not too many," she answered briefly.

Darlene waited. When Annie failed to supply details, she continued. "Well, I guess practice was interesting today. But you probably know all about that."

Annie rolled her eyes in exasperation. Darlene sounded catty. "All about what, Darlene?"

"Didn't you issue an arrest warrant for him?"

Annie winced in dismay. "Was he arrested?"

"Yes, he was," Darlene said with poorly concealed delight. "In front of everyone. And a restraining order was read out loud to him in front of the whole team. He must have been mortified."

"I see," Annie said weakly. "Darlene, I had no power over how he was served. I signed criminal complaints against him and asked for a restraining order. The judge issued the warrant. I had no idea they would serve him at practice."

"Not only serve him," Darlene said emphatically, "but take him away in handcuffs. Pretty embarrassing."

"I was pretty embarrassed myself at the Emergency Room." Annie stopped herself. Darlene had a big mouth. It was possible Kevin would hear every bit of this conversation. "Still, I'm sorry it happened that way." She forced herself to refrain from asking questions.

"Yes," Darlene continued. "I guess the coach followed them down to bail him out."

"Well, then, he did not have to stay too long. That's good," Annie said politely. "My main concern was the restraining order."

"Annie, are you sure you didn't overreact just a little bit?" Darlene said. "I mean, Kevin moved out of the apartment. Did you really have to get him arrested?"

"I thought so," she answered with a sinking heart. There would be no friendship with Darlene. She was obviously discussing the matter with Greg, Kevin, and the team. "I did ask Kevin not to attack me, Darlene. You were the one who called to warn me. Remember? You didn't want me to come over because Greg was afraid of him. Greg thought I could handle him, though. Well, as you can see, I couldn't. I don't want that to happen again, Darlene. He told me if I ever left him, he would kill me. I think he meant it." Annie closed her mouth firmly. Darlene would not understand. Most people did not. Caroline had warned her about squandering valuable emotional energy.

"I know you guys had a major fight. But it's over now. Let it go, Annie. You've got him out of the apartment. What more do you want?"

Annie finally understood. Greg was sitting with her. Darlene was calling to get Annie to drop the charges. For Kevin. "I want to start school next week and take care of my daughter. In peace. I don't think Kevin will let me do that unless he's forced to."

"It seems cold. Don't you think?" Annie speculated that Darlene was enjoying her role in the drama. She would give Greg plenty of fodder for tomorrow's practice.

"Apparently you do, Darlene. I'm trying to do what's best for all of us." Annie's voice was sharper than she intended.

Darlene jumped in hastily. "Don't misunderstand me, Annie. I think Kevin has a horrible temper. But why torture the guy? All he wants is to get back together. If you're going to abandon him, you could at least do it kindly."

"I'm trying to, Darlene. See you later." Annie hung up. She was shaking with rage and despair. Annie guessed Darlene was delighted with the opportunity to get Greg's attention. She could castigate Annie's actions and thereby raise her own self-esteem. *Well, let her,* Annie thought wickedly. *She'll always be insecure. Judging me will only give her temporary satisfaction.* Few understood Kevin. She would have to live with that.

Annie cleared the table quickly. The bills were taken care of, and her life was in order—on paper anyway. She had registered for school and was starting on Monday. Mary was enrolled in the nursery. Both Mary and Annie would attend school from nine until noon. That was a full load and satisfied the terms of the scholarship. Financially, Annie would be solvent for three months. During that time she would need to get another job. She had lost the old one, and resolved to begin looking next week. Once the baby came back, it would be more difficult.

The next morning, Annie took laundry down to the washhouse. The small load was done in no time, and Annie began to pack up her soap. A slamming door announced company. Darlene staggered in with two highly stacked baskets.

"Let me help," Annie offered, wrestling with the top basket.

"Thanks." Darlene panted, putting down her load. "I'm glad I ran into you. Were you mad last night?"

Annie averted her eyes. "Not at all. I do feel like you're completely sympathetic to Kevin. That's your business, though."

"Annie, that's not true. All I'm saying is this: It's over. He knows that. He's heartbroken. Maybe he deserves to be. But criminal charges? Come on! That's a bit much."

"Darlene, do you really think he's going to leave me alone?" Annie struggled for words. "I know him better than you. He won't. If I could have gotten the restraining order without the charges, I would have. Until I'm convinced he's willing to let it go . . . I have no choice."

Darlene changed the subject. "How's your arm? Does it still hurt?"

Annie shrugged. "Not really."

Darlene took a breath. "Annie, I've got to tell you honestly. Kevin wants me to feel you out on something. He wants to get counseling with you. He thinks you two can work it out."

Annie felt her heart twist. "Don't do this to me."

Darlene exclaimed hastily. "He knows he was wrong. He's sorry, Annie. He really is. He's willing to forget the whole incident."

"I'll bet he is," Annie retorted sarcastically. "Darlene, try to understand. I'm not mad at him. But I can't give him an inch. Not even a millimeter. He's too manipulative. Tell him if he loves me, he should leave me alone."

Picking up her belongings, she turned and left. She would have to avoid Darlene now that she was Kevin's ambassador. The stairs leading to her apartment were littered with belongings. Annie gingerly stepped around boxes. She must be getting a new neighbor. As she neared the top, someone came out of the door next to hers.

"Hello," said a friendly voice. Annie glanced up. A tall, tanned woman in her mid-twenties stood with the door propped open. She had long, flowing brown hair and beautiful green eyes.

"Hello," Annie responded. "My name is Annie Griffin. Are you my new neighbor?"

"Yes. I hope I'm not bothering y'all with the mess on the stairs."

"Not at all. Are you and your husband moving in today?"

"It's just me. And my six-year-old daughter. I'm divorced, but I'm eligible for married housing because of my daughter."

Annie felt her spirits lift. "Are you? I'm sorry to hear that. I'm getting divorced, too."

The woman rolled her eyes and extended her hand. "My name is Marty. And I'm sorry that you're getting divorced, but if you're anything like me, you're probably relieved."

Annie burst out laughing and shook the woman's hand. "Something like that. Can I give you a hand?"

"No, I'm taking a break. Come on in for some iced tea."

Annie spent the next thirty minutes talking to her new friend. Marty was in the nursing program and had waited for this apartment two years. One year remained of her studies. Then she had to serve an internship. Annie was delighted with Marty. A native Texan, she was warm and genuine. A summary of Annie's dilemma prompted Marty to give Annie her phone number. If Annie had any problems, she should call. Annie thanked her sweetly. It would be nice to know that a friend was so close.

Leaving Marty to her unpacking, Annie went in and called Chicago. Mary was fine, having a wonderful time, according to Eileen. Annie hung up quickly. She wanted to save her long-distance calls for when she was lonely or depressed. She readied herself to go shopping. Groceries were necessary, and she had resolved to buy herself a new pair of jeans for school. She drove away feeling content and hopeful.

The first week of school flew by. New notebooks and texts were neatly stacked on the desk. By Thursday afternoon, Annie felt as though she had been in college forever. She was just sitting down to lunch when the phone rang. The caller identified herself as a paralegal for Annie's attorney. She informed Annie that there was an emergency hearing at two. Annie's presence was required.

Annie replaced the telephone with shaking hands. Dialing Caroline's number, she instructed the secretary to cancel her afternoon appointment. She gratefully accepted an appointment for the next day and changed into a skirt and blouse.

An hour later she was again walking up the steps of the courthouse. Uncertain of a final destination, Annie paused in the vestibule.

"Annie?"

She turned with a sinking heart. "Hello, Kevin," she said weakly. "I don't think we should be talking."

For a moment, his look of pain pierced her armor. "What happened to your arm?"

Annie hardened her heart. "You broke it."

He looked at her in misery. "I'm sorry. You can't know how sorry I am." His brown eyes welled up. "Please listen to me. I love you. I can change. I've done it before."

"Annie," rang out a female voice. Annie turned to see Madeline Freeman walking briskly down the hall. "Come this way."

Turning shakily, she followed her lawyer. Kevin followed them. "Annie, you've got to talk to me. Right now!"

The lawyer turned abruptly on her heels. "No, Mr. Griffin. You're wrong. She does not have to talk to you. Following her like this could be construed as harassment, which you'll find has been prohibited by the restraining order that was served on you."

Annie held her breath. Glancing back at Kevin, she saw the look of rage on his face. Instinctively, Annie began to walk, leaving her lawyer to deal with him. She arrived at the courtroom door and looked back. Kevin was pointing his finger down into the face of her lawyer. Annie made out the words *dyke* and *feminist bitch*. Her face flushed in humiliation.

The lawyer turned and walked quickly toward Annie. Kevin went the other way.

"Are you all right?" Annie asked sympathetically.

"Fine," Madeline answered through tight lips. "I can certainly see why you're divorcing him."

"I told you," Annie said in dismay. "I'm so sorry."

"No." Madeline held up her hand. "You have no reason to apologize for him. You've done nothing wrong, Annie. Now I can go in and tell the judge exactly what we're dealing with." Taking a breath, she laughed shakily. "Hello, Annie. How are you today?"

They both laughed. "Fine, thank you. And how are you?" Annie said.

The lawyer smiled. "Great. Thanks for coming on short notice. Kevin has hired an attorney. The bottom line is this: Kevin's attorney is petitioning the court for emergency relief. He feels that the restraining order, which precludes him from entering the residence, is placing undue hardship on him." Seeing Annie's look of horror, she went on hastily, "I'm sure this judge will refuse to amend the restraining order. It's not his jurisdiction. Another judge is presiding over the criminal charge and the restraining order. Let's see what happens."

They entered the courtroom and sat down. Moments later, Kevin entered with his attorney and sat down on the opposite side of the room. Annie put her hand on her stomach. She was terrified she would become sick. She felt her knees shaking and clamped them together.

"*Griffin* vs. *Griffin,*" bellowed a clerk.

Annie's lawyer rose and indicated that Annie should follow her. Her peripheral vision assured her that Kevin was doing the same. A middle-aged judge read through a file in front of him. The four parties stood before him silently. Everyone waited while he leisurely familiarized himself with the motion.

Finally, he looked up. "What have we got here?" He addressed Kevin's attorney.

"Your Honor," answered the man with Kevin, "my client has been thrown out of his home and denied access to his daughter for over two weeks. We're asking for immediate relief."

The judge turned to Annie's lawyer. "Your Honor," Madeline responded in a firm voice, "Mr. Griffin was legally removed from the residence by a restraining order signed on the twenty-sixth of December. That order is running in tandem with a criminal charge of battery under Judge Melbourne. The respondent is currently out on bond. We would strenuously object to any change in the status of that order."

The judge sighed heavily. Turning to Kevin's lawyer, he said in an aggravated tone, "What do you really want, Counsel? You must know I'm not going to change another judge's order."

The man assumed a placating air. "Your Honor, my client wants to see his daughter. It's my understanding that the petitioner does not even *have* the child. She sent her out of state without consulting my client. Now, if the petitioner wants to relinquish custody, my client would be glad to raise his little girl."

"This is outrageous. Your Honor," Annie's attorney said, jumping in. "The child was taken back to Chicago temporarily while my client recovered from injuries sustained when the respondent assaulted her. I'd like to add that the injuries included several broken bones and two lacerations requiring stitches."

"Your Honor, give me a break here," interrupted the opposing counsel. "We're not trying the battery case."

"I'm not trying anything. Your Honor," Annie's lawyer said calmly. "I'm merely familiarizing the court with the facts. As for the child, she'll be brought back within the next two weeks. Judge Melbourne denied the respondent access to both the mother and child in the interest of their safety."

"Under the circumstances, Judge Melbourne's

denial seems reasonable to me," said the judge. "What else can I do for you today, Counsel?"

Annie was trying to breathe slowly. Her anxiety was at such a level as to stop her from breathing if she let it. She wondered idly how Kevin was faring. She dared not hazard a look in his direction.

"There is another matter, Your Honor," said the attorney without missing a beat. "My client is interested in preserving the marriage. He would respectfully ask the court to order some kind of counseling before the marriage is terminated."

"That also seems reasonable," said the judge, turning to Annie's lawyer. "What say you, Madame Attorney?"

"No, Your Honor. Absolutely not. My client is only interested in protecting herself and her child. Her decision to file this petition for dissolution of marriage was well thought out and remains irrevocable."

"Your Honor," said the opposing counsel, "would it be too much to ask that my colleague not answer for her client? Surely she can say whether or not she wants counseling."

The judge nodded. "Mrs. Griffin?" he said, looking at Annie, "are you willing to give this boy one more chance? You look like nice folks. It's hard to be married when you're young. Maybe you two are throwing in the towel too soon. How about seeing a counselor and finding out for sure?"

Annie looked helplessly at her lawyer. The

woman winked at her. "You can talk, Annie. Tell them what you think about additional marriage counseling."

"Well, Judge," Annie answered in a shaking voice, "it did not work out the last time. I don't want to."

Annie's lawyer spoke quietly. "Are you afraid of Kevin, Annie?"

"Your Honor!" shouted Kevin's lawyer. "She's putting words in her mouth. Maybe she should let the lady answer."

Annie spoke up. "Yes. I'm afraid of him. And no. I have no desire to attend counseling with him. I'm seeing a counselor right now for myself. I won't change my mind."

"Nobody is talking you into this, are they?" queried the judge.

Annie's lawyer tapped her pen in annoyance. "Your Honor, contrary to what my colleague thinks, I do familiarize myself with my clients' wishes before bringing a case before the bench. The reality is this: My client has petitioned for divorce and, by her own admission, has no desire to attend counseling with the respondent. I would also like to ask the court at this time to admonish the respondent to refrain from threatening me. Either in this building or outside it. He threatened me in the hallway before this hearing."

"Your Honor," exclaimed Kevin's lawyer, "this is outrageous. Counsel is attempting to slander my client."

"I'm attempting to protect myself and my client, Counsel."

"*Hold it!*" the judge roared. "Stop this nonsense." Turning to Annie's lawyer, he said heavily, "He better have, miss, or you're in trouble."

"I'm married, Your Honor, so you can call me ma'am." Annie looked down and noticed that her representative was now clutching her pen tightly. "The respondent was harassing my client, saying 'You have to talk to me.' I informed him that she did not *have* to talk to him. At that point he told me to mind my own business or I would get hurt. Specifically, I was told to mind my own 'fucking business' because I was a 'dyke lawyer' and a 'feminist bitch.' I have no interest in being hurt by this man, Your Honor, and would ask the court to firmly admonish the respondent. If he harasses my client in the courthouse, Your Honor, we can only imagine what he'll do outside of it. Additionally, if I am threatened again, I will bring charges against him."

"Your Honor, Your Honor," said Kevin's lawyer, putting his hands out in a placating manner.

"Yes, I see," the judge said noncommittally. He gave a deep sigh and addressed Kevin directly. "Young man, I'm sorry for you. You don't want this divorce. I can see that. I wish I could change your wife's mind, but I can't. Most young people today have no sense of commitment. Obviously, your wife has made a decision. She may be abandoning you without giving you a chance. There's nothing I can do about that. Now, I know you're feeling angry about all of this. I don't blame you. But you can't threaten people or call them names. Try to behave." With this he winked at Kevin. "Send some flowers and hope for the best."

Annie's mouth dropped open. Had she heard him correctly? She began to giggle.

"Court's in recess," said the judge with a bang of the gavel. He left the bench.

"I'm serious about the charges," Madeline said to Kevin's lawyer.

Annie was surprised to see Kevin's lawyer nod his head affirmatively. "I'll sure make that clear to him, Madeline. I myself will firmly admonish him."

"Thanks, Bob," said Madeline gratefully. "See you next month."

Kevin was already walking out of the room. Annie was confused. Was Kevin's lawyer being nice now?

"Madeline?" Annie asked. "I don't understand. Is that guy a friend of yours?"

The lawyer smiled understandingly. "We've been friends for years, Annie. Just because we're enemies at the bench doesn't mean we don't like each other. It went well. Nothing has changed. Are you okay?"

Annie shook her head, dazed. "I guess so. I'm shaking. What was all that about flowers?"

The older woman snorted in disgust. "Just be grateful your restraining order is in criminal court. This judge likes to think he's a traditionalist. That means he's a male chauvinist pig. We're going to keep the divorce simple and leave your restraining order where it is. It will be fine."

They talked some more. Annie's queries were vague, and Madeline told her to write down future questions as she thought of them. They walked together to Annie's car, making certain Kevin was not around. As Annie pulled out, she saw Kevin talking with his attorney. It looked as though they were arguing. She put on her directional and left quickly.

Annie arrived home and plopped down on the couch. Minutes later there was a knock on the door. Her stomach lurched as she remembered she had not put the chain on. In the split second it took to make a decision, Annie was on her feet and heading for the back door.

"Annie?" called a female voice.

Annie let out her breath in relief. It was Marty. She turned and opened the door. "Hi," she said warmly.

"Hi, yourself. You look like you've seen a ghost." Marty was carrying two large glasses of what looked to be Kool-Aid.

"Come in," Annie said, stepping back. "I thought you were my husband coming to kill me."

"Good God. Why would he want to kill you?" Marty stepped in with the glasses, and Annie motioned her into a chair.

"I just got back from court. He was not pleased." She sighed heavily. "I'm afraid of what he'll do."

"Here, drink this," said her neighbor, extending a glass. "It's my own concoction. Raspberry iced tea with gelatin. It's supposed to be good for your nails." Annie smiled and took a deep drink. "Do you really think he's going to come after you? Even with the restraining order?"

Annie rolled her eyes. "I don't know. That's what's so scary. A friend says he's sane and rational. She swears he won't bother me unless I tell him it's okay. Then again, he just called my lawyer a dyke and a bitch. He did not seem very rational to me."

Marty's eyes were round. "He didn't! What a nut!"

The two young women talked for another hour. Annie explained some of what had gone on before, and Marty shared her story of marital woe. Annie felt much better. It was good to talk. Marty reminded Annie to call her if she got frightened.

After a shower and a light dinner, Annie sat down to her homework. A ring of the telephone interrupted her. Annie hesitated. Darlene would upset her. As would Kevin. Resolving to make short work of either of them, she answered.

"Hi," said Annie's lawyer. "This is Madeline Freeman. Are you by any chance looking for a job, Annie?"

"Yes, I am. Why?"

"Well, I've got a friend," Madeline began. "Her elderly mother recently had heart surgery. She's not dying, but they can't leave her alone. They need someone from one till five Monday through

Friday. It pays five dollars an hour cash. It would start next month. What do you think?"

Annie was delighted. "It sounds perfect. I would have to line up someone to watch my daughter."

"I told them about your little girl. That's no problem. You can bring her along. They think it might be good for the patient to have a child around."

"Yes, yes, I definitely want it," Annie said with surging hope. "My daughter is very good, and she sleeps every afternoon. I could change her bedtime so she would sleep longer during the day."

"You can work that out with them, Annie. You'd also take her to the hairdresser once a week. Things like that. I'll give you the number, and you can arrange an interview. These are great people. They'll love you."

Annie took down the number. She thanked her lawyer emotionally. After collecting herself, Annie dialed the number. A woman with a soft Southern drawl answered, and Annie briefly introduced herself. A ten-minute conversation followed during which it was determined that Annie would come next week for an interview. She hung up the phone with high hopes. The woman sounded warm and friendly. Annie marveled that she was meeting so many great people. She called home and informed Maureen that life was falling into place beautifully.

Later, Annie turned off the lights in the living room. She was checking the locks on the front door when she spotted an envelope on the floor. It was addressed to her in Kevin's handwriting. Annie picked it up and put her ear to the door. No sound. She went back to the phone and shakily dialed Marty's number. After hearing the situation, Marty agreed to check the hallway. She told Annie that if she spotted Kevin, she would say loudly, "My goodness, you scared me." That would be Annie's signal to call the police.

Tense moments followed while Annie listened at the door. She heard Marty walking down the three flights of stairs. Running to the front window, she watched as her neighbor walked around the building. Annie ran to the back door and saw Marty coming up the back stairs. She opened her door.

"No sign of him, Annie. Did you read the note?"

Annie held the door open for her friend and then opened the letter. Marty watched while she read the contents.

Dear Annie,

I am writing to beg you for forgiveness. Surely we have some good memories. After all we have been through together, I can't believe you would let it end this way. I'm willing to see a counselor, and I have promised to change. What else can I do? You are not completely innocent in this. You know that. I understand about the criminal charges, but I do wish you would drop them. Annie, this is not necessary. If you do not want to give it a chance, I will understand. But drop the charges. You owe me that much. Call me. My number is at the bottom of

the page. Please. Call me. You'll never find anyone
who will love you like I do. Call me. I'm still your hus-
band. All of my love forever,
Kevin

Annie handed the letter to Marty. Weakly, she lowered herself into a kitchen chair. He was not going to let it go. Marty read the letter quickly and patted Annie's hand sympathetically.

"It does not change a thing, Annie. He can write anything he wants. He's really trying to get you to drop the charges by making you feel guilty. 'You owe me that.' Throw it in the garbage and forget it," Marty advised. "Better yet, call the police and tell them he was here. Isn't that a violation of his restraining order?"

Annie looked at Marty in surprise. "I don't know. He's not supposed to be here, but couldn't he say he had someone else drop it off?"

Marty was thoughtful. "Yes, I suppose he could. But he's kind of threatening you to drop the charges. Surely that's wrong. Annie, you better give me a picture of him. That way I'll know him if I see him around."

Annie remained pensive as she looked through the desk drawers. The recent pictures were kept there. Strangely enough, she could not put her hands on them. "They're gone. I'm sure they were here a couple of days ago. I must have misplaced them." Annie went to the hall closet and pulled out a photo album. After flipping quickly through the pictures, she selected one and gave it to Marty.

"Here is an older shot. He has shorter hair now. I have a roll that's half taken. I'll get it developed tomorrow and give you a current picture."

Marty studied the photo and nodded. "He looks like a big guy. I'm sure I'll know him if I see him. There's a one-hour developing place at the mall."

"I'll run it over there tomorrow afternoon."

The women talked for a while longer. Marty offered Annie her couch for the night, but Annie declined. Kevin would be waiting for her phone call. She felt she would be safe enough.

Rain fell steadily the next day as Annie made her way to the mall. She had finished her first week of college. The course work was not difficult, and she had little concern about retaining her scholarship. Annie was eager to get Mary back. The days seemed strangely empty without the constant gurgling of her toddler. She told herself it would not be long. Another ten days at the most. If the job came through, she would be completely settled by the time her daughter returned.

After locating the photo shop, she pulled the camera from her purse. She started to unload the film and glanced down at the counter. It read zero. Puzzled, she shrugged and took the roll out. She thought Maureen had said there was half a roll left. Annie checked it in and promised to return in an hour.

Post-Christmas bargains tantalized her as she wandered through the mall. Today she would window-shop. If she landed the job next week, she would splurge and buy herself a whole new outfit. The hour quickly passed, and she returned for the film. She was certain there was a shot of Kevin holding Mary. She remembered it was the first picture she had taken on the new roll.

Annie left the shop and opened the package as she walked. Sure enough, there was Kevin holding Mary by the washhouse. Annie smiled as she flipped through several silly shots of Maureen and the baby. Next was a terrible photo of Annie cleaning the toilet. Courtesy of Maureen, the comedienne. The next picture mystified her. It was a picture of the inside of the refrigerator. Had Maureen taken it? Annie shrugged and went on. The next photograph set off an alarm in her head and caused her to quickly flip through the rest. There was a picture of the inside of her underwear drawer. Another shot showed her marriage license propped up against the dresser. The fourth showed her divorce petition on the kitchen table next to her textbooks. As startling as they were, it was the fifth that turned her blood cold. Placed on her pillow was the daily newspaper. It was opened to the obituary page.

Chapter Twenty

Shoppers swirled around Annie as she stood holding the photograph. Her frozen face belied the furious activity of her mind. Kevin was sending her a message. He was going to kill her. The death notice resting on her bedroom pillow made that clear. Also, the marriage license and the divorce decree. He felt justified because she was divorcing him. He had often reminded her of her marriage vow. Now he would kill her for breaking it.

Annie shuffled the pictures again. The underwear drawer. What was the message there? Also, the inside of the refrigerator. Her thoughts jumped darkly. Maybe he was going to kill her in her underwear and stuff her into the refrigerator. Annie giggled nervously. *Oh, no*, she thought. Inappropriate laughter. She stuffed the pictures into her purse. Kevin had been in her house. Recently. He had the key. Annie could hardly chain the door from the outside.

Jogging across the lot to her car, she threw her purse in and started the engine. A terrible thought struck her, and she opened the door and jumped out. Checking the backseat, she was relieved to see it empty. She settled in again and gunned the engine. She had to do something. He fully intended to kill her. Annie knew most people would think she was unbalanced. But she knew how Kevin's mind worked. He had a criminal charge pending. He was outwardly on good behavior. Annie shuddered at the probable depth of his internal rage.

Annie drove home with a deadly serious frown on her face. She scolded herself for becoming complacent. From now on she had to be aggressive. She could not sit and wait for him to kill her. Not only would she not drop the charges, she would add another charge. He had obviously violated the restraining order this time. He had broken into her home.

Pulling up to the apartment, she allowed another thought to crystallize. Kevin had written a predictable note by normal standards. "I love you," "I miss you," "Give me another chance," etc. He was not afraid of the note's being scrutinized. That was why he left the message on the camera. Only Annie would understand it. Kevin was not acting impulsively. He was thinking things through. The thought chilled her.

Annie was putting her key in the door when another horrible thought struck her. What if he was inside? With shaking hands, she knocked on Marty's door. In seconds, Marty answered, looking fresh and uncomplicated.

"Hi," she said brightly. Seeing Annie's pallor, she frowned and stepped back. "What happened to you?"

Annie entered and haltingly filled her in. Marty

looked at the pictures. She, too, paled.

"Annie, this guy is worse than weird. Do you realize that means that he left the letter after he had taken the pictures? I mean"—Marty frowned in concentration—"does he think he can threaten you into a reconciliation? He's certifiable."

Annie met her new friend's frightened eyes. "I know. That's what scares me. It's like he is trying to say 'Get back with me or die.' Do you get that feeling?"

Marty stood up abruptly. "Call the police. Right now."

Annie followed her to the telephone and dialed the number for the police department. The dispatcher sounded bored. He asked Annie if she was in immediate danger. Annie said no, then added, "Unless he is hiding in my apartment across the hall."

"*Is* he hiding in your apartment?"

"I don't know. I'm afraid to go in."

"Well," said a bored voice, "if you go in and he's there, call us back. That *would* be a violation of the restraining order."

Annie stared at the wall. "He's not going to hand me the phone, you know. If he is there, his intentions are not lawful."

"Lady," the voice snapped, "we can't come over every time you get paranoid. I don't know who took those pictures. And neither do you. Those are the facts. And you're complaining because he wrote you a letter? He did not threaten you; he just wants to get back together. Sounds like a perfectly normal divorce to me. Call your lawyer." The phone went dead.

Annie looked at Marty with her mouth open. "Can you believe this?" she asked her friend. "He told me Kevin sounds perfectly normal and I should call my lawyer."

Marty was furious. "That bastard. I can't believe this. What's the point of giving you a restraining order if they blow off every violation?"

Annie shook her head. She had no answers. "Can you walk me home?" she asked in a pitiful voice. Both burst out laughing.

"Well, I guess so. We may as well do it while I'm good and mad," Marty said jokingly. "I'll kill him if he's in there."

They opened the door talking loudly. The idea was to warn Kevin that they were coming so he would have a chance to run out. Marty went around checking closets. Annie checked the bathroom and then went back and pulled the shower curtain open. The apartment was empty. They threw themselves onto the couch in relief.

"Honestly, Annie," Marty began, "I thought my ex was nutty. I don't know if you're safe. Are you sure you don't want to go home?"

"I thought of that," Annie answered honestly. "But it makes me so mad! I've got a good setup here, Marty. If I leave now, I'll mess up the divorce and lose the scholarship." She frowned in concentration. "It's not fair. Why should I have to drop my life? I mean, he's the one causing all the trouble. Why can't we make him leave?"

Marty's eyes brightened. "I hadn't thought of that. Let's ask him to leave." The joke was lost on Annie.

"Screw him," Annie swore bitterly. "He's a spoiled baby. And, Marty, he'll follow me anywhere. Especially back to Chicago. I swear I'd be afraid he would hurt my father or something. You know? He's disturbed enough to do it."

Marty sighed. "What can I do?" she asked warmly. "I'm going to leave my front door open. That way you can come in if you need to."

Annie smiled gratefully. "That's great, Marty. If I get paranoid again, I'll stop at your place first."

Rising to her feet, her neighbor sighed again. "Okay, Annie. I'm going home to study. My daughter is coming back next weekend, so I'm trying to get ahead as much as possible. Call me if you need anything."

Thanking her, Annie closed the door and turned the deadbolt. She contemplated calling home but knew that the latest developments would only underscore her family's opinion that she should load up the car and come home. How she wished it was not too late to reach Caroline. Annie felt lonely. She pulled out her books, fighting back tears. They came anyway and filled her with rage. She would not let Kevin ruin her life. She would fight back. It was all she could do to restrain herself from calling and telling him. Thoughts of Kevin in the courtroom stopped her. She could not give him ammunition. He would say she was harassing him or something.

The weekend passed uneventfully. Annie spent most of it in the library after deciding Marty's strategy was sound. She wanted to be ahead in her studies when Mary returned.

Monday morning Annie dressed carefully for school. The job interview was scheduled for 12:30, so she would have to leave right after her last class. Annie was also seeing Caroline after the interview. It was going to be a busy day.

Shortly after noon, she crossed campus. Her car was back at the apartment, and she was not certain about the directions. She hustled accordingly. The weather was warm and sunny as usual. Annie lifted her face to the sunshine and smiled. It was exhilarating to be on her own. She was amazed at the changes in herself. In a few weeks' time, she had regained much of her lost confidence. She also felt attractive again. Men smiled at her, and she smiled back.

Arriving at her car, she opened the back door and threw her backpack over the front seat. Glancing up at the apartment, she froze. Had she seen the drapery move? Either way, she had to go. Annie started the car and pulled around the circle driveway. She looked up again and saw nothing. Surely it had been the glare of the sunlight. *I can't deal with this now*, she thought sternly. *I have to look sane for the interview. I'm paranoid, paranoid, paranoid.*

The interview went well, and Annie was asked

to begin in mid-February. The elderly lady was quite genteel, and Annie loved her at once. She was proudly informed that her patient belonged to the Daughters of the American Revolution. Annie smiled and nodded her head admiringly. A middle-aged woman, the patient's daughter, winked at Annie. Apparently, this was a big deal, so Annie looked even more impressed. Gratified, the elderly woman informed Annie that her little girl was most welcome. They offered her a salary and asked if it was sufficient. Annie schooled her face and nodded affirmatively. Quite literally, it was twice what she had expected.

Spirits soaring, Annie drove to her counseling appointment in prayerful gratitude. Things could not possibly be working out any better. With the salary and the stipend, Annie would be completely independent. She rolled down her window and let the dry air blow her hair into a mess. Thoughts of Rene filtered into her head, and she resolved to call her that evening. Annie missed her. Now that she was on her own, she could call whomever she pleased as long as she stayed within her budget.

Annie drifted into Caroline's office on a cloud. Caroline rejoiced with her. She told Annie she was very proud of her, and Annie choked up. She had never understood Caroline's unwavering faith in her. She filled Caroline in on the phantom photography session. The older woman was concerned.

"I don't like it, Annie," she said, shaking her head. This set off a round of tinkling jewelry, and

Annie laughed. "What are you laughing about?"

"Your jewelry. It's lovely. Does the noise ever bother you?"

"No," Caroline answered vehemently. "I love the noise. Remember I once told you that I would tell you why I helped battered women? Well, I'll tell you now. You have probably guessed that I was in a violent marriage."

Annie's eyebrows shot up. "You're joking! I would never have guessed."

Caroline nodded her head affirmatively.

"But you look so normal."

Her counselor rolled her eyes. "How is a formerly battered woman supposed to look, Annie? You look pretty normal yourself."

"I don't feel normal," Annie said, chagrined. "I feel half cracked most of the time."

"That's temporary," Caroline promised. "You'll feel normal again, and people will never guess that you married a homicidal maniac the first time." They both laughed.

"Back to my jewelry . . . My first husband never let me wear any jewelry. He said only tramps wore jewelry. So when I got divorced fifteen years ago, I went out and bought myself all kinds of jewelry. I've worn it ever since."

"What does your current husband say about it?"

"He says I'm eccentric and that he adores me." Caroline shuddered. "To think I might have stayed with my abuser . . . I still have nightmares sometimes. Anyway, I have two wonderful children, and my marriage is better than I ever thought a marriage could be. So there you are, Annie. I never forget what I went through, and I will probably help battered women for the rest of my life. It gets in your blood. I have high hopes for you."

Annie smiled. "That's wonderful, Caroline. I would love to think that I could be as together as you are someday."

Caroline reached over and placed her hand on Annie's. "Annie," she said seriously, "I have no doubt that you will far exceed what I've done. You've got the right stuff, Honey. Much more so than I did at your age."

Annie struggled with tears. "Thank you, Caroline. You saved my life, you know."

"No, Annie. You saved your own life. I'm only pointing out the right roads. Now, when you get home, call Grady and tell him dispatchers are blowing you off. See what he says. I'll call him, too."

They spoke a few minutes longer. Caroline warned Annie not to underestimate the danger. She made Annie review her safety plan and nodded approvingly at Marty's offer to leave her front door open. Annie left with undiminished optimism. Kevin would back off. What else could he do?

Annie pulled up to her apartment and fairly danced up the stairs. She could hardly wait to get to the phone and tell her family about the job. She would insist they bring Mary back this week. There was nothing standing in the way now. No more job interviews or appointments.

Opening the front door, she threw her bag of books onto the couch. She suddenly noticed that she was starved. Grabbing an apple from the counter, she went into her bedroom and kicked off her shoes. She was just peeling her nylons off when she noticed the toe of a very large athletic shoe sticking out from the closet. Everything immediately stilled.

Her mind, unlike her heart and lungs, was still working. Annie assessed the situation. Kevin was hiding in her closet. The slow motion thing kicked in, and she pulled her nylons off with her head lowered. There was a crack between the panels of the door. He could be watching.

"There now," she said casually, as if she were talking to herself. She rose from the bed and started for the bedroom door. *Slow!* she cautioned herself. She was just leaving the room when she heard a frantic shuffling. Annie ran for the front door with a sinking heart. This had never worked yet. She was just unbolting the top lock when she heard him yell.

"Bitch!"

The door opened as if by magic, no thanks to her violently shaking fingers. Annie flew across the vestibule. Thanks be to God, Marty was as good as her word, and the large wooden door across the hall opened easily. Annie slammed it shut and turned to bolt it. With one hand on the lock, she felt the door pushed violently in. Kevin's hand was on the inside, and Annie reached down and bit it. She heard him swear violently as she tasted blood. The arm was withdrawn for a second. That was all she needed. The door closed easily, and she slid the bolt home.

She heard Marty's voice scream from behind her, "The police are on the way. You won't get away with this, you bastard."

Marty put her arm around Annie tightly, and they listened. A moment's silence was followed by hasty footsteps on the stairs.

"You call the police," Marty said tensely. "I'll see what he does and lock the back door."

Annie flew to the phone. Her mind was blank so she pushed O. The operator came on the line and rapidly connected her. In a shaking voice, Annie told whoever answered what had happened. The dispatcher agreed to send someone over.

Annie and Marty stood by the window and waited. Both young women shook violently. "It's okay," Marty repeated. "They'll arrest him now, and it'll be okay."

Nodding her head, Annie tried to calm her stomach. "I feel sick, Marty," she said in a trembling voice.

"You watch the window, Annie. I'll get you something." Seeing Annie's white face, she added, "The back door is bolted. He can't get in. They'll be here in a second. It's going to be fine. I promise."

Annie gazed out over the campus. Kevin could be anywhere.

Marty came back shortly with a glass of ginger ale and some crackers. "Sit down, Annie," she urged. "He's not coming back. He's psychotic, but he's not stupid. My grandmother always swore by ginger ale. She said the ginger quiets an upset stomach."

Allowing herself to be shepherded into a chair, Annie sipped at the ginger ale. Realizing she had not eaten, she forced the crackers down. In moments she was feeling stronger. "Thanks, Marty," she said solemnly. "I would have been dead if you had not left the door open."

Marty was chalk-white. "I know, Annie," she said, equally solemn. "I almost forgot. I had to go back and unlock it this afternoon." The girls looked at each other. Both felt chills. "I would have heard you banging," Marty said to reassure them both. "I would have opened it right away."

"Then there would have been three of us in here," Annie said quietly. "No," she amended. "He would have dragged me back into the apartment and locked you out."

"I would have called the police, Annie." They both glanced up at the clock. Ten minutes had elapsed, and there was no sign of them. Annie looked at Marty meaningfully. Marty shook her head in disgust. "I know," she said, reading Annie's thoughts. "If he intended to kill you, he could have."

Marty looked again out of the window. "They're

here. We might as well let them walk up so the neighbors don't hear."

"I'm sorry, Marty. We'll go into my apartment. This is embarrassing for you." Marty gave a snort of disgust. "Well, considering you're my only friend, I'm not too concerned. Was he in there when you got home?"

"Marty, I was taking my nylons off, and I noticed his shoe sticking out of the closet."

Marty held her stomach. "Oh, my God. Now *I* feel sick." She opened the door in anticipation of the officers' arrival. "We're up here," she yelled down the stairs. "They're talking to the downstairs neighbor," she said with a giggle. "The one with the crazy eyebrows and the husband with the roving eye. Do you know her?"

Annie shook her head.

"She thinks I'm a harlot because her husband always looks at me. People like that suspect any divorced woman."

Annie smiled. Marty's irreverence reminded her of Maureen.

Two officers plodded slowly up the stairs. Annie's heart sank when she recognized the older officer who had responded with Officer Grady the first time.

"What's all the hullabaloo about?" he asked tiredly.

Marty took offense. "The hullabaloo is that this woman's ex-husband, who has a restraining order against him, was hiding in her closet when she got home." Both officers looked bored. "He would have killed her if she had not run to my apartment."

Annie stepped forward. Officer Grady had warned her about appearing hysterical in front of police officers. "Thank you for coming," she began calmly. "My husband and I are separated. I've filed for divorce, and I have a restraining order against him. He's not allowed near this property. When I got home, he was hiding in the closet, and I ran here. He tried to follow me in, and I bit his hand and locked the door. He left when Marty"—she indicated her friend—"threatened to call the police."

The older officer took the lead. "Where is this restraining order?"

"It's in my apartment. I'll go get it," Annie replied, moving toward the door.

"Let's all go over," the officer said, making a move to follow her. "Thank you for your help, ma'am," he said, dismissing Marty. "We'll handle it from here."

"I'm sure Annie would prefer me to go with her," Marty said coldly.

Annie smiled gratefully. "Thanks, Marty. I would."

The group stood silently while the police officer scanned the restraining order. He finally spoke.

"It does say that he should not be here. Plain as day."

"Yes," Annie agreed. "Can you go and arrest him?"

The older man exchanged a look of patient

frustration with his partner. "Well, ma'am, it's just not that easy. Did anyone actually see him?"

Marty piped up. "I saw him running into the campus. I can tell you exactly what he was wearing."

"You know this man?" asked the second officer.

"I've seen a picture of him," Marty said defensively.

"Officer," Annie began, "I saw his shoe. It was his shoe. I *do* know this man."

"No offense," said the older officer, "but from what I've heard so far, neither one of you can positively identify Kevin Griffin as the man who pulled these shenanigans."

Annie tried hard to control her temper. "Sir, I've known this man for seven years. He called me a bitch. It was his voice. He also stuck his hand in the door. I know my husband's hand."

"But you did not look out of the window. Your friend did. And she doesn't know him."

"Officer . . ." Annie spoke with thinly veiled contempt. "I recognized his hand, his voice, and his shoe. In addition to that, I can't offhand think of anyone else who would be waiting in my closet to kill me. Can you?"

"Well, little lady, I don't know anything about what you get up to in the evenings. For all I know it could have been anyone."

Marty exploded. "How dare you? This woman has a perfectly valid order against this man. Why do you even grant these orders if the offender can do whatever he likes? She bit him. Check his hand.

It will have a bite mark on it. Is that positive enough for you?"

Both officers began shifting uncomfortably at Marty's verbal onslaught. Now they turned their backs to her and addressed Annie. She spoke quickly. She told them about the pictures and the letter. They were unimpressed.

"Let me remind you," spoke the older officer sharply, "you filed for divorce, lady. In my experience, divorce is ugly. This is what you get. I understand you already filed a criminal charge against him. Haven't you done enough?"

"Hasn't he?" she asked incredulously. "Does he have to kill me before you'll do anything?"

"You're getting a little excitable." Annie's mouth dropped open. "Calm down, and I'll tell you what to do. Call your lawyer and have her deal with it. It's not a criminal matter as far as I can see."

"How did you know my lawyer was a woman?" Annie asked, watching him intently.

The officer averted his eyes. "This is not a big town, Mrs. Griffin." The officers turned to leave, and Marty lifted her middle finger at their backs. Annie could not even smile. "Officers," she said calmly. "One more thing. What happens if he breaks in and I shoot him?"

The younger of the two turned and spoke lightly. "If you wound him and he runs out, drag his ass back in. That way you're in the clear." Both men burst out laughing as they ambled down the stairs.

Annie and Marty stared after them, stunned. "I'll be," said Marty. "He can do whatever he wants, Annie. You may as well use that order for toilet paper." At that moment Marty's phone rang from across the hall. "Come on," Marty said. "I don't want to be alone yet."

Annie heartily agreed and followed her back into the apartment. She threw herself down on the couch only to be interrupted by her friend.

"It's for you, Annie," Marty said suspiciously. "A very polite man. Maybe someone from the police department. Don't you have a friend over there?"

Annie sprang up hopefully. It had to be Officer Grady. "Hello," she said brightly.

"Annie." Kevin's voice was tight. "I see you called the police." He laughed shortly. "Let me guess. There is nothing they can do, right?"

Holding her hand over her stomach, she signaled Marty. "No, Kevin. There's not. How did you know? How did you get this phone number?"

Kevin laughed again. "Think about it, Annie. The cops won't touch me. They think the whole thing is pretty shitty. Those guys love my coach, and they told him not to worry. As far as the number? Do you really think I don't know everything about you? I know what you wore yesterday, and I know what you're wearing today. Did you get my message on film?"

"You're not clever, Kevin. You're twisted. I thought you wanted me back. Is this how you think I'll change my mind?"

"Well, I do want you back." He sounded uncertain. "Are you ready to come back yet?"

"After this, Kevin, I'll never come back. I can't believe you would even ask me."

"Annie . . ." He spoke in a soft voice that was horrifying. "Despite what you think, I still love you. You don't deserve me; you never did. But I do still love you. I don't care how many guys you're sleeping with. I also liked the old lady you're going to work for. I'm up-to-date."

Annie drew in her breath sharply. She felt hair prickling the back of her neck.

"You're very quiet," he continued. "Do you understand? You can't hide from me. I will always find you. And you're not going to get away with this. Now, if you drop the charges I might let you live. Call me tomorrow and tell me that they're dropped." Annie remained silent. She was thinking frantically. "Tell me you understand." He waited again. "Do you realize that right now you could be lying on your bedroom floor dead? I'm going to strangle you. That way there's no evidence. I won't get caught, Annie. I'll get custody, and Mary and I will live happily ever after. Trust me."

She tried a different tack. "Kevin, how can you even talk like this? We've been best friends for years. Okay, our marriage did not work out. But do you really want to hurt me that badly?"

His voice cracked. "No, Annie, I don't want to hurt you anymore. It would be better if we both died. We'd be together forever. I'm sorry about all of this. But you're forcing me to do it."

"But, Kevin, if you're so intent on killing us, what do you care if the charges are dropped?"

"I don't know for sure if I want to die. But I can't let you get away with this. I have no choice."

"So if I drop the charges, you'll leave me alone?"

"I'll try to, Annie, I really will. If I can, I will."

"Kevin," she pleaded, "get some help. You sound terrible."

He turned ugly. "Fuck you, Annie. You get help. You're the one who needs it."

The line went dead. Annie stood holding the telephone in her hand. Marty stood staring at her tensely. "Marty, he's not making sense. He's going to kill us both so nothing matters. On the other hand, maybe he'll let me live if I drop the charges." Annie's whole body began to shake violently. Marty led her to the sofa. Annie sat and put her head down into her own lap. Cold sweat dripped across her back. Caroline had talked about anxiety attacks. This must be one of them. Soon she felt a cold cloth on the back of her neck. The result was immediate. Annie sat up. "Thanks, Marty," she said quietly. "I'm better."

"Well, I don't wonder you feel sick," Marty said gently. "I feel sick myself, and it's not happening to me."

Annie smiled warmly at her friend. "Marty, you've been a lifesaver. I'm really okay. I'm going to go home and call my lawyer. Maybe she'll have an idea."

Annie rose to leave. Marty's look of concern was genuine. "Are you sure you want to go back in there?"

"Yes, I'm fine."

"I'll check on you in a little while. Annie," she added, "make sure you answer the door, or I'll be scared silly."

Annie promised and crossed the hall. She dead-bolted both doors. Next she sat down at the table. Dialing the police department, she asked for Officer Grady. She was informed that Officer Grady was on vacation for the next ten days. Annie politely thanked the woman and hung up.

After a few minutes of deep thought, she dialed her lawyer's number. She was told that Madeline was on another line and would call her back. Annie hung up and remained motionless. When the phone rang, she answered it dully. She did not care if it was Kevin. Instead she heard her attorney's crisp voice.

"Madeline," she asked clearly, "what would happen if I went back to Chicago?"

"You mean before the divorce?"

"I mean tonight," Annie answered flatly.

Madeline grasped the seriousness of the situation and answered professionally. "If you leave the state without notice to the court, he can file in your absence and be granted pretty much anything. For example, I know your first concern is the child. Kevin could go in tomorrow morning and get custody. It happens. Technically, you could be accused of abducting the child. Then he shows up at your father's house with a squad car and takes her. He would have the right to do that. We're working on a law that says a victim can flee from an abusive spouse with her children, but frankly, Annie, we're not there yet." The woman paused. "Tell me what's going on."

"Well, he was hiding in my closet when I got home." Annie heard the sharp intake of breath and told her the details. "The policemen said there was nothing they could do."

"I see," Madeline answered in disgust. "About the best I can do is take it in front of the divorce judge and ask that Kevin be further admonished."

Annie felt as if someone had just clicked off the light at the end of the tunnel.

"That didn't get you very far last time, Madeline." Realizing how that might sound, she added hastily, "I'm not blaming you. . . . I'm trying to be realistic."

"I know you are, Annie. Don't worry about offending me. The system here is pretty much a Good Ole Boys club. Is there somewhere else you could stay for a while?"

"Yes," Annie said, in a hurry now to hang up. "I think so, Madeline. Don't worry."

"You're not going to do anything drastic, I hope."

"Not at all," Annie said. "I'll be in touch."

She hung up and went to the bedroom. Pulling a chair to the closet, she climbed up and rummaged around on the high shelf until she felt the gun. Annie pulled it down and replaced the chair. Calmly, she opened the linen closet and felt around on the top shelf. Locating the box of sanitary napkins, she reached in and grabbed the bullets and clip.

She mentally thanked Danny and proceeded to load the gun. How naive she had been to think Kevin could be controlled by the courts. The system had made a fool of her. Far from feeling shaky about handling the weapon, she felt calm and secure. When the gun was loaded, she checked the safety and set it down on the table.

Annie rose to get her purse. Her movements were unhurried. In a way she was relaxed. *Yes*, she told herself, *it has really come to this*. She pulled Buddy's number from her wallet and calmly made her last call of the day.

Chapter Twenty-one

A knock on the door made Annie jump. Shadows darkened the little dining room, and Annie noticed the clock she had been staring at. It was nearly seven. Two hours ago she had hung up with Buddy. Lifting the gun, she faced the door.

"Who is it?" she asked in a confident voice.

"Marty."

"Hold on, Marty. I'll be right there."

Annie placed the gun in the top drawer of the desk. She was walking to the door when she thought of Danny. Mechanically, she turned back and opened the drawer again. Turning the gun over, she checked the safety and replaced the gun in the drawer. She must know where she stood at all times. Satisfied, she admitted her friend.

"Have you recovered?" she asked Marty lightly.

"Never mind me," Marty said emphatically. "How are you? Have you eaten anything?" The young woman held a plate in her hands. When Annie shook her head negatively, Marty offered the plate. "Great. I figured as much. I brought you some Texas barbecue with beans. It's legendary, and I have a fridge full of it. Granny again. She figured I might neglect myself with the move and all."

Annie smiled and took the plate. "Will you join me?"

"No. I ate. But I'll sit and talk a while."

They sat at the table. Annie lifted the tinfoil and realized she was ravenous. She barely noticed when Marty rose to double-check the bolts on the door. In less than ten minutes, she sat back with a sigh. Strength coursed through her body.

"Marty, once again, you saved the day. I had no idea how hungry I was. I'm ready for anything."

Marty took her chair again and grinned. "That's how it is in a crisis. You forget to eat and then wonder why you feel so weak. What did your lawyer say?"

Annie outlined the dismal legal situation. Marty's look of concern prompted her to continue.

"Don't worry, Marty. I called a friend of my brother's. He's on his way."

"What's he going to do?" asked Marty hesitantly.

Annie frowned. "I don't know. He sounded normal on the phone." Her frown deepened. "I have a feeling he's going to threaten Kevin or something. I don't care anymore. Kevin's going to kill me if I don't do something. I'm out of options."

Marty became brisk. Standing, she cleared Annie's plate and bustled around the kitchen. "I'm making hot tea. Annie, don't worry about what he does. Leave it to him. Is he from Texas?"

"Originally, I guess. Now he lives in New Orleans. I don't know anything about him. It's kind of weird."

"Not at all," came the smooth response. "Texans have a way of handling these situations, and it does not involve the courts. He'll probably scare the hell out of him. Kevin needs to deal with a man on this. Let him take on someone his own size."

"I couldn't agree with you more," Annie stated firmly. "I don't care who he deals with . . . as long as it's not me. I thought of going home, but that muddies up the divorce waters. Kevin will do anything. He's scary."

"Hey," Marty said suddenly, "how did the interview go?"

Annie brightened immediately. She filled Marty in on the details and cheered herself in the process. "So you see," she continued, "if I can just get Killer Kevin to settle down, I should be fixed up pretty nicely."

The girls sat and talked for another hour. Shortly after eight, Marty rose and stretched. "Are you sure you won't take my couch?" she offered. "I'd feel a lot better if you did."

"No," Annie said flatly. "Thanks, but this guy might show up during the night. Buddy, I mean. He said he was leaving right away. How long does it take to drive here from New Orleans?"

Marty pondered. "At least twelve hours, I would guess. Depends on whether or not there are highway patrols out. He won't get here till morning, Annie."

"Still," Annie said firmly, "I'll stay here. I have the doors bolted."

"What you need is a gun, Honey. I've got one, but it's at Mother's. Yanks aren't used to them, but here in Texas we're raised knowing how to shoot. Do you want me to bring it out next weekend?"

Annie internally debated how much to tell Marty. Coming to a decision, she shook her head slowly. "I don't think so. Thanks, though. Let's see what my Buddy can do."

Marty took her leave, promising to leave her doors unlatched. Annie thanked her for the dinner. The emptiness closed in upon the apartment. Annie turned on all the lights. She wanted to watch television but decided against it. The noise might cover sounds she needed to hear. A bath and a book would have to suffice.

The hot tap blasted on full. Annie watched the tub fill and remembered another night in this bathroom. Blood had splattered all over the floor. Her face hardened, and she went into the dining room and pulled the gun out of the drawer. She scolded herself for going even into the bathroom without it. Instinct warned her she would have little time if he struck again. Danny had counseled her to shoot first and reminisce later. Tonight it sounded like good advice.

Setting the gun on the toilet, Annie stripped down and climbed into the tub. It was perfect. Scalding hot. She had the bathroom door locked and the gun within reach, but she could not relax. Glancing at the weapon, she realized it was pointing directly at her. She shot out of the tub naked and checked the safety. The room filled with steam. Would moisture interfere with gunpowder? Was gunpowder what made it shoot? Danny had told her how to clean it, but Annie had not listened. At the time she had no intention of using the weapon. Swinging the door open, she wrapped herself in a towel and moved the gun into the living room.

In minutes she was sitting in the recliner. Warm, soft pajamas provided comfort, and Annie reprimanded herself. The bathtub was a dangerous place to be. The only worse location would be the shower. She had seen the movie *Psycho* and had scarcely enjoyed a shower since. She checked the clock. Roughly eight hours to go. She determined she would sit in the chair until Buddy arrived.

Contemplating the mysterious Buddy, Annie wondered if Danny had paid him. A cultured drawl had thrown her when she called him. What had she expected? Honesty prevailed, and she admitted she'd expected a tough, shady voice. Maybe a mafia type. Voice-wise, Buddy sounded like the first judge Annie had spoken to. Educated and gentle. For a while she considered her brother. Was he tough? Danny was a gentleman in her experience, but how would she know? By his own admission, he carried a gun. Maybe he had been too long in the South. Texans carried guns. Most were law-abiding citizens. Annie seldom heard of shootings here, while in Chicago they were rampant. She gave up the attempt to categorize men.

By nine o'clock she was equally tired of checking

the safety and chasing her thoughts. She fought the urge to call Chicago. It was only ten there, but Annie knew she could not keep the situation to herself. Maureen would get everything out of her, and they would be worried sick. They would also think she was demented. Annie wrestled with the concept of craziness. Was she nuts? She was sitting in a living room, thirteen hundred miles from home, with a gun on her lap. It did not sound good. On the other hand, what would be a better response? If she left, Kevin would follow her and disappear with Mary. He was unstable. Annie decided she was too weary to scrutinize the situation any longer.

Reaching down, she grabbed the first textbook she touched. Psychology. She would study. Opening the pages randomly, she landed on a chapter titled "Avoidance." "Denial" was the first subheading, and she threw the book down in disgust. There was such a thing as too much thinking. She needed light reading. Perhaps a Gothic romance. No. Something more modern. A book where the heroine wielded a .22 and took grief from no man. *I'm losing it*, she thought humorously.

She toyed with the idea of calling Kevin to make sure he was at home. At least she would know he was not lurking around in her vestibule. No. That might inflame him. Buddy had begged her to go stay in a hotel until he arrived. Annie had been adamant. She would stay in her home with the gun ready. Maybe she was behaving irrationally. Too late now, though. Annie was too frightened to open the door and run to the car. *Imagine a lifetime of this*, she thought in dismay. A person would go stark raving mad. She had done the right thing, she told herself. Danny had seemed to think Buddy was the man for the job, and Danny was almost always right.

She thought about saying a rosary but decided her situation was a bit nebulous for prayer. A real Christian martyr would relish the thought of offering herself to a brutal death. Annie would never make sainthood because she was determined to do some damage to Kevin before he killed her. If she prayed, there was no telling where she would end up. She had a sneaking suspicion God frowned on the whole murder-for-hire thing. Now, in fairness, she had no idea what Buddy had planned. She had emphatically told him she did not want Kevin hurt. He had understood completely. Even so, spiritually speaking, she felt the waters getting deeper and murkier. She thanked God for taking care of Mary and then mentally put her fingers in her ears.

"It's not that I'm not interested. God," she said politely out loud. "I'm just too tired to hash it out now."

With a guilty feeling she grabbed her history book and began to study.

At two o'clock she had a glass of juice with a Hostess cupcake. At three she had hot tea. At four she made soup, and at five she downed two Cokes. Completely wired, she decided to clean out her silverware drawer. Moments later, she decided the job was too loud. Also, she could not see the front door from the kitchen. He could sneak up on her. Annie left the forks, spoons, and knives on the counter and went back to the living room. She had just settled back in her chair when the phone rang. Annie leaped from her chair, spilling her pop, and ran to the phone. Her heart raced as she picked it up.

"Hello?"

"Annie?" asked the soft drawl. "It's Buddy. I'm down the street. I did not want to scare you by coming up. Are you in the apartment with all of the lights on?"

"Yes," Annie said, giggling. "I didn't want him to think I was sleeping."

"Okay. I recognized Danny's old car. I'll be right over. My car is a blue Thunderbird. All right?"

"Thanks, Pal . . . I mean, Buddy." Annie closed her eyes in dismay. "I'm a little tired."

He chuckled, too. "I'll bet you are. See you in a minute."

Moments later, headlights pulled into the drive. Finally a soft knock came, and Annie swung open the door.

"Hello, ma'am," said a tall, athletic-looking man.

Annie looked him over. He was well dressed in a casual, collegiate way. Light brown khakis were paired with a tan sports shirt. The inevitable belt buckle was small and did not sport a horse. Annie smiled up at him and extended her hand.

"Call me Annie," she said sweetly.

"I will," he replied. "Thank you, Annie. Your brother is a good man, and I owe him. So don't think you need to be thanking me."

"Well, I'm glad you owe him, Buddy." Annie smiled impishly and stepped back. "Enter the hold-out."

He smiled back and preceded her into the apartment. "Is that your gun?" he asked as he walked over to the easy chair.

"Yes," she said, ruffling her bangs. "I've been sitting there holding it most of the night. Danny gave it to me."

Buddy picked it up and looked it over. "It's a beauty. I'm sure glad you didn't need it, though."

"Why?" she asked in surprise.

"Because the clip isn't in all of the way. It won't fire like this." He looked at Annie. She gave him a look of comical dismay, and they burst out laughing.

Annie was still wiping her eyes when she spoke. "Well, the joke is on me. That's what I get for thinking I'm so tough. What can I get you?" she asked suddenly. "You must be exhausted."

"Nothing," he said politely. "I've been drinking sodas all night. What are your plans this morning?"

Annie sat down on the couch and waved him into her chair. "Well, I guess I'll go to school in a couple of hours. Why?"

Buddy's clear, handsome face crinkled. "I'd rather you didn't, Annie. From what you've said, this guy is on a mission. Danny had no idea he was this far gone, or he would never have let you stay."

Annie considered for a moment what Danny could have done. Thrown her over his shoulder?

She dismissed the thought as uncharitable, and paid attention.

Buddy continued, "The picture thing is pretty telling. Until I have the chance to talk to him, I'd rather you stayed close to me."

Annie wavered. After making him drive all this way, she could hardly start quibbling about details. "That's fine. Do you think he'd hurt me at school?"

"No," Buddy answered patiently. "He's not brave. Any guy with a little pride would do time before begging you to drop the charges. Of course, any normal guy would keep his hands to himself. He's not a hero, Annie, but he could grab you on campus and haul you off somewhere. I'd feel better if we played it safe."

"Me, too," agreed Annie. "But when will you talk to him?"

"Don't worry," he said with a grin. "From what you told me about yesterday, he's feeling pretty cocky right now. He'll make a move today."

"You think so?" Annie asked with rounded eyes. "He expects me to drop the charges today. Should I?"

Buddy frowned. "No. Only because I don't feel like going down to the courthouse. I've had enough of courtrooms to last me a lifetime. After I talk to him, you can do whatever you like. But let's make him unhappy. Okay?"

"Whatever you say," Annie said complacently. It was wonderful to have someone else take the lead. "How about some breakfast?"

"No, thank you. Annie, go ahead and get some sleep. I'll stretch out here on the couch for a while. You can leave the gun with me."

"I'll never sleep," she said gloomily. "I'm too nervous."

"Give it a try," he encouraged her. "You look tired."

Annie sighed. "Are you sure you don't mind?"

"Not at all. You'll feel better. I'll take you to lunch when you get up."

Annie smiled widely. "That would be great." She was thanking him again when the phone rang. "Who would that be?" she asked Buddy irrationally. He shrugged pleasantly. Annie looked at the clock. It was six o'clock in the morning.

"Hello?"

"Annie," Kevin said calmly. "How are you doing?"

Annie motioned to Buddy. He walked over and stood by her. He shook his head negatively, and Annie understood she should not tell Kevin she had company.

"I'm fine, Kevin. What do you want?"

"I'm reminding you that you need to be at the courthouse."

"Why?" Annie asked innocently.

"Annie," Kevin said venomously. "Do it today! I'm tired of being nice about this. Drop the fucking charges."

"So if I don't drop the charges today . . ." she

said for Buddy's benefit. Buddy smiled. Annie suspected this was what he wanted.

"You die, Annie. Any questions?"

"Screw you, Kevin. I hope you rot in jail." She hung up the phone. Her hands were shaking, and she knew that her face was pale.

"Perfect, Annie," Buddy said pleasantly. "Now, go get some sleep and we'll talk about it when you get up."

"I'll lie down," she promised. "But I know I won't sleep."

Annie climbed into her bed and stared at the closed bedroom door. How comforting to know he was out there. She wondered what Danny had done for him. He'd said he was sick of courtrooms. Was he a criminal? Annie tried to think about Kevin, but her mind refused. She was too tired. Certain she would lie awake for hours, she promptly fell into a deep sleep.

Chapter Twenty-two

At three thirty in the afternoon, Annie sat up in bed. Shaking her head groggily, she made a grab at the day's reality. Was there really a strange man sitting in her living room? What was that thing about Kevin? Oh, yes. Today he was going to kill her. It came back to Annie in a sliding way, as things sometimes do when big events precede a deep sleep.

Annie rolled out of bed and groped in her drawer for clothes. Jeans and a T-shirt seemed appropriate. Glancing in the mirror, she grimaced at her hair. A shower was mandatory. First she would check on her bodyguard.

Annie peeked around the corner. Buddy was looking right at her.

"You're awake," she said in surprise.

"I could say the same about you," he answered easily. "Did you have any trouble sleeping?"

They both laughed. "No, I guess not," she responded ruefully. "I guess we missed lunch. Are you hungry?"

Buddy was sitting on the couch reading one of her textbooks. "We'll get dinner whenever you want," he said politely. "I made myself a sandwich. Annie, do you have an address for Kevin?"

"No," she said apologetically. "I'm sorry, I don't.

He'd be at practice right now until five. I have a picture."

Her houseguest smiled and nodded. "Great. Can I see it? I'm going to wander near the gym and see if I can get a look at him. I won't be long." He rose and stretched. "By the way, I met your neighbor, Martha."

"Marty?" Annie asked. "She's been a great help to me. He might have killed me the other day if she had not left her door open."

Buddy smiled. "That's what she said." He took the picture Annie offered and put it in his shirt pocket. "Deadbolt the doors after me, Annie. I won't be long."

Annie locked the doors and headed for the shower. The phone rang. She decided to ignore it. She thought of her father saying "I can't think of a soul still on earth I'm interested in talking to."

After showering at high speed with the curtain half open, Annie dressed. She was replacing her silverware in the drawer when she heard a knock on the front door. She walked to the living room and stood uncertainly.

"Annie?" she heard Marty say.

"Hi, Marty," she responded easily. "Just a minute." Annie unbolted the door and swung it open. "How are you?"

Marty stepped in and looked around. Large curlers rested on her head. "Where did he go?"

Annie laughed. "He's gone out to stalk Kevin. I heard you met him."

Marty rolled her eyes. "That's the understatement of the day. Are you in love? He's gorgeous!"

Annie frowned. "Yes, I guess he is. I hadn't really noticed."

"Let me check your pulse. You must be dead." The girls heard footsteps outside. They froze. A soft knock landed on the door, and they looked at each other in dismay.

"It's Buddy," he said softly.

Annie made a motion to open the door when Marty grabbed her arm. Her neighbor gestured to her hair and headed for the back door. Annie grimaced and first followed Marty back through the kitchen. After locking her out, Annie returned to the front door and unbolted it.

"Hi," she said, smiling. She crushed the urge to giggle but knew her smile was too wide.

Buddy stepped in. He, too, sported a grin but said nothing. Almost immediately the phone began to ring. Buddy went to the couch as Annie reached for the telephone.

"Annie," said her neighbor tensely, "find out if he's married."

Annie turned her back to Buddy and said flatly. "Not right now, Marty."

"*Whenever*. Find out or I'll kill you myself." Marty hung up, and Annie felt her face warming up. She replaced the telephone and turned to Buddy innocently.

"Did you see him?"

"Yes," Buddy answered. He was acting normal,

but Annie sensed he knew. Her face burned hotter. "He was working out," Buddy continued nonchalantly. "I spotted him right away. I'm going to head back there in fifteen minutes and see if I can find out where he lives. I wanted to let you know what I was doing. If you want to go shopping or anything, Annie, this would be a good time. I'll be right behind Kevin, so you'll be safe."

Annie searched for a way to ask her question. "I don't know how to ask you this, Buddy. I don't want to be rude." Buddy's features were inscrutable. Annie dove in. "You're not going to kill him, are you? I know that sounds ridiculous. Of course, you would never do a thing like that . . ." Annie was babbling, and she knew it. Buddy rescued her.

"Annie," he said kindly, "I know that in spite of everything, you don't have any hatred for this guy. I'm not a killer. I'm only going to talk to him and make sure he understands that you're not alone. He needs to know he's accountable to someone. That's going to be me." At Annie's look of relief, he continued, "I might throw a few punches if he's not listening. Nothing big. He'll survive. I need to make sure he gets the message. Okay?"

"Yes," she said, still hesitant.

"What's the problem, Annie?"

"Well, I wouldn't want you to get hurt, either. He's very big." Annie looked up at him in concern. "I've never seen him lose a fight."

This made Buddy chuckle. "Don't worry, Annie. He's not going to hurt me."

Something about his complete confidence unnerved her.

"What do you do for a living, Buddy?"

"You mean when I'm not killing Yankees?" He spoke innocently, and they both laughed.

"There's nothing mysterious about what I do. How about if I tell you over dinner? I'll be back in an hour, and we'll get something to eat."

"Fine." Annie smiled up at him.

Marty was right. He certainly was likable. After he departed, Annie telephoned next door. A firm scolding was followed by thirty minutes of speculation about Annie's visitor. Annie had noted the absence of a wedding ring, but Marty said that was meaningless. Something about Buddy made Annie remember that her hair needed to be cut. For the first time in weeks, she wondered where her makeup was. Marty said she was a fool if she did not at least flirt with him. Annie said she felt guilty even thinking about another man. Marty's snort of disgust was audible.

"Get real, Annie. You're getting divorced. If you live through it, you're going to date other guys. Your brother's best Buddy is as good a place to start as any."

Annie found herself laughing hysterically.

"Tell him that my anatomy teacher is looking at me funny," Marty said playfully. "I'd like it handled."

Annie ended the conversation in another fit of giggling. She would have to rid her mind of these thoughts or she would be terribly uncomfortable. She firmly reminded herself that Buddy was here for one reason. He was Danny's friend. He looked young, but Annie guessed he was at least thirty. He carried himself with the confidence of an older man. It was possible he was an "unclaimed treasure," as Marty called him, but it was equally possible he had a beautiful wife and eight children. Nevertheless, Annie told herself she was going to begin wearing makeup every day. She might as well start today.

An hour later, she was still waiting. The phone rang. Buddy kept it short. Kevin had stopped at a bar. Buddy would remain with him until he headed home. At that point Buddy would come back for Annie. He would call again if it got late. Annie said she was going to go get groceries.

Annie ran through the grocery store as though she were being chased. Her mind raced. What if Kevin got hurt? How would she feel? Emotions ebbed and flowed, and the contents of her grocery cart mystified her. Forcing herself to look at a different scenario, Annie stopped in aisle seven. Buddy had been a last resort. Kevin was dangerous. The loving and kind friend she remembered was gone. It was time to be concerned with her future and Mary's. She would have a whole different set of worries if Buddy were not there. No, she thought doggedly. She would not worry. Danny was smart, and he would never have suggested Annie call a man who would kill Kevin. Promising herself it would come out all right, she sifted through the non-sense in her cart and concentrated. She would cook dinner for Buddy at home.

Another hour passed, and Annie sat alone with her tossed salad. Finally, she heard footsteps on the stairs. A soft knock told her Buddy was back. Still, she checked. After positively identifying him, she opened the door.

"Hi," she said brightly. "Are you starving?"

"Yes, are you? I'm sorry I was gone so long. Let's go to dinner."

"I thought we'd eat here," Annie countered. "If you don't mind."

"Even better," he said cheerfully. "I'd rather we stayed by the phone."

"Why?" Annie asked nervously.

"So that you're here if he calls. He's drunk, but somehow I don't think he went to bed. There were a couple of people at the apartment he's staying at. Let's eat."

Annie nodded and waved him into a kitchen chair. The table was set. She pulled the salad from the fridge and put the steaks into the broiler. Conversation flowed more easily than Annie expected. Buddy had attended Texas A&M University. His degree was in law enforcement. Right now he was working on starting his own business, but he did not say what it was. Annie asked him artfully if his wife worked, and he shook his head.

"She stays at home?" Annie probed.

"No," Buddy answered. "I'm not married."

"I see," Annie said innocently. "Did you like Texas A&M?" The subject had to be changed quickly. Buddy liked college but had been glad to finish. All that was years ago, he said. Annie refrained from asking how many years ago and changed the subject. How did he know Danny? Buddy said Danny formerly worked for an oil company that had internal troubles. He did not elaborate except to say Danny was a "stand-up guy" and not easily intimidated.

"That worked to my benefit," he added mysteriously. Deftly changing the subject, he asked about Annie's classes. After dessert, Buddy thanked her politely. He then folded his napkin with the air of a man who was getting down to business.

"Annie," he said slowly, "here's what I have in mind. I think Kevin knows you did not drop the charges today. I also think he's pretty wired right now. Let's see if he shows up here tonight. If he doesn't, I'll run over and talk to him in the morning. How does that sound?"

"Fine," Annie said thoughtfully. "But if he's had a few drinks, he'll be even worse. I mean . . . he won't be in a good mood when he gets here."

"I'm certain of it," Buddy agreed, poker-faced. "From what I saw at the bar, he's feeling a lot of hostility." Annie smiled nervously at his obvious understatement. "When he comes, you head for the bedroom, and Kevin and I will take a ride. There's nothing to worry about." Seeing Annie's pale face, he continued. "Annie, I know what I'm dealing with.

I doubt Kevin is carrying a gun. Even if he is, it's not a problem." He paused and selected his words carefully. "I've done this kind of thing before with tougher guys than your husband. You see, Annie, Kevin is deadly with you. There's no doubt. But when he's up against a guy who's not afraid of him, he's not so scary. Do you mind if I shower?"

"Not at all. Let me get you a towel."

Once Buddy was supplied with what he needed, Annie cleared the dinner dishes. A dropped plate nearly sent her through the roof, and she screamed. Buddy immediately opened the bathroom door a crack.

"Are you all right?"

"Fine," she said, wincing. How embarrassing. "I dropped a plate. Sorry."

"I'll be out in a minute, Annie."

"Great," she said, fearing she would drop dead from mortification. Walking into the kitchen, she put her hands over her face. Annie decided sternly to be completely calm and rational from this moment on. No more second-guessing. Buddy was possibly saving her life, and that was that. She would behave sanely if it killed her. Determined, she put the dishes in the sink and blasted the hot water. Hearing him yell, she turned the water off. Wincing again, she walked within five feet of the bathroom.

"Sorry," she shouted.

"That's okay."

Annie's shoulders began to shake with silent laughter. There was something unnerving about having a man in the shower. She went back to the kitchen and tried to stop giggling. *Wouldn't Maureen love this story?* she thought ruefully. The exact moment she heard the water shut off, she turned on the sink and began to wash dishes industriously. She worked quickly and was finished before he came out. Hesitating only a moment, she dumped all the dishes back into the soapy water and began again. Buddy came out of the bathroom looking as well-kept as before except with wet hair. He carried an overnight bag and had changed clothes. He smiled at her, and she smiled back.

"Buddy, I have to admit I'm a little nervous."

"I would never have guessed that, Annie." They laughed. "I think you're holding up remarkably well. This must be horrible for you."

"It's not so bad anymore," she said in surprise. "I guess I feel relieved that I called you and you're here. I thought about calling you a lot."

Buddy looked genuinely sad. "I'm sorry any of this happened to you." After a moment he continued brightly, "Don't worry, Annie. I know that being a single mother is probably rough, but at least I can guarantee you that from now on he won't bother you. You'll do great in school."

Annie grinned. "I hope you're right. On both counts."

The tension broken, they relaxed. After an hour watching the news, Annie yawned in spite of herself.

"Go to bed if you want, Annie," Buddy said kindly. "I put the gun under your bed. It's loaded, and the safety is on. I'm leaving the deadbolts off the doors, and I'm going to grab a nap on the couch here." Annie made a move to get him bedding. "Annie"—he stopped her—"no matter what you hear, stay in your room. Promise?"

She looked directly into his eyes. "If you say so." A thousand questions flitted through her mind. She shrugged and let them go.

Silently, she went to the closet and pulled down some bedding. She set it on the couch next to him.

"Sleep well, Annie," he said.

"I'll try," promised Annie. "Be careful, Buddy."

Chapter Twenty-three

Sometime after midnight, Annie heard the screen door close downstairs. She sat up. Unable to resist, she opened her bedroom door and peeked out. Buddy's voice came softly from the darkness.

"I heard it, Annie. You promised."

"I know. I'm sorry."

She closed the bedroom door and sat on the bed. Her stomach tensed, but she was not shaking. She wondered if this had been a good plan. On the off chance Kevin got past Buddy, she was a sitting duck. She remembered the gun and felt for it under the bed. She felt better holding it. Listening intently, she heard nothing. There was no sound whatsoever. She was just lying back down when she heard Buddy speak.

"You must be Kevin," he said in a normal voice. "I've been waiting for you."

Annie heard Kevin yell in surprise. "Who the hell are you?" She noted from his voice that Kevin was far from sober. Her stomach knotted with abandon. Praying incoherently, she clicked the safety off the gun.

"I'm a friend of Danny McGowan," Buddy said conversationally. "He was worried about his sister so I told him I'd stop by and see her. Are you supposed to be here, Kevin? I thought there was a restraining order against you."

Annie listened tensely. Buddy was being extremely polite.

"It's none of your business," Kevin snapped. "Where's my wife?"

"She's sleeping," Buddy said. "And I don't want you to wake her."

Annie noted half hysterically that Kevin lowered his voice. "Get the fuck out of this apartment. I've got business with my wife."

"I don't think so, Sport. You've got business with me. Let's go for a ride." Annie heard Buddy stand up. Kevin laughed. Next she heard a scuffle, followed by a yelp and a thud.

"Now, get up and let's try again, Kevin. I'm serious about this. You do what I say. That's the only rule. Do you have any questions about it? Ask now. If you make noise, the neighbors might call the police. And you're not supposed to be here. I don't want the police to come. That would be bad for you. Let's try it again."

Annie heard the door close behind them.

Two hours passed. Sleep was not an issue as Annie watched out the window. Buddy and Kevin had gotten into Buddy's car. Kevin was driving. Initially, Annie could not imagine why Kevin was so cooperative. Then something occurred to her. Kevin was afraid. *Good*, she thought. *Let him see how it feels.*

Shortly after three A.M. she heard a car. Racing to the window, she watched as Buddy jumped deftly from the driver's seat. Annie had the door open and met him in the hallway.

"Is everything all right?"

"Fine, Annie. Everything is fine." He smiled. "Are you still up?"

Annie backed into the apartment. Buddy followed.

"Strangely enough, I had trouble sleeping."

Buddy closed the door behind him. He turned to Annie. "I'm going to take off, Annie. It's a long drive, and I might as well get started."

"So soon?"

He smiled. "Yes. I have to stop by and see my folks in Abilene. Annie, are you calm?"

She looked up at him. "Why? Should I be calm?"

He nodded. "Absolutely. I just want to explain a few things. Kevin will be calling you in the morning. I told him to. And I have his phone number. I'll call you in the afternoon to see how you're doing. After that I am going to check in with you every so often. And you should call me if anything worries you. Anything at all. I'll be back in two weeks to see you."

"In two weeks? Why?" Annie felt like she was repeating herself. Wrapped in a bathrobe, she was having trouble taking it all in.

"To make sure you're okay, of course. I promised Danny I would keep an eye out for you." He gave her a reassuring smile. "Kevin sees that he was wrong, Annie. He promised not to bother you anymore."

"Are you sure he won't?"

Buddy gave her a sardonic grin. "I'm nearly certain. You see, Annie, these guys aren't brave when they're dealing with other men. Actually, they're cowards. Kevin does not mind messing with you, but he will think twice before he messes with me. And now he understands that if he messes with you he not only messes with me, but he messes with Danny. And he doesn't want to do that."

Annie was still uncertain. "Where is he now?"

"At the hospital, I believe. He fell and hurt his wrist. It's nothing serious, Annie."

Buddy turned and grabbed his bag, which was by the door. "Annie, my friend, I wish I had met you under different circumstances. But who knows? Life's not over yet."

Annie nodded her head. He was leaving. He walked out into the hallway. Turning one more time, he gave her another grin. "I'll be in touch. Good night, Marty."

The last sentence was spoken loudly. Buddy was barely out of the building when Marty's door swung open.

"How did he know I was there?" she demanded.

Annie shook her head numbly. It had all happened so fast. He was gone. Kevin had hurt his wrist. Buddy wished he had met her under different circumstances.

"I'll talk to you in the morning, Marty. Okay?"

"Sure," Marty said just above a whisper. "You're okay?"

Annie nodded and shut the door. She went to the window and watched his car disappear. Sitting down weakly on the couch, she wondered what to do. Kevin was hurt badly enough to go to the hospital.

"I'm tired," she said aloud. "I'll go to bed." And so she did. It was too soon to unload the gun, so she checked the safety and left it on the dresser.

A ringing telephone dragged her from a sound sleep. She stumbled from her bed and answered with half-closed eyes.

"Annie," Kevin said weakly, "you don't have to drop the charges. You can if you want. But you don't have to. I'll plead guilty."

"Kevin, are you all right?"

There was silence. Then Kevin spoke with bitterness. "Just fine. I had a car accident last night and had to go to the hospital."

"I'm sorry to hear that," said Annie with her hand over her stomach. "Were you hurt badly?"

"A sprained wrist and four stitches in my lip. I guess I don't even know you anymore, Annie. I cannot believe you would let someone do this to me."

Momentarily speechless, Annie slumped under waves of guilt. Then something snapped inside.

"Kevin, it's okay for you to send *me* to the hospital. That's okay. It's just you having a few stitches and a sprained wrist that's the problem. It's over, Kevin. You can do whatever you want but don't think I'm going to take it nicely anymore."

He slammed down the phone.

Two days later Annie headed home from her appointment with Caroline. The sky toward the southwest looked ominous, with black clouds moving quickly toward the town. Annie increased her speed in an effort to beat the storm. Tornados blew up out of nowhere here, and she had no wish to be caught without shelter on such flat landscape.

The counseling session had been productive. Caroline focused on practical realities and cautioned Annie to tread slowly with romance. Too bad, she'd thought. Maybe Buddy would be around when she was ready.

Large angry drops pelted the windshield as Annie pulled into the parking lot of the convenience store. Tornado or not, she was getting a newspaper to act as her dinner dining companion. Maureen was bringing Mary back from Chicago tomorrow, but until then Annie was on her own.

Grabbing the paper, she joined the line, wiping away the water that dripped from her hair. A couple ahead of her spoke in tense voices, and Annie politely looked away. The woman was a little older than Annie and spoke in a conciliatory tone.

"Shut up," her husband ordered. "Shut your mouth."

Startled, Annie looked to the woman for her response. With flushed face, the woman looked away, refusing to meet her gaze. Annie resisted the urge to hit the man over the head with her newspaper as she watched them leave.

Shortly after, she pulled into her parking space at home. With her sweater over her head, she made the dash to the doorway

She threw her things on the couch and turned on the television. Sure enough, there was the outline of a tornado in the bottom right-hand corner of the screen. That meant a watch, and Annie relaxed. She turned the volume up a little, just for the noise. She was lonely today.

The nearly dark apartment seemed menacing, and she glanced out the back window. What if there was a tornado? Normally, Annie did not fear storms. On the contrary, at home the McGowan girls often left their beds in the night to watch a good thunderstorm. But her sisters were far away and it was quite dark outside. She turned on the lights.

"Stay busy," she directed herself.

Grabbing her sweater, she shook the rain off and opened the closet. She hung up the sweater and attempted to close the door, but had to push hard against the pile of books and papers that shifted inside. Resisting the urge to put her weight into the job, she opened the closet door again and took stock.

Many of the papers and notebooks needed to be thrown out. Annie had a tendency to put things in piles and forget about them. A pile soon became clutter, which she then shifted to various hiding places like closets. She sorted and sifted and thought about Kevin. Was it him she missed? Or, more likely, "it"?

Caroline defined "it" as the relationship, the companionship, the marriage. Being part of a couple. Having someone there with you. *Yes*, Annie thought. *I miss "it." Not "him."*

"Garbage, garbage, garbage," she said as she sorted.

A new-looking notebook caused her to pause. It was the notebook she had bought at the college bookstore, what seemed like years ago. Annie ran her hand over the embossed logo. New notebooks offered such possibility and hope. Annie recalled how happy and hopeful she had been that day, intending to begin a journal. She heard Kevin's voice in her head, shaming her for buying the notebook. She remembered his fist hitting the wall above her head. Such a little thing, this $1.50 notebook. Kevin must have known it represented hope to Annie. She began to cry, in spite of herself. It was a perfectly good notebook, clean pages, no writing. Despite this, Annie placed it gently on the garbage pile.

Stopping long enough to get a box of Kleenex and the garbage can, Annie continued to sort through the cast-off debris. *It could be worse*, she thought. *I could be that wife in the convenience store.* She thought of the woman's humiliated look. How she would have loved to take that woman by the arm and run. Nice husbands did not tell their wives to shut up in a convenience store line. No doubt the woman right now blamed herself, thinking she had made him mad. Along with millions of others, she was probably being abused. Feeling helpless, Annie threw out papers with a vengeance. It was an overwhelming problem, but what could one person do?

She thought of Caroline. Caroline was just one person. Caroline hadn't rid the world of the problem. But she had saved Annie. Caroline would reject this notion, claiming Annie had saved herself. Annie knew better. By telling her the truth, and giving her information, Caroline had helped Annie see the pattern, which set Annie free to leave. Without that knowledge, Annie would have continued to blame herself. Most likely, she would have been murdered. She had come that close.

Shuddering, she took a deep breath and looked down at all of the college papers and books. She knew what she would do. The university in Chicago had a renowned counseling program. Annie was going home. She would be like Caroline. Some girl was starting high school right now, destined to end up in Annie's shoes. There was nothing she could do about that yet. But in a few years, she would be one more Caroline.

Annie stopped sorting, picked up the whole pile, and dropped it into the garbage. The closet door closed easily.

"There," she said with satisfaction. "It's finished."

Understanding Dating and Domestic Violence

Following are some concrete tools to help you understand dating and domestic violence. Be aware that while most victims are female, some are male. There are abusive females, and they wreak the same havoc on the lives of their partners as male offenders. Additionally, there are batterers within same-sex relationships. The dynamics are the same. The only difference is that the victim in a same-sex relationship is likely to feel even more isolated, more fearful, will be less likely to seek help, and possibly remain in the relationship longer because of a fear of exposure.

Please keep this information with you for as long as you are dating. Reread it periodically so it is fresh in your mind. Dating and domestic violence can happen to anyone. Don't let it happen to you.

One more thing. Many people fear that because they do not come from a perfect family, there is something wrong with them. This is nonsense. First of all, there are no perfect families. Secondly, you can be whatever you choose. If you witnessed or experienced violence in your family, you can be that much more determined to choose a healthy and nonviolent partner. Don't let a tough childhood define you. Your future is up to you!

Profile of an Abusive Partner

- *Low self-esteem.* At the same time this person may appear cocky and boastful on occasion.
- *Trouble trusting others, particularly you.* In spite of this, they may say that they know you would never be unfaithful.
- *Jealous and possessive.* Initially, the abuser may say others were coming on to you. Eventually, though, you will be accused of being attracted to other people, flirting, or being unfaithful.
- *Controlling.* Sometimes this can be subtle. You may be changing your behavior without realizing why. For example, you may "decide" not to see your friends too often because you don't want your partner to get mad.
- *Usually comes from a family where there was violence, although they may deny this.*
- *Passionate!* The abusive relationship is intense and passionate. There is usually a Romeo and Juliet quality, which may be noticed by your friends. This intensity does NOT mean you are fated lovers. It means someone is holding on too tightly.
- *Dr. Jekyll and Mr. Hyde personality.* Loving and supportive one minute and cold and hostile, accusing, or distant the next.

• *Mood swings or explosive temper.* You think everything is going fine, and suddenly your partner is furious.

• *Macho or supermasculine.* This is sometimes present in male abusers. This boyfriend will have strong opinions about how a man and woman should behave. He will be rigid. You may find yourself saying, "Well, yes, this happened, but there are reasons why." The abusive partner, male or female, will not accept reasons or explanations. Everything is black or white.

• *Isolating.* These partners may want to isolate you from your friends or family. They may always want to be alone with you. Often they will start trouble between you and your best friend. They will be threatened by any relationships you have with members of the opposite sex and may attempt to destroy those friendships by criticizing your friends or pointing out ways in which they have wronged you.

• *Emotionally and verbally abusive.* Sometimes there is no physical abuse until something like a commitment is made, i.e., you have sex, get pregnant, or cut off your friends and family. It could also be as simple as your agreement not to date other people. You don't have to have bruises to be in an abusive relationship.

• *Denial.* This partner will attempt to minimize the violence or behavior, saying:

"I barely touched you."

"I was just messing around."

"You can't take a joke."

• **Blamer.** Abusive partners will blame others for their mistakes or problems. Again, it may be subtle. They will blame others for fights if they can.

"You know how mad I get when you talk back."

"You make me crazy."

"I love you so much I can't help being jealous!"

"If you weren't so beautiful/handsome, I wouldn't be so worried about losing you."

"Your friends are trying to break us up."

"That person was coming on to you."

• **When you have a fight, they may try to blame outside stressors.**

"My parents are making me crazy!"

"My teachers are making me crazy."

"I feel like I'm under so much pressure."

"You don't understand. Nobody does."

These are pressures with which we all must cope. They are not an excuse to be violent or *abusive*.

• **Alcohol or drug user.** This partner may abuse alcohol or drugs. If so, he or she has a built-in excuse. Remember that many people abuse alcohol and drugs and never become violent or abusive. It's no excuse.

"I was totally wasted."

"I don't even remember this. Did I really do that?"

"I'll never touch that stuff again!"

"I'm such a jerk. Why do you stay with me?"

They may also say things like:

"Hey, you pushed me first."
"What do you expect when you say the things you said?"
"You were just as violent as me."

This can get confusing for you. Don't let it. When you are in an abusive or dysfunctional relationship you may begin to act in ways you normally would not.

Behaviors of an Abusive Partner

• They may keep track of your time.
• They may show up somewhere you have said you'll be. They will call this "surprising" you. If you get angry, they will act as though you were doing something you did not want them to see.
• They may stalk or follow you, sometimes calling your home to see if you are there and then hanging up.
• They may buy you a pager or cell phone so they can always reach you. This can start fights if you don't answer or call back right away.
• They may try to intimidate you by punching something close to you, (a wall, car, window) or by driving dangerously, breaking your personal property, shouting in your face, pointing down at you, kicking walls or doors, or threatening to tell secrets to your family or friends.
• They may criticize your clothes, hair, or mannerisms. They may try to take charge of whether or not you drink, use drugs, smoke, or use birth control.
• They may challenge your femininity/masculinity.
• They may act as if they are the boss or in charge. They may want you to talk to them before making

decisions about your activities or friends.

• They may invade your privacy by reading notes; going through your room, purse, or wallet; eavesdropping on telephone conversations; or playing back messages on your answering machine.

• They may push your boundaries by tickling you until you are uncomfortable. Another way is wrestling in an aggressive manner that they call playful but you find painful or upsetting.

• They may be pushy about sex. Even though you have agreed on a cut-off point, you may find that they do not respect the agreement. When confronted, they will say you are overreacting.

• They may pressure you to quit your job or outside activities because they do not want you around members of the opposite sex.

• They will be overly jealous. Remember, JEALOUSY DOES NOT EQUAL LOVE!

• If you do not do what they want, they may threaten to break up with you or possibly end the relationship for a while.

• If you try to break up with them, they may threaten to hurt you or your family, to tell your friends or parents that you had sex or did drugs, or even to commit suicide, killing you first.

• Remember that violence progresses in a gradual way. If a new partner slapped you and called you names on your first date, you obviously wouldn't go out with him or her again. It usually starts with emotional abuse and progresses to shoving, grabbing, or restraining. The next step could be slapping, then kicking or biting. Punching and choking may follow, after which the abuse usually escalates to beatings with repeated kicks, slaps, and punches.

ONCE A PARTNER IS VIOLENT, HE OR SHE IS USUALLY VIOLENT AGAIN!

Types of Abuse

Emotional Abuse
- Criticizing
- Calling you insulting names
- Ignoring or ridiculing your feelings
- Making fun of the way you speak or express yourself
- Manipulating you with lies or distortions of the truth
- Leaving you at a party or somewhere dangerous
- Putting you in situations where you get in trouble, for example, keeping you out later than your curfew, making you late for work, etc.
- Ignoring you or embarrassing you in front of others
- Criticizing or teasing you in front of your family or friends
- Telling friends or family things you have said (or allegedly said) about them
- Telling you things that family or friends have said (or allegedly said) about you
- Threatening to break up if you do something they do not like
- Threatening to break up if they feel they need more control
- Mimicking you

- Teasing you
- Minimizing or ridiculing your accomplishments
- Challenging your femininity ("A real woman would not do this") or masculinity ("Only a wimp would act like this")
- Breaking items that are important to you
- Ridiculing your friends or family
- Calling you a liar or repeatedly asking you to "tell the truth"

Sexual Abuse
- Telling jokes that put women or men down
- Treating women as sex objects
- Acting pushy or aggressive about sex or sex acts that make you uncomfortable
- Forcing you to have sex (rape)
- Calling you names like slut, whore, lesbian, or frigid, fag, wimp, or baby
- Publicly showing interest in members of the opposite sex (the flip side of this would be acting intensely loyal to you and showing no interest in other people at all)
- Acting as if you would have sex with other people
- Telling others about your sexual relationship
- Giving you excessive or unwanted "hickeys" or bite marks (they may say they are marking their territory or want everyone to know you are taken)
- Reading or asking you to read or watch pornography

Physical Abuse

- Pushing
- Shoving
- Slapping
- Kicking
- Biting
- Punching
- Pulling your hair
- Throwing things at you
- Excessive tickling
- Aggressive wrestling that makes you uncomfortable
- Restraining you by holding you by the shoulders or pinning you to the wall or car
- Keeping you in a car or home against your will
- Shoving food or liquid in your face, mouth, or hair
- Hitting you with a weapon or object
- Banging your head against the floor, ground, or car
- Any forceful sex is considered physical abuse as well as sexual abuse

Teasing

Many people have talked about teasing that is disturbing and humiliating. Others have wondered about an appropriate response. People sometimes fear being labeled a brat, baby, or someone who lacks a sense of humor.

For example, one woman's boyfriend repeatedly called her a wench. When she asked her boyfriend to stop, he said she had no sense of humor and was being a baby. He also suggested she "lighten up." She felt embarrassed and decided she was taking it too seriously. At the same time, her boyfriend continued to address her this way, to the point of never using her name. Eventually, the relationship ended.

How do we know when teasing has crossed the line? Simple. When it stops being funny. If you find yourself going along with the joke but feeling hurt or embarrassed on the inside, a line has been crossed. The teasing is not funny and must stop.

Another person asked, "But how can we make them stop?"

This, too, is a simple answer. You tell them it's not funny and you don't like it. If they continue, you have a bigger problem than the teasing. They are not respecting your wishes. In this case you say you cannot stay in a relationship with someone who is intentionally hurting you. Overreacting? Not necessarily. If you stay in this type of relationship, you will eventually observe your partner behaving disrespectfully in other areas. The relationship will probably become abusive or end.

Remember also that partners are not mind readers. It is possible your partner is just being playful. If you don't like what they are doing, tell them. Be clear and unequivocal. "Don't call me that. I don't like it."

Be aware that you also must be careful about teasing. Anything that might hurt or insult your partner is out of line. You should treat your partner with the same respect you expect and deserve from him or her.

Cycle of Violence

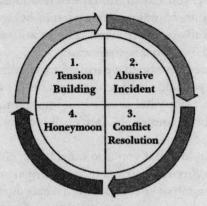

1. Tension Building	2. Abusive Incident
4. Honeymoon	3. Conflict Resolution

1. Tension-Building Phase

Characterized by:

- Walking on eggshells
- Criticism

"I'm trying to do everything right, but my partner keeps getting mad at me."

Depending on how far advanced the cycle has become, this phase may include minor incidents such as pushing, tripping, inappropriate tickling, etc. More apparent may be criticism of the victim's behavior. The batterer may get mad quite often and ignore the victim or leave him or her in social situations. (See *Behaviors of an Abusive Partner* for specific behaviors during this phase.)

Victims sometimes think they can diffuse the situation by doing what their partners want and keeping them calm. The victims will try hard during this phase to please the abusers, attempting to see in advance what might anger them.

This phase may be hard to see in the beginning of the cycle but later become more pronounced with the victim often being able to detect when the abuser is getting ready to "go off."

2. Abusive Incident Phase

Characterized by:

- The big fight
- The explosion
- The break-up
- The violence

"My partner's totally crazy. He/she just exploded!"

Depending on how far advanced the cycle has become, this phase may include violent behaviors such as pushing, shoving, choking, slapping, punching, etc. (See *Types of Abuse* for more specific acts of physical abuse.) The abusive incident is sometimes characterized by the abuser's rejection of the victim, even breaking up with him or her. The abuser may appear out of control during this phase, and the victim may become frightened. The abuser may say someone was "coming on" to the victim or that the victim was flirting with another person. The victim may be called names such as whore, slut, fag, or wimp. Sexual assault may occur during this time.

In the beginning, this phase may seem romantic to the victim, particularly if the abuser is reacting in a jealous way and the violence is limited to shouting, punching walls, restraining, or grabbing. The victim may see it as a sign of the partner's deep love and attachment.

Later, as the cycle progresses, the accusations will become more serious, more frequent, and more violent. This phase is typically short and explosive, but toward the end of the cycle it can become longer, with the abuser even holding the victim "hostage" somewhere for hours or even days while beating and berating him or her.

3. Conflict Resolution Phase

Characterized by:

- Apology and explanations
- Shared feelings
- Excuses and denial
- Spelling out the rules
- Forcing the victim to admit he or she was partially to blame

"My partner was under a lot of stress, and it didn't help that I was talking to somebody else. He/she is just a little insecure. We worked it all out."

In the beginning of the cycle, the abuser may take full responsibility for his or her behavior, apologizing profusely and offering a list of excuses and reasons for the "fight." "I love you so much that I get crazy with jealousy. I was drunk. You made me furious. I misunderstood something." (See *Behaviors of an Abusive Partner* for more on this.) Along with this, there may be denial and sharing of feelings, along with explanations. "I barely touched you. You're overreacting. It's just that your friends make me crazy."

As a rule, abusers can be uncommunicative, and the victims may stand on their heads trying to get feelings out of their partners. This phase can lead the victim to think the couple is making progress with intimacy because the partner is so open and responsive. As the cycle advances, though, this phase will be characterized by spelling out the rules. "If you don't do these things, then I won't be violent. It's as much your fault as mine." Initially, the victim may see this conversation as normal struggling to maintain a relationship.

This phase must happen before moving on to the next. Sometimes couples will simply break up. It can be a painful time for the victims while they desperately attempt to figure out why the violence happened and what they should do about it. Reality is shifted in that the victim may know the truth but buy the abuser's explanations. Initially it is a short period, maybe one long conversation, but later, usually after marriage, is characterized by such things as vacations, counseling, and possibly voluntary restrictions in the abuser's alcohol or drug use.

4. Honeymoon Phase
Characterized by:
- Falling in love again
- Getting back together

- Passion

"We were meant for each other. My partner loves me so much."

The abuser is kind, contrite, and, in summary, kissing the victim's backside. If you are a woman, expect things like flowers, candy, compliments, and kindness. If you are a man, you will receive affection, tenderness, and compliments. The relationship is now passionate, and the victim will feel cherished. This is very romantic, and it will not last.

In the beginning of the cycle, this wonderful phase assures the victims that they did the right thing by reconciling. It's so good to be back together, and the abuser couldn't be nicer. Later in the cycle, the victim will enjoy this phase but will know that it will not last. He or she will feel guilt, anxiety, and fear of the next incident.

With most abusive dating relationships, this phase is initially very long. Because of this, the victim thinks that this is the *real partner* and the other behaviors are isolated incidents. As the cycle progresses, this phase becomes shorter and shorter, eventually disappearing altogether, being replaced by blame, blame, and more blame.

Risk Assessment

Warning Signals

1. Does your partner call you names?
2. Does your partner say things that will hurt you, then act angry if you get upset?
3. Does your partner tell you things your friends or family have said about you?
4. Would you describe him or her as more jealous or possessive than most people?
5. Does your partner get mad if you have a good time without him or her?
6. Does your partner talk about breaking up when you do something he or she does not like?
7. Does he or she sometimes mimic you or ignore you when you are talking?
8. Does your partner have sudden mood swings?

Abusive Behavior Low Risk

If you answered yes to any of these questions, your partner may be emotionally abusive.

Most abusive relationships begin with emotional abuse and escalate to physical abuse. If you don't feel you can break up, set some guidelines or boundaries and see how they react. Call them on the emotional abuse. For example, tell them you will not tolerate name calling. Then, the next time they call you a name, walk away. Let them know they owe you an apology. Remember, if they restrain you when you try to walk away, they are being physically abusive. Tell them so. If they threaten to break up with you because you demand respect, let them. It may be difficult to do, but if you do not set limits now, their behavior will get worse.

Danger Signs

1. Does your partner say he or she trusts you but still accuse you of flirting or fooling around?

2. Does your partner check up on you? Does he or she surprise you by showing up somewhere you have said you will be?

3. Does your partner track your time? For example, does he or she ask where you were for an hour if it only takes twenty minutes to get home from somewhere?

4. Does your partner isolate you from your friends? Do they hate your best friend or say that your best friend has talked about you?

5. Have they pushed, shoved, slapped, kicked, or punched you? Have they grabbed you by the shoulders to "make you listen"?

6. When you defend yourself, do they say you are "talking back"?

7. Does your partner say he or she would not get so jealous if he or she did not love you so much? Do they say that you know what makes them mad and you do it anyway, so it is really your fault?

8. Do you apologize to others for your partner's

actions? "They didn't mean it; you don't know them. They were just upset."

Abusive Behavior Medium Risk

If you answered yes to any of these questions, you are in an abusive relationship.

It is not normal for someone to feel the need to check up on you. A classic sign of an abuser is dislike of the people closest to you. Typically, an abuser will try to separate you from your best friends by pointing out their faults. It starts with emotional abuse and moves to physical abuse. After a fight during which they are abusive, abusers may become apologetic and contrite. They may be extremely loving and promise all kinds of things. At the same time, they may subtly blame you for the violence by saying you are making them jealous or that they love you so much they cannot help themselves.

If your partner is behaving like this, you need to get out. It will only get worse. Chances are your self-esteem has already been affected, and you are beginning to feel badly about yourself. Being in an abusive relationship is confusing. You are never really sure if it is your fault or theirs. You may be thinking, "They have a point about some of their arguments." That may be true. You are probably not perfect. Nobody is. But often an abuser will take the truth and twist it so you do not know which way is up. You will find yourself trying harder and harder to please them and being less and less able to. This relationship could destroy you.

Red Alert Red Alert Red Alert

1. Has your partner become so jealous that you could describe him or her as paranoid?

2. Do you often find yourself trying to convince them that you did not do anything wrong?

3. Have they ever kept you somewhere against your will (car or house)?

4. Have they ever repeatedly commanded that you "tell the truth" even when you were not lying?

5. Do they say they will die if you leave them or that they cannot live without you?

6. Have they ever talked about killing themselves?

7. Have they ever threatened to kill you?

8. Have they forced you to have sex when you did not want to?

9. Do you have to justify your actions, activities, and time with your friends?

10. Do you want to break up sometimes but feel afraid of what they might do (hurt you, harm your family, or tell others personal things about you)?

Abusive Behavior High Risk

If you answered yes to any of the questions above, you are danger!

Run for your life! Your partner is extremely abusive and could seriously hurt or even kill you. If your partner is behaving like this, it is no longer safe to date him or her. It is time to get help and end the relationship. You will never convince him or her that you are innocent of his or her accusations. Until you break up. Then they will say they realize that you are the best thing that has ever happened to them and they are sorry. But that means nothing. As soon as you go back to them, it will all start again.

Many abusers threaten to kill themselves when you try to break up. Will they? Usually not, but it is possible. They need professional help, and you need to tell someone you trust. (See *Safety Plans*.) YOU CANNOT HELP THEM. In cases of dating/domestic violence in which a woman is murdered, the abuser often kills his partner and then himself. This also happens with male victims, though not as often. That is why it is so risky when your partner is suicidal. The most dangerous time for a female ending an abusive relationship is *when* she tries to leave.

Show your parents this risk assessment and make a safety plan. Then call the nearest domestic violence hotline. They can advise you about protective orders and safety strategies. Do not minimize the danger in this situation. It could mean your life!

Red Flag List

Check all that apply:

☐ Your partner has followed you, spied on you, or kept you under surveillance. (This is stalking.)

☐ Your partner seems extremely upset, agitated, or paranoid, accusing you of being sexually active or unfaithful with someone else.

☐ Your partner has access to weapons.

☐ Your partner has told you how he or she will kill you, your family members, or someone else.

☐ Your partner is very depressed.

☐ Your partner is obsessed with you.

☐ Your partner has been physically abusive in the past.

☐ Your partner has raped you or forced some kind of sexual activity against your will.

☐ Your partner has injured or killed a pet.

☐ Your partner abuses alcohol or drugs.

☐ You are pregnant. (Seventy percent of pregnant teens are abused.)

☐ Your partner has threatened to kill you.

☐ Your partner is suicidal.

☐ You are afraid to disagree with your partner.

☐ Your partner may accuse you of talking back.

☐ You are afraid of your partner or of what he or she might do.

☐ You are attempting to break up with an abusive partner.

The more items you checked, the more dangerous your situation.

These are serious danger signals, and you should get professional help. Also reread the *Red Alert* list of the *Risk Assessment* section.

"But I Was Violent, Too..."

Identifying the Primary Aggressor

When police officers respond to a domestic violence call, they often must determine who is the bad guy or the primary aggressor. In relationship violence, often both parties get violent. This can confuse the victims, who may think they are as bad as their partners because they fight back or defend themselves. Following are some points to help keep the issues clear:

- People have the right to defend themselves. Often when someone is attacked, he or she instinctively strikes back.
- When a victim becomes involved with a violent person, his or her behavior may change. When someone is yelling, it's tempting to yell back. When someone is violent, it's tempting to respond violently. These behaviors are learned and can become habits. With a well-adjusted partner, an emotionally healthy person is likely to respond in kind.
- Every relationship has problems and conflicts. Getting angry is not an excuse to assault.
- Nobody is perfect. Many abusers will try to per-

suade the victim that the abuse is caused by the victim's behavior or faults. This is not true.

• Abusers encourage victims to feel insecure and inadequate. This is manipulation and can cause feelings of jealousy. Unless the other behaviors are present, a victim is not abusive merely because he or she, too, gets jealous.

• Who is usually the abuser or aggressor? The fact that someone hits back during a violent incident does not make him or her abusive. The person who is usually violent is normally the abusive party.

The most telling factor to consider is really very simple. Who is afraid? Are you afraid of your partner? If the answer is yes, then he or she is probably abusive. If your partner is not afraid of you, then you probably are not abusive.

**DON'T GET CONFUSED! IF YOU ARE
AFRAID, GET OUT NOW!**

Safety Plans

What Is a Safety Plan?
A safety plan is a series of actions you can take when you feel threatened or afraid. If you are not ready to end the relationship, you can prepare for the next violent episode. If you are breaking up, you can prepare for the violence and stalking that may follow.

Why Bother?
If a plan is prepared in advance, it can maximize safety and prevent panic. Because every relationship is different, safety plans will vary. For this reason it is important that each safety plan be designed by you, the victim, to suit your circumstances.

How Is It Done?
After identifying your resources and potential danger signals, you can devise your own individual safety plans, including one for breaking up.

A. AVAILABLE RESOURCES
The first step is to identify your resources. What might you possibly need? Who can help and how?

Look at the following list and add anything or anyone that might be helpful to you.

Code word or phrase. A code word or phrase is chosen by the victim to convey a message to family or friends. It can be as simple as, "I'm kind of tired tonight." The meaning is decided on in advance and can mean "Don't leave us alone." There can be varying degrees. For example, "I'm exhausted" can mean either "Come over right away" or "Call the police." You may be with the abuser or in the same room. The code word will help you indicate danger without tipping him or her off.

Cell phone. A cellular phone is a good idea because you can carry it with you as opposed to finding a pay phone and struggling to locate change. On the other hand, it is a well-known fact that victims go through a lot of phones. The reason for this is that the abuser is not likely to hand you the telephone and wait patiently while you call your parents or the police. (This problem is so prevalent that the state of Illinois enacted a law that prohibits an abuser from interfering with a victim either calling the police, seeking medical attention, or reporting domestic violence. But quoting statutes won't help you at the moment.) Put important numbers, such as parents, friends, police, on the speed dial. And give yourself a couple of options in case of a busy signal. On the flip side, an abuser can use your cell phone or pager to harass you. Part of your breakup plan may be to get a new pager or cell phone.

Answering machines. Use these to screen calls if your abuser begins to harass you by telephone.

Friends. Let them know your situation and give them the code word or phrase. They can also ensure that you are not left alone with your partner when the situation seems likely to escalate. Friends can run for help and should be told to call police if an assault is occurring. It is a good idea to let them know just how violent your abuser gets so they will take the situation seriously.

Parents. I know. You're thinking, "No way am I going to tell my parents." But if your partner is really dangerous, you'll have to. They have the power to do lots of things that you cannot. Like change your phone number, pick you up wherever you call from, contact the abuser's family, help you to get charges filed. (Last on your list, I'm sure. But it may come to that, and it is better they be somewhat prepared. Also, the abuser may threaten other family members, and they *must* be made aware of that.)

Teachers, counselors, and school officials. This is important because the abuser may come to your school looking for you. If he or she attends the same school, he or she may be violent there, and you have the absolute right to attend school without being afraid. Also, if school personnel are informed of the problem, they will be more likely to react positively and quickly in a dangerous situation. If you get an order of protection, make sure school personnel have a copy. This will enable them to call the police and get immediate action.

Crisis lines or battered women's shelters. These organizations provide a wealth of information and give you a place to talk. You can call a crisis line anonymously and bounce your situation off someone who is knowledgeable about the problem. Many people call and say, "These are the things my partner is doing. Do you think that is abusive?" Shelters can provide you with legal information about your area and will even go with you to court if you end up there. Call them for help or just to chat.

Police Department. This may be a hard step, but if you are being assaulted or see someone *else* being assaulted, you need to call the police. Policemen are experienced in dealing with domestic violence and have seen everything. Your situation will neither shock nor surprise them. And they have the power to intimidate where you may not. Also, a run-in with police will indicate that the situation is serious and convey a message to the offender: violence is against the law, and the abuser is going to suffer consequences.

B. WARNING SIGNALS

The next step is to identify when you may be in danger. Let's review your abuser's warning signals. What are signs that he or she is in the tension-building phase? What does your abuser do when angry? Does he or she:

- raise his or her voice?
- go silent?
- stamp around?
- throw things?
- punch walls?
- drive aggressively or dangerously?
- behave in a sexual manner that is pushy or embarrassing?
- get jealous?
- call you names?
- bang on the steering wheel?
- stare at you?

At this point anything can trigger a violent episode, and you need to be one step ahead. Put yourself in different situations and decide which courses of actions you can take, what kinds of safety plans you can make. For example, if you are:

At a party

1. You can use your code word or phrase to indicate to your friends that it is not safe

to leave you alone.

2. You can go to the bathroom and use your cell phone to call your parents. Ask them to pick you up.

3. You can pretend to have a stomachache and ask to be taken home, making sure that you do not go alone with your abuser.

4. If you cannot get away from them for even a minute, you can tell them you have to call home for some reason and use your code word to let your parents know you're in danger.

5. You can sneak away and ask a friend, or better yet a few friends, to walk or drive you home.

6. You can approach adults at the party, or the host if you are an adult, and either tell them you're sick and would like to be taken home or tell them the truth—that you're afraid.

The nice thing about parties is that there are other people there. Make the most of that and do not leave with your partner to "talk it out." Chances are they are going to say they want to talk to you privately. Stand your ground and do not get into a car alone with them! Also, try to avoid getting trapped in a room away from everyone else. Tell them that if they want to talk privately, they can go home and call you on the telephone or even call you the next day. As soon as you see your partner escalating, get away and refuse to talk, even if he or she persuades you he or she is now calm. You know the person. If you saw signals, you're probably right, and they are moving toward a violent phase.

In the car

1. Say you're feeling sick and ask to be taken home. Pretend to throw up if you have to.

2. You can act as though you are going along with your partner and wait until you are at a light. Then jump out. Run to the nearest public place like a restaurant, hospital, or even a busy intersection and call the police, your parents, a friend, or maybe a taxi to take you home. Ideally, all of these numbers are on your cell phone's speed dial.

3. If he or she is dropping off friends, get out at one of their houses and refuse to get back in. Then use their phone and call for an alternate ride home. Or try to insist you be taken home first. Chances are he or she won't do this, saying, "Get back in the car. I want to talk to you." Refuse. Better a scene at a friend's house than in a deserted parking lot where there is nobody to help you.

4. Think back to what has helped you in the past. Is it better to cry, beg, reassure, stay silent? If you fight back, do you have a chance? If not, you may be in the unfortunate position of going along with them or trying to get through it without getting hurt. Try to get out, but odds are they may restrain you or lock you in. Do what you can.

5. Think of an excuse to call your parents or a

friend and use the code word or phrase.

6. Scream for help. Wave for help. Act hysterical. Go crazy and see if that works.

The best way to avoid being trapped in a car with an abusive partner is to stay out of the car in the first place. This cannot be stressed enough. Cars are dangerous places to be because you can be taken anywhere and be kept in there. He or she can also get you killed by driving dangerously.

In your house

1. Stay out of the kitchen. This is a dangerous room because there are items that can be used as weapons.

2. Move the fight to a safer place like the living room.

3. Call a friend and use the code word or phrase.

4. If anyone else is in the house, call for help, loudly and repeatedly.

5. If the situation is still at a low level, for instance, they are not violent yet but you feel it is escalating, move the fight to a room within easy hearing of anyone else in the home. This should force them to quiet down and give you easy access to help if they get violent.

6. If you are alone there, try to move the fight out on the porch, particularly if there are neighbors around. This will give you the chance to run for help if necessary.

7. Say you have to go to the bathroom and call

the police with the cell phone.

8. Try to call 911.

At school

1. Move to a hallway or other public place.

2. Call for help.

3. If you leave school and your partner is waiting outside, go back in and inform a teacher or administrator, or call your parents to pick you up. You can leave by another exit if you're sure he or she won't spot you.

4. Stay with a friend so your partner cannot get you alone.

5. Refuse to go to a secluded spot. Insist on talking in a public place or tell your partner you'll only speak to him or her if your friend stands close by.

C. PERSONAL SAFETY PLAN

There are unlimited situations you may find yourself in. Think of them and write safety plans for each one. Following are a few good ground rules.

1. Don't get in a car alone with an abusive partner.

2. Insist on talking in a public place. If you have things to discuss, do it at a restaurant.

3. Keep a cell phone handy if you can.

4. Do not go anywhere alone if you're afraid.

Breakup Plan

Suggestions

1. Use the buddy system. Have friends with you everywhere so the abuser cannot get you alone.

2. Carry a cell phone with the numbers of people who can help you on speed dial.

3. Inform school and work personnel that the situation is dangerous.

4. Use your answering machine to screen your calls. Also, since telephone harassment is a crime, save answering machine tapes. Keep a notebook by the phone and record the time, date, and whatever the abuser says. It can also be helpful to record your responses to him or her, such as "Don't call me again" or "I've asked you not to call here. You're harassing me." Put the abuser's statements in quotes, such as "You've got to talk to me." Or "If you don't see me, I'm going to kill myself." Or "I'll kill you, you _____." It's extremely important to record threats.

5. Lock your doors and make sure your family is aware that your former partner may come over.

6. If you get an order of protection, keep a copy in your purse or wallet and on the refrigerator. Make sure that your family knows to call the

police if they see the abuser. Also, drop off a copy to your boss at work and to the principal or security officer at school.

7. Ask your parents to consider changing the phone number and getting an unlisted one.

8. If you feel he or she may kill you, go into hiding. Stay at a relative's or friend's house. The abuser cannot have access to you when he or she is dangerous or you may end up dead, along with your family members.

9. Either you or your parents should call your partner's parents and see if they can affect his or her behavior.

10. Make sure your partner knows, via friends or family, that any further violence or harassment will be dealt with legally. Threaten.

11. Stalking, which means following you or keeping you under surveillance, is a crime. Make sure to tell someone that this is occurring. Document any incidents and report them to the police.

12. Try to avoid giving your former partner any reason to think you might reconcile. Because victims sometimes feel guilty or think that they are partially at fault, or because they feel sorry for the abuser, they may agree to see the abuser in an attempt to "make things better." You cannot do this without giving him or her the idea that he or she can still get to you. Be strong and do not see or talk to him or her. Try not to get sucked back in.

Personal Breakup Safety Plan

Now it's your turn. Sit down with a piece of paper and do your own personalized safety plan. Do it with someone else if possible, because he or she may have ideas that can help you. Following is a rough guide.

1. List your resources.
2. List the possible situations or places where you may be threatened.
3. List your responses to those situations.
4. Have an alternate place to go if it's not safe to go home and tell the person in advance that you may be showing up.
5. List the things you have to do to make your safety plan work (get cell phone, set speed dial numbers, get order of protection, inform school and work, talk to parents or family members, etc.).

Remember that anything you have to do to stay safe is okay. Never feel guilty for anything you do to get out of a bad situation, including acting crazy. Many victims end up having sex with the offender to stop an assault. If you find yourself in a situation like that, don't feel guilty. You know best how to take care of yourself. Also, in spite of all of your precautions, you may get hurt. It's not your fault. An aggressive response might protect you.

Victim Blaming

Myths About Dating Violence

Violence in dating relationships rarely happens. Not true. Statistics show that one in every three dating relationships is violent. (Levy, B., ed., *Dating Violence: Young Women in Danger*. Seattle: Seal Press, 1991)

Dating violence occurs only with drug users or poor people who come from "bad" families. Not true. Dating violence can occur whether or not a partner uses alcohol or drugs. And it can happen if a partner is poor, rich, respectable, an athlete, or a good student.

Dating violence means a couple having a "fight." Not true. Dating violence is not about a couple having a fight. It is about one partner threatening, abusing, controlling, and assaulting another.

Young women are just as violent as men. Not true. While young women can be violent, statistics show that young men are more violent.

Dating violence is usually an isolated incident. Not true. Dating violence is a "pattern" of abuse and control, and once it starts, it almost never stops.

Stress causes dating violence. Not true. Many people are very stressed and never assault their partners.

Drinking causes dating violence. Not true. Abusers will use alcohol as an excuse for their violent behavior but will eventually also be violent when not drinking. Additionally, the manipulation and controlling behavior are normally present even when an abuser is sober. Also, think about it. Many people get drunk, but most do not assault their partners.

People who batter cannot help it. They lose control. Not true. Usually people who batter do not assault anyone else. They get mad at others but control themselves. They assault their partners because they can get away with it.

If victims wanted to leave, they could just break up. Not true. Often abusers will threaten to kill the partners if they break up and will later stalk them. Also, victims feel sorry for their partners and sometimes even feel guilty, thinking the abuse is their fault.

If you love someone enough, you can make him or her change. Not true. It's not that easy. The decision to change must be made by the abuser, and usually this does not happen.

If the victim did not make the partner angry, he or she would not hit the victim. Not true. Victims are assaulted regardless of their behavior. If it's not for one reason, it's for another.

IN SUMMARY, ANYONE CAN BE A VICTIM OF DATING/DOMESTIC VIOLENCE.

Why She Stays

Why does a woman stay in a violent relationship? Below are some possible reasons.

1. He has threatened to kill her if she leaves.
2. She is afraid of him.
3. She thinks he'll get better.
4. He has promised to change, and she believes him.
5. She thinks it is partially her fault because she did want to make him jealous.
6. She loves him.
7. She is afraid she won't get another boyfriend.
8. She thinks he loves her.
9. When he is nice to her, he is wonderful.
10. She doesn't want to be alone.
11. She believes she can help him to change.
12. She has seen this type of violence at home and accepts it as inevitable.
13. She feels that his extreme jealousy is a sign that he really loves her.
14. He has never really "hurt her." She's received just small bruises, and she doesn't really think that low a level violence is abuse.
15. She feels sorry for him.
16. She has a low self-esteem as a result of the abusive relationship.

Why He Stays

Why does a man stay in a violent relationship? Below are some possible reasons.

1. She has threatened to kill him or tell secrets about him if he leaves.
2. He is afraid of her.
3. He thinks she'll get better.
4. She has promised to change, and he believes she will.
5. He thinks it is partially his fault, because she tells him so.
6. He loves her.
7. He doesn't want to be alone.
8. When she is nice to him, she is wonderful.
9. He believes he can help her to change.
10. He has seen violence at home and accepts it as normal.
11. He feels the abuser's extreme jealousy means that she really loves him.
12. She has never really hurt him. She just screams, yells, says mean things, and sometimes pushes or slaps him. He does not realize these behaviors are abusive.
13. He feels sorry for her.
14. His self-esteem is low as the result of the abusive relationship.

Helping Friends

What can you do when your friend tells you they are experiencing dating violence?
- Listen, listen, and listen.
- Do not judge. Use helpful statements and avoid unhelpful statements.
- Do not give them a list of solutions right away. Move slowly.
- Do a safety plan with them, even if it is an informal one (for example, what they will do if the abuser follows them to school).
- Stress that they have the right to break up if they are ready.
- Convey that the violence is not their fault, regardless of what they said, wore, or did.
- Give them information about the cycle of violence, risk assessments, and the profile.
- Give them the phone number of a local shelter or a hotline. They can remain anonymous or say they are working on a paper for school, if they choose.
- Continue to be their friend if they go back.
- Call the police if you witness an assault. Then honk a horn or scream for help until police arrive.

Because these situations can be dangerous, you should be acutely aware of your own safety. Do not put yourself at risk!

Helpful Statements

1. You don't deserve to be treated this way.
2. It sounds as if your partner is acting worse and worse.
3. I know how much you like him or her. It must be hard for you.
4. It sounds scary.
5. Your partner is acting abusively.
6. Have you thought about breaking up?
7. Jealousy is one thing. He/she is out of line!
8. Nobody should be pushing or shoving you.
9. Can I help? Is there anything I can do?
10. This sounds familiar. Let me give you some information about this.
11. You're right to be upset. I would be, too.
12. You cannot argue with them if they act like that. It's not fair.
13. You should be able to get mad without getting hurt.
14. I'm worried about you. I think this person could be dangerous.
15. You are too good to be treated like this.
16. There are plenty of people out there who don't act like this.
17. I'm afraid he/she is only going to get worse.
18. I don't think you can help him or her.

19. This must be awful for you.

20. If you don't feel as if you can break up now, make sure to say that if he or she hurts you again, it's over.

21. Let's call someone who knows about this kind of thing.

Unhelpful Statements

1. What a big jerk! What a bitch!

2. At least your partner cares enough to get jealous.

3. You're lucky to have somebody, even if the person is not perfect.

4. So . . . wear what he wants. At least he notices.

5. You should just break up. I told you this before.

6. Don't talk back.

7. All people are like this when you get to know them.

8. He's really cute, though. She's a fox.

9. If you don't do something, you're as bad as your partner.

10. It's not like he/she punched you or anything.

11. I think it's kind of romantic. Give him another chance. He said he was sorry.

12. He loves you so much. I wish somebody loved me like that.

13. He is not usually like that. Focus on his good qualities.

14. Stop making him mad. Don't talk to other people if he's around.

15. He wouldn't get so jealous if he didn't care so much.

Healthy Relationships

The following are characteristics of a healthy relationship:

- Respect
- Dignity
- Trust
- Consideration
- Communication
- Good conflict resolution skills
- Emotional safety
- Consistency
- Honesty
- No physical violence

In a good relationship you will be able to:

- say no to physical closeness or sex without feeling guilty.
- change your mind.
- go out without your partner.
- have your own goals and interests.
- express your opinions.
- have control over your life.
- be equal.
- be safe.

- be respected.
- break up without feeling afraid.

A good relationship does not mean a conflict-free relationship. Conflict is healthy and inevitable. Disagreements should be resolved without violence, though, and each partner should feel safe enough to voice his or her complaints.

Often, people who have been involved with abusive partners think that a healthy relationship sounds boring. *You should not be bored!* There should be chemistry. But a good relationship is constant. It should not have the wild roller-coaster ups and downs usually seen in an abusive relationship.

Unhealthy Relationships

The following are characteristics of unhealthy relationships:

- Suspicion
- Mistrust
- Lack of consideration
- Emotionally unsafe
- Inconsistent
- Poor conflict resolution skills
- Poor communication
- Lack of respect
- Dishonesty
- Verbal, sexual, or physical abuse

Think in terms of fair. If you find yourself thinking your relationship is not fair, you've probably got trouble.

In a poor relationship, you'll often begin to feel unsure. Your partner will keep you guessing and may encourage you to feel insecure. A good rule of thumb is that your partner should make you feel good about yourself. You should not always feel as though you have to try to please your partner. You should not always have to wonder about whether or not your partner will be in a good mood. You

should never be afraid during an argument, and
your partner should not do things to humiliate or
embarrass you. Physical intimacy should never be
forced, uncomfortable, or beyond whatever limits
you have set.

Questions to Ask About
the New Person in Your Life

Following are some guidelines for determining which people are potential abusers. While you probably won't quiz your dates, be aware of the following problem indicators:

1. Do your new partner's parents argue a lot? Are they divorced? If so, what happened?
2. Does your new partner have a violent father or mother? An overly critical father or mother? While they may not come right out and tell you this, you can usually get a sense of whether or not anyone in the family is afraid of a parent. You should try to spend some time with your partner's family, certainly before a serious commitment is made. Domestic violence runs in families!
3. How was your new partner disciplined? Anything more than mild spanking when very young is suspicious.
4. Does your new partner get in physical fights with siblings?
5. Does your new partner get into fights with others?
6. Was your partner violent in other relationships, even if he or she contends it was not his or her fault?

7. How did your new partners former relationships end and why?

8. Is your new partner disrespectful or demeaning toward all women or all men?

9. Are they overly interested in pornography?

10. Are they sometimes pushy about sex?

11. Do they abuse alcohol or drugs?

12. Do they ever try to intimidate you emotionally, physically, or sexually to get their way?

13. Is your new partner sometimes rigid about how women and men should behave? For example, the way they dress or whether or not mothers should work?

14. Do they have mood swings?

15. Is your new partner extremely possessive or jealous?

16. Do you find yourself surprised by the seemingly innocent things that make them angry or upset?

17. Does your new partner have strong negative feelings about either his or her mother or father?

Questions for You to Answer at the Beginning of a New Relationship

Often young people spend a great deal of time wondering what other people are thinking. Do they like me? How much? Will they want to see me often? Do they still want to date other people? Take some control! When starting a new relationship, spend some time thinking about the following questions. Decide what *you* want before you get into it.

- How often do I want to see this person?
- How much time do I need for myself?
- Am I willing to date this person exclusively?
- What is a comfortable way to resolve conflict?
- What actions will cause me to end the relationship? (Disrespectful behavior, violence, forced intimacy, or simply falling out of love are a few.)
- How far am I willing to go sexually? (Important tip here. Make a decision about this and stick to it. If you're feeling ready to extend your limit, decide well in advance. Trying to decide while you're in someone's arms is like deciding whether or not to swim after you've jumped off the diving board!)

Questions for Your Partner

If you fear your partner may be struggling with these issues, copy this questionnaire for him or her.

1. Do you have trouble controlling your temper?
2. Do you get into fights?
3. Are you violent when you use alcohol or drugs?
4. Do you believe you are only violent when you are provoked?
5. Are you afraid that if you don't control your partners, they will control you?
6. Do you sometimes throw or break things to get a partner's attention?
7. Are you afraid your partner will be unfaithful?
8. Do you spend a lot of time worrying about where your partner is and whom he or she is with?
9. Have you ever grabbed your partner by the shoulders or arms to make them listen?
10. Do you feel that you would not get so angry if your partner would do what you told them?
11. Have you ever followed or spied on your partner?
12. Have you ever pushed, shoved, slapped, hit, kicked, or choked your partner?
13. Have you ever thought you might kill yourself if your partner broke up with you?

14. Do you sometimes call your partner names or say things you know will hurt them?

15. Do you ever pretend that you're going to break up with them if they make you angry?

16. Are you more jealous than most people?

17. Do you get angry when your partner does things without telling you?

18. Have you ever forced your partner to do more sexually than they wanted to?

19. Do you believe you are supposed to be in control?

20. Do you believe women or men are manipulative?

If you found yourself having to think about these questions, you may have a problem with relationship violence. Get some help. It doesn't have to be this tough. Talk to someone who is experienced in this field. Violence is a learned behavior that can be unlearned. One person struggling with this problem said the best thing that ever happened was learning they did not have to be in control. You can learn that, too.

Date Rape

Author's Note

This topic has been directed primarily to women, as they are more likely to be raped than are men. In spite of this, men can also be victimized in this way and should familiarize themselves with the information. Pay special attention to *Date Rape Drugs* and *If It Happens to You*.

Men should also be aware that a woman has the right to say no at any time! If you feel that a woman is "a tease," maybe you should be with a different woman. Rape and chemically assisted rape (using date rape drugs) are crimes that can put you in jail.

Date Rape Facts

- 25% of college women were found to have been victims of rape or attempted rape.
- 90% of these victims knew their assailants.
- 47% of rapes were committed by first dates, casual dates, or romantic acquaintances.
- 90% of the victims did not report the rape.

(1985 study by Dr. Mary Koss of Kent State University. Students were polled at thirty-five college campuses.)

It can happen to anyone! Remember that you have the right to say no at any time. Practice the following safe behaviors:

1. Group dating is best, at least until you are comfortable with a new boyfriend.
2. Limit your use of alcohol and drugs so you can remain in control.
3. State your limits CLEARLY, even if you feel a little silly.
4. Say NO at any time you are uncomfortable or feel a situation is moving too quickly. Do not try to be nice. Say NO loudly and unequivocally so your partner is not confused.
5. Beware of date rape drugs (see *Date Rape Drugs*).
6. Trust your instincts!!! If you're feeling uncomfortable, there is a reason. Get out of the situation.

Beware of the man who:
• takes everything sexually, even if it is not intended that way.
• is overly aggressive or violent.
• is disrespectful of women.
• tries to get you drunk.
• won't take no for an answer.
• consistently tries to talk you into sex.
• feels women ask for rape by being provocative.

If It Happens to You . . .

If you said no and sex was forced upon you, you were raped. You may want to report the assault to the police. If you are not sure about reporting but want to keep the option open for later, the following will help you to preserve evidence:

- Do not eat or drink.
- Do not wash your clothes.
- Try not to go to the bathroom.
- Do not douche.
- Do not take a shower or bath.

You should get medical attention as soon as possible to check for injuries and to test for pregnancy and sexually transmitted diseases (STD). Being seen by a doctor or at an emergency room does not mean you have to make a police report, but if you tell medical personnel that you were raped, they are required to contact the police. Even then, you do not have to make a report or file charges. You can refuse to talk to the police or simply tell the doctor you had unprotected sex and want to be checked for STD and pregnancy. If you decide to file criminal charges, you have the right to drop them at any time. The decision to proceed legally is yours and yours alone.

Do call a rape crisis line. It can only help you. Women experienced in sexual assaults will answer your questions and assist you in identifying your options. They will even accompany you to court if you choose to go that route.

Victims of sexual assault feel many different emotions afterward. This is normal and should not alarm you. Following are common reactions: fear, anger, guilt, shock, denial, depression, anxiety, embarrassment, shame, helplessness, confusion, and betrayal.

Additionally, many victims also experience trouble sleeping, nausea, nightmares, the need to shower or bathe repeatedly, difficulty in concentrating, bedwetting, loss of appetite or overeating, and difficulty with touching or being touched.

Please do not blame yourself. It is not your fault!

If Your Friend Tells You She Has Been Raped . . .

• Advise her to get medical attention.
• Let her talk about the experience as much as she needs to, but do not press for specific details if she does not share them.
• Tell her that her emotions are a normal reaction to the experience.
• Advise her to get professional help and give her the number of a rape crisis line.
• Do not judge her actions before, during, or after the incident. (Don't tell her she was foolish to go home with him or that she should have fought harder, etc.)
• Advise her about the importance of preserving

evidence if she wants to proceed legally.
• Be patient while she recovers. It will take some time.

Date Rape Drugs

Be aware that young women are being raped with the assistance of various "date rape drugs." Sometimes called "chemically assisted rapes," these assaults leave their victims with little or no recollection of the attack.

Rophynol and gamma-hydroxy-butyramine (GHB) are two of the most common drugs to be misused in this way. Similar to Valium, Rophynol is ten times stronger. It is known to cause temporary amnesia, muscle relaxation, sleep, and impaired motor skills. Additionally, alcohol will intensify the effect. These drugs are extremely popular in the Rave scene. People under the influence of these drugs can become agitated, excited, uninhibited, dizzy, confused, have slurred speech, and lose their judgment. Also possible are breathing problems, unconsciousness, and even comas. Fast-acting, Rophynol can take effect in as little as ten minutes. If Rophynol and GHB are combined and alcohol is also present, death can occur. Following are some tips to avoid being attacked in this way:

• Do not take an open drink, especially one offered from a stranger.
• Drink only from tamper-proof bottles or cans. Insist on opening them yourself.

- Never ask someone to watch your drink. Take it with you everywhere, even to the bathroom.
- If a friend asks you to watch his or her drink, hold it or watch it closely.
- Try to avoid mixed drinks or any drinks from wide-mouthed glasses.
- Use the buddy system. NEVER leave a friend who seems wasted. The bigger your group of friends, the safer you are. Stay with at least one other friend at parties or bars and agree that you leave together. Period. Do not let the plans change later in the evening.

Acknowledgments

I would like to acknowledge the following persons:

My father, Richard Jennings, who told me not only that I could write this book but that I should. He is a knowledgeable writer, an able mentor, a source of constant encouragement, and my dearest friend.

My husband, Jimmy, the ultimate team player, who makes me laugh and smile every day. He gave me the time and the courage.

My brothers and sisters, Bobby, Richy, Michael, Mary, Therese, Veronica, Nancy, and Julie, who make my whole life, even the rough times, so manageable. I truly cannot imagine a world without their laughter and wisdom.

My mother, Mary, R.I.P., who was generous enough to give me such a large and humorous family.

My children, Maggie, Annie, Bob, Mary Kathryn, Frank, and little Veronica.

Colleen, my friend, who suffered through the chapter reads, the rewrites, the typing, and everything else in my life.

Celeste, my friend, who helped me subdue the personality disorder lurking in my computer.

Sister Margaret Johnson, RSM, who liked me when nobody else did.

Father Bill Quinn, for his tremendous kindness and support.

Jane Gomulka, for her encouragement, guidance, and energy.

Karla Fiaoni, Bridget Healy, and Paul Pavlus, for their tireless commitment to and enthusiasm for domestic violence prevention.

For Mary Pat McWalters, just because I like her so much.

For Linda Smagoc for countless unseen kindnesses, like blue curtains.

Molly Magill, my editor at HarperCollins, for patience and professionalism.

I would like to acknowledge in a special way the late Roberta Sheehan, a lovely woman, who did her part to move *The Breakable Vow* forward. She will be missed and remembered.

To all of the unsung heroes who work tirelessly in the cause of domestic violence. May God strengthen, bless, and reward you.

To each and every battered woman and man. May you find the courage and strength to bring peace back to your life.

A curriculum guide/prevention manual and video and audio training series are available for use when presenting *The Breakable Vow* as part of a dating/domestic violence instructional program.

Domestic Violence Prevention, Inc (DVP, Inc.)

Visit us at
www.thebreakablevow.com